Carole Leret

Elspeth

novum pro

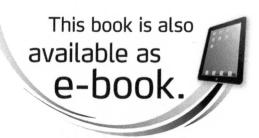

www.novum-publishing.co.uk

© 2021 novum publishing

ISBN 978-3-99107-491-5
Editing: Rachel Jones, BA Hons
Cover photos: Antonio Guillem, Natalia Bachkova | Dreamstime.com
Cover design, layout & typesetting: novum publishing

www.novum-publishing.co.uk

To my husband

Prologue

....

*"In the beginning was the Word.
The Word was with God and the Word was God."*
(John Ch 1 vs 1-3)

Leah was sitting in front of the tent. It was her favourite hour when the day was almost over. The sky was full of stars. She rested with little Eve, her sister Rachael's child. Her sister had died in childbirth and her little girl had attached herself to her aunt. Now she was nestled against Leah's knee half asleep.

Leah was crippled, her foot had been twisted since birth, but she managed to walk albeit with a limp. She was not considered marriageable and this suited her well. She had never been like others. She was content. This time of late evening her spirit was at peace. She loved the silence, the vastness of the heavens, the myriad of stars. The work of the day was over and she could be alone and undisturbed, lost in her own thoughts. Leah thought of it as 'the time before time' and a time she considered her own. Tonight there was a full moon and Leah remembered another moonlit night when her neighbours and tribal family members had shattered the quietness of the night with loud clashing cymbals as they danced around a golden idol they had made. They had collected and melted down golden rings and trinkets and with the gold, they had crafted a calf saying they wanted a god they could see. They were angry and full of complaints about Moses who had apparently deserted them, he had been away so long he might even be dead and they were being left to die slowly in the wilderness. They had been better off in Egypt! Leah had watched as many of them cavorted around the golden calf many of them appeared unconscious and danced as if they were

7

in a drunken stupor. Then suddenly above them there had been a fearful sound of crashing stones and Moses' cry of fury, followed by deadly silence.

Leah sighed, her peace for the present had been broken. Little Eve stirred and Leah drew back the dark curls from the sleepy child's pretty face and then led her into the tent and lay down beside her. They slept.

Chapter 1

....

"And every human heart that breaks,
In prison cell or yard,
Is as that broken box that gave
It's treasure to the Lord,
And filled the unclean leper's house
With the scent of costliest nard.

Ah! Happy they whose hearts can break
And peace of pardon win!
How else may man make straight his plan
And cleanse his soul from sin?
How else but through a broken heart
May Lord Christ enter in?"
(Oscar Wilde: Ballad of Reading Gaol)

Elspeth awoke suddenly, the window was rattling loudly against the window pane. She got up and closed it and glanced at the clock, it was half past five. Her student's room was sparse not unlike her school dormitory. She climbed back into bed knowing she would not get back to sleep and hoping the noise of the window had not disturbed her friend in the next room. She and Louise were in their first weeks at university and studying English. As their rooms in the residence were also next to each other's they had become friends.

Elspeth had opened the curtains and now looked out at the dawn sky as it brightened into morning. She wondered yet again if shock could stop one from crying, her whole being was an anguish of unshed tears. What might her new friend think if she knew?

She liked Louise, indeed it would have been difficult not to she was open, friendly and warm. She reminded Elspeth of her oldest friend Belinda. She and Belle had shared their childhood and school-days and secrets, but not the present one. Belle was not academic and had left school at sixteen and this was where the likeness with Louise ended. Her new friend had a lively face alight with intelligence and would very likely be an understanding confidante, but Elspeth could not confide in anyone. She felt a stab of pain when she thought back at the last four months – was it really such a short time ago that her life had been turned upside down! She sighed, twisted and turned and finally got up, another night without rest.

Thankfully, Louise chatted away despite the lack of information coming from Elspeth, but Elspeth knew that her friend was insightful and aware of her sadness. She had caught a look of concern on her friend's face from time to time and had asked her in the first day or two whether she had any siblings and whether she was missing home. When Elspeth had replied rather hastily that she did not and that she would rather not talk about home, Louise recognised there was clearly something very amiss but did not press her and instead spoke about her own home and family.

'I'm one of eight, I'm the fourth! You might come and meet the Donoghue clan sometime. They are all around apart from Callum, my eldest brother is in a seminary training to be a priest.'

Elspeth sensed the pride in Louise's voice.

'You're Roman Catholic?'

'Yes. You're not I take it.'

'I'm not a church goer.'

'My eldest sister, Bridget is married with a baby, Antony, born last Easter and my sister Ann – she graduated in the summer – is planning to become a nun. We are going to have a family celebration in three weeks' time before she goes.'

'Your sister's going to be a nun!'

'Don't sound so alarmed, nuns didn't die out in the Middle Ages! Ann is going to join the Order of Mercy nuns and they'll train her to be a teacher. We've always been very close so I'll miss her.'

Elspeth quickly found out a lot about Louise's family? She learnt that Louise's mother was Irish and had come over to England to be a waitress in the café her aunt had opened. She had met Louise's father at a church social so she stayed and they had married. Her father had been a bus driver in the early days of the marriage but had worked his way up and was now an inspector. There was never very much money, Louise had explained, it was understandable there would not be with so many children, so it had to be scholarships, hand me down clothes and home knits. The house frequently seemed to be bursting at the seams, but they were a close family and were always there for each other.

Elspeth felt she should make some contribution, 'My father was an officer in the Air Force, he left sometime after the War and now runs the UK side of the family business. My mother was a concert pianist and my father met her at a recital she was giving'.

'There's something top drawer about you Elspeth, no I have no intention of prying, but I'm curious – those amazing eyes of yours! The fellows at tutorials can't take their eyes off you and as for us females, well your beautiful clothes are definitely not hand me downs!'

If Elspeth intrigued her fellow students, Louise was growing in popularity with them. She took a friendly interest in people that inspired confidence; they liked her and were soon inviting them both to join the groups they had formed for coffee. Elspeth knew that they accepted her because of her friend, she also knew that this would not have been the case a few months ago, she sensed that the other students considered her aloof, possibly snobbish and she inwardly suffered.

Louise also had a ready-made social group in the Catholic Chaplaincy where she attended mass two or three early mornings a week. She told Elspeth that a debate was held there once every other week of term.

'I think you would enjoy it, you don't have to be Catholic, everybody's welcome, agnostics, atheists and Protestants'.

Elspeth declined. She didn't say what she was thinking that the debates were perhaps a ploy to recruit new converts, then she dismissed the thought Louise was above any kind of deception and would not countenance it, it had simply been, on her part, a wish to take her friend out of herself.

'I visit the chapel for half an hour or so during the week. It's a beautiful chapel, very peaceful and the chaplain, Father Dominic is a star! So much suffering and so many problems in the world, I can't cure them but I pray in quietness, something I got used to doing in my Parish at home.'

Elspeth sighed, 'and the suffering continues after you leave'.

'Don't be cynical, Elspeth'.

'It wasn't intended as cynicism'.

'More things are wrought by prayer than this world dreams of...'

'Wherefore let thy voice rise like a fountain for me night and day! For what are men better than sheep or goats'.

Elspeth finished the lines off for her. Louise was genuinely surprised. 'Do you believe in what the poem is expressing then?

'I'm not sure what I believe, I do like Tennyson though and Browning and I have always been drawn to the Victorian period. I sense it's not so much in vogue at present, there always seems to be a tendency to stress what is negative about the Victorians, poverty, workhouses, the oppression of women all brought to our attention by Charles Dickens and rightly so the social conditions he describes were deplorable, of course, but there were so many positive things in the nineteenth century too. The Abolition of slavery, the Pre Raphaelites, the Arts and Crafts movement, and then there was Darwin putting everybody in a spin, and Cardinal Newman to counteract him with the Oxford Movement and Cardinal Manning, another one of yours, taking up the cause of the Dockers!

My grandmother is not religious but she told me that her family, as late Victorians, held Cardinal Manning in high regard. I always think that if we were able to go back into the past we'd find people there like ourselves and the same diversity of life as we have now. History fascinates me I almost more than half wanted to read history at university. I can't help thinking that every period of history is like a huge tug-of-war with one end, the positive and good, pulling humankind forward and the negative and bad tugging at the other end with rebels goading things on and the indifferent standing on the side-lines.'

It was the most Elspeth had expressed of her personal views about anything and her friend was impressed but she made her own addition.

'There are also big movements in history, the Reformation, the Enlightenment, and the ideologies of this century, Fascism and Communism, that rather call for 'outsiders' and criticism'.

'Yes, of course you're right! There are a few things I would be happy to be outside of!'

Louise was going to continue then once again she saw the sad shadow on her friend's face and changed the subject, but she remained more convinced than ever that her friend was hiding behind some deep sadness or tragedy.

Elspeth met Louise at breakfast that morning and asked if the rattling window had disturbed her.

'I'm dead to the world once I'm asleep', her friend assured her. I'm off home this weekend for the family's celebration I told you about. What are you planning to do?'

'I have work to catch up on.'

'Elspeth are you sure you're OK. You look as white as a sheet!'

'I'm fine, I didn't sleep very well.'

Louise shook her head in concern, 'well I'll off then but make sure you take care.'

II

Elspeth went to the library but could not concentrate. Towards late afternoon she decided to take a walk. The dark came earlier in the north and it was very cold, Elspeth shuddered against it, thrust her hands into her pockets and drew her coat around her. She wandered without purpose and stood for a while looking over the bridge at the river. Two students were rowing one of them had a shock of red hair that stood out in the half light. Absent minded Elspeth stood watching them as they approached the bridge. The student with the red hair had a thin, sensitive face, a poet's face Elspeth half speculated, before walking aimlessly on. She turned into the crescent where she knew the Chaplaincy was that Louise had described. She found herself in front of it before she knew it and was curious despite herself so she did not hear the approaching footsteps until they stopped close to her and a male voice spoke, 'it's much warmer inside it's freezing out here'.

He stood aside for her and she found herself going up the steps in front of him. The young man, presumably a student spoke again, 'are you a first year?'

Elspeth murmured 'yes'.

'You've not visited the Chaplaincy before?'

'No'.

Elspeth wished he would move on and leave her so that she could make her escape. It was a mistake; she should not be there – she did not belong.

'The chapel is beautiful; we were so fortunate to get this building five years ago.'

He stopped and dipped his fingers into a holy water stoup and crossed himself and then opened the door of the chapel for Elspeth to pass through.

The chapel was dimly lit with flickering candles, Elspeth moved into the front pew and as she sat down she watched the student light a candle and kneel down. After a minute or two he stood up and left, he probably had other things to do in the building she thought.

Elspeth asked herself for ever afterwards whether it was by chance she had sat down where she had. As she grew accustomed to the light in the chapel her eyes were drawn to the statue of the mother and child in front of her. She had, of course, seen many statues and paintings of the mother and child they were all different but this one was unlike any she had seen before. The mother's face was calm and serene as she held the child out in front of her. The sculptor had been skilful and had caught the innocent, trusting expression on the child's face. It seemed to Elspeth that the child's mother was holding the child out to her, for her to take.

Elspeth sat transfixed and her eyes welled up with the tears she had been unable to shed for so long. They now streamed down her cheeks.

She was half aware of someone sitting down next to her and then she was being spoken to.

'You look very lost and forlorn.'

Elspeth wiped the tears away with her hand and she saw a priest was sitting beside her. He began speaking again.

'I rather think a hot cup of tea might be in order, come.'

It was the last thing Elspeth expected to hear but she found herself following him. Outside the chapel the priest called to another girl, presumably another student, 'Claire please bring two cups of tea.'

He opened a door on the other side of the passageway; the room they entered was quite small and contained two chairs and a low table. The priest took a box of matches from his pocket and bent down to light an old looking gas fire, 'Ah! That's better, it'll soon heat up'.

He straightened up and smiled. Elspeth was above average height but the priest towered above her. He was an impressive figure she thought in his black soutane, he brought to her mind one of El Greco's elongated figures of a saint. He had a fine face with well-defined features and a scholar's forehead and reminded Elspeth of a photograph she had seen of Cardinal Newman. She thought Oxbridge educated, probably Cambridge and she felt a sudden twinge of regret.

'I'm Father Dominic by the way.'

'Yes, I know, my friend Louise Donoghue said,' her voice trailed off.

'Ah! And you, what's your name?'

'Elspeth, Elspeth Penrose, but there's a mistake, I shouldn't be here, I'm not Catholic'.

'Well never mind, many of my friends are not Catholics – you're very welcome'. Father Dominic smiled again, it was the most tender smile Elspeth thought she had ever seen, it reached his eyes and his face appeared to be lit with some inner light.

She was confused, this was not what she expected. She was not sure what she had expected but not this.

The tea was brought in and put on the table she picked a cup up and tried to take a sip but her hand shook and she put it down.

The priest was speaking again, 'If you are a friend of Louise then I can take it that you are a first year student. Are you homesick is that why you are so distressed?'

'No.'

If only that was all it was!

'But you are very unhappy, perhaps I can help'.

'It's too late, nobody can. I can't talk about it.'

'Try'.

The concern in his voice and his gentleness made her eyes fill with tears again. He was someone with a gentle authority that made people do as he asked and so very slowly and brokenly and then with increasing confidence she began to open her heart to him and to tell him what had happened.

'I'm not usually an unhappy person; I mean I wasn't unhappy until four months ago that's when it all went wrong. Last year at this time I was very happy indeed! Everything was going well, I was used to things going well. I was in the Upper Sixth of my Girls' Public School, Oaklands and I had a conditional place at Oxford University. In October, at a friend's party I met Rob my first boyfriend – no, it's not what you might think, a tale of un-requited love, I had considered Rob a friend. I have a very good singing voice and was frequently given solos to sing in my school's choir and I was asked last year to sing a solo in the Christmas concert that is held every year in the city's Cathedral. My parents were sitting near the front, my Gran was sitting next to them looking very proud – she almost brought me up – and Rob was there looking very happy, but Jamie wasn't there! Jamie was my brother, he was mentally handicapped, brain damaged or some-thing, nobody really knew what was wrong. He was a beauti-ful baby and looked perfectly normal, he was always beautiful to me'. Elspeth's voice broke and she struggled to gain control, 'I loved him more than I loved anyone else, when he was very lit-tle – he was three years younger than me, he followed me every-where and I told him stories and looked through picture books with him. My parents realised by the time he was two years old that there was something seriously wrong.

'My mother was always sweet to him but my father couldn't ac-cept him. Last year I begged my father to let Jamie come to the concert but he refused, he never allowed Jamie to attend social functions with us. It was wrong Jamie would not have caused any disturbance but my father was ashamed of him, and he was forever trying to discipline him. Mealtimes were worst it would be, "can't you eat quietly, don't slurp your food, what do you think the napkin's there for?" and my mother would sit next to Jamie saying, "try to eat nicely darling and please daddy".

The one person that Jamie never failed to respond to was Grandpa. He would play football with him even when he was old and Jamie would laugh and laugh, he would also let him help him in the garden planting things and Grandpa would say, "there's more in the boy's head than you think!" but Grandpa died suddenly two years ago and Jamie lost a very good friend. After his death Jamie began to close in on himself. I don't know where he got the maths book from, perhaps from his school. I was a weekly boarder at my school, I went home for weekends because the school is in the same city not far from home. Jamie attended a private school, outside the city, it has residential provision, but Jamie came home each night, my mother used to go and collect him.

Jamie treasured that maths book and he used to fill notebooks full of numbers and strange drawings. Nobody knew what they meant but they were clearly important to him. I used to sit in his room near him, reading. He didn't speak much but he was happy for me to be there. His room was full of his 'treasures', old toys, cuddly animals from his early childhood, dead flowers that he still picked from my grandparent's garden, even old pieces of broken pottery – he refused to throw anything away and refused to let anybody else tidy them away either. That room was so important to him, he was such an innocent – that's what made me cry in the chapel, the face of the Christ Child, the innocent expression of trust it was so like Jamie, I couldn't bear it'.

This time Elspeth was sobbing and Father Dominic waited quietly for her to continue.

Finally, she went on, 'I'm sorry; I haven't been able to cry since it happened. I finished my 'A' Levels at the beginning of June and later on that month Rob suggested that I should spend a weekend at the home of his aunt and uncle and his three cousins. Rob's parents are divorced, he told me his mother had left when he was seven years old – he is now twenty-one – he said she more or less abandoned him, she's married again with other children. He lives with his father and his father and uncle have a joint family construction business in the next town and Rob works there.

I had already met his uncle's family, they are warm and friendly, they have three sons, Pete is eighteen, Greg is fifteen – the same age as Jamie – and Jack is thirteen and Rob suggested that I should bring Jamie along with me. He said his uncle and aunt would be more than happy and his cousins would love to have him visit and so that is what was arranged. It was unbelievable! Jamie was transformed! Back like he was with Grandpa. The whole family were so kind to him and Rob's cousins played football with him and he laughed and laughed! When we were ready to return home they said, especially to Jamie, that it had been a pleasure to have him and they would love to have him visit again very soon. The look of joy in my brother's face! It just lit up! That's why what happened next is so dreadful and unforgivable.

Immediately we arrived home it was back to the old routine, we were hardly through the door when my father started, "look at those shoes – what have this family allowed you to do, roll in the dirt? Take them off at once and wash those hands thoroughly, supper is ready we expected you home an hour ago". Then over supper the bombshell fell. Poor Jamie! My poor darling brother! My father said that while we were away my mother and Elsie, one of our cleaners, had cleared and cleaned his room which my father added was a frightful mess. Jamie just sprang to his feet and dashed upstairs and he just went berserk! All his treasures were gone. He picked up a chair and threw it at the window and began throwing the furniture around shouting and screaming!

My father bounded up the stairs saying "the boy's hysterical" and he slapped Jamie hard across his face, my father was harsh but I had never known him to be violent before. My mother and I had followed my father up the stairs and I saw Jamie sitting on the bed whimpering. I can't get it out of my head, that sad sound. My father told us to leave him alone and said the boy needed to learn his lesson. When my father came downstairs he said that Jamie must become a resident at his school as my mother would not be able to cope with him as he grew older.

My mother didn't protest, I think she thought when he calmed down she would be able to dissuade him, she usually managed to make him think things over he adores her, she's the only person he listens to, but this time he meant what he said and made the necessary arrangements with Jamie's school. I went up to see him before they were ready to leave, I hugged him and kissed the top of his head the look he gave me is branded into my mind, it was a look of hope, but very brief, then he looked down and I knew he was just lost.

A fortnight later the school rang to say there had been an accident. Jamie had climbed out of the window of his first floor room and had sustained serious head injuries, by the time my parents arrived at the hospital he was dead. It seemed untrue, a nightmare that I couldn't wake up from. My father, I'm sure out of guilt was angry with the school and threatened to sue them for negligence, but my mother stood up to him for a change and prevented him from doing so. I just think he was responsible for my brother's death and nobody else!'

By this time Elspeth was sobbing uncontrollably and Father Dominic handed her a crumpled white handkerchief, but Elspeth had more to tell and she knew she must get what had followed out into the open.

'I have something else to tell you but I'm so ashamed,' and she covered her face with her hand.

'I hear many confessions, Elspeth and I won't be shocked, I can assure you of that – go on when you're ready'.

'My father's parents live in Switzerland, with my aunt and uncle and three cousins, they moved there after the war and they came over for Jamie's funeral. It was given out that Jamie had had an accident, he'd deliberately climbed out of that window! Gran, of course attended along with several friends and Rob also came. The following weekend I met up with him. My aunt and uncle and cousins were taking a train to the airport but my parents were driving my grandparents there, they asked me to join them, if only I had!

Rob had arranged a visit, and everything seemed fine, we went for a walk and then I invited him in for a drink. It was then things changed he put his arms around me and told me he loved me and wanted to marry me. I tried to laugh it off, I said, hold on a minute I am going up to university and that he was a friend and we would probably both meet up with other friends. He became angry saying that I didn't think he was good enough for me and that my wealthy, stuck-up parents would never allow me to marry him and that he could tell that my father didn't like him. He pointed to the room around him saying, 'who do your family think they are?' and then he took hold of me, I was terrified he was out of all control. He forced himself onto me I tried to push him away and begged him to stop. He wouldn't. He raped me.'

A groan came from somewhere deep inside her, she felt an unbearable agony; she was reliving the horror of it as the scene she was describing past in slow motion before her mind. She felt as if she had survived her own murder – that she'd never be clean again and that something too precious had been forcefully stolen from her. She was silently weeping now. The priest waited for her to go on and eventually she continued.

'Then he tried telling me he was sorry, that he didn't know what had possessed him but that I had had no right to reject him and if I told my parents he would deny it or say that I had consented to it. I just begged him to leave and he just got up and slammed the door as he left. I crawled to the bathroom, I was bleeding and hurt I tried to wash myself clean. I was numb inside as if something had died inside of me I kept telling myself that I was somehow to blame. I knew I never wanted to see him again as long as I live.

'During the summer and at Christmas we go to Switzerland and Gran goes to visit her sister in Cornwall for six weeks from July 'till the end of August, but my mother didn't want to go abroad she was mourning my brother and so we went to the Lake District. It was very miserable, I just took myself off by myself for long walks and buried my head in books.

We returned home to receive my 'A' Level results. They seemed to belong to another life! I had had excellent results and had achieved my place at Oxford. My parents congratulated me and my father said I had made him proud and that they would be buying me my own car – I had had lessons and had passed my test around Easter time. Then I had to take my mother aside and tell her that I wouldn't be able to take up my university place because I was sure I was pregnant. She said I had to tell my father and she would stand by me whatever happened. I knew my father would be horrified but I honestly believed that he would say that I would have to go to Switzerland and stay there and put off going to university for a year.

It had earlier been suggested that I should take a year off and spend it abroad. I was wrong! He seemed to have become another person. It was the very worst encounter I had ever had with my father! He went white with anger and said that he was disgusted with me. He said I was still in his care and still his responsibility and that he would not allow me to bring shame on his family, that he and my mother had had more than enough to put up with but that he would not allow me either to ruin my life.

He said, 'as for your glorified bricklayer or was it carpenter, if he ever sets foot in this house again he'll be thrown out into the gutter where he belongs and don't even think of contacting him, I'll make arrangements, there are ways around the situation and sympathetic doctors, abortion is in the pipeline of becoming legal and will be very soon. You can stay in your room. You'll have your meals brought up to you there'. He disconnected the hall telephone and made me a virtual prisoner. I hate the whole idea of abortion I can't say I wanted to have a child and certainly not with someone I hated, who had raped me – but I would never have agreed to an abortion. In the end it wasn't needed anyway, I had been mistaken but it didn't excuse the way my father had reacted.'

Elspeth was exhausted, she'd talked nonstop and cried herself dry.

The priest was silent for a while digesting what she had told him, she thought he looked sad, then he spoke quietly.

'I can't condone your father's harsh treatment of your brother or the actions he took with you, abortion is wrong in my eyes and in yours too, I think, but I believe you may be wrong about your brother wanting to kill himself. I think it more likely that he was wanting to, perhaps find a way of getting out of the school – escaping if you like – maybe even trying to get home and he misjudged the height of the window. Did you ever consider that?'

'No, no I didn't', in a moment another perspective on her brother's death had opened up and Elspeth wondered why she hadn't thought of it as a possibility before. She was so angry with her father.

'I think your father was right about your brother's school being negligent. Any residence dealing with very vulnerable young people should have made sure that its windows were secure. As for what has happened to you, Elspeth, it is a very serious matter indeed. Rob I think is a deeply troubled young man, you have said that his mother had more or less abandoned him as a child and it has left him unable perhaps to take rejection or what he thinks is rejection, but he should not be allowed to get away with what he has done, he could behave in the same way again. I take it you have kept all this to yourself?'

Elspeth shook her head.

'When my grandmother returned home she said I looked ill, she couldn't understand why I had turned down a place at Oxford and told her that I had my reasons and that I wanted to get a long way from home and that this university had been my second choice. She told my parents that she thought I needed a time away, a holiday before I left for university and she arranged a holiday for us both in Spain.

She said that she had always planned to visit Spain and this was an opportunity, she said we wouldn't go to any beaches where she felt I would mope but that we would visit the cities and keep busy. She thought that I was just grieving for my brother. So we went but I just felt that I was sleepwalking through days, I can't explain it, everything seemed, and still feels, unreal as if I'm numb inside. One day, Gran asked me to tell her what was wrong, and what had happened to Rob. I said I would tell her if she promised not to tell my father.

She was outraged when I told her what had happened. She said that he had raped me and that my parents should be told. I told her that I didn't want him charged because it would mean I had to see him again and that I had not been able to believe that he could have behaved the way he had, he had been so kind to Jamie and that was the last time I had seen my brother happy with his family.

If what had happened had happened with a stranger it might have been very different but I felt as if I was implicated and to blame.

She said she would say nothing, because she had promised but she wanted me to think about it very seriously because like you she thought the same thing could happen to some other young girl and she thought that he needed help'.

'I want you to tell your parents,' said the priest. 'It's right that they should know and you owe it to yourself. Rob can be cautioned it would mean the police speaking to him. A caution would mean that his name would be kept on file and it could be put to him that he needed to seek help. But tell me about your other grandparents? Do they have any influence on your father?'

'I have lovely grandparents! Nan – my grandmother is actually called Nancy and everybody calls her Nan not just her grandchildren – she told me once that the war had changed my father. He had been in the Air Force, he had only ever wanted to fly and he joined the Air Force when he left school and he did fly all during the war, at some stage he became an Officer. His only brother, James, qualified as a doctor just after the war started and he was called up and became a medic in the army and he was sent out to the Far East and was captured. He died in a Japanese Prisoner of War camp and when my father learnt of his death after the war he never got over it.
Nan said that he and his brother had been inseparable.

'When Jamie was born, she said that my father had been overjoyed and had named him after his brother and then he couldn't face up to Jamie being mentally disabled. She said that Jamie was physically very like James so much so that it was heart-breaking. Nan said my father helps anyone in need but can't deal with himself, she said he was her son that mothers see their children in ways that others who don't know them do. She said that my father had attended church until he had learnt of his brother's death but had then said that he could no longer believe in God. Nan had Jamie and I baptized she said that my father just shrugged his shoulders but had not objected. His mother might excuse him but I can't.

I'll never forgive him!' and as for Rob I'll never forget, it's impossible for me to forgive him!'

'Never is a very long time, Elspeth. We are not being asked to forgive the sin, but the sinner, and this doesn't happen overnight, it may take a very long time, God is patient He understands your pain and anger. Rob has committed a dreadful crime against you but when we don't forgive the past we can so easily allow it to poison the present and the future and in the end our suffering is twofold and becomes coupled with bitterness and I don't want this to happen to you.

There comes a time for all of us when we need to re-evaluate our past lives, to forgive and discard what was bad and profit from what was good. I would like you to try and pray for those who have so seriously wronged you. You are very young still, but as you go through life you'll find that everybody has a Cross to carry, some heavier than others, and yours at present is very heavy, but at the end of the day it is not the weight of the Cross that matters but the way we carry it and an important part of that is that we learn to understand and empathize with the pain of others as they try to carry theirs. I have never met any worthwhile person that has not suffered and neither have I known any wise person who has not learnt to forgive. For now I hope that you will find that talking and tears will help to release some of the tension of the past months and enable you to grieve and feel the sorrow that needs to be expressed in order for you to find healing.'

The priest spoke quietly and slowly. His expression was serious but filled with kindness and the understanding of experience. What he said was heartfelt, he was not just reciting a formula. Things she had been unable to speak about she had spoken about to him and she felt calm but also utterly tired as if she had been on a long journey.

'And now Elspeth, if I might suggest, there is a Girls' cloakroom at the end of the passage, go and splash some cold water on your face and then go back into the chapel where I found you and stay there a while. Our Lady has been listening to our sorrows and joys for two thousand years and she will help you if you ask her. If you ever need to talk, at any time, you know where I am.

So Elspeth found herself once more in the Chapel. She closed her eyes and begged for help and felt a sense of peace that had evaded her for so long. She was not sure how long she stayed there, time seemed to stop, or ceased to exist at all. When she finally got up to go her step was lighter. She felt that she had learnt something of infinite importance and that the shackles that held her prisoner were, if not broken, loosened.

Chapter 2

. . . .

'The seasons bring the flowers again,
And bring the firstlings to the flock;
and in my breast
Spring wakens too; and my regret
Becomes an April violet,
And buds and blossoms like the rest.'
(In Memoriam, Alfred Lord Tennyson)

It was a late sunny August morning and Elspeth stood in front of her brother's grave. It was the first time that she had visited the graveyard since the funeral and she had brought a bunch of roses. She noticed that the grave was tidy and well kept, flowers that were just beginning to fade were in a stone vase and she thought that her mother must visit regularly. She bent down and placed her own flowers on top of the grave and then stood for a while quietly.

Elspeth had been a very pretty girl and she had grown into a beautiful young woman. Her blue grey eyes wore a grave expression this summer morning with just a shadow of the old sadness standing where she was and reflecting on the last three years that had so changed the direction of her life. She was aware that she was still frequently considered aloof by those who knew little of her, it was a wrong assessment, an air of detachment was natural to her. Her thick brown hair was cut short and her dress, as always, was simple and understated, this morning she wore a white, long sleeved lawn blouse, a cotton skirt and sandals. She wore no ornamentation.

She told herself that she had come home only semi-permanently. Her grandmother had suffered a severe attack of influenza during the winter, followed by a bad fall and had been persuaded to move in with Elsbeth's parents. She had her own independent living space with a pleasant living room at the back of the house which looked out on the garden and she was able to maintain her independence. Elspeth had been very shocked at Easter, her grandmother looked so frail but when she had caught sight of her granddaughter's expression she had said, 'it's just old age, don't look so anxious child!' But Elspeth was worried, Gran had been the mainstay of her childhood, more her mother than her grandparent, and she knew that she would stay close by all the time she was needed.

Following her graduation Elspeth had called in to see her old headmistress. Miss Cresswell had seemed a distance figure to her in her days in the Lower School but she had taught English to the Sixth Form and loving her subject she had inspired her young students. She had encouraged them to consider the intentions of the writer and how successful he or she had been in conveying those intentions. She had led them to recognize the complexities of life and how characters reacted to them. A brilliant teacher she had made her subject not just an Arts subject but a Humanities subject too. It was Miss Cresswell that had inspired Elspeth to read English at university and who had been so disappointed that Elspeth had turned down her place at Oxford. However, they had kept in touch and she greeted her star pupil warmly.

'Congratulations my dear on your Degree, being awarded a First was no more than I expected! What are your plans?'

Miss Cresswell had, Elspeth thought, never been pretty, but her grey hair now added to a certain air of distinction and her soft brown eyes wore a permanently kindly expression. She was wearing the same tweed jacket and skirt that Elspeth remembered from her Sixth Form days, so familiar that they seemed an integral part of her. She was neat and dressed with care.

Elspeth quickly explained that at present she was staying at home to be close to her grandmother but she was planning to teach in the future – it was always what she had wanted to do.

'I wrote telling you that I had become a Roman Catholic and I am thinking that I will apply to teach in a Catholic school, I suppose that I have some wish to teach less fortunate, disadvantaged children but I haven't applied anywhere yet'.

'Yes, I was interested in your becoming a Catholic and mentioning it to Mrs Manasses, we both agreed that we weren't really surprised, you always had something otherworldly about you. Your wish to teach less fortunate youngsters I think must be the influence of your grandmother – she was always one for championing the underdog as I remember! but y'know we also have very needy children here, not financially needy, of course, but poor little rich children and a few arrogant individuals who consider themselves superior to us lesser mortals! Remember Mr Brocklehurst, the clergyman in Jane Eyre and his two frightful, frivolous daughters – they in their way were more in need than Jane who had a strong moral sense and a capacity to empathize with others suffering, possibly because she had suffered so much herself'.' The assessment was so typical of her old headmistress that Elspeth inwardly smiled. She wondered who else, reading Jane Eyre, would think that the two frightful sisters were needy, or give them a second thought, let alone think that they might benefit morally from a sound and corrective education.

'I am Church of England myself – high church – and I do love a beautiful ritual. My father was a clergyman in the Suffolk country town where I was brought up. I like to think that a Christian teacher brings a sense of empathy towards children with her, it's not always the case, of course, but when it is it creates a special atmosphere in the school. My father was a gentle soul who like your grandmother, had a special love for the poor and oppressed. He was a classics scholar, and bookish with a study crammed with books always disordered, and my mother's despair, but he never turned anyone in need from the door. He was childlike and some might have said naive, but he had earned the love of his parishioners and when he died the townsfolk all turned out for his funeral and the church was full on that occasion at least.

I had such a happy, tranquil and secure childhood despite it including a World War and it's that sense of security that many of our pupils don't experience in their lives away from here, in their own families. I'm aware that things change with the times, of course, but I think it's important that some traditions are kept and passed on. I believe they make for a sense of security in a frequently insecure world. It's what I've tried to do here, make something of a haven at Oaklands.'

'And you have succeeded!' Elspeth had loved her school and knew that enjoying school days was not the case always.

'I would like to think I have a happy school that prepares girls to go out in the world and take their place confidently there. Oh! I wonder – you say that you are staying at home for the present – I hope you won't think I'm being presumptuous but would you consider helping out here? Mrs Fraser's retirement is long overdue and she's eager to leave and I haven't managed to find a suitable replacement for her as yet.'

Elspeth had taken in the room as they were talking. The polished desk, the freshly cut flowers. Miss Cresswell had dedicated her life to Oaklands and her influence was clear to see around the school; the careful placement of artwork and flowers. The peaceful atmosphere had much to do with her.

'I think I would be delighted, and consider myself very fortunate to come and teach here. I have a lot to learn, I haven't taught before and have no experience, but if you are willing to take me on then yes!'

'Then I'll speak to Mrs Fraser and arrange for you to meet and sort things out between you.'

So the necessary arrangements were made and Elspeth's immediate future was decided.

....

When Elspeth left the Chaplaincy that cold late autumn evening she was aware that something pivotal had taken place in her life. She felt drained of energy and had no desire to join a communal meal. She stopped at a corner shop that remained open and bought something to eat and back in college she made a hot drink and took herself early to bed. She woke late on the Saturday morning with a weak, winter sun shining through the curtains.

The first thing Elspeth became aware of was that the dreamlike state where she had felt her soul to be in a place of inert slumber that had enveloped her for months had gone, she found herself once again in the present reality. She spent the day mainly alone dwelling on the encounter with Father Dominic, knowing that she must consider what she should do regarding Rob.

By evening she had decided to ring her grandmother and tell her that she had received some good counsel and that she wanted her to tell her parents. However, she also decided that she would write to her parents herself. She knew that she was unprepared to let her father get away with his treatment of his blameless, mentally disabled son or of his treatment of her. She reasoned that Jamie had been rejected and that that rejection had lead to his death, and that rejection by his mother had been, perhaps, the unconscious cause of Rob's behaviour to her. She wanted her father to read between the lines and so she described more fully than she had explained to Father Dominic how she had trusted Rob because it had been with his family that she had seen Jamie happier than she had seen him since before Grandpa's death; Rob had been very kind to her brother.

She never wished to see him again but she wanted him cautioned, not charged. She argued that he needed help and she wanted them to see he got it. She felt hatred towards Rob and dread, but she did not think he was a totally bad person.

Once the letter was written she posted it quickly, giving herself no time to change her mind.

The grief over her brother's death remained undiminished. Sometimes during the course of that weekend and for long afterwards her brother's face would come to mind, sometimes he would appear to plead with her, at other times and worse, he would be laughing and happy and then she would bury her head in her hands in an anguish of grief. The trauma of the rape was still overwhelming; it was fused in her mind with the tragic death of her brother the two things would always be welded together, how would she ever learn to trust again?

The letter to her parents had an almost immediate effect. They wrote that they were horrified and wanted Rob charged but they would follow her wishes and make sure that he faced a caution. Her father did not exactly apologise but neither did he make any lame excuses for himself. Elspeth felt that it was not all she hoped for but it was for the moment enough.

II

When Louise returned after her weekend at home she found a change in her friend and thought perhaps she had had some pleasing news from home or that she had resolved some matter she had been wrestling with and which she did not wish to share. As for Elspeth she was not ready to confide in her friend and she did not want to talk about her visit to the Chaplaincy. She did what she had done in the past and diverted the attention from herself by getting Louise to tell her about the family celebration.

'It was great! My grandparents came over from Ireland. My parents had hired the church hall and had laid on some refreshments and in the end many of the guests came with contributions of food and so we had a regular feast. My youngest brother, Patrick, plays the fiddle and he and my uncle Seamus played some Irish reels. My two youngest sisters do Irish dancing – I used to be in a group myself when I was younger but I wasn't as enthusiastic as my sisters, especially Maeve – they arrived with their dancing troupe and entertained us and my aunty Peggy sang, 'Danny Boy' and 'Take Me Home Again Kathleen', In the end everybody was singing and joking. No one parties like the Irish!'

III

So the term went on and Elspeth became more involved and willing to add her own comments in tutorials. She loosened up but made few friends. The last Saturday of term, out of the blue, she asked Louise if she could accompany her to Mass the following morning. Louise was surprised but said that yes, of course, she was more than happy for her to. She added once again that the Chapel was beautiful and if Elspeth enjoyed singing she was sure that she would enjoy the Gregorian Chant sung by the choir. Elspeth said simply that she thought the Chapel beautiful as she had visited it one afternoon.

'You never said!'

'No'.

The greatest surprise came after Mass when Father Dominic was shaking hands and wishing them 'A Happy Christmas' as they left.

'You'll be going home, Louise.'

'I will indeed',

Louise was just about to introduce her friend when Father Dominic greeted Elspeth: 'You too will be off home this week Elspeth?'

'We'll be going to Switzerland – we always go to visit my grand-parents over Christmas.'

'Ah! Yes I remember you saying. So you'll be skiing?'

'Two of my cousins are very proficient, my youngest cousin, Esme and I stick to the lower slopes but we enjoy the winter wonderland.'

Louise was astounded and outside turned to her friend, 'I must say you're a dark horse, Elspeth'.

'I'm sorry, I was in a very dark place when I came to universi-ty, my brother – he was fifteen and mentally handicapped – was killed back in June and I didn't want to talk about it. I was pret-ty desperate and I called in at the Chaplaincy, I wasn't even in-tending to really and Father Dominic saw how miserable I was and helped me. There were other issues too which I don't want to talk about'.

'No! Elspeth, I'm so sorry, I knew there was something wrong, and there was me going on and on about my family!'

'I was happy you did, I wanted you to, it was like an antidote'. Elspeth's eyes had misted over and her voice shook.

Louise didn't speak, she squeezed her friend's arm gently and sympathetically and they walked back to college in silence.

IV

After the Christmas holiday, Elspeth joined her friend each Sunday for Mass and became increasingly involved in the life of the Chaplaincy.

In February Louise invited her for a long weekend at her home. The afternoon they set off was cold and overcast. The two travelled by bus and looking out of the bus window the scenery was bleak, Elspeth saw rows upon rows of poor, mean looking streets and wondered how families managed to survive in such cramped conditions. The damp weather heightened the sense of desolation, there was a greyness that enveloped everything. The clouds were low and seemed to shroud the rooftops and the heavy industry added to the general gloom. Later a closer knowledge of the people was to change Elspeth's ideas about the North of England. The people were open and hospitable. Louise spoke up for her fellow townsfolk and North Country people generally, 'England is divided down the middle, this side we talk. Here in the North you'll learn how the other half live'.

She was right the people were hardy and open and the ones she met were uncomplaining. They did not seem to be constricted by the reserve so common in the South and talked about themselves and asked questions of acquaintances with genuine interest.

Louise had told her that her home sometimes seemed to be ready to burst at the seams and Elspeth did wonder how her parents and eight children had managed to fit themselves in. However, Louise's mother welcomed her and seemed unfazed by having another body to accommodate.

Louise's sister Ann, unfortunately, had had to give up her vocation as a nun. She had apparently never been strong and had suffered pneumonia soon after Christmas. She was at home recuperating and looked pale but Elspeth found her thoughtful and intelligent as indeed all Louise's siblings appeared to be.

However, Elspeth also sensed an undercurrent of tension particularly when Louise's father was present. The children were more highly educated than their parents and perhaps more outward looking. Mr Donoghue had greeted her respectfully enough but his welcome had lacked warmth and knowing she was not Catholic he was wary of her; she felt he did not approve of her and probably thought her not a suitable friend for his daughter.

When Louise's sister Bridget and her husband Tom arrived with their toddler, things relaxed. Tom was a pleasant looking man with bright blue eyes and he smiled, and laughed easily particularly when he looked at the antics of his baby son. Louise's father relaxed and talked cordially with his son-in-law, perhaps Tom had the right Catholic credentials. Elspeth thought Tom wore his faith with a lighter and perhaps greater grace.

On Sunday morning Elspeth accompanied the family to church and afterwards they all sat down to lunch together. During the meal a discussion arose. Louise's youngest sister, Catherine, began asking Elspeth about the Protestant Bible and why it stated that Christ had brothers. Catholics apparently thought that if a person was not a Catholic then they must be Protestant. Ann chipped in to say that in Hebrew, as she understood, the word for brothers was the same as for cousins. Catherine not unreasonably asked why then did the Protestant bible not use the word cousins. Elspeth said that it may have been a ploy of the Reformation to downgrade the mother of Jesus. Then she went on to describe the explanation her Scripture teacher had given.

She told them that her teacher, Mrs Manasses, was Greek Orthodox having married a Greek and converting to that faith. Her teacher had said that it was a very early Orthodox tradition that St Joseph was a widower and already had children when he married Mary. She said in all the early icons of St Joseph he is portrayed as an older man and that in the Greek church calendar they have an important feast day for St James, the Brother of the Lord, but they certainly do not believe that St James was a son of Mary to whom they give the same honour as does the Roman Catholic Church.

Elspeth wondered if she had spoken out of turn but Ann immediately came to her rescue saying that she had not heard this explanation before but she thought that it was very interesting and she added that no doubt many important traditions had been lost since the Schism.

Mrs Donoghue asked Elspeth if she was a protestant and Elspeth said somewhat to her own surprise, 'No, I'm not, I'm not altogether sure what I am at present, but I'm not a protestant.'

'But you believe in God?'

'Yes, yes I do!'

'Well then, my dear, the Good Lord will lead you to His truth in His own good time.'

Elspeth had Louise's father down as sanctimonious or bigoted, but was surprised when she and Louise were ready to leave, he smiled and shook her hand and said that it had been a pleasure to have her and they all hoped she would come again soon.

Louise had sensed something of her friend's discomfort and explained her parent's position. Things were in a state of change, her younger siblings were saying things that even five or six years ago she and her older brother and sisters would not have said. The Convent school she and Ann and Bridget had attended and which Maeve and Catherine now attended had seemed unchanging and her parents had felt secure but this sense of security was now being threatened.

When a nun retired she would now be replaced by a lay teacher and Church teaching which they had never particularly questioned was now being questioned and her parents found it unsettling. Her father was vulnerable and although his own faith would never be shaken he felt the changes of the Second Vatican Council might threaten the faith of his children. Louise added that she too felt that greater liberalisation may not necessarily make people happier.

Elspeth was amazed at this new way of approaching life. In her experience parents educated their children for life, but left them to make up their own minds about what they later did with that education and education was always considered more important than religion.

Elspeth asked Louise what the Second Vatican Council was, she had never heard of it, and Louise explained briefly and said there was even talk of a new rite of Mass and she wasn't happy about it. She also went on to explain that her father, particularly, may have felt some discomfort because Elspeth was from the South of England and decidedly Middle Class and his home and position were humble by comparison from what he would assume were hers.

Also she added, her father had been somewhat alarmed by her own choice of English as the subject she had chosen to study and might, therefore be questioning her choice of friend. He'd been horrified by some of the literature he had found her reading as a Sixth former and which she hastened to add, had not led her to question her faith, all the opposite. Her father had wanted her to study Latin or Medieval History as Ann had; The Middle Ages had, after all, taken place before the Reformation! The parish priest had finally spoken up on her behalf and her father had reluctantly given in.

It was all amazing to Elspeth not least because she was being allowed to see herself through the eyes of others. Louise's life had been, indeed, very different from her own and yet she had suffered during the past year, with her financially secure and apparently sheltered background, what she hoped Louise would never have to suffer; wealth did not safeguard one from death and harm. It was too soon to ask herself if suffering had deepened her appreciation of life, but with all her expensive education and material goods, she was the one who had felt humbled by Louise's home.

V

At Easter, Elspeth invited Louise to visit her home in the South West and Louise had readily agreed. Now it became Elspeth's turn to feel a degree of trepidation. Rob's accusation rang in her mind, 'Who do your family think they are?' She had told her grandmother what he had said and her grandmother had assured her that while she did not see eye to eye with her father about some things, he was not guilty of looking down on people.

Elspeth's visit to Louise's home and her meeting with her friend's parents had opened up a whole new world for her and led her to consider her own parents objectively, particularly her father. On coming home that Easter she had looked around for the family photograph album which her mother had put together at some point. She was eager to look for early photographs of her parents, she felt in a sense that she knew little of them.

The big players in her early life had been her grandparents. Her mother was frequently away accompanying her father on family business and social events.

She turned the pages and found a photo of her father as a young airman standing in front of his plane in his pilot's gear, a cigarette dangled from his fingers. He looked young and rather handsome and for the first time she considered the date: 1943 and the words below the photo, Flying Officer. She knew her father had piloted fighter bombers throughout the War but it had never really been talked about – few things were discussed in her home! But now she wanted to consider what the photo was telling her. Her father, she knew, from Nan had been awarded for courage and he must have witnessed friends and comrades being burnt alive when their planes were hit in enemy combat. She had only a vague idea as to when her father had retired from the Air Force, sometime soon after the War and after his marriage in 1945.

He had learnt of the cruel circumstances of his brother's death. Had he been war weary? Disillusioned? She realised that she had no idea. Had his training in discipline suppressed his emotions? He was, after all, of the generation that subscribed to the 'stiff upper lip'. She knew it happened and she had read that many World War survivors lived on, traumatised, unable to follow a normal life. Many found that the intensity of life lived during the war never reached that pitch of intensity again and this brought its own problems.

Where did her father fit into all this? Why had she never asked herself these questions in relation to him? She knew her parents were happily married – her father had once said he had fallen in love with her mother on first sight – but when she considered the families of friends her parents' marriage seemed somehow exclusive, for the most part of their children. They had never discussed anything meaningful with her and her mother appeared to agree – certainly she never openly disagreed – with her father.

She realized that he was a stranger to her. She had learnt much more about her mother from her grandmother who was very openly proud of her daughter; her mother was a beauty and accomplished. She was kind and could be generous to a fault, but was it acceptable to have stood by when her father had harshly treated her son? Gran had once told her that her daughter and indeed she herself, believed that human beings were born good and that it was the circumstances of life that caused them to do bad things, and that if her daughter had been called onto a jury she would have had difficulties in passing judgement on anybody and half-jokingly she had added, 'your mother would have wanted every defendant reprieved'. Now for the first time Elspeth asked herself if this was justice.

She was also beginning to subscribe to the belief that human beings are born with dispositions that were bad as well as good and that they have the capacity for both good and evil. Her father had wanted to sue the school for negligence and have Rob charged. Her mother had refused calling the school to account, was it because she felt in her heart that her father was guilty or that she didn't want any unpleasantness? Did she understand her father's inner insecurities and was she dedicated to giving protection? Did her mother actually lack moral courage? Would her mother stand up to be counted if the occasion demanded it? All these thoughts occupied her and she sighed deeply and turned the page of the album.

There she found a photograph of herself holding the hand of her little brother. He was looking up at her while she was staring directly ahead at the camera. She felt her heart lurch – she had no memory of the photograph but she remembered how her brother would rush towards her clapping his little hands in welcome if she had been away from home for any time. He had loved her and she had loved him with all her heart! The house was quiet now, the silence was empty.

Her father was generally charming to her friends, particularly her best friend, Belle, and both her parents liked Belle's family, so Elspeth knew they would welcome Louise. But something went on bothering her, she realized that her father rarely smiled, let alone laugh. She had never consciously thought about it before.

Her fears that Louise would feel critical of her home and her family's obvious wealth were thankfully unfounded, Louise was full of admiration. Elspeth met her at the station and her friend enthused about the architecture of the city on the way home. When they stood outside her home Louise was openly delighted, it simply didn't occur to her to make a comparison with her own humble home because for her, her family would always be a source of love and pride; she had nothing to envy.

'Elspeth your home is palatial! – it's beautiful.'

Over the threshold her admiration continued, 'what a beautiful house!'

Where Elspeth had been reserved on meeting Louise's parents Louise greeted her parents with open enthusiasm, 'I've been so looking forward to coming, I have never visited the Southwest before.'

'We've been looking forward to meeting you.'

During dinner Elspeth's mother asked Louise about her family, 'do you have brothers and sisters?'

'I have four sisters and three brothers – there are eight of us. Elspeth has met my brothers and sisters with the exception of my eldest brother who is studying for the Priesthood in Rome, he is going to be a Jesuit and it takes a number of years.'

'So you are a Catholic – I hope you didn't require a dispensation to visit our godless home', this from Elspeth's father.

'No dispensation was required, your home is not Godless, where Love is, God is.'

Louise's remark was half complimentary, with just a hint of admonishment, her Catholic faith would always be on the side of the Angels.

Elspeth noticed her father half start, he looked at her friend appraisingly as if he was considering her seriously for the first time.

'I've noticed a display of fine family photographs in the hall; I'd be so interested to know who the people are'.

I'll be delighted to introduce you to them'. Elspeth could see that Louise's honest, straightforward manner had won her father over.

After the meal they went into the hall. Central to the photograph display was a Victorian family scene. The husband and wife sat in the centre of the group and Louise said the wife looked a little like Elspeth.

'It's Elspeth's great grandmother, another Elspeth. This was their house. My grandparents inherited it. My father was brought up here and so was I. When my parents moved to Switzerland in the 'Fifties I just went on living here, it was my home and became the home of my family. Perhaps Elspeth will take it over one day.'

'It's Elspeth as a young girl in the photo with the little boy, isn't it?'

'Yes, the little boy was our second child, he died last summer, Elspeth will have told you, I think.'

Louise nodded.

Elspeth was glad that her father had used the word 'child' and not 'son'. Jamie was a child, a little child and would remain so always.

Louise looking at the photograph of Elspeth's mother remarked on her beauty.

'My wife is very beautiful, and very accomplished. I'm sure that we can persuade her to give us a piano recital during your stay'.

Elspeth's mother required little persuasion, she loved music and she played Chopin – her favourite composer – for them. It was a professional and exquisite rendition. Louise was over-awed.

Elspeth was most eager for Louise to meet her grandmother who lived close by and they called the following day. While her mother was an accomplished pianist her grandmother produced excellent pastries and cakes. She had done her best to interest her daughter into the arts of her kitchen with no success and she had been even less successful with her little granddaughter. Elspeth didn't like getting her hands sticky and was content to sit reading a book in the kitchen while her grandmother baked.

The old lady lay on a fine tea and Louise was delighted, she loved baking and cooking. She and her brothers and sisters had been required to help out in the kitchen from being very young. It had been a matter of necessity, but fortunately, she had always enjoyed it.

Gran immediately warmed to Louise when she expressed her appreciation of her baking. The two were soon exchanging recipes and cooking hints. Her grandmother was happy to tell Louise about her failed efforts to interest her granddaughter in the culinary skills. Elspeth she said had always been a bookworm, her life from being very small had been a world of books.

'I used to think poetry and singing songs was her second language – she could recite verse and sing songs long before she could read and when she learnt to read that was that, she would sit with a new book every week trying to engage me in the life-cycle of the butterfly or the frog. Her best friend, Belinda, was the one for animals and wildlife and Elspeth would find the books to inform her friend of habitats and habits of a range of creatures. I've watched Elspeth with Belinda on one side and her little brother, Jamie, on the other informing them about a range of topics, and they would be engrossed.

Belle's father came to collect his daughter one afternoon and he laughed and said Elspeth would make a wonderful teacher one of these fine days. She asked Louise about her family and once again Louise was obliged to describe her brothers and sisters. Gran looked sad for a moment and then said that she and Elspeth's grandfather had longed for more children but that none had come. At this Elspeth was very surprised when Louise told them that while her father was one of a large family her mother was an only child. She said her grandparents had also longed for children but none had come and after ten years of marriage they had given up hoping and then her grandmother had found herself pregnant. She said that her grandparents had several brothers and sisters and so her mother had been brought up on their farm in Ireland surrounded by uncles, aunts and cousins.

The visit proved a great success and Louise asked Elspeth if, as she had once said, her grandmother was not religious why she had a religious text on her wall.

'One of her sisters gave her it. I think my grandmother would say that the Labour Party was her church. As a young child, at the beginning of this century, her mother used to take her to suffragette meetings with her, Gran joined the Labour Party when it was formed and has remained a member ever since. She's all for the poor and women's rights!'

'In the North people who vote Labour are almost always poor your grandmother isn't'.

Elspeth's grandmother's house also looked very fine. It was large, comfortable and tastefully furnished.

'No, I think far from it! I questioned her about her political beliefs once and she said the poor needed the rich, because if everyone was poor it would be like the blind leading the blind. The rich were able to buy the products of the poor but one should never allow money to become the be-all of existence. One had an obligation to give generously to those in need.

I questioned her about artists dying in garrets in poverty when no one bought their works and how designers got very wealthy through the success of their designs and she had a ready answer, she said that they had provided employment for thousands and the aeroplane for example had helped to win the war, so she didn't think she would want to deprive its designers of their profit. I suppose she has a point. She has spent her life running charities of one kind and another and helped for years looking after children in a local orphanage. She's the most caring of the caring and I love her to bits'.

VI

The summer term went by without incident and Elspeth and Louise along with her sister, Ann and two friends from the Chaplaincy, agreed to go to Lourdes to help with the sick and disabled. When Elspeth told her parents they said that they were disappointed she would not be joining them in Switzerland and afterwards on a holiday in Italy. So Elspeth agreed to go on from Lourdes to Switzerland and then join them on the last part of their holiday in Sicily.

The girls threw themselves into the work. Ann was so much better and was in her element and Elspeth, much to her own surprise discovered that she loved the French Shrine. How different things were from the year before! She felt as if she was on a different planet.

Helping the mentally and physically disabled helped her in facing up to Jamie's death in a way she could not explain. She found herself doing for these disabled people, especially the children, what she could no longer do for her own young brother, and the experience became a catharsis, a great release of her pent up emotions; helping the sick she could not dwell on her own sadness. She felt that she was being healed. She thought if cynics were only to come and experience this place for themselves they could not fail to be moved and to question their disbelief. But then she dismissed the thought. She was well acquainted with the Scriptures and had an 'O' Level in Scripture knowledge, she had not gone on to take it as an 'A' Level subject but had continued attending the lessons when she was free; her Scripture teacher had always been able to keep her interested and the subject itself had always engrossed her.

She had always believed that human nature was constant in so many things. She had once sat down and read the Old Testament Book of Wisdom and was intrigued by its second chapter she thought it could have been written yesterday it was so modern sounding and the same could be said of the Gospels and much of the Epistles how else could one so easily understand them? Like all great literature it was timeless. Time was another concept that intrigued Elspeth.

By the end of the summer vacation she found herself longing to return to the Northeast. She told Louise that she loved the Northeast and Louise had replied 'if it wasn't for the winters it would be great'. Elspeth was succeeding at university, her grades were excellent and she was by nature perceptive and this was essential in studying Literature, but with the exception of Louise and one or two others, she felt that most of her fellow students held her at arm's length. It distressed her and she expressed her feelings to Louise one afternoon in Lourdes when they found themselves free and alone.

'You give the impression that you are holding back and they think you are superior – I know you don't think of yourself in those terms but it comes over to them that you don't regard them as – well good enough for you.'

Elspeth was horrified! It was what Rob had said.

'I'm sorry, I think I've really hurt you'.

It was then that Elspeth related to her friend the 'other issues' that she had not wanted to discuss with her in her first months at university. Without tears and passion this time, she told her friend about the events of the previous summer and what had happened to her, 'it's so difficult for me to trust anyone', she said.

'I'm glad you've told me now. I knew you were grieving for your brother but I couldn't have imagined that you had experienced such a depth of suffering! And this is what you told Father Dominic?

'Yes'. I thought I had sobbed it all out of my system but I don't think I will ever fully come to terms with it. I'm afraid to be alone with any young man – Rob looked so open and honest. I try to put it behind me but it's always there, far from feeling superior I feel the opposite – sometimes I feel like crawling into a hole and hiding away as if there's something wrong with me.'

'There's nothing wrong with you! I have found you looking so much happier here in Lourdes. When you first came to university you looked very pale, distant and so very sad I knew there was something very wrong. If only I'd known! I cannot begin to imagine how I would have reacted if it had happened to me! I think you're very brave. Give yourself time. I know people say that time is a great healer but sometimes it just sounds like a platitude made by people who have not experienced the same loss and suffering or something to say because they feel they've got to say something. I just think you have got to be patient with yourself.

I liked your parents a lot, by the way but I felt your father was very sad, I thought it must be because of your brother's death. While your mother was playing the piano I looked at him and thought he had the same sad expression you had last year. You say that your father was a Bomber pilot during the War, he must have seen terrible things, friends and comrades burnt to death and survivors scarred and disfigured for life, he must have been afraid every time he stepped into a plane to go on a bombing raid. There are the physical effects of war which we so sympathise with because they can be seen but we should not forget the mental effects. Then there is the terrible death of his brother. I think so many survivors of war have what must be an impotent rage inside of themselves, they need help. Of course one should not take one's anger and frustrations out on the innocent but I can empathise with your father in a way that it's very difficult for you to – I can be objective. You are very special to Father Dominic, I realise now why that is, I thought he was, well if you must know, I thought he was more than a little in love with you'.

Elspeth was taken aback, 'Louise he's a priest!'

'One of the finest, but he is also a man.'

'I was a lost sheep that he found and saved, that's the whole truth of it. I'll owe him a debt for the rest of my life'.

'I heard down the Catholic grapevine that Father Dominic's eldest brother was killed during the evacuation of Dunkirk.'

'It doesn't surprise me, I have the impression that he has suffered himself' and understands the pain of others,' said Elspeth.

That autumn she approached Father Dominic and requested instruction; she had decided that she wished to become a Catholic. The following Easter she was received into the Church and Louise and Ann acted as her sponsors. That night she wrote in her diary the verse of St John of the Cross:

I had no light, no guide
But that which burned within my heart,
And yet that light did lead me on
More clearly than the noonday sun,
Unto a place where waited One Who knew me well.

When she told her parents her mother looked surprised and her father said, 'I knew two Catholic chaplains in the Air Force during the War they were very fine human beings, two of the bravest men I have ever known.'

Gran, however, voiced her disapproval in the strongest terms. 'My parents had spent their lives helping the poor and the Working Man, and they spoke well of Cardinal Manning standing up for the London Dockers but they did as much themselves giving their time and financial assistance to the Charity Organization Society that was set up in Victorian times to help the very poor. They didn't need holy statues and incense! I don't go along with it! And I'm sorry that you have been caught up in it. I like your friend, Louise, but I expect she has been the main influence in all this!'

But when Elspeth showed no inclination to convert her, and when she remained the same loving granddaughter she had always been, she relented and finally said that she knew she had gone through a serious trauma and if religion had helped her face up to things then she would say no more on the subject.

It was Nan's response on being told that most surprised and gladdened her granddaughter. She embraced her and said how happy she was for her and how important her own faith had been in her life, 'it kept me sane after learning of James' terrible death – there are folks who say that people who are religious are just fulfilling a need. That's always seemed an illogical argument to me, I don't refuse food and drink because I need them, would it really mean I was strong if I chose to starve myself? I've prayed all your life for you Elspeth hoping that you would find a faith in God and now I believe those prayers have been answered,'

VII

Elspeth's third year at university was her happiest, she extended her circle of friends and slowly became less reticent. The Chaplaincy became important to her and apart from the choir which she had joined, she discovered that she enjoyed the Debating Society which sometimes held joint debates with the university. One evening Father Dominic spoke to the group about a debate which the university was organising about abortion and the motion that had been decided on was: 'Abortion is a Necessary Evil' and he requested that one of their group should speak against the motion and Elspeth volunteered.

She wasn't used to speaking in public but she felt that she could put forward convincingly a strong argument, and on the evening of the debate she sat on the platform feeling very nervous. She heard all the arguments put forward by a third year student who had a reputation as a feminist and for the first time she listened to the case of 'Women's Rights"; 'the previous horrors of back-street abortionists;' 'the profoundly handicapped with their limited quality of life and the burden they placed on families;' and 'the extensive growth of populations and the unsustainable pressures placed on poorer countries in their efforts to feed them,' These became over the coming years the stable arguments in favour of abortion but this was Elspeth's first introduction to some of these arguments and she wondered how the simple case she was putting forward would sound in comparison.

Then it was Elspeth's turn to speak against the motion and she stood up.

'I'm going to begin by making a short digression and I would like you to be patient while I explain why I have reached a different point of view. My oldest friend, we've been friends since we began school at four and a half, is a great lover of wildlife and animals and one day when we were about six or seven years old, we were allowed by her father to pick up some cabbage from his vegetable patch to feed my friend's guinea pig. Under one of the cabbage leaves we discovered a cluster of cabbage white butterfly eggs and we asked her father what they were. We were amazed and my friend said, 'do butterflies grow inside of the eggs then?' Her father enlightened us by telling us that they grew into caterpillars first and made themselves a feast on his cabbages, so he added they should be destroyed because they were a pest. There was no way that my friend was going to allow that and she pleaded with her father to save them. Her poor father, who has spent years having to give way to his daughter's desperate lifesaving of creatures great and small either stood to see his cabbages eaten or look like a murderer in his little girl's eyes. And since I've always been something of a know-all I compounded the situation by finding a book that described the lifecycle of the butterfly. The moral of this tale is to draw attention to the minute size of butterfly eggs and to the beautiful life forms that emerge from them.

'Biologists tell us that each one of us began as microscopic cells and those cells contain everything that we would later become, a much more complex life form than a butterfly! Those microscopic cells determine the hair and eye colour, the intelligence, personality, mannerisms, of not just any child but an individual, unique child, your child or my child, you or me. By the time most abortions take place at around twelve weeks the growing baby already has a heartbeat and all its organs including its brain is in place, in other words it is a human person.

'It is not a jelly-like substance that proponents of abortion are suggesting in order to make the procedure more palatable and acceptable. We should not forget that the Nazis put forward propaganda to make believe that Jewish people were subhuman because that was the only way they could convince their followers to commit their inhuman crimes.

The more we learn about the human brain and its functions the greater the wonder of life becomes. When we crush a chrysalis we kill a butterfly when we carry out an abortion we kill a child. The world has plenty of resources to go round if they are used as they should be and not monopolised by particular trading groups.

I would like to conclude by saying that the unborn have 'rights' too, most particularly the right to life. Disabled children have been mentioned, I should like finally to say that my mentally disabled brother died as the result of an accident four months before I came to this university. I loved him more than I can say and I wish that I could turn the clock back and have him alive. His innocent, trusting smile could light up a room and melt a human heart, my heart! He gave me the best thing in my life, so much more than I could give back. I'll mourn my beautiful brother for the rest of my life. Love doesn't have a price it's above price as life itself is, it's precious, and disabled children are precious and give and receive the love that we should be prepared to give them, it brings enormous rewards.'

Lots of questions followed. Some students put forward the suggestion that the unborn had no knowledge of their fate and no one could say at what point they had a soul or an identity as such. Few debates were so passionately argued it was said and at the end the opposition won by a small number of votes and Father Dominic and the Chaplaincy were encouraged by the outcome. Elspeth's speech with its inclusion of personal details and its engaging of people's emotions was thought to have gone down particularly well. Father Dominic thanked her and students who had previously considered her standoffish changed their minds and her reputation improved.

Chapter 3

....

'My true-love has my heart and I have his.
By just exchange one for another given:
I hold his dear and his I cannot miss.
There never was a better bargain driven:
My true-love has my heart, and i have his.

His heart in me keeps him and me in one,
My heart in him his thoughts and senses guides:
He loves my heart, for once it was his own,
I cherish his because in me it hides:
My true-love has my heart, and I have his.'
(A Ditty, Sir P Sidney)

Elspeth left her brother's grave that late August morning to make her way to her friend Belle's house to have her last fitting for her bridesmaid's dress. Belle was going to be married in September. She drove there in the car she had been promised three years earlier and which had finally been given her for her twenty-first birthday and for achieving her degree.

Belle's home was in a small country town that had grown up around an old village not far from the city. Elspeth looked at her friend's house fondly as it came into sight. Belle's father had had it built in the 1950s to accommodate his growing family, it was large and sprawling and built more for comfort than for any architectural merit and Elspeth loved it. Belle's father had gone into his father's business with his brother when they had left school. The family owned a chain of Grocery shops across the city. During the Fifties and early Sixties they had bought up new premises and opened a new shop every other year and even had shops in nearby towns. These would inevitably be swallowed up in the next two decades by supermarkets, but for the present they were thriving.

Belle had worked in the offices attached to the main shop after leaving school, but her heart had not been in the work. Belle's life-long passion was animals and wildlife and at eighteen she had finally achieved her dream and been offered a job as a receptionist in a small veterinary hospital. In a fortnight she was to marry the veterinary surgeon who ran it. Elspeth had spent hours helping to look after a succession of her friend's pets and in making graves for them when they inevitably expired. Many times Jamie was also invited to help out. Belle looked on Jamie like one of her pet animals, 'he doesn't understand like the rest of us and we have to be patickuly kind', she would say in her childish voice and she would let Jamie hold her beloved guinea pig saying, 'be very gentle, he likes you to stroke her', – or him as the case might be. So the guinea pig, Dot, when she finally died was put to rest in a grave in the garden and Belle was inconsolable. 'I called her Dot,' she had told Elspeth 'because Mummy said it was short for Dorothy and I like that name and we didn't know if it was a girl guinea pig or a boy because daddy forgot to ask the shop and he said Dot could be a name for a boy or a girl.' The guinea pig had been so smothered with love and constant affection he or she would not have objected either way. Sid the hamster soon followed after Dot's demise and on passing was mourned for a long time.

Elspeth remembered being invited to go on holiday down to Devon with the family and Belle pleaded with her father to let her take the hamster with them, 'he'll be no trouble, I promise, please daddy!' But daddy on this occasion was firm and put his foot down. He had three daughters, and his wife always ready to overrule him and being reluctant to deny them anything being the most indulgent of fathers this time he flatly refused, 'Sid is going to your auntie Daisy and she'll take great care of him, and if you stop moaning you can telephone her while you're away and ask how he is'. But when Sid finally died she continued to mourn him for months until her birthday when she was given Harold and Bill, two angora rabbits, and her father built a hutch for them. Belle's animal stories became legendary in the family and Elspeth smiled with nostalgia as she remembered them.

Elspeth rang the doorbell and soon heard Mrs Honeyman, Belle's mother, hurrying to answer it proceeded by Skip, their golden retriever, barking loudly. Skip knew Elspeth and as soon as the door was opened he barked louder and jumped up at her. 'Down you silly dog! Elspeth doesn't want you all over her'. Elspeth bent over and stroked him and they moved along the hall into the living room.

The room reflected the exterior of the house, it was furnished for living comfortably in. Large sofas with plenty of cushions, it had looked the same for years and was as dissimilar as could be from her elegantly furnished and ordered home. The family's two cats were sharing the rug in front of the fireplace. One of them got up to see who it was, arched its back and lay down again, the other one lazily opened an eye, saw that it was no one worthy enough of its attention and closed it again. Tim, Belle's sister Meg's husband – they had married the year before – was reading a newspaper, he lowered it when Elspeth entered the room, nodded and smiled at her and went back to reading.

'The dressmaker and the girls are upstairs waiting for you, they are in the guest room, you know where it is. You'll be staying for lunch afterwards I hope'.

'If it's no trouble.'

'Trouble! You're like one of the family!'

When Elspeth opened the door of the guest room, the three sisters and the dressmaker greeted her. Chloe, Belle's youngest sister was in the process of her last fitting. Belle's dress was already finished, along with two small dresses that were intended for their cousins, they were hanging on a rail. Elspeth had not seen Meg, Belle's eldest married sister for a while. She now had a home of her own and Belle had told her that she was expecting her first child in the spring. As always she was the picture of contentment, she was comely and resembling her mother she would one day be buxom too. She worked happily for her father, she enjoyed the camaraderie of the office and she now congratulated Elspeth, 'You have done so well at university Elspeth, Belle told me!'

'Thank you. I understand Congratulations are due to you too, what month is your baby expected?'

'March, if it arrives on time'.

Belle, spoke up, 'Alistair is going to train me as his assistant, Elspeth, I'll be a veterinary nurse'.

'You'll be a natural!'

Belle looked radiant. All three girls were fair-haired, Belle was wearing hers shoulder length. When they were very young children, Elspeth thought Belle was the most beautiful girl in the school and longed to look like her and wanted to have blonde hair and to wear the same clothes. Elspeth's hair was, of course, dark and Mr Honeyman used to call them, Snow White and Rose Red, the names stuck for a long time and it brought the children closer together. They would always be friends. Belle never questioned Elspeth, she admired her cleverness without understanding the complexities of her mind and this suited Elspeth, it allowed her to relax they were always there for each other; at Jamie's funeral it was Belle she clung to, she did not have to explain.

When they had not seen each other, sometimes for months on end, on meeting up again they took up where they had left off as if they had met the day before. She was so happy that her friend was marrying Alistair. He was quite a large young man but he had she had noticed, delicate hands and she could imagine how gentle he would be dealing with her friend. Mr Honeyman had commented to her, 'those two fit together like a hand in a glove, there's not an unkind bone in either of their bodies'. Sitting on the bed, waiting to be fitted, Elspeth wondered whether that was the secret at the heart of her parents' marriage, that her mother did not question her father, she accepted him for what he was, the words of the psalm came into her head, 'he maketh me to lie down in green pastures: he leadeth me beside the still waters. He restoreth my soul.' She hoped her friend's marriage would be forever in green pastures and beside still waters.

Now it was Elspeth's turn to be fitted. The shot silk of the older bridesmaids' dresses was in a flattering shade of turquoise, the little cousins were wearing white decorated with floral sprays and turquoise sashes and they would all wear plain turquoise headbands. Chloe had helped with the designs and colours of the dresses, she was the youngest sister at eighteen and she had just left Oaklands School having gained 'A' Levels in Art and English. She was about to go to college to study fashion design. She wore her fair hair long, she had dreamy grey eyes and frequently appeared to be lost in pleasant day dreams, she liked Elspeth and admired her dress sense, she had once remarked, 'Your clothes are so beautifully understated, next to you women feel overdressed'.

Elspeth slipped her blouse and skirt off and removed her sandals and was about to help the dressmaker to put the long bridesmaid dress over her head, when Meg spoke, 'Tim and I met Rob the other week, you went out with him for a while before you went to university didn't you? Tim was at school with him. He asked after you and I told him that you had gained a First Class Degree and he just said, I always knew she was well out of my league. He said that he is engaged to a farmer's daughter called Fiona.'

Elspeth pulled the dress down over head and was glad her face was hidden, she felt her stomach muscles tighten, 'I'm glad for him', she said. She managed to keep her voice calm, she still felt the horror of him. She had received a short letter from him eighteen months ago. He had written that he was very sorry and he hoped that she would find it in her heart to forgive him, he said that he had received counselling, that he had decided to see a counsellor because he hot been able to live with himself. It was many years before Elspeth learnt that it had been her father who had paid for the help he had received. She surmised that the letter had been written about the time he had met Fiona.

'You haven't got any new boyfriend yourself, Elspeth?'

'No, I've not met anybody special.'

'Well don't you go and bury yourself in books. I must say I'm surprised, with your looks, I would have thought you would have young men lined up outside your door! I can see I'll have to take on the job of matchmaking! That dress is looking lovely on you, what do you think Chloe, it is your design?

'If I'm not careful Elspeth's going to steal the show', remarked Belle.

'You don't see yourself as others see you, Belle, all eyes are going to be on you', returned Elspeth.

II

The wedding was to take place in the village Parish Church. Elspeth loved the atmosphere to be found in old churches. They had a particular musty smell of something indefinable and the church in Belle's village church had centuries of history; it had a quietness undisturbed by outside events, it had withstood the test of time. Elspeth had accompanied Belle and her sisters to Sunday school when they were younger and when she had been invited to their home on a Sunday. Mr Honeyman was Church Warden and Mrs Honeyman saw to the flower arrangements along with two other women. The family were regular churchgoers but they had never attempted to influence any of their friends they did not talk about religion or politics; they regarded it as an infringement of another's privacy.

The part they played in the lives of others was to be there when their friends and neighbours needed them; they were upright and decent and very English. When Elspeth told Belle's family that she had converted to Catholicism, Mr Honeyman said, somewhat uncomprehendingly and clearly embarrassed, Elspeth thought, 'Well there are worse things, I suppose, we can't all be the same.' And then he had asked what her parents had said about it.

'They are fine about it, Gran disapproved, but my Nan was very happy about it'.

'Well, of course your father's parents live on the Continent – '.

The comment was left in the air and Elspeth was left wondering what he had meant, but did not ask.

III

The day before the wedding there were squally showers. Elspeth arrived at Belle's home to spend the night on a put-up bed in her friend's bedroom and they talked long into the night.

'I hope tomorrow's fine'.

Belle said it would not spoil anything whatever the weather, 'we can't expect everything'.

The household were all up by seven o'clock and when Elspeth drew the curtains she was pleased that the day, though still overcast, was dry. They all had breakfast and a hairdresser arrived at nine o'clock to dress their hair. They could hardly contain their excitement. The Marriage Service in the church was set for eleven o'clock and they were all ready for half past ten when the flowers arrived. The two small cousins were wide-eyed with happiness and two little male cousins were dressed up as page boys and were laughing at each other in their top hats. By eleven o'clock a weak sun was just beginning to make an appearance and the wedding party began to make its way to the church, which was a mere stone's throw from the house.

Elspeth saw her parents and Gran as they processed up the aisle and she smiled, Gran was leaning on a stick but was determined that she would stand up with the others; she was arthritic and her legs were feeling their age. The Church of England Marriage Rite was lovely Elspeth thought – the Language in the Book of Common Prayer along with the Authorized Version of the Bible Elspeth would always consider beautiful – today it had a solemnity that matched the occasion. She liked the choice of hymns to – with the exception of the inevitable 'All things Bright and Beautiful', and wondered what was going through her Gran's mind. The offensive verse had been removed from the modern hymn book: her grandmother had once returned from a Labour Party church service incensed, she had hardly crossed the threshold when she reported her horror.

'I can't believe it, they sang 'All things bright and beautiful' and one of the verses actually says: 'The rich man in his castle, the poor man by his gate, He made them high and lowly, and ordered their estate'. What do you make of that!? It's surprising they didn't include workhouses or slaves on plantations!'

'They wouldn't mean any harm Emmy, I mean the writer of the hymn wouldn't'.

Grandpa was used to these outbursts and slowly filled his pipe lit it and drew on it. It relaxed his nerves.

'What do you mean he didn't mean any harm! Keir Hardie and Emmeline Pankhurst would turn in their graves! And those silly women singing with gusto!'

Keir Hardie and Emmeline Pankhurst were Gran's heroes she had been called Emmeline after the suffragette, as she frequently reminded them, and she ignored for the moment that the 'silly women' were among her closest friends.

The wedding reception took place in a country hotel and there were speeches and clapping and general rejoicing and then an orchestra arrived and there was dancing.
Today the entire world was a wedding!

When the couple were ready to set off on their honeymoon Belle threw her bouquet into the crowd, she aimed it at Elspeth but it was Chloe who caught it and Elspeth laughed with the rest.

Would she ever be a bride she wondered ruefully? Next year she had been asked to be bridesmaid for Louise who had met and fallen in love with Jerome while she and Elspeth were in Lourdes for a second year. Jerome a Double First from Cambridge was working with the sick along with them. He was kind, clever and impractical and the disabled loved him because they recognized the efforts he was making and how hard he tried to help them. Louise stepped in for him and managed his efforts with a bright smile. He needed to be managed and Louise liked to manage and so Elspeth thought, it would continue throughout their married life. Louise announced their engagement to Elspeth telling her that Jerome was not ambitious and was joining his family's firm of Solicitors in the Cotswolds, 'Would you believe it, we'll be practically next door'.

Chapter 4

....

' – there came wise men from the East – and opening their
treasures they presented unto Him gifts,
gold and frankincense and myrrh.'
(Matthew Ch 2 v11)

Oaklands School had originally been an eighteenth century stately home set in extensive grounds comprising parkland and gardens. During the nineteenth century the family that owned it was left without an heir and the entire property had been bought by a Victorian philanthropist who turned it into a Girls' School. Over the following century it had become an exclusive Public School largely owing to its expensive and prohibitive fees. There were places allocated to girls in the city who had passed a scholarship and the school was notable for its high standards. An ancient oak tree of some renown stood in a small copse in the grounds and it was this that had given the school its name. During the nineteenth and early twentieth centuries a housing boom had taken place so that the school was now surrounded outside its gates by a large residential area made up of Victorian and Edwardian houses and the school was no longer seen to be part of the country estate it had originally been.

Elspeth had entered Oakland's preschool at the age of four and a half years. The small building that housed the nursery or kindergarten had been built in the 1930s and stood just inside the gates. Oaklands had been a huge part of her life from almost as far back as she could remember. Every part of it was familiar to her. She had spent time when she could, sitting under the oak tree and thought and read books and dreamed dreams and wondered how many others over the centuries of its existence, had sat beneath its branches when it was perhaps part of a woodland or a village. It presented an unbroken link with the past.

Now as she prepared herself to teach in her old school she asked herself if she was living in a bubble and that a return to Oaklands was escapism. She was living in a culture of 'Rock and Roll' and she realised that many of her new pupils would be enjoying that culture and not for the first time she felt that she was on the outside looking in at a cultural world that she had never fully embraced. At university she knew that she had been considered as something of an elitist and she also had enough knowledge of herself to recognise that the traumatic events that had taken place in her life in the months before university were not the sole reason for her feeling an outsider. However, she was not anti-social, why then did she have these doubts? Was Oaklands a microcosm in much the same way as any other school or institution? And was she being unnecessarily hesitant? In any case, she told herself the arrangement was semi-permanent and she wanted and had always wanted to teach and very soon she would find out if her self-questioning was indeed baseless.

It was in this frame of mind that Elspeth entered her new life early in September a few days after Belle's wedding. It was an early autumn day and the sun was lower in the sky but it was bright and warm and she took it to be a good omen. Her uncertainty was left behind, teaching was her vocation, and she knew that she wanted to make a difference to her pupils' lives and prepare them for the world they would one day be entering; she could not, of course, change the world but she could make a small contribution. She would take the example of her old Headmistress who greeted her affectionately, she would teach English Literature as reflections of life made by great writers and she would share the poetry she loved.

She had prepared herself for teaching by reading some educational theories during the long vacation and she was determined that she would not pigeon hole her subject but would make herself take a full part in school life and learn to see her pupils as whole individuals not just her English students. They came she knew from very different walks of life and indeed from different parts of the world and she was determined to find out as much as she could about them; she would become interested in them as people. Opportunities for putting this approach into practise came almost immediately.

Elspeth had never been particularly involved with sport, she was not in the least competitive and during the sport events trials in summer she had mainly been a spectator, cheering her special friends on and as soon as she could legitimately escape she had wandered away or sat on the grass of the school field making endless daisy chains lost in reverie. Now she was determined to change this attitude of hers and to learn about her pupils by attending sports and games events that were important to the young people who she considered were, in a broad sense, in her care and she very soon found that it paid dividends.

Dinah was fifteen and in her third year in lower school. She was from an African Chieftain's family and a natural athlete. She ran as swiftly as the wind and spent as much time as possible out on the track trying to improve her timings. She was as elegant as a young gazelle and each time she was first in a competition her beautiful black face would glow with happiness. Her whole physical being exuded confidence and delight. Elspeth's Scripture teacher who had befriended her at school was standing next to Elspeth one afternoon watching Dinah being congratulated on winning yet another race and seeing the girl's beaming joy had quoted half to herself, the words from The Song of Songs: "I am black but lovely, daughters of Jerusalem – I am the rose of Sharon, the lily of the valleys."

'There's no guile in Dinah, Elspeth, one always feels so pleased for her. She may not be the cleverest girl in the school but she is one of the pleasantest, most genuine and altogether lovable'.

Dinah had stayed behind briefly after an English class and with a good natured whinge said, 'I'm off for some Maths coaching! I'll never make head nor tail of Algebra. The coach is a nice woman so at least I'll provide her with employment all the time I'm here. To tell you the truth Miss Penrose I'm not one for books either!'

Elspeth laughed, 'I was never one for sports when I was a pupil here, I was the despair of Miss Jones.'

'You were a pupil here?'

'I think I must have left shortly before you arrived on the scene, but watching you run and compete I am beginning to see what I might have missed, even if I lacked the ability to succeed.'

Dinah raced off and Elspeth thought, she may not be one for books but she is African and she is black and I can remember one of the novels that made a lasting impression on me when I was her age, I'll find the copies of Alan Paton's 'Cry, the Beloved Country', and see if I can rouse Dinah's interest in one book that will surely be at least meaningful for her.

Elspeth rummaged in the cupboard and found the set of books and the following term she introduced them as the class reader. The copies were paperbacks and somewhat the worse for wear and she saw one or two girls handle them with less than enthusiasm.

'You all know the saying, 'Don't judge a book by its cover,' said Elspeth, 'this was one of my favourite books when I was fourteen and fifteen'.

The girls opened the books and one of them exclaimed, 'My copy has your name written inside the front cover Miss Penrose!' and half the group got up to take a look.

The girls liked Elspeth and she noticed them making a quick calculation of her age, she was young, they considered her beautiful and she was one of them; she went up a notch in their estimation.

She read parts of the novel to them herself and also called on different members of the class to read aloud. She sensed that the book had caught their interest by their deep level of concentration. When they reached the last chapter, Elspeth said that she wanted them to read it quietly on their own, she still found it profoundly moving, the poor black clergyman going into the hills to be alone in the early hours of the morning of his son Absalom's execution. She took a stealthy look at the expressions on the girls' faces, they looked very young and impressionable and she thought one would have to have a heart of stone not to be deeply moved by the undeserved and agonising grief of this poor African priest whose very poverty added to the pathos of this last chapter. She could see at a glance how Dinah was reacting. She was close to tears. She allowed time to elapse before she spoke.

'I want to discuss the novel with you at our next lesson. I am going to write these headings on the board for you to consider before we meet: Capital punishment, Racism and Justice and after we have fully discussed them then I will set a piece of written work for you'.

Dinah stayed behind after class, 'Thank you, Miss Penrose, I think you must have chosen the book for me. I may never become a reading ace but I think I might change my mind about books. This book has certainly made me think and I will never forget it.'

The city had a small cinema club that showed old films every week and Mrs Fraser, Elspeth's predecessor had been responsible for looking through the forthcoming programmes and when she saw a suitable film listed she advertised it on the school notice board and organized small groups of interested pupils and staff and booked seats. Miss Cresswell was pleased it was the kind of project that she happily promoted and she asked Elspeth if she would like to continue with organizing it and she had readily agreed. She obtained a booklet that gave the films for the coming months and Miss Cresswell went through it with her.

'Oh that's fortunate they are showing, 'Westside Story' in a fortnight! That might prove helpful! I have a problem I would like to share with you, something that arose a few nights ago. It involves two young girls in your second year class: one of them Hephzibah, is a young Israeli who is new this term. She's a boarder here while her parents are studying in a nearby college, the other is Maryam who comes from a political family in Jordan and we almost had a riot on our hands the other night,' she told Elspeth. 'Apparently Hephzibah's young cousin was murdered by a Palestinian and Maryam unknowingly, in their dormitory, was voicing her views about the state of the lives of the thousands of Palestinian refugees that were camping in her country and for which her country has been providing a refuge, food and facilities to, for over two decades. She had more than implied that it was a total injustice and Hephzibar was absolutely furious at what she alleged was Maryam's ignorance of Israel's position. It got quite ugly and the house mistress had to call me. We really want this situation resolved peacefully, this is a school where I want young people to feel secure and to develop a greater understanding of others. Hephzibah is a very bright girl who is also showing an aptitude for games and Miss Jones has placed her in the school netball team which are playing an 'at home' game this coming Saturday against a visiting team, and completely by chance Maryam's elder sister Nina is also in the team; the two don't know each other so we'll see what happens there, but including the two girls in a group going to watch 'Westside Story', well who knows, at their age a love story might teach

70

them something about the disastrous outcomes brought about by blood feuds and vendettas. One never knows and we can but try and take every opportunity to diffuse a situation that shows every sign of igniting again! They spend their time in class looking daggers at each other'.

'Yes, I've noticed. They sit as far apart as possible,' replied Elspeth.

So Elspeth agreed, she thought it was a long shot but she thought it was worth inviting the two girls anyway and she could always follow it up in a class discussion afterwards. They continued looking through the programme and choosing films, and in this way the girls were enabled to see a range of early Shakespeare productions with a mixture of comedies and musicals.

'They are showing the Russian version of 'War and Peace', in two parts in January, I've seen it and it's excellent', said Miss Cresswell enthusiastically. The fifth and sixth forms should be given the opportunity of seeing it.'

'I'll get things organized,' said Elspeth.

'You won't have any difficulties, these outings are very popular and you can use a little innocent manipulation to make sure our two young firebrands are included.'

That Saturday Elspeth stood next to Miss Cresswell for the netball match 'at least it's not hockey, I hated the hours spent on a freezing cold field in the middle of winter!' I must say,' said Elspeth.

'Running around was intended to keep you warm,' and Miss Cresswell laughed.

A lot rested on this netball match. The Beeches, a local state school had won an outright victory the previous year and taken the county's prize trophy and Oakland Girls' were determined to win this match. By half-time it didn't look too promising for them, the other school team was ahead. During the second half, things improved but only just. Hephzibah was certainly good and had scored, and Nina too had scored and evened the match and the two girls grinned at each other. In the end it was a draw and they had to be satisfied with that. Elspeth saw the two girls they were particularly watching, smile happily at each other, then she watched as Nina turned away for a moment to find her sister in the group of spectators that had gathered and to receive her congratulations. Hebhzibah stood and gazed at them while it slowly dawned on her that the two were sisters. She looked just slightly shocked and then walked indoors with other members of the team and their rivals.

'Neither of us has been active in sports, well apart from tennis in my case, Elspeth, but it's true that sports attract a global following and should always be above politics. It plays a huge part in bringing people together and hopefully it's worked a little magic here today', said Miss Cresswell.

The musical worked its own magic too, all the girls who were fortunate enough to get a seat at the film club enjoyed themselves. As for the two young firebrands, it may have been too much to expect them to end up friends but they were no longer sworn enemies either and no one was required to read the Riot Act to them.

III

It was the first evening of term after the Christmas holiday that Elspeth learned something about 'poor little rich children'. She had been asked to go up to the first floor to collect something, and feeling curious she had looked into what had been her own dormitory to see if things had changed very much. She wandered by the cubicles until she came to the one which had been next to hers and she heard sobbing. It was a private space and she hesitated to intrude but then she thought that she could not leave a child so obviously distressed so she spoke up and asked if there was anything wrong. The young occupant tried to answer and say she was alright but her voice choked on a sob.

'Do you mind if I come inside a minute?' This was met with a muted response so Elspeth took it as an agreement. Sitting huddled up on her bed was one of her first year lower school pupils. Imogen Beaumont was small for her twelve years and sitting as she was she seemed tiny, it was as if she wished to take up as little space as possible.

'What is it, Imogen? Are you unhappy to be back at school?' This opening gambit reflected so closely Father Dominic's question to her, 'are you homesick, is that it?' Had she looked as miserable as this little figure?

'No, I wanted to come back.'

'Why is that?'

'It's just,' Imogen made an effort to stop crying, 'I'm not wanted'.

'What makes you think that?'

'My parents, they want me out of their way. They're divorced. Mummy has remarried, she lives in America, she is American, and her new husband has two sons. I had to spend the summer with them. The boys are quite nice but they are older than me and they wanted to be with their friends and I felt I was in the way. Christmas was daddy's turn to have me. He has a new girlfriend called Karin, she's very beautiful but she's not kind. One evening I heard them talking, I was just going to go into the room and I stayed outside, I didn't mean to listen in on them. Karin said

73

that she had wanted to go to New York for Christmas, she said it's lots of fun there at Christmas because she has plenty of friends there and she said that she was bored. She said,'why do we have to stay here with your little waif!' What's a waif Miss Penrose?'

'A waif is a neglected or abandoned young child, and I don't believe you are quite that.'

'It feels like I am. She said I was like a shadow creeping about the house turning up unexpectedly. She said it was unnerving having me around and then she said, are you sure she's yours? She doesn't look anything like you, in fact she's not like you in anyway at all when I come to think of it, and by what you've told me about her mother, well I'd say you might well have been taken for a ride!'

Elspeth was horrified. 'What did your father say to that?'

'He said, of course she's mine. She's just a child. Then he said that he would ask my grandparents, his parents, to have me for New Year and that they would go off to New York together. So that's what happened.'

'Were your grandparents happy to have you stay with them?'

'I think so. Granny had a lot of preparations to make for guests, it's a busy time for her but my grandfather liked having me I think. He taught me to play chess when I was quite small and we played a few games together, then my uncle and auntie and my three cousins came for dinner on New Year's Day and my cousin Amy is the same age as me and we are good friends. My auntie said she was surprised that my father was not with me and granny said he had gone off to New York with his new lady friend and I saw them exchange looks and my auntie looked annoyed. My uncle is always kind he calls me his mini mouse because I'm small but I don't mind because he says it kindly, there's a difference isn't there Miss Penrose?'

'Yes, there is!'

'I've been invited to stay with Barbara for half term, she's a good friend, but then I have to go to my father's for Easter because my mother is expected to have me all through the summer holidays.'

Elspeth felt the poor little girl was being passed around like a parcel and she felt she had to say something to help her without being critical of her parents. She felt very critical but she knew it was not her place to say anything negative about them. She thought carefully before speaking. 'I think that you can do something perhaps to change, or improve the situation, Imogen. Put what Karin said out of your mind, she was very wrong, you are your father's daughter and his house is your home, it's not Karin's home if she is not your father's wife or your mother. Try not to be too upset, I know that's not easy, you do have every reason to be unhappy, I would feel the same, but try while you are away this term not to dwell on it.'

'I mustn't be self-pitying, must I Miss Penrose?'

Elspeth was amazed at the twelve-year old's maturity, 'that makes you sound much older, I would have been impressed if a much older person had said that. I think your parents are very fortunate to have such a child. Be confident and walk tall!'

'The little girl laughed, 'that might be a little difficult for me, but I know what you mean Miss Penrose and I will try'.

'There's the gong for your evening meal, give your hands and face a quick wash and brush your hair and I'll walk down the stairs with you'.

The little girl washed her hands and face and brushed her hair quickly and the pair walked down the stairs together, Imogen smiled and thanked Elspeth, and walked off a lonely little figure trying hard to be brave.

At home Elspeth thought back on what she had learned, she felt angry at parents whose selfishness had led to their child feeling unwanted. It was inevitable that she thought about Jamie but he had never been totally abandoned, her mother had loved him, she had adored him and all her grandparents had loved him too. She would never be sure about her father, he she felt increasingly was caught up in miseries of his own. She felt comforted. Her own childhood had been on the whole happy when she compared it with Imogen's childhood. She sighed, Prometheus, she mused, was believed to have stolen fire from the gods to give to human beings, but his gift came with a warning, a misuse of fire could bring about destruction. How many people including little children went to bed and lay sleepless and unhappy night after night through the misuse of love, an even greater gift?

Elspeth had put this evening aside to clear her old Christmas cards, she should have done it the week before. She looked through them and one or two caught her attention. One pictured the Wise Men in garish exotic clothes with crowns perched above their turbans. But they weren't kings, or at least not as far as anyone knew. She had wondered as a child what, 'If I were a wise man I would do my part,' actually meant, she had wondered if it meant giving riches. Now she decided it was their Wisdom they were meant to impart. They must have been astronomers, and men of great learning and knowledge. She had received help and understanding from a wise and caring priest and she went over in her mind her short encounter with Imogen, had she said the right things? She would keep a special eye on her. Suddenly she felt very happy to be a teacher and at her old school. She felt she could make a difference to the children and young people she taught. She wanted to make a contribution, she wanted their lives to be enriched by the works of Literature that she presented to them. It did not matter if they were from wealthy backgrounds, she had learnt that lesson. The most important gift she could give was love and understanding and to never lose sight of that.

The term went on as terms do, days became weeks and weeks months. Elspeth did her best to help Imogen to respond in class and she learned that the little girl was bright and sensitive, she was also good natured with a pleasant sense of humour; she had not been wrong Imogen was mature for her years.

Elspeth had experienced some trepidation at teaching the sixth form, she thought they might remember her as a sixth former herself and she had approached them cautiously knowing that she was not much older than they were. Her fears proved to be groundless they respected her and while she respected them she was determined not to allow any lax informality. She gave her time to any student who sought her help and she was diligent in going over the work and helping students who had difficulties with obscure, perplexing or ambiguous pieces of literature. She encouraged discussion and questioning but she was also adamant about deadlines being met. She thought privately to herself, 'I'm going to end up a staid old school ma'am if I'm not careful!'

IV

During the Easter vacation Elspeth travelled up to the North-East to act as bridesmaid for Louise. It was a very different wedding from Belle's wedding where everything had been carefully choreographed down to the last detail. Louise wanted her sister Ann and Elspeth as her only two bridesmaids, and she didn't want to choose between her two younger siblings so had decided to have neither of them. She was to wear her sister Bridget's wedding gown which only required a minor alteration, Ann was wearing the bridesmaid's dress she had worn at Bridget's wedding and Elspeth was wearing the bridesmaid's dress she had worn at Belle's wedding. In a short discussion it was decided that the colours of the two dresses would blend rather than clash and the flowers chosen would bind the group together. The main emphasis would be placed on the Nuptial Mass and the church hall was chosen for the reception and the family had planned to decorate it the evening before. The Parish Priest, who had known Louise and the family for many years would celebrate the Mass and Louise's brother Callum, home for the wedding, would act as altar server.

Louise's house was full, her grandparents over from Ireland were the guests of her other grandparents, aunts and uncles were accommodated by other aunts and uncles and Jerome's family, who were altogether better off than the Donoghues were staying in local hotels. Louise's brother Callum was staying at the presbytery with the priests who had known him from childhood and regarded him as their special protégé.

The morning of the wedding was sunny if chilly and despite Elspeth's anxiety that things were somewhat chaotic Louise was calm and unruffled and everything went like clockwork, the happy bride and groom arrived at the church exactly on time. The church was quite large Elspeth thought and Italianate in design but not over ornate. It had been built at the beginning of the century and did not have the attraction of age that Belle's village parish church had but there was something more Elspeth realised.

The church was full to overflowing and she sensed the awe and reverence inherent in the liturgy. She felt that it held them all in a huge all-embracing whole that drew in the diversity of peoples, living and dead, nations, and worlds. It was inclusive, and classless, cosmic and timeless.

The two now sacramentally one and followed by bridesmaids and the Best Man were greeted joyously and at the Church door were showered by greetings and covered in confetti. It seemed to Elspeth that the whole town had turned out.

Photographs were taken in the Priest's garden and then the wedding party made its way to the Church Hall on the other side of the road. Long trestle tables were laid out and Elspeth was amazed at the number of guests, there were extended family members, friends, parishioners and children, lots of children. Louise had said her wedding was to include everyone and it seemed that everyone had turned out! Elspeth was seated next to Ann and after the meal and the speech making were over they chatted amiably together then Ann went off to talk with an old friend and Elspeth was left alone.

Mrs Donoghue came to sit next to her, 'I've been so busy I haven't had the chance to speak to you. I am so pleased that you have come. Louise tells me that she won't be living far away from you, I'm glad! It's difficult to see her leave home and go to the other end of England, but of course it's what I did leaving Ireland and my parents, Callum has been living away for many years now but well I'm very fortunate to have so many children and family around so I mustn't complain. We do like Jerome and we think he will make a fine husband. But you are an only child now, Louise told me that your only brother was killed before you left for university. That must be very hard for you, Elspeth'.

Elspeth took in the sea of friends and family and thought of all Jamie had been denied, there was always this lonely space inside of her, 'yes, I will always miss him,' she replied simply.

'Perhaps I shouldn't have mentioned it.'

'No I'm glad, I want Jamie remembered, I think of him every day, he's never far from my mind'.

'After Louise told me about Jamie, well, I've kept you both in my prayers and I was so pleased when you decided to become a Catholic because we always pray for our dead loved ones. It's one of the things I've always found so strange in England where death almost seems to be treated as somehow unseemly and folks refer to dying as passing away or use some other euphemism that they think will not offend. There's no shame in dying and I think it's sad that people might be offended by referring to death and calling it what it is. It's not like that in Ireland we believe our dead are close to us. I have a lovely Irish prayer that you might like to have.'

'Oh, yes I'd like to have it.'

'Then I'll copy it and send it on to you. Dear me! Look at our Maeve! We've never managed to instil into her any sense of propriety'.

Maeve had drawn the tablecloth back and had climbed up onto the table with a younger cousin and had begun an Irish dance.

Elspeth laughed and Mrs Donoghue said, 'they say when children are young they are a headache and when they grow up they become a heartache. I don't think there's any real harm in Maeve other than high spirits but she keeps her father and me on our toes. She's very different from her sisters but then they can't all be alike.'

At this point Callum came up to say that he was about to leave with Father Moran the Parish priest and Louise's mother introduced them, 'This is Elspeth, Louise's friend from university.'

He shook her hand, she had of course noticed him in the church and she thought him strict looking. The family were clearly proud of him and ring-fenced him, they treated him with something close to reverence. Mrs Donoghue explained that Elspeth had gained a first class degree and was a convert. He nodded and looked, she thought, rather sharply at her, his look was penetrating and she thought edged with steel. She assumed that he knew she had studied English Literature and wondered if he considered it an unsuitable subject as Louise's father had thought. Did he believe that many of the books up for study were on the Index? He's not very much older than me and he makes me feel like a ten-year old, Elspeth thought. She felt trivialised and she stiffened. He said he would see them all at Mass the following morning and unsmiling he left.

'Callum passed a scholarship to Stonyhurst Public School, it's a Jesuit run school', said Mrs Donoghue.

'I see'. Elspeth had never heard of it and had no idea where it was she thought it must be well known, she would ask Father Dominic who she had decided to visit on the following day, but her introduction to Callum had left her with a feeling of unease and she was thankful that he had left the reception.

....

Elspeth took a bus the following day, shortly after lunch, it was a relatively short journey and she planned to return for the night before taking a train home the next morning. Father Dominic greeted her warmly and she offered to make them both a cup of tea. They went into the library, it was quiet, there were only two or three students around.

'You are looking well Elspeth, how did the wedding go?

'It was wonderful. Quite an event, most of the Parish were there! And the family is, well to say the least, extensive. Where is Stoneyhurst School by the way, is it somewhere around here in the North East?'

'No, it's in Lancashire, quite some distance away. Why do you ask?'

'Callum Donoghue, Louise's eldest brother was home for the wedding, he's studying to become a Jesuit priest in Rome and

Louise's mother introduced him. He is so stern looking! And he's not that old.'

'Ah yes! One of the assistant priests in their parish is an old friend of mine. Callum is brilliant apparently, I understand he won a scholarship to Stoneyhurst School and the family all made sure that he took up the place and had everything he needed. He is about ten years older than Louise so she would have been very young when he gained the scholarship and apart from being at home for holidays he was away, I imagine, for most of Louise's life. He's expected to go far.'

He had caught something negative in Elspeth's tone and he said, smiling, 'Saints come in different guises and some are not the easiest of people. His Parish Priest, my friend Father Sullivan, has a very high opinion of him.'

'I haven't seen him smile the whole weekend!'

'You wrote saying you have your grandmother living with you, how is she?' asked Father Dominic, changing the subject.

'She's frail but as fiercely independent as ever. She has her own rooms and can spend time in the garden, she used to be a keen gardener.'

'Has she accepted your conversion?'

'She doesn't oppose it but that's not quite the same as accepting it! I've been Gran's golden girl all my life, I can't do anything wrong for her, she'd love me no matter what!'

'And your parents, how are they?'

'They're well. I went to visit my brother's grave one morning to take some flowers and I noticed how well kept it was, I thought my mother must visit regularly and mentioned it to Gran and was surprised when she told me that my father goes every six months or so and clears Jamie and Grandpa's graves'.

'So you are learning to forgive him, Elspeth?'

'I'm trying to understand him. All my friends think he's wonderful, including Louise who also thinks he's sad, Louise would pick up something like that. I feel I know so little about him. I don't feel angry anymore.'

'Good! And you are enjoying teaching. Have you put your doubts behind you about going back to your old school?'

Elspeth told him briefly about her little pupil, Imogen Beaumont and how she had come to realise that wealth and status did not necessarily cushion one from problems and neglectful parents.

'I love teaching at Oaklands, it's an oasis in many ways, I really enjoy my pupils. I felt nervous about teaching the sixth form thinking they would remember me as a sixth former myself but things have gone really well.'

'What about your Parish Church?'

'I only attend there for one or two early morning Masses a week, I drive myself to the next town and attend the Traditional Mass and I have joined the choir there, the people are determined to keep the old practices and I find that I'm not too happy with the new modern Mass.'

Father Dominic did not reply but she felt that he agreed but would not say anything that might sound disloyal to the Church.

The conversation went on and Father Dominic recommended some spiritual books she might find useful and he gave her a copy of one of Cardinal Newman's books. He was considerate of her as always and they talked easily together. He saw her to the door when she was ready to leave and a student arrived at the same time, 'I'll be with you in a minute Joanna,' Father Dominic said to the student as he shook hands with her and just for a brief moment Elspeth felt bereft. She was no longer a student or a lost soul in need of saving, she felt alone entering unchartered waters, then she gathered herself firmly together and made her way to the bus stop.

The day had been sunny when she set off and she had noticed the shadows as they played on the grey roofs of the small houses, the bright sunshine warmed the atmosphere and lifted her spirits. But the sun had disappeared by the time she made
the return journey and the towns as they passed looked altogether greyer and gloomier, the sky seemed to be bearing down on them, it was oppressive and weighed down on her. There were no trees.

She had been met with so much kindness and friendship in the North East, she liked the people and yet this late afternoon on the way back to Louise's home she felt an outsider, having no longer a part in its life. She imagined the lives of the people living out their lives in the mean narrow streets as they passed. The houses had been built close together to house as many of the workforce as possible and they had been built in a hurry. They had been constructed with no thought for the people who would have to spend their lives there. There were no trees. They at least would have broken the relentless monotony. She felt these houses had been built for pitiless convenience that spoke nothing of beauty. Nature and beauty had been forgotten and regarded as a expensive nonessential commodity. Little wonder that those who could rented allotments and tended their gardens if they were fortunate enough to have one. She thought, is there a desire in all of us to grow and produce new life on the land and this goes hand in hand with parenting children? The longing for continuity was strong, was inherent within it a longing for immortality?

The countryside within walking distance of the towns was magnificent and the people were justly proud of their villages and country towns where so many of them had their roots, they were spiritually tied to them. The people thought nothing of leaving the towns behind when they were free, and walking for miles into the surrounding lanes and fields and woodlands of home. She had not known them to whinge and she admired their stoicism for she knew that many of the people who occupied these houses and towns were living out lives of hardship. She thought back to the wedding the day before and thought that not all of Louise's neighbours would have such fulfilled lives as the Donoghue family enjoyed. Louise had said to her the first time she had visited their home, 'Here you'll learn how the other half live'. Had she learned? She thought now she had been no more than an outsider looking in she had not experienced their lives in any real way, she had not lived with them and hardly alongside them. She had read novels that portrayed the lives of those faced with the conditions brought about by the Industrial Revolution, coal miners, cotton workers in factories, railway workers, frequently housed in poor and unhealthy conditions, her understanding of them was second hand or virtual reality, she had deceived herself into believing that it her knowledge was experience. They did not want her pity or anyone else's, they were proud and rightly resented being patronised. She was aware of what that felt like, she had experienced something akin to it in the unspoken criticism of herself 'those that hadn't needed to get their hands dirty'. It cut both ways. Yet she highly esteemed these people, and knew that many of them looked back on their lives and their hardship positively they were hardy and she could appreciate even envy their sense of community. They were happy together and they shared their joys and sorrows together and cared for their neighbours, they enjoyed close knit communities but it would be wrong to romanticise their lives. Their close communities allowed them to value their shared experiences of life and why they tended to look at outsiders as 'them' and themselves as 'us'. Is that what she was doing, the same? People who had lived through the War had experienced Comradeship, being part of something, sharing the same experiences together, being close to each other. Was that why many of the survivors did not share their wartime experiences and enjoyed meeting up with other veterans that did share them and understand? Are we closer to others when we share the same fate and the same suffering?

This evening she felt lonely, isolated and vulnerable and she knew how loneliness and isolation imposed its very real suffering too. All at once she wanted to be home, it was where she belonged. She thought I want to see Gran I want to be welcomed and understood, I don't want to explain myself I don't want to feel guilty for my 'privileged' way of life, Gran has lived so much of her life for others; she's a loving and good example. And I want to see my parents. She needed them and suddenly it was important to show them that she loved them. Perhaps her father needed to know that despite everything she cared. Had she forgiven him? The past was the past she thought and I am not going to allow it to poison my today or my tomorrow.

Refusing to forgive her father would not help Jamie, her beloved brother had his place in her heart forever, no one could change that. She felt older as if she had passed an important milestone but then on an altogether much more prosaic level she realised that she was also very hungry and she thought about the leftover food from the wedding which had been gathered up and returned to Louise's family home. There was enough left for a feast she thought and she looked forward to the evening meal.

V

The first day back at school she was surprised when Imogen ran up to her in the corridor, she looked radiant.

'I have something to tell you, Miss Penrose! It's about Karin, she's gone!'

Elspeth was startled, 'Gone'.

'Yes, Miss Penrose, daddy's got a new girlfriend, she's French, she's called Monique and she's ever so nice and she's really kind to me'

'Well that's very good news, I'm very happy for you'.

'Thank you Miss Penrose I thought you would like to know. I've told daddy and Monique all about you and they are going to try and get here for Sport's Day and they will be able to meet you'.

'I'll look forward to it!'

VI

The saga of her little pupil continued. When Sport's Day arrived, true to their promise, Imogen's father and Monique made their appearance and Imogen dragged them over the school field to meet her. Elspeth had thought she would nurse an inner anger for the father that had neglected his daughter, but she found instead that she immediately liked the suave, good looking man she was introduced to. He had that masculine appeal that attracted women and he smiled while openly appraising her, 'My daughter has talked endlessly about you! All good things, English has become her favourite subject'.

Monique hanging on his arm was silently making her own assessment, 'what's this beautiful young woman doing in this closed environment?' Then she seemed to make her mind up, Elspeth was not posing any competition, she just might as well be wearing a label round her neck, the French woman thought, saying 'Look but don't touch', and her assessment complete she smiled brightly. She was not particularly pretty but she had a lovely smile and was very well groomed and Elspeth wondered, not for the first time, how it invariably was that a French woman could nonchalantly throw a simple scarf around her neck and look at once chic and striking.

VII

When the summer term ended Imogen again ran up to her, 'I'm leaving Oaklands Miss Penrose'.

Elspeth was sorry but her young pupil looked very happy and assured her that she was very pleased. 'I'm going to live with my grandparents and attend a private girls' day school and I'll be in the same class as my cousin Amy. I know Barbara will miss me but she's also good friends with Val and we are going to write to each other, and I'll never forget you Miss Penrose.'

'Then I'm delighted for you and I'm sure you are going to be very happy '.

'I don't even mind going to America for the summer because I know it's only for two months!'

How sad, Elspeth thought, she is going to visit her mother who she has not seen for twelve months and she is less than enthusiastic about it, but her father had proved to be the kinder and more caring of her parents in the end and she was pleased. All's well that ends well, she thought. Her first year of teaching was over and it too had gone well.

Chapter 5

....

"Thou shalt not make unto thee any graven image, -"
(The second Commandment: Exodus Ch 20 vs 3 and 4)

"The Times They Are a'Changin'", was the Bob Dylan song that encapsulated the 1960s for Elspeth. She had bought the record when it was released, and she had sung it and hummed it over and over again. It was one of her favourite lyrics and she loved it; Bob Dylan was her hero. But now she was growing increasingly perplexed by the changes and the pace of the changes, taking place in the Catholic Church, they were beginning to cause her some dismay.

She remembered Louise explaining her father's uneasy misgivings about the future and how the changes in the Church might affect his children's faith and now she found herself beginning to commiserate with him.

Only four years ago she would have wondered what all the fuss was about – how she had changed! – she had entered what she now regarded as a global family, one in faith, belief and practice and in these earliest years of her conversion when she longed for stability she was finding the Church and the society around her in a state of flux; she began to fear that the unity of the Church was threatened with rupture. Her own loyalty to the Church was not in question but this did not stop her from feeling a sense of unease.

The first time that she had felt really disturbed was when she had attended the new Rite of the Mass, she had come away feeling distinctly unsettled. The priest was celebrating facing the people! In the tradition that had first held her soul captive the priest was turned to the altar and saying the beautiful words: 'Brethren, pray that my sacrifice and yours may be acceptable to God the Father Almighty', had prepared the people to enter the holiest part of the Mass. The image brought about a sense of unity, the priest at the elevation was making both his own offering and that of the people and the grace flowed from the host down from the priest to the people in one unbroken movement. Now, it seemed to Elspeth that that unity had been broken; the imagery was saying something different, the priest facing the people seemed to be making an offering only on behalf of the people, for the people, and in so doing he was also standing with his back to the crucifix. Something of the meaning and mystery had been lost. This was the age increasingly of the 'image' and a simple analysis of this image was stating something decidedly different from the long, unbroken Tradition of the Church; the image was broken. The Language of the new rite also distressed her. Elspeth, found herself looking around and she discovered a group in the nearby town that celebrated the Old Mass and she drove herself there each Sunday and joined the choir, she loved Gregorian Chant. On Wednesday and Friday mornings, before school she attended a quiet early Mass and she bought herself a chain of Rosary beads which she prayed before going to bed. Louise had given her a copy of Thomas a Kempis', 'The Imitation of Christ', and she read a passage each day. He had written, 'All of our lives we are subject to change, even against the will', and she considered it. Father Dominic had given her a copy of St Therese of Lisieux's 'The Story of a Soul', at the time of her reception into the Church and she discovered whole new spiritual depths of faith. 'The Story of a Soul', became profoundly important to her in her journey of faith and like millions of Catholics the world over she was to remain devoted to this young saint and 'her way of spiritual childhood'. Therese had died at the age of twenty-four of tuberculosis and had said prior to her death, 'I shall spend my eternity doing good on earth and after my death I will let fall a shower of roses'. The spirituality in the writings of St John of the Cross, became perhaps most important to her and as she slowly learnt more and more about her faith she began to internalise it. She had sworn her allegiance to her Catholic faith and she would remain faithful to it until death despite the changes taking place. She knew she had made the right choice; it had brought great blessings and she would never for a moment regret her acceptance of the Catholic Church.

II

Elspeth's Scripture teacher, Mrs Helen Manasses had befriended her when she had been a pupil at Oaklands and now they were colleagues they became close friends and it was to her that Elspeth increasingly turned and they discussed religion together.

Helen's Greek husband was a Lecturer in a local Teacher Training College and very soon she became a frequent visitor to their home. Helen told Elspeth that she had been diagnosed with cancer of the uterus in the very earliest years of their marriage and consequently could never have children but she said the circumstances had brought her and Johannes even closer together. Theirs had been a love match she said and they both agreed that they had married the love of their life, 'I am very fortunate, Johannes is the best and kindest of men'.

The word that most aptly described Helen Manasses was serenity. Elspeth felt such a calm sense of certainty in the older woman who never seemed to be agitated. She had been denied motherhood so would care for the children she taught with special devotion. Elspeth had profited from her when she herself had been a pupil, she always had time and would always engage with her pupils; she respected them and they in turn respected her. Schoolgirls at Oaklands like schoolgirls everywhere liked some teachers more than others and could dislike and criticise teachers they did not like with the same zeal expressed in schools from one end of the globe to the other, but Elspeth had never heard any unkind criticism of Helen Manasses, she was sincere and her pupils liked her. Helen was deeply committed to her subject and this is what had initially brought Elspeth to her special notice as a pupil, now as colleagues they had cemented their friendship.

Johannes Manasses had studied firstly in Athens and had come to England to study for a PhD in Political Science. He had met Helen who had been attending a course at the same university, had fallen in love with her and on finishing his Doctorate had settled in England and established his home. He remained, however, essentially Greek, unapologetically proud of his Greek culture and feeling himself the inheritor of a noble ancestry. Greece, he said had produced Literature and Philosophy that was still influencing the world after two millennia. The New Testament Scriptures had first been written in Greek and had had the greatest influence on the spreading of Christianity; Greece was the cradle of Western Civilization.

Elspeth found Johannes a fascinating personality. He was slight and of average height, and clever, his face was expressive and his eyes which were his most impressive feature, were a very dark brown almost black. When he argued a point his eyes shone with intelligence. Where his wife had a stillness about her Johannes was like quicksilver. They complimented each other.

Elspeth asked Helen early on in their friendship about her conversion to the Greek Orthodox Church and she told Elspeth that it had taken place almost immediately on her first visit to Greece after their wedding. Johannes had accustomed himself to spending several weeks a year in a Greek Monastery and they had visited a Monastery of nuns in Thessalonika for a special festivity of a saint together – she pointed out that in Greece the word monastery was used for women as well as men they did not use the word convent – and she had listened to a liturgy that had continued during the night. She described the nuns singing and had felt she was in heaven the music came in waves and she had known that this was where she belonged, it was she said like arriving home. They went to Greece every year to stay with Johannes' family in the mountainous region in Northern Greece and planned to retire there. She told Elspeth that for Johannes four things were of importance, his religion, his family, politics and education and in that order and that he was passionate about all four.

Elspeth knew nothing about politics, she had never been interested, she thought it meant Party Politics and she thought that she would continue to vote for the Labour Party as Gran did. She did not know for certain what her parents voted for they had never said and she had never thought to ask them. She was only vaguely aware of the candidates and had the impression generally that it was too much like a knockabout the manner in which the opposing candidates exchanged insults with each other and scorned each other's policies.

Helen pointed out to her that it was not party politics Johannes was interested in – and in fact as a Greek National he was not eligible to vote in the United Kingdom's General Elections, only Local Elections – but in the political ideologies that underlay them and this sparked an interest for Elspeth. Louise had once said, 'you look at things and sense undercurrents and have to investigate'. She had to question the things that were important to her, she had to know, it was her being, her life, her mind was always active and inquiring.

One evening at their home she expressed her concern about the new rite of the Mass and the discarding of the old altars and their replacement by others that were usually plain. Johannes spoke up:

'It's a form of iconoclasm, the Eastern Church had its iconoclasm in the eighth century,' said Johannes.

'Wasn't the Reformation iconoclastic? Images that were considered idolatrous were destroyed along with monasteries', asked Elspeth.

'Yes, indeed you are right of course and I suppose it all came to a head from the time of the Enlightenment onwards when there was a movement to dismantle what was considered at the time to be authoritarianism promoted by the Roman Catholic Church, and in the centuries since they have replaced it with another subtler form of authoritarianism, with the downgrading of religious beliefs and the attempt to replace them by political ideologies such as Communism, National Socialism – Fascism – and Liberal Democracy. Over time they each become the ruling class of ideas and ideals, and being the constructs of the mind they lend themselves to becoming idolatrous. We in the West think that we are too sophisticated and too civilised to bow down and worship graven images in blocks of wood and stone, nevertheless idolatry is alive and kicking'.

Elspeth was astonished, 'I don't understand'.

'Ideology – the logic of ideas –. Ideologies can be worshipped as readily as any beliefs or religions.

Elspeth was not sure, 'I understand that well may be so in the case of Fascism and Communism – the newsreels taken in the Germany of the 1930s with mass rallies acclaiming Hitler certainly appear idolatrous and I can recognise idolatry in Communism. Both these ideologies end up as totalitarian states where people are deprived of free speech and other freedoms for that matter but surely that is not the case with Liberal Democracy.

'The Russian people in 1917 didn't recognise the endgame of Communism and neither I suspect do the Chinese who hail Mao in their millions. The German people on the whole at the beginning had no idea where National Socialism would lead them and people here don't suspect where Liberal Democracy will lead us'.

'But Liberal Democracy enshrines the ideals of Freedom and Equality,' said Elspeth.

'There are no ideals in Christianity, there are Commandments only,' said Johannes quietly. Elspeth was shocked but allowed him to go on.

'Christ said that he had not come to destroy the Law or the Prophets but to fulfil them and he condensed the Ten Commandments into two positive Commandments, "You shall love the Lord your God and you shall love your neighbour as yourself". He also taught, "Love your enemies", and "One Commandment I give unto you that you love one another as I have loved you". In Christianity, therefore, Love is the fulfilment of the law that is, when we Love God and observe the Commandments in our relationships with others. Christ's: 'Be perfect even as your father in heaven is perfect' is not a call to aim at achieving some ideal or other and Christ by addressing each and every one of us is allowing us to recognise that perfection is not beyond any of us and that we – even the weakest among us – is loved by God. Perfection is infinitely more than ideals and love is infinitely greater than idealism. Christianity is not a mismatch of different ideas and ideals and Love is not a construct of the human mind.'

'All this is new to me', said Elspeth.

Johannes had not finished, 'Liberty, Equality and Fraternity', the proud slogan and aims of the French Revolution underlie the ideologies of National Socialism, Communism and Liberal Democracy and they are flawed. There are obvious limits to personal freedom which we usually find out quickly enough and to our own cost! But perhaps what Aristotle had to say about Equality should be borne in mind: "The worst form of inequality is to try and make unequal things equal". My fear is that as this century proceeds and we enter a new Millennium, Liberal Democracy will increase in popularity. It will appear to offer broad-mindedness, a lack of bias, and magnanimity. But sadly, along with the liberal utopia it seems to offer is a darker reality underlying it. Liberal Democracy believes that one person's belief system is equal to another person's belief system and that one person's truth is equal to another person's truth.

'It leads to an acceptance of some mythical common denominator and where there is no black or white we become enmeshed in shades of grey. There well might be a difficulty in recognising truth from falsehood and confusion about what constitutes good and what is evil in human affairs. Where we make an equal playing field for all, there is a danger that excellence in the Arts for example, ends up with society rewarding mediocrity, in short there will be attempts to make unequal things equal! In such a climate of opinion as new liberal laws are passed, those of us who offer a Christian understanding of life will be looked upon increasingly, as intolerant, prejudiced, small minded and bigoted. Free speech will be limited to expressing what the Liberal Elite deems acceptable, we are not there yet but with an increase in the Ideology of Relativism I fear it is in the pipeline. There will be increasing efforts made to silence religious beliefs, most particularly Christian beliefs and those that go against the status quo. Silencing the free speech of an opposition by a liberal elite among the powers that be, puts all citizens and society as a whole into jeopardy. Laws are passed, with more to follow based on tolerance for all and that means serious divisions will follow. Liberalism is a subjective philosophy, where the line between right and wrong becomes blurred and consciences along with them. Moral boundaries will be eroded and Liberal Democracy, firmly grounded as it is on Liberalism may eventually end up like Communism or Fascism because the greatest danger of Liberalism, I believe, lies in its capacity to deceive. It appeals to the best in us and to our desire to understand others and it holds out the promise of a fairer society for all with the added promise of 'fraternity', a universal brotherhood of men and sisterhood of women. In attempting to achieve their ends these Political Ideologies, Communism and National Socialism, have produced in this century the greatest wars in human history! Liberalism, underlying them, is a father of Lies. The second Commandment states that we 'do not make for ourselves any graven image or likeness',

Liberalism, it seems to me, is 'likeness' or 'similarity' and appearing to be a secular virtue equivalent to Christian love, compassion and goodness, and it is being paid homage to the point of worship. I think it can be justly perceived as idolatry.'

'And so we could end up with something like George Orwell's 1984 a world of 'News Speech' and 'Hate Speech' which in the end stifles 'Free Speech'.

'That threatens it altogether! Paradoxically it is freedom destroying freedom! Liberalism is insidious it is spreading itself almost imperceptibly around the globe. It appears irresistibly attractive. It's like a giant spider weaving its gossamer web and drawing the peoples of the world in. And here is a very potent warning given by Christ, "For there shall arise false Christs and false prophets, and shall show great signs and wonders; in as much that, if it were possible, they shall deceive the very elect. Behold I have told you." What makes me feel that I am right about what I am saying is that if anyone of the three of us broadcasted this discussion in the public square and made a case for Christian teaching being undisputed truth we'd be regarded as not just 'absolutists' but we'd meet with laughing scorn, people would say that we were crazy and walk away in embarrassed disgust. We would be considered as dogmatic bigots and silenced.

'Imagine the headlines in the morning papers the day after saying, Christianity is a Religion of Commandments! The response would be one of glee, people would come back at us with,' we always said so, Christians and especially Catholics are indoctrinated', and fail to realise that it is they that are not only being indoctrinated but silenced because they don't question Liberalism and Democracy, they may not believe they have perfection but they do believe they have near enough to it.'

'I've always wondered about this other saying of Christ,' said Elspeth, "If the light that is in you be darkness, how great is that darkness!" It suddenly has meaning. But you have described such a very bleak picture of the future that I am wondering if you see any possibility for optimism? We do have to have government.'

'So we do, we render unto Caesar the things that are Caesar's, but it requires constant scrutiny both of the politics involved and most particularly of politicians. The electorate is not homogeneous so it can never be a case of one size fits all! And I think we are required to be involved with the political process. But our laws, which were originally based on a Christian ethos, are becoming increasingly less so and I believe there are some very worrying trends in today's society which are reflected in the liberal political ideology of Western governments. On a personal level, love will have the last word in the individual lives of people – it is love and caring for others that has kept societies in the West caring and dutiful during the centuries of the Enlightenment – it means keeping The Commandments as best we can. It has been said that if there was no God man would have invented him, the same cannot be said, however, for Love. Love is the Alpha and Omega of existence; Love is the reality of God', said Johannes.

Elspeth gazed at him and saw the essential goodness of him, his conviction, his clarity and lack of ambiguity. He was neither arrogant nor overbearing. She recognised in him a deep peacefulness, he had spoken with humility and she felt that she would never look at life in the same way again. Her encounter with Father Dominic had been a pivotal experience this discussion would also remain with her, forming her outlook on life, she would never forget it.

Chapter 6

"we're made so that we love
First when we see them painted, things we have passed
Perhaps a hundred times nor cared to see;
And so they are better, painted – better to us,
Which is the same thing. Art was given for that –"
(Fra Lippo Lippi – Robert Browning)

Elspeth's friends were determined that she should break free of what they considered her closed circle. Belle's sister Meg had told her that she must not bury herself in books and Belle herself wanted her friend to fall in love and marry, she longed for Elspeth to have all that she had in the way of conjugal bliss. Louise too felt that she should do something to extend her group of friends. She suggested that she should take up an evening class.

'I remember you saying that you liked painting but had never been given the opportunity to take art seriously because your timetable had been given over to academic subjects. Now's the time to do something about it. I would suggest singing but I know you have already joined a church choir'.

Elspeth did feel restless, she loved her work but her friends were right, it was not enough and at the beginning of her second year of teaching she joined an art class that was mainly devoted to still life painting though occasionally they met up on a Sunday afternoon, particularly in the summer, at an appointed place in the countryside on the edge of town and painted Landscapes. The group was made up of older members who had been together for two or three years and knew each other. There was one eighteen-year old boy who had joined the group at the same time as

Elspeth and who was applying for an Art College place for the following year and two older men, Elspeth reckoned they were the same age as her father. They had taken the teenager under their wing and for a time Elspeth thought they must be related. There was a young married woman and the rest were women in their late thirties and forties mostly married though two she later learned were single.

At the time Elspeth joined the group there were some ten members and they welcomed her warmly and she immediately felt at ease and would look back at her two years in the art class as a delightful interlude. She certainly did not meet the love of her life but she met people and enlarged her circle of friends and she was happy. She had never painted in oils before and she soon discovered that some members of the group were very proficient and had their still life paintings in oil and landscape paintings in watercolour – exhibited in a local art gallery. Felix Murray their teacher was a fine landscape artist and two of his paintings had sold for considerable amounts of money.

Felix Murray was an Art Historian who taught in the college during the week. There was some mystery attached to him, he had a 'a past' and was known to be divorced. He had a mildly sardonic manner with a seductive charm and the women had decided among themselves that he might prove 'dangerous' where young women were concerned though they knew nothing certain about his past at all and Elspeth noticed that they were silently pleased when he bent over them to correct a piece of work.

'I wouldn't want one my girls left alone with him. Watch it Elspeth, we can tell he likes you'.

This remark was made by Kate one of the self-appointed leaders of the group, she had shortened her name to Kate rather than to Cathy because she felt it had a certain artistic flair about it and Cathy sounded too much like Wuthering Heights and it wasn't the persona she wanted to cultivate. Had she been born some fifteen years later than she had been Elspeth thought she would have been a Sixties hippy. She wore her dark hair long and held back with a brightly coloured scarf and dangly earrings and she came to class in denim jeans and whatever the weather, she wore what looked like a Scandinavian Cardigan over a T-shirt. She worked as a Lollipop lady during the week and recounted anecdotes to them all during coffee breaks. She was she firmly stated, still very much in love with her husband Mike who gave her lifts to the Art classes and she was equally proud of her daughters. Abbi was at college studying Home Economics and Jill was a nursery school assistant.

'The three of us are best friends and people we meet when we are together think we're sisters, they tell me everything!'

Why do parents think that their children tell them everything? Elspeth knew her mother would never think that and even Gran that she shared most things with would never assert that she was told everything. But Kate was good natured and took to Elspeth immediately and dubbed her, 'Mona Lisa', not because she had considered the enigmatic smile the painting was famed for, but because she considered it an expression of universal beauty and Elspeth was flattered.

'If I'd been born with your looks, Elspeth I'd have been looking to Hollywood for a career', she said in admiration.

'I can't act!' Elspeth had replied.

'Since when did that matter?' Kate replied and they all laughed.

This was followed by a discussion about the famous painting. One of the class asked who the model, Mona Lisa was and some said that no one knew. Kate said she thought it was one of Leonardo Di Vinci's mistresses, 'Italians! Can't trust them near women'. This was followed by mildly lurid stories about past Italian holidays. It was generally agreed that womanising was a national pastime among Italian men and none of them were to be trusted.

'They make wonderful ice cream though!' this from Sue.

'They should stick to what they do best then,' said Lillian.

Elspeth did not talk a great deal but she felt she was accepted and it was important to her not to be considered detached and distant. She accepted them and they were happy to pass on small hints that improved her work. She would be lucky, she thought, if any painting of hers was exhibited, she was destined to remain very average as far as painting was concerned and she learned to respect the dedicated members of this little group and to like them for their lack of pretentiousness, certainly as far as their art work was concerned.

A first glance at Kate and Lilian would have placed them poles apart, but Elspeth learned that they were old friends. Kate had never made it academically, but she was a talented artist and Lillian admired her and they were the chief spoke leaders of the group.

Lillian – never Lil or Lilly – the use of her full name gave her just that sense of sophistication and decorum she was intent on maintaining – much as a shortened form of her name added artistic verve for Kate. Lillian worked on perfume and make-up at a large department store. She had worked there from leaving school and was now head of her department. She had a trim figure that she was very proud of, her hair was cut short and stylishly set and her nails were perfectly manicured, she wore black slacks and demure sweaters and always attended class wearing a string of pearls. Elspeth soon learnt that she had met her husband, – Ernest, never Ernie or Ern – at Ballroom dancing classes and she had married him when she was nineteen.

'I was a teenage bride,' she proudly told Elspeth, 'Ernest never looked at anybody else and never has.'

At Ballroom Dancing classes they had won several awards, but had had to give dancing up when Ernest had a fall that permanently damaged his back, so she had joined this Art class.

'I've always had a creative streak and I have an O Level in Art,' she told Elspeth whose dress sense she admired along with so much else, the cultured voice and the education that went with it and she teamed up with Elspeth whenever possible feeling they had things in common.

She and Ernest had only ever been able to have one child – she did not go into details – and they had named him Oliver. Lillian went on about this wonderful son who was now in his early twenties and engaged. The fortunate young woman, Brenda, was on Handbags and Scarves and Lilian blamed herself that they had met at all because she didn't think the young woman was anywhere good enough for her carefully brought up son. They had had him privately educated at a local direct grant school, and he was working with his father as a fully qualified electrician. When his father was recovering from his fall, Oliver had accompanied her to the store's Christmas party and it was there he had met Brenda.

'I only hope she can look after Oliver properly,' – Oliver had been thoroughly cosseted his entire life – 'I invite her to lunch frequently and it's clear to me she has no idea how to boil an egg! I don't know how young women are brought up in nowadays' and Elspeth thought guiltily of her own abysmal cooking ability.

'Of course I never criticise her in front of Oliver, it wouldn't do, he might just end up defending her and taking her part against me and he's always been very close to his father and me and I know all about loyalty! I don't want to end up losing my son and eventually grandchildren. I make sure if we are on a coffee break together that I sit next to her although I'm much more senior, of course, and I hope she appreciates it'.

They enjoyed their gossip times during their coffee breaks but the gossip was never malicious and showed no envy of each other and they were genuinely pleased with each other's success. In this the group were unusual and Elspeth was pleased that she had joined them.

At the beginning of January, Kate could hardly contain herself until the coffee break to inform them about what she had learned at the beginning of term.

'You won't believe it! Felix arrived at the crossing with his little boy who has begun school this term. He arrived at the crossing with another mother and her little son Keith, who I know from last term. After school Felix's little boy was picked up by his grandmother and I was able to ask Keith's mum about Felix. She told me that it wasn't Felix that ended the marriage it was his wife! She met an old flame shortly after Josh – that's the name of his son – was born and made off with him and Felix has never got over it. Keith's mother and her husband are old friends of theirs and she said that his wife, Charlotte, even told her that Felix had been a good husband but had added 'the heart has its reasons'. What do you make of that?'

'Where's his wife now?'

'God knows, the hussy! That's all I can say about a woman like that, up and leaving her husband and child, she didn't deserve to have a child. Josh lives with Felix, poor little mite, he has that look of a motherless child.'

Kate did not define what exactly that 'motherless look' was but the other mothers in the group nodded their heads knowingly and with a shared understanding and they were incensed. It was inevitable that Elspeth should recall another son whose mother had abandoned him and she hoped that Josh would grow up without feeling his rejection so badly that he displayed the behaviour that she had been subjected to. How is it she thought, when other memories fade that she would have loved to recall in detail but couldn't, that this one never faded? It was branded indelibly into her mind, every detail of the violation she had suffered and which she could never erase. She thought it will be with me all my life like a nightmare that never disappears on waking. She didn't know Charlotte but what she had learned filled her with frustrated anger.

From that time on the small group considered their teacher in a different light and were altogether kinder in their appreciation of him. At the same time they considered his ex-wife a scarlet woman and no better than a harlot and they asked Kate to give them regular updates on little Josh.

II

Elspeth learned that the group when they met up during the summer always got together on a Sunday afternoon to accommodate, Liz, a mother of five and a Catholic and Janice a practising Anglican who wanted to attend church.

'That woman's a saint!' said Kate of Liz and the others readily agreed, she's a wonderful mother.'

When they discovered that Elspeth was a Catholic one of the group said, 'I'm not surprised you look like one of those holy pictures,' and Elspeth thought irreverently that Mona Lisa had acquired a halo. She thought back at one occasion at school when a girl in her form with a spiteful reputation had told her that she looked like a Catholic and when she had retorted that you could not look like a Catholic the girl had replied mockingly, 'yes you can, they have their eyes sewn in with black cotton!' Catholicism was still viewed with suspicion even in 1960s Britain and secretly disliked. All incense, bells and superstition, it was after all what her grandmother thought.

During the summer it was the two older men that Elspeth came to know well. The class met one Sunday afternoon close to a wooded area outside of the city and found a spot they wished to paint. The two older men turned up with black berets and they had obviously made an attempt to look like what they considered were Artists in the mode of Picasso and Elspeth was secretly amused. At the end of these outdoor sessions the class came together as a group and discussed each other's work and the painting they all agreed was the best for that session was given a name. This particular afternoon, one of the older men's paintings was highly praised. Elspeth was asked to give her opinion and she said that the painting reminded her of days she had spent as a child walking in the woods and how she had loved how the sunlight had sent shafts of light through the branches. She said she thought Doug's painting had caught something of that sunlit atmosphere and that she would name the picture, 'Halcyon Days'

'Well done, Doug', said Felix and the group applauded him, and Doug turned pink with pleasure.

Elspeth joined Doug and his friend Phil during the next coffee break and they told her that they had been friends since their schooldays. They told her that they had never had the opportunity to do art work earlier on in their lives.

'We both had woodwork lessons, youngsters at school in the thirties didn't have the same opportunities as they do now it was all about doing work that was best fitted to get a job and earn a living, it was difficult enough finding work back then,' stated Phil matter-of-factly.

'Did you find work?' asked Elspeth.

'We were both lucky, said Doug, 'Phil had his uncle who was a plumber and he took him on, and our other friend from school – the three of us always went around together – was George Honeyman. He was going to work in his father's grocery store and he asked his father to take me on. The shop is now part of a chain but back then the family only had the one shop and I was proud to work for them. They still run their business as a family and look after their employees, there's not a finer man anywhere than George Honeyman.'

Elspeth was delighted to hear her friend's father praised.

'George Honeyman is the father of my oldest friend, Belinda, we all call her Belle.'

'Well I never did! Belle as you call her worked in the office for a while, a pretty little thing, we heard she was married to a vet last summer.'

'She was, I was one of her bridesmaids', said Elspeth.

'It's a small world', replied Doug. 'Her sister, Meg worked in the main office but has a young'un now but she drops in now and again to see us all. I have a lot to thank the Honeyman's for, after the war they gave me my old job back when thousands were left on the dole.'

'Were you both in the services during the War then?'

'We were. George was turned down from active service due to some minor physical defect so he trained in First Aid and worked as an Ambulance Driver on some Air Field, I reckon he saw as many awful sights as we did', said Phil.'

'My father was in the Air Force during the war but I didn't know about Belle's father,' said Elspeth.

'Well you wouldn't know, George has never been one for blowing his own trumpet. After the war, with us married with young children, Phil went back to working as a plumber and I went back to the shop and worked my way up to be manager in the main branch.'

Elspeth thought these are two humble and thoroughly decent men trying to take back something of their youth that life has deprived them of, yet they don't complain and it doesn't cross their minds that they have anything to feel resentful about. Doug nor Phil had expressed any envy of their old friend George that life had treated so much better than it had them. She felt humbled and the next time she saw the Honeyman's she told Belle's father how she was sharing art classes with his two old friends and that both of them had had paintings exhibited in a local Art Gallery.

'So the two of them have taken up art, Doug has never said, I'm glad for them they haven't had much from life either of them. I don't know what Doug was doing to marry the woman he did, we all knew her she lived in one of the streets nearby and she didn't have much to commend her even then as a young woman. Always sloppy, she works as a charwoman in some local offices, nothing wrong with that, of course, but I've never seen her without a cigarette in her mouth and she's let Doug down on so many occasions at Christmas Parties and the like, she drinks too much and she's coarse in her manners and speech and embarrasses Doug and he's too loyal to complain. Their two sons are well enough, the eldest is married and the second one works as a car mechanic and the daughter works in the office of the garage but unfortunately she's just like her mother, never without a cigarette in her mouth, I perhaps shouldn't say it but she looks slutty. She and her mother think we are snobs, they expected I would give Maureen a job in our main office but I couldn't we have to keep up standards. I know they think we've gone up in the world and have forgotten our origins since we were all brought up in the same streets, but nothing could be further from the truth.'

George Honeyman looked stricken and Elspeth quickly came to his defence, 'Doug doesn't think that he spoke very highly of you, he said that you had given his job back after the war and that you have been a great friend to him, but what about Phil you say life hasn't been very kind to him either?'

'Phil's wife is a fine woman, poor thing is an invalid, she has a very bad heart and has been in a wheelchair for years. He has two fine sons they are both married and live close by and their wives help out. It'll be how Phil manages to get away and follow these art classes. But what are you doing Elspeth attending classes with two old men, you should be with young people your own age? I'm surprised you haven't joined the town choir you always had a beautiful singing voice and the choir is very big, me and Vera go to their concerts.'

'The art class is quite mixed and I enjoy it though I'm not as good as your two old friends, I'm learning a lot there'.

Elspeth thought she was learning some invaluable lessons about life too. She enjoyed the other members of the group. She thought, individuals, families, groups of one sort and another are all like different worlds interacting and mingling with each other.

Chapter 7

....

"No Spring, nor Summer Beauty hath such grace,
As I have seen in one Autumnall face."
(Elegie IX Jon Donne)

It was Christmas and her parents had decided to stay home as Gran was looking very frail, she protested but not too strongly as it was obvious that she could not make the journey to the home of either her eldest or youngest sister. Her eldest sister was also by this time growing old and was planning to spend Christmas at home, her husband although still in good health was feeling his age and did not wish to travel far from home, they would be spending Christmas with their son's family who lived close by. Elspeth's parents suggested inviting Gran's youngest sister, also widowed, and her mother's favourite aunt as it happened, along with her daughter, Freda and her husband Frank and their daughter, Jackie. Their son was an archaeologist and abroad on a dig but Jackie was home from university, she was in her second year and planning to become a journalist. Elspeth liked her she was very lively and good company. They took up the invitation and it was decided that they would stay from Christmas Eve until New Year.

Their family's two cleaners – helpers and carers, more like – could always be called on to give a helping hand they had been with them for so long that they were like members of the family and they prepared the house for the guests between them. Christmas, of course was their time to spend with their own families but once guest rooms were set up and plenty of food had been ordered and delivered, everybody could be expected to help out and Elspeth looked forward to the holiday.

Elspeth had always liked her great aunt Maude unlike Gran she had strong religious beliefs and had joined the Salvation Army as a teenager. It was there that she had met and married her husband, who was an officer in the Salvation Army and her mother always spoke well of him. She said that he had been the kindest of people and one who put his faith into practice. He had worked she said with some of the poorest people in the London slums when he and Maude were young, he was incapable of turning anyone in need away and although Gran did not share their religious beliefs she and Grandpa had helped them out frequently because they had chosen a life that did not provide them with real financial security. It was her sister Maude who had given Gran the religious text that Gran had on her wall and which Louise had commented on. Freda and Frank were also Salvationists and Jackie was certainly a sympathiser, though whether she still attended services with them she did not know.

They ended up having a wonderful Christmas and Elspeth was very happy to see Gran enjoying herself she looked better than she had for months. Her parents were also looking as if they were having a good time. Aunt Maude and Freda were very good at preparing the Christmas Dinner, they were good cooks as Gran had once been and Elspeth and her mother did all they could to help.

Elspeth got to know Jackie much better during the course of their stay and they took occasional walks together. Jackie was thin and by comparison with Elspeth she was like a live wire and very quick witted. She had quite a mass of dark auburn hair and an elfish – Elspeth couldn't make up her mind whether Jackie's look was elfish or impish – mischievous expression. She had small features and a pointed chin and although kindly Elspeth thought she was unlikely to take fools gladly, she did not miss a thing and clearly had journalism in her blood. It was perhaps for this reason she was excellent company and when they were all together she entertained them with anecdotes about her university life. She had a boyfriend who worked on one of the National Newspapers and she had a fair amount of gossip which she shared. She was hoping that her boyfriend would provide an opening for her into journalism and Elspeth thought that this was the focal point of the attraction, her second cousin was unapologetically ambitious and Elspeth could imagine her reporting scandal and gossip with relish, although she liked her she found herself being very cautious about what she prepared to discuss with her and she told her little or nothing about herself.

By the time the visit was coming to an end she was beginning to weary of the never ending chatter and her thoughts turned to her other cousins in Switzerland. She had never had a great deal to do with her two older cousins who were three and four years older than she was. Max was working with his father – Elspeth's paternal grandparents had bought up hotels on the continent after the War and her father's sister had married an hotelier – and Ursula was a Psychiatrist. Her youngest cousin, her friend of the lower ski slopes had always been her good friend, she was a year younger than she was and she was studying medicine. She was fun loving but essentially serious and wanted to do good in the world and help her fellow human beings and Elspeth was slowly realising that she had never really had to explain herself to those she termed her 'Swiss family'. They knew her instinctively and at an altogether deeper level and Nan especially understood her. No one could ever take Gran's place, she thought, but in the end I am my father's daughter and have more in common with his family.

II

Their guests finally left the morning after New Year's Day and the following day Elspeth's mother asked her if she would accompany her to the shops to buy a dress that would be suitable for an evening dinner party that she and her father had been invited to. Elspeth needed little persuasion, she enjoyed a shopping spree, and after lunch the two of them set off together. Her father was relaxing with his daily newspaper and Gran was sitting before her living room fire filling in a crossword puzzle.

She and her mother drove to her mother's favourite boutique that Elspeth thought had never heard of sales. It sold exclusive designer labelled outfits now but before the War it employed dressmakers and reproduced clothes that had been designed for the top Paris Fashion Houses. Her mother tried on three dresses before she decided on the one she finally bought; it was a light navy blue. It was in two layers; the lower layer was topped by a silk layer. It was simple, elegant and beautifully cut and her mother looked magnificent. Elspeth and the sales lady expressed their approval, her mother said it was more expensive than she had planned, but Elspeth knew she invariably said the same, and as she could not resist it the dress was duly packaged and they left the shop.

'I don't have any shoes that I can wear with the dress, I'll have to find a pair'.

Elspeth knew that her mother had numerous pairs of shoes that would be perfectly suitable but she declined from saying so and they made their way to shoe shops and in the third one they found the very pair her mother thought fitted and completed the outfit.

'I think we both deserve tea after all this, darling,' and Elspeth agreed.

They walked to the large department store which was close to the car park where they had left the car. The perfume and makeup area was just inside the main doors and Lillian was there as neatly presented as always. Elspeth was pleased to see her and introduced her mother and Lillian was thrilled. Her mother felt they should not leave without buying some perfume and said she would treat Elspeth too, 'you've been so patient accompanying me'.

Elspeth said it had been a pleasure and then they finally made their way to the small restaurant. As they were about to leave the shop her mother caught sight of a counter with a display of Cashmere sweaters in the sale and could not resist looking through them.

'This is a lovely colour and style Elspeth, it would look so nice on you, try it on, I'll treat you!'

'You already have, mummy,' but she did not refuse and it did indeed look beautiful. Her mother had found another in the same size but a different colour and she insisted on buying them both for her. When they left the shop it was already dark but they were both so pleased with the way the shopping had gone that they talked happily all the way home. Elspeth had never felt that she was close to her mother but they enjoyed a long familiar and easy companionship and she loved her, her mother's generosity and outrageous extravagance amused her. After a particularly expensive shopping spree she would always say, 'I really must tighten my belt, I'm not spending on anything else for months', but more often than not the 'months' proved to be weeks.

Arriving home, she and her mother rustled up some supper and Gran joined them, afterwards Elspeth washed the dishes and the four of them settled down to watch a drama on the television. By ten o'clock they were tired and Elspeth got up to give her Grandmother a kiss before her mother went with her to help her to bed. Elspeth said what she said to her grandmother every night, 'I love you,' but then added, 'Make sure you sleep well'. She was to wonder forever afterwards why she had used this phrase, she never had before. Then after saying a general 'goodnight', she had climbed the stairs to her room happily carrying her shopping and planning to try on the two new sweaters her mother had bought her that afternoon. However, she decided she was too tired, they could wait for the following day, she quickly washed and climbed into bed and went straight to sleep.

III

She was still fast asleep the next morning when her mother began shaking her and asking her to wake up. One look at her mother's face and dishevelled appearance made her realise at once that something was very wrong, she was immediately awake and out of bed.

'It's mother – Gran, I went to take her a cup of tea, I couldn't rouse her, Elspeth, she's died in her sleep'.

Elspeth grabbed her dressing gown and pushed her feet into her slippers and without any further word between them she hurried in front of her mother down the stairs. Her grandmother's bedroom was on the ground floor and she pushed open the door and entered. For a moment she thought it was a mistake and Gran was just asleep, she looked peaceful and defenceless as sleepers do. Her silver hair was carefully parted and she was wearing the lacy sleeping jacket her sister Maude had given her for Christmas. Her hands lay one over the other above the covers. She is beautiful, Elspeth thought, she bent over and kissed her and drew back as the shock hit her. What was she expecting? Not the icy cold she was met with as the realisation and inevitability of death struck her. Her darling, loving Gran was dead, she could no longer respond. All that warmth and love that she had lavished on her all her life had passed beyond her. Elspeth felt again that shroud of unreality envelope her as it had after Jamie's death and the cruel event that had followed it. It could not be real and at the same time it was only too true. She and her mother still not exchanging a word left the room. Her father was standing outside, 'I've made you both a hot drink and I've rang Doctor Pearce, he'll be here as soon as he can make it.'

Then the front door opened and Elsie came in to begin her morning's work and life and the world came into focus again.

'She was a lovely old lady, I'm so sorry.' Elsie wasn't flustered, if a thunderbolt had passed through her house, Elspeth thought, she would have carried on where she had left off and neither thankfully did she indulge in euphemisms about death that offered no comfort for the bereaved. Instead she turned her mind to practicalities and said that they needed to eat, that they needed to stay strong. Elspeth felt she could not eat anything and said she was not hungry.

'I'm not suggesting you eat a full breakfast', and she prepared them some buttered toast and it helped to make things feel a little more normal.

After eating, she and her mother quickly got washed and dressed and were ready when Doctor Pearce arrived and she and her parents accompanied him into her grandmother's bedroom. He felt her hands and seemed to move her fingers and established a possible time of death, saying that she had very possibly died soon after she had fallen to sleep. He took a look at the medicine bottle on the bedside table and her mother told him that she had given her mother one of the sleeping pills, that he had prescribed, when she had helped her to bed the previous night.

'Will there have to be a post-mortem?'' Elspeth's mother asked.

'No. Your mother was old and her heart was weak and she has been getting steadily more frail. Death was to be expected. She has died of natural causes and I will sign a death certificate to that effect. It's a shock for you all and you have my sincere sympathy. She was a fine lady and much loved.'

Elspeth knew that it was not a tragedy, her grandmother was old and she had had a long and happy life but Gran had been more her mother than her grandparent. Her mother was lovely, loving and generous but as Elspeth increasingly realised somewhat frivolous. She did not take anything deeply seriously. Perhaps her light-heartedness was what her father needed from her and she herself frequently welcomed it. She was inclined to be too serious and lacked the optimism of her mother.

She knew her mother would be sad for a month or two then she would gather herself together and get on with her life, for her tomorrow was always another day! It was different for her, she would mourn her grandmother for as long as she lived. Perhaps Mrs Donoghue was right, we cannot all be the same and for the moment she had to face up to the funeral and she shrank from it.

IV

Elspeth was surprised how quickly things were organised. Her grandmother was laid out simply and placed in a coffin and to her granddaughter she appeared smaller and just very vulnerable. She stayed with her for a while then wandered back into the room where her parents were and where her father's words shocked her and she felt the horror of what he was saying.

'I'll need to get in touch with the crematorium and arrange the funeral.'

'No! Gran's not going to be cremated! I couldn't bear it.'

She thought her blood was being drained from her face and she was going to faint, she swayed and her father rushed to her and held her, 'It's alright Elspeth, there, there child,' and she wondered when he had last called her 'child,' not since she was one she thought, and he helped her to a chair. Was this the same father who had been so harsh to her brother and to her when she had been in trouble?

'I don't like cremation either, but it is what your grandmother was very clear about wanting and we must respect her wishes.'

Elspeth thought that he must remember planes bursting into flames and plummeting towards the ground, knowing that inside them a pilot and crew were going to be incinerated.

'Grandpa wasn't cremated'.

'He didn't wish to be', said her mother, 'we will put the urn containing Gran's ashes in the grave with your grandpa, they will be together'.

Her father then said that he was going to pour them each a brandy, 'It'll put the colour back in your cheeks Elspeth, you're shocked'.

She had to be content with that, but she was horrified. If only her grandmother had spoken to her she would have persuaded her against cremation, but could she have done so? Her grandmother was very strong willed about what she believed or disbelieved.

That night she went to sit by the coffin and because she knew that there were Catholic groups that went to pray by a dead loved one she said a rosary for her grandmother who had disliked and spoken against established religion all her adult life but who was now rendered powerless to protest.

Afterwards she climbed the stairs and crawled into bed but she was unable to sleep. Images kept coming into her mind of her recounting some minor achievement and receiving Gran's congratulations, happy memories of Jamie and herself being joyously welcomed into the home of her grandparents, her brother's smile and laughter and her parents somewhere in the background waving as they hurried off together on a social outing or a short break without their children. She tossed and turned and at six o'clock in the morning she went downstairs, took a glass of water and made herself a strong cup of coffee then she went back to her room, but not to sleep. She opened the curtains and stared down at the winter garden, it was still quite dark but she could see the outline of the silver birch against the grey sky.

Trees usually lifted her spirits but today the tree was dark and the garden was shrouded in mist and the barrenness of winter, it was desolate, it mirrored the way she felt, she thought that she could have borne it better in spring or summer. Then she felt slightly ashamed, Gran would not approve of such weakness. She washed and got ready quickly and went down to breakfast.

In the afternoon her parents were receiving visitors that had heard about her grandmother's death and she decided that she wasn't needed so she rang her old friend, Belle and went off to see her. Belle was now the proud and doting mother of a nine-month old little boy, Jonathan, and she and Elspeth spent the afternoon laughing at his antics. He smiled and gurgled contentedly and Belle was in her element. The visit lightened Elspeth's spirits, life is a continuum she thought, when one set of players leave the scene others take their place and she hoped she saw hope for the future in the little one's face.

V

On the morning of the funeral it was raining, there had been a steady downpour all night and Elspeth felt her resolution to stay strong dissolve. The cemetery was quite large, it was where Jamie and her grandpa were buried and she had formerly found it a peaceful place there were trees that on a spring or summer's day lent a sense of growth and life so that death did not altogether dominate and claim the place for its own. This morning it wept. The Crematorium stood in the centre of the cemetery and Elspeth hated it. She felt that it was designed to sanitise death and it was hygienic she thought rather than clean. Her mother had asked her if there was a hymn she would like to have sung and she had said that the words of 'Lead kindly light,' were written by Cardinal John Henry Newman, and she had always seen Gran in a way as a Victorian.

When it came for the coffin, during the singing of the hymn, to pass through the curtains into the flames she could not stay to watch and with her handkerchief held to her eyes she walked out sobbing and stood in the portico outside. Belle followed her.

'Please don't be so distressed, Elspeth, your Gran won't feel anything, she's not there, she's in Heaven now.'

'Gran didn't believe in heaven; she didn't believe in God'.

'But that doesn't mean He doesn't believe in her. All those people here for her funeral, you heard some of them speak about her, people who were once orphans, people she helped. Everybody loved and spoke well of your Gran, do you think God won't love her too, didn't Jesus say, "For as much as you do good to the least of these my brethren you do good to me?"

Elspeth looked at her friend and recognised in her a simplicity that was profound.

'That's the best, most beautiful and comforting tribute I've heard from anybody I think I can be brave now. Thank you Belle.'

VI

The guests at the funeral were invited back home where caterers had prepared refreshments. Gran's eldest sister, Christabel and her husband Tommy had managed the journey, driven by Bill, one of their sons, and they left quite quickly. Her youngest sister, Maude, had clearly been crying and her eyes looked red, Elspeth's mother had told her that she had always been very soft hearted and of course they had all been together such a short time before. Jackie was surveying the room with her journalist's eye, taking everything in, Elspeth thought that her second cousin saw life in terms of newspaper coverage, she introduced her to Belle and her parents and left them talking together while she went about the room speaking to Gran's friends. Belle came to her and said she had to leave early because she had left her baby with her sister Meg and he would soon need to be fed but she told Elspeth to visit them soon. The funeral had been early in the morning and by noon the guests had left apart from Nan and Grandda, they had made the journey from Switzerland and they were planning to stay with them for several weeks. This had, of course, been their home where they had brought up their children and Nan said that it held bittersweet memories for her. Elspeth was pleased they were staying.

VII

Two days following the funeral the family's solicitor turned up to read Gran's will and apart from small legacies made to her sisters and her favourite charity, she had left everything to Elspeth and her granddaughter was shocked and looked at her mother. Her mother, however, was pleased and told her that she and Gran had discussed it and that she had been given two or three pieces of jewellery and other momentoes and those were all she required.

Elspeth was not sure what she felt. She would never go out in the world and make money but was glad, if she was honest, that she was not poor, something of her Grandmother's philosophy of life had she thought rubbed off on her. But she had not thought to be rich and she now most certainly was. Gran's own house had never been sold when she had moved in with her parents, it was large and stood in an expensive location close by. It was being rented to short stay tenants and her father suggested that it should remain unsold as it would appreciate in value. In addition to the house, Gran had considerable investments in property around the city and she felt confused. Her father said he and her mother would be more than happy to continue dealing with the management of her estate, which they had been doing since Grandpa had died, along with their own. Elspeth knew that her father and his family owned a large number of properties and land in the area and she was relieved and happy to leave it in their hands. He said that they would sit down with her and explain everything to her and she was more than happy for them to do so.

Elspeth went up to her room after this conversation with her father, to mull things over, she had never had to face a need for money and she had always accepted the situation because the money had never been strictly hers, now she was wealthy in her own right and she felt that it brought with it a moral responsibility that she was determined to face up to. She sighed, she was getting older and life was becoming very much less simple.

VIII

Within days she was back teaching but she had told herself when she had returned home from university that she was staying on a semi-permanent basis to be close to her grandmother, now that Gran had died she had to face up to a new future.

At home one evening she looked into the library and Nan who was sitting reading looked up from her book and smiled. Elspeth and her grandmother shared a love of books and when they had left England for Switzerland a considerable number of books had been left behind and Elspeth had found them a source of pleasure.

'What are you reading, Nan?' she now asked.

'I'm really into reading biographies and autobiographies these days and quite a lot of history, straight history not historical novels. I find it really well written and absorbing. You're looking very perplexed, dear, can I help, I don't want to intrude but I've watched you looking very serious?'

'I feel that I've been thrown in at the deep end suddenly and I'm trying to think of what I should do. I love teaching at Oaklands but it's not enough I want to spread my wings'.

'There's no young man in your life I take it, so you're not ready to settle down. Perhaps you could go abroad for a while and have a complete change of scenery. Of course I know that your Gran's death was to be expected but it has nevertheless been a shock and I think a break from this house and environment would do you good.'

'You're right. I do love this house, I don't want to leave it forever, at least I don't believe I do. I'll want to come back one day for my parents'.

'It has its difficulties being left as an only child but your parents are still young and able to look after themselves and hopefully one day you will marry and have children of your own and no doubt you will want to make this your family home. It will come down to you'.

'When you left here did you ever want to come back?'

'Yes and no! This had been, as you know, where we had brought up our children and it's full of memories which I cherish. I can remember your father and James sliding down the banisters and kicking balls around in the garden and making a mess and annoying Grandda because the garden was his pride and joy. He planted the Silver Birch and the Magnolia and built the rockery and they are still doing well. I used to feel sorry for your Auntie

Elspeth because she felt left out and Grandda spoilt her, she was always bossy and your father and James when they were home from school – they boarded as you know – used to tease her, but believe me she could hold her own. She's still bossy now, she treats me like an infant. When she went off to boarding school I was on tenterhooks but I needn't have worried she took to it like a duck to water and loved it, she became Head Girl and kept everybody in their place. She runs the local church now and I suspect she drives folks mad but if there weren't women like her, the rest of us might just sit back and do nothing. It's not just the flowers she takes care of she organises committees and fund raising. She's a hive of activity and also helps your uncle with the business. She's a good soul and she's been an exceptional mother. She took things in hand when we left here. I was grieving for James and was fit for nothing and John, your father, had lost his best friend. God knows what he experienced himself during the War, it was a bad time, so many lives were destroyed. I can remember being worried almost to death when the pair of them bought motor bikes and went tearing around the countryside, then the war came and it was almost impossible to sleep at night wondering what frightful news the following day would bring'.

'He never talks about it.'

'He never has but I am seeing a difference in him lately. This visit I have seen something of his old self and I'm glad. Your mother has always been good for him. Our family has always been very serious, me especially I'm afraid, and your mother came to live in this house because your father couldn't bear to leave it though I'm sure she wanted something smaller and more modern. She gave up a very promising musical career for him and has always stayed by his side and of course, despite what might be supposed, she has considerable business acumen. She's optimistic and looks on the brighter side of life and I think your father has a lot to be thankful for, she saved him from himself.

As a child he was a daredevil and very carefree for a Penrose, he caused me some anxiety, but now how much I would like to have those days back.'

So she had been right, her mother's natural optimism had been a foil for her father and she had always noticed how indulgently he looked upon her extravagance.

'Elspeth here I am talking about myself when I should be talking about you and your future plans. I feel sure that life will open up for you and you will find what you are looking for before you know it. It's the way when we are young.'

'I am very interested in teaching mentally disabled children and have been reading up a lot about Maria Montessori's teaching methods, I suppose I'd like to combine them with assisting in a Catholic school for the mentally or physically disabled'.

'You are still thinking about Jamie?'

'Yes. I really loved helping out at Lourdes. My Italian is good so perhaps I could find a place in Montessori's homeland. She has schools all over the world now, but I have been considering working in Italy for some time'.

'Do you still blame your father for Jamie's death, Elspeth?'

'I have been determined to put it behind me, being angry and critical of my father doesn't help Jamie.'

'He's angry enough with himself and guilty too. Has your mother told you that he makes regular large contributions to a charity that works on behalf of the mentally and physically disabled?'

'The last thing I knew was that he was going to sue Jamie's school for negligence, I thought my mother changed his mind.'

'He didn't need anyone to change his mind, he knew that he had treated his young son badly. It's a pretty dreadful thing to live with. Your father has his own demons.'

'I'm learning to see that, slowly'.

Chapter 8

....

"Blue Moon
You saw me standing alone
Without a dream in my heart
Without a love of my own

Blue Moon
You knew just what I was there for
You heard me saying a prayer for
Someone I really could care for"
(Rodgers and Hart)

During the February half term Elspeth went to stay with Louise and Jerome and their one-year old daughter, Eleanor. They had settled in a Cotswold's country town and their nineteenth century house was built of the stone notable in that area. The day she arrived the air was crisp and inside a wood stove was burning which gave off a pleasant heat and lent a comfortable and altogether welcoming atmosphere to the room.

'This is lovely, such a state of domestic bliss. Where's Ellie?' asked Elspeth.

'Having her afternoon sleep. But my domestic bliss has been disturbed by a family crisis. I arrived back only last week from my parents. Things came to a head after New Year and I knew you were in a sorry state following your grandmother's death so I didn't say anything. Let's have some tea before Ellie wakes up and I'll tell you all that's happened.'

'It sounds ominous'

'It has been. It's what my parents always feared might happen! It's Maeve. She has always been one for getting herself into scrapes of one kind or another and my parents have regularly been called upon to sort things out. For the most part her escapades were none too serious, smoking on the school premises with her friends, behaving badly on the way home from school, again with an undesirable group of friends. She hated school and mocked the nuns and was determined to leave at the earliest possible moment. It wasn't very pleasant for Catherine, two years younger and very different, she was frequently embarrassed. Maeve is bright enough and managed to scrape reasonable exam results and she took a job in a large department store in the fashion department and my parents sighed with relief. She was an excellent saleswoman, people like her and take to her and wearing thick make-up and dying her hair and smoking were the least of their problems! The store has a very good reputation in the town and they were planning to train her as a Manageress. That was eighteen months ago, she's twenty now.'

'What's happened?'

'She started staying out 'til late, then she told my mother that she was staying overnight with her friend, Gabby. One night something happened and she was needed at home and my mother rang Gabby's mother to be told that Maeve had not been round to their house for some months. When Gabby picked up the phone she said that she had met Maeve in town during the week with her boyfriend, Ed, and she supposed that Maeve was probably with him. You can imagine my parents' reaction they knew nothing of this boyfriend. When she turned up home the next day and they confronted her she became furious, said she was nineteen and could please herself that they were old fashioned, catholic fanatics and she was sick and fed up with the church and everything to do with religion. When they asked her why she had not brought her boyfriend home they learnt that he was divorced, 'the devil incarnate as far as you're concerned', she threw at them and he had a five-year old son and that she loved him and was going to marry him! And she stormed out and announced that she was going to live with him!'

'Is he Catholic?'

'No, and neither had he any intention of marrying her. To cut a long story short she'd got pregnant and when she told this Ed fellow who, incidentally, is in his mid-thirties, he told her it was nothing to do with him. When she pleaded with him he beat her and threw her out. She crawled home badly bruised, distraught and contrite.'

'How did your parents take all this?'

'They treated her like the prodigal. They rang her place of work and told them she was unwell and that she would return to work when she was feeling better. Once the bruises healed she went back to the store put in her notice and left before her pregnancy was too far advanced.'

'Is she staying at home?'

'No, I went up home to help them sort things out and to support my mother. My parents have made arrangements for her to go to her Godmother in Dublin. Liz is my mother's old school friend and Godmother to Ann and Maeve. She was a doctor's receptionist but retired early to look after her mother who has rheumatoid arthritis. As I told you, my sister Bridget and Tom have moved to Dublin. Tom's mother died last year and he managed to get a teaching post in Dublin and they are living with his father. They have three children by this time but will be willing to help out when Maeve's baby is born and when she is ready to go back to work!'

'Is Maeve planning to keep the baby, she's not going to have it adopted?'

'She's determined to keep it, I actually think she'll make a good and caring mother. There's so much to like about her and despite the problems she's given my mother, she was the closest to her when she was younger. She's not a bad person we just hope that she will be wiser after this experience. My mother is hoping it will be the making of her, who knows! I don't suppose that one can have such a large family without problems of some kind or another. My parents have handled things really well, all credit due to them, my father confided in Father Moran and when Maeve thought she should get up and accompany my parents and younger brothers to Mass – Catherine is in her first year at university, I think I told you – my father stopped her saying he understood that she was twenty years old and free to decide about her religious beliefs and she should no longer accompany them if she no longer believed. He said that he wanted her to take her time and to think things through and they would not put any pressure on her'.

'I hope she realises how lucky she is! When I was eighteen, after the rape I thought I was pregnant and my father made me a virtual prisoner while he made arrangements for me to have an abortion. Thankfully I'd made a mistake. That's the part I didn't tell you'.

'Your father's handling of your experience led you to the Catholic Church, hopefully my father's handling of Maeve will lead her back to it. God writes straight with crooked lines!'

'God writes straight with crooked lines! I like that, I've not heard that before', said Elspeth.

'It explains things when reason fails to!'

'I'll remember it. I like your family, especially your mother and I'm really sorry that she has been facing such a trying time.'

'Now about you Elspeth, you said that you were planning to spend some time abroad?'

'I have more or less decided what I want to do. When we were in Lourdes there was a school group of mentally disabled children who make a pilgrimage there every year from Italy. Sister Maria Rosa is in charge of them and acts as Headteacher at their school. You might remember her. We have kept in touch and I want to work voluntarily in the school. I don't need a salary or anything, I told you that Gran has left me more than well provided for and I think she would strongly approve of my helping out – she would have preferred it not to be in a Catholic school, of course, but that's all water under the bridge now. I have been taking time to think it through but I am going to write to Sister Maria Rosa when I get back, I remember her saying they could do with all the help they could get, and I'll try to arrange something for this coming September. I am hoping that I can join them in Lourdes and journey back with them. It's not totally without some self-interest, I love Italy and I would love to spend a year or so in Rome. So we'll see.'

'I'm hoping that you are going to meet the love of your life, I can just see you falling in love with a Latin!'

'You're an incurable romantic Louise.'

Just then Ellie woke up and Louise went to bring her downstairs. Ellie still half awake and clutching a teddy bear entered and eyed Elspeth warily. After a minute or two she livened up and Elspeth gave her a toy panda she'd brought her as a gift. The little girl smiled but soon put it down and turned to the family's cat; there could be no rivalry for her attention between a toy animal and the real thing. The cat, no doubt would have preferred it differently. When she was stopped from pulling its tail she tried, unsuccessfully, to gather him up in her arms. 'Stroke him gently', went unheeded and the cat did not protest until Louise decided that it had had enough of her daughter's care and telling Ellie that, 'Pussy Cat was tired' she removed him to his basket at the side of the fireplace, before he ended up smothered and she replaced him with a box of toys. Ellie had different ideas and much preferred opening the cupboard doors within her reach, Jerome happily entered at this point and took charge of things while Louise went into the kitchen to prepare the evening meal and Elspeth followed her there.

II

The next day was Sunday and after Mass, Jerome again took charge of Ellie and suggested that his wife and Elspeth should go for lunch in the town and spend the afternoon together.

'Do you miss the Northeast Louise? Asked Elspeth when they were alone.

'I realised just how bleak the winters really are last month when I was home, but yes I miss the community I was brought up with and my family. It was good being with Ann she's settled into teaching, as I think she will have told you, she's still living at home and seems contented enough. There is a community here, of course but I think it takes longer to be fully accepted. In the north, folks willingly tell you their life stories from one bus stop to the next, here I've noticed that people think you're being nosy when you're simply being interested. I love this part of the country though the Cotswolds are really beautiful. The West Country is more Jane Austen than the Brontës with their wild dramatic countryside, and it has its own appeal which I may not have acknowledged so easily when I was younger.'

After lunch the pair left the small town and set off on a walk into the countryside.

'You are so different from the person I thought you were when we first met and you said that you were not a church goer, now you are immersed in the Catholic faith,' said Louise.

'I have told you about my Orthodox colleague Helen and her husband Johannes we discuss religion a lot. Apparently when Miss Cresswell, the Headmistress told Helen that I had become a Catholic she had said that it hadn't surprised her that she had considered me to be otherworldly! I think I'm probably naturally religious!

But my Catholic faith is basically centred on belief in God and the Eucharist. When God in the Old Testament gives His name to Moses, He says 'I Am the One that Is' and this is what He becomes for us in the Eucharist, 'the One that Is. At the Elevation the congregation becomes silent and to me it's not just because I have been told and believe that the bread and wine have become the Body, Blood, Soul and Divinity of Christ it is because they Are and Christ Is. And from this acceptance of God everything in life and nature takes on a deeper significance, I'm not sure if I'm making any sense, but nature and everything that grows speaks to something deeper in us, to our souls, it's mystical, and that can become in turn a prayer that allows us to commune with God. Bread and Wine are the fruits of the natural world and they are taken and become the Reality that is Christ Himself.

To consider that the Eucharist is only symbolic, which the Protestant churches believe, denies the fullness of Truth. Symbolism eventually becomes reality once removed and gradually over the centuries several times removed, ultimately it allows beauty and even love to be less than they might be. It is serious reductionism. Denial of the reality of God in the Sacraments becomes in a sense a betrayal by failing to believe and trust in the words of Christ and the people's faith in religion – generally that is, I'm not talking about particular individuals, like my old friend Belle, and Nan as there always seems to be a remnant left of past traditions upheld by a number of the faithful – weakens over time and there is increasing indifference to all things religious. Religion is set to decline further and replacing God with materialism and all things secular is idolatry.'

'I agree. 'There is a beauty deep down things', is the line Gerald Manley Hopkins writes describing what is deeper and mystical in nature.

....

On returning home Elspeth got down to carrying out her plans and she was pleased and relieved when things began to fall into place, it was easier than she had thought it would be. Sister Maria Rosa told her that if they met in Lourdes in mid-August there would be some weeks before the school reopened in September. She suggested Elspeth book into a guest house nearby or alternatively there was a convent that offered accommodation but in the end Elspeth's mother said that she would be happy to join her in Rome and together they could look around for a small, furnished apartment that she could rent.

Miss Cresswell said how sorry she was to lose her but she understood and she added when Elspeth told her, that while she remained Head Mistress at Oaklands there would be a place for her if she wished to return some time in the future. Helen and Johannes Manasses said how sorry they were to see her go but they intended to keep in touch.

Elspeth was amazed how quickly the time passed and the last week of the summer term arrived. She was moved by the number of cards and small gifts given to her by her pupils. Miss Cresswell gave her a copy of John Donne's poems and Helen and Johannes gave her a book of the Church Fathers but the gift that moved her the most deeply was the gift made by Doug on behalf of the Art group. Doug had had his picture that Elspeth had so admired and named 'Halcyon Days', framed for her. Elspeth was close to tears as she accepted it along with her art friends' good wishes and she said that she would treasure it all her life and would always remember them. And so the term ended and she set off on the next stage of her life.

III

The school group she was joining always booked into the same hostel and Elspeth joined them there in mid-August. Several parents accompanied their children who were staying for ten days and this year Sister Maria Rosa introduced her to her cousin who had joined the party to help out, 'This is my cousin, Anton, he teaches singing and music at a college in Rome but comes into school voluntarily for an hour every other week and introduces the children to some music therapy, the children love it.'

'I'm only staying for five days, a small choir in Rome I'm in charge of are making a short tour of some of the Northern Italian towns'.

Elspeth was interested, 'I love singing, do you sing solos?'

'Yes'.

'I was in the choir of the church I attend; the church still celebrates the old Mass and sings Gregorian Chant'.

'Very good! I have never taken to the new Mass, the Church was never intended to give up Gregorian Chant, it's a treasure of the Church'.

Elspeth thought, I may have met a soul mate!

'You speak very fluent English with a slight American accent, I think'.

'I studied English at school and I spent a year in America on a singing scholarship and I have considered going back to America or perhaps working in England.'

He was tall with dark brown hair, slightly fairer than her own, it was straight and thick and a shock of it lay across one side of his forehead. He had boyish good looks and misty blue eyes and she thought he was probably about twenty-six or twenty-seven and she liked the way he behaved towards the children, they clearly loved him and treated him like a friend.

In the evening they joined the candlelit procession as it wound its way around the grounds of the Grotto, a river of light against a darkening sky, and afterwards Elspeth helped the nuns and parents to get the children ready for bed.

One afternoon, three or four days later, she climbed up to a grassy area above the grotto grounds and was sitting quietly thinking when Anton approached.

'A penny for your thoughts, isn't that what the English say? May I join you?'

'Of course, please do.'

'So you sing well, perhaps you might like to audition for my choir in Rome'.

'I think I would like to very much'.

'You read music? Anton asked.

'I do yes, my mother is a pianist and was professional, she gave up her career when she married. She taught me but I never reached her standard of competence.'

'My cousin says you came here to help with two of your friends when you were a
university student, and now you're planning to help in the school.'

'Yes, I enjoyed working here with disabled children. I've been teaching for the last three years at the school I attended as a pupil and I thought it was time to try something new. I have been read-ing about Maria Montessori's teaching methods applied to disa-bled children. My young brother was mentally disabled, he died as a result of an accident when he was fifteen but he had attended a special school that really developed his ability, there were sev-eral things he could do well. When my grandfather, my mother's father was alive he used to help him in the garden planting seeds and bulbs and looking after them as they grew. He also loved football, and animals and responded to music as these children do here. I really believe that children like my brother benefit from being stimulated and given an education suitable for their needs. I love teaching and that's the main reason that I want to work for a year or two in the school in Rome. I am also looking for-ward to living for a spell in Rome, my Italian is quite good, not as good as your English, but it's a beautiful language and I want to perfect it. Are you seriously considering returning to America or working in England?'

'I do think about it, America is an obvious choice, I suppose, I have family there and there's an extensive Italian population which works at all levels of society. I'm not sure that's the case in England. I may be wrong, of course, things will have changed but I grew up believing that apart from Opera singers Italians in England are most well known for their ice cream! We were also given to believe that Italians working during the war were im-prisoned in Scottish islands and on an island off the English coast and these stories tend to stick'.

'I know that Italians and Germans were sent to the Isle of Man during the war but it wasn't a concentration camp exactly, though I'm sure that it was understandably resented. I have never heard any prejudice against Italians or ordinary German people for that matter, though the horror of the Holocaust still resonates, but there is, I think on all sides a desire for reconciliation. My fa-ther was an Officer in the RAF and a bomber pilot during the war but he hasn't expressed any hostility towards Germans. He is somewhat tight lipped, however, about Japan as his brother was brutally treated, possibly tortured, before dying in a Japanese Prisoner of War camp. War casts long shadows'.

'My family helped their Jewish employees and neighbours to find refuge in 'safe houses' and convents and monasteries, but yes, war as you say casts long shadows. If I'm not destined to be looked upon as an ice cream vendor, as wonderful as our ice cream undoubtedly is, I might be tempted to gain some experience of life in England, since England is internationally admired. Well it's time I think to join the rest of the party for the evening meal, I'm leaving tomorrow but I'll look forward to meeting up with you again in Rome'.

IV

Elspeth's mother was already in Rome when they arrived and she happily introduced her to Sister Maria Rosa and some of the mothers that had been in France with them. They instantly liked her mother and said how pleased they were that Elspeth was going to work with their children. When Elspeth explained to them that her mother's young son had been mentally disabled, but had sadly been killed, they warmed to her even more and said that they hoped that she would visit them in the future and they assured her that she was leaving her daughter in safe hands and they would see to it that she would not lack for friends.

Elspeth and her mother settled into a small hotel close by and during the following days they searched for a suitable flat for her to rent. It wasn't difficult and they soon came across a furnished one-bedroom apartment on the second floor of a block of flats. It had a small balcony that overlooked a square and they both felt that it was more than adequate and a more than pleasing prospect and Elspeth took it for a year. She and her mother shopped for the things she needed to set up 'home' and she was excited about having a place of own and living by herself for the first time in her life. All the same she was sorry to say 'goodbye' to her mother, she felt naturally apprehensive about this preliminary step she was taking into an unknown future.

The school she was to work in was run by an order of nuns but it was not a school in the usual understanding of an educational establishment. The parents along with the church met the financial costs of running the school which provided practical occupation for their mentally disabled children and Elspeth was given a fairly free hand in assisting the nuns and teachers. She had plenty of ideas and her own financial means to put her ideas into practice. When the school lacked the equipment required she provided it, she was assigned to a group of ten children who were not in wheelchairs and so mobile.

Five of them she already knew from Lourdes and what she most liked was the atmosphere of happiness that pervaded her small class and the school as a whole. Paolo and Lilliana were Downs Syndrome and she instantly loved them. Paolo had never managed to speak very well and his mother longed for him to acquire speech so that she and the rest of his family could communicate with him better and Elspeth set about spending some time with him every day and going through simple picture books and words with him. Every time he succeeded with a new word Elspeth praised him and was rewarded herself by his smile.

Both Paolo and Lilliana were excellent mimics and kept the good natured group happy. She went home each evening and prepared the small class with improvised worksheets, drawing their name in dots and getting them to draw round them. She taught the ones that could to count by drawing small pictures and getting them to colour them in. She gave them colouring in books and encouraged them to colour in neatly without going over edges. There was a garden surrounding the school yard and she brought along plants and helped them to plant them. During that first autumn she helped them to plant bulbs in plant pots for inside the school and supervised the children as they cared for them.

One of the things she had so admired at Oaklands was the placement of flowers and paintings around the school, here there were holy pictures and statues and now she made sure that there were fresh flowers placed before them. She wanted the children to be presented with beauty because she sensed implicitly that beautiful surroundings aided tranquillity and were spiritually uplifting. Like all Catholic environments she had become acquainted with in England they were always clean and ordered and she found the same was true in the school here.

Elspeth had admired Sister Maria Rosa in Lourdes now she warmed to the nun's dedication and kindness. The nuns and several of the mothers were excellent at knitting and Sister Maria Rosa organised a knitting circle and sold the things they knitted to raise funds. They held raffles and once a year held a bazaar. Sister Maria Rosa encouraged the mothers to bring in clothes that their children had outgrown and these were made available for needy children. These things created a very real sense of family and Elspeth was made welcome and was happy to become part of it.

A fortnight into the term Anton came into the school and helped the children to make music. The school had some percussion instruments, triangles, castanets, drums and a xylophone and the children enjoyed a happy hour. They also sang simple Italian folk songs and Elspeth was given a copy of the words and joined in.

Before leaving, Anton asked her if she still wished to join his choir and she said that she would love to and he asked where she was living and agreed to collect her on the evening of the next choir practice. He was as good as his word and she was already waiting outside when he arrived. Elspeth had enjoyed singing all her life and knew that she had a good voice and she was very pleased when Anton praised her. At the school she had thought him easy going but with the choir he was exacting and demanded a high standard and the members of the choir responded. It was an amateur group but there were singers within it that reached professional standards and she felt fortunate to have been accepted.

Anton was soon inviting her for coffee after choir practice and one Sunday soon after they had met up he asked her if she would like to join him at Mass. He attended a church that had retained a close observance of the rubrics, he pointed out to her that the Mass was a holy and public performance and that the vestments should be beautiful and 'up for the job'. He hated any failure or a slack observance of the ritual feeling that it expressed an undisciplined approach to the liturgy which should demand the highest and the best and which he felt the modern church was frequently falling short of. Elspeth felt that replacing the Latin with the vernacular had weakened the unity within the church, while Latin had been used there was a sense of universality that had now been lost. She felt she had much in common with Anton and the friendship between them deepened.

Sister Maria Rosa had said to Elspeth after the first session that Anton had visited the school, 'My cousin is a good person, though something of a troubled soul, we've been close all our lives. He has not had the easiest life or the happiest.' She had not given any further details and Elspeth was naturally curious especially as she was seeing more of him. He didn't strike her as an unhappy person, he occasionally expressed frustration about his job but she considered that was nothing out of the ordinary and he could be amusing and he had laughed out loud when she described the visit she had made to the Sistine Chapel with her mother.

'I was sitting at the back of the chapel with my mother admiring its beauty when a group of American tourists came to stand near us and one of them exclaimed, "Is this the Sistine Chapel, is this all!" I think I'll be relating the incident into my old age, the reaction of one sightseer to Michelangelo's masterpiece. Do you visit the historical places?'

'We're surrounded by so much history and I suppose we're living history ourselves and so we pass it almost without thinking about it most of the time. We are proud of all of it, of course'.

'I have been brought up myself in an historical city – not so world famous as Rome – but I know what you mean, you tend to take it all for granted. When I first invited my college friend home she was full of admiration.'

She found herself becoming increasingly fond of him but she was not swept off her feet, this was not what her parents had experienced, a love at first sight, this was more like slow glowing embers, a developing friendship that might or might not ignite into flames.

Chapter 9

....

"Two roads diverged in a yellow wood,
And sorry I could not travel both –

And both that morning equally lay
In leaves no step had trodden black.
Oh, I kept the first for another day!
Yet knowing how way leads on to way,
I doubted if I should ever come back"
(The Road Not Taken, Robert Frost)

It was a late autumnal Sunday afternoon and Elspeth and Anton were sitting together in a quiet place on the outskirts of the city when Anton began to speak about his life and background. She had noticed that he was particularly quiet and reticent throughout lunch and she asked him if there was something wrong.

'I find this part of the year sad, it's the anniversary of my mother's death, my father's too as it happens, but I don't mourn him!'

He spoke with some bitterness and his tone shocked her, 'Why not?'

'My father was one of life's failures and my mother and I were his victims'.

'Aren't we all failures in one way or another?' Elspeth asked.

'Yes, but we don't all destroy other people's lives.'

'What did your father do? You don't need to tell me if you don't wish to'.

The relationship had reached a stage of shared confidences and Anton clearly trusted her and wished to tell her about his family and background. 'My family has secrets,' he said.

Elspeth didn't reply but allowed him to tell her in his own good time his family's story, which he plainly wished her to know.

'The events I am going to tell you begin way back with my great grandparents – My father's family are Sicilian and Giulia and Francesco Spadaro, my paternal great grandparents lived and brought up their family in a small coastal town in Sicily. They had three sons and two daughters and the family had a good name in the town, they were devout and well thought of and they brought their children up to be responsible citizens. Their eldest son, Giovanni, followed his father into carpentry; Giorgio, their second son married and joined his wife's family in Rome, his wife's family ran a restaurant and my great uncle worked for them before buying a restaurant of his own; their third son, Angelo, my grandfather, was a policeman and their two daughters were teachers before they married. I have not told anybody about the secret that my father harboured, I don't think anybody apart from my mother and of course, his own family, knew'.

'What about your cousin, Maria Rosa?'

'My mother's family knew about his treatment of her and of myself but I don't believe that she ever broke his confidence about his early life and what occurred that made him leave Sicily and never return'.

Anton was quiet for a while, thinking how to go on and Elspeth waited for him to continue.

'My great grandmother's youngest brother had emigrated to America and travelling as it was then, made it difficult to visit somewhere as far away as the States. When my grandfather was nineteen and possibly restless before settling down or perhaps even considering emigrating himself, the family arranged for him to visit his uncle's family for some three months that finally ended up as six months. During his time in America his uncle had become friendly with another Sicilian, Fabio, from his own town, though previously unknown to him. Fabio had opened a bar in New York and married an American wife and they had three daughters. The youngest of the daughters, Lena, was seventeen at the time of my grandfather's visit and they fell in love. When my grandfather returned to Sicily six months later he returned with Lena. They had been married on her eighteenth birthday. My grandfather was just twenty.'

'Did your great grandparents know of their wedding?'

'No and sons and daughters married young at that time, their two daughters had married very young and they accepted the marriage happily enough, initially. My grandmother was American and had been brought up expecting a greater degree of freedom to that she found in my great grandparent's home where they lived to begin with. She found their home rigid, the house was dark and there were large religious pictures on many of the walls and she found it oppressive. My great grandmother was always dressed in black and though by nature, kindly, she was not given much to merriment. My grandmother, Lena, on the other hand was young and light hearted she had been allowed to sing in her father's bar and had been spoilt and pampered and she must have felt like an imprisoned bird, but she truly loved my grandfather and they remained happily married. My great grandparents, however, were growing increasingly concerned. They had become aware of Mafia connections in Lena's family who still lived locally. They heard rumours of protection money being obtained by extortion and the involvement of an uncle and cousins who lived in a town close by.

They knew Lena was completely innocent but they would have liked to have prevented her from making any closer association with her father's family, but this, of course was impossible. My grandmother was pretty – I'll show you some photos sometime – and quite delicate looking, but she was stronger than she looked and she soon gave birth to two healthy boys, Andrea and Luigi. Her third birth of my aunt, Maria, was however difficult and over the following nine years she had two miscarriages before her last successful pregnancy.

My aunt Maria was almost ten years old when my father, Antonio was born. The birth was particularly difficult and my father should have been delivered by Caesarian Section but the labour was too advanced. Despite the fact that her life had been in danger, my grandmother, who had been an indulgent mother with her older children now fixed all her doting affection on this her youngest and last child. He was soon the family's darling! He was beautiful looking with large laughing eyes and a head of dark curls. Even my great grandmother was enchanted and said he was the sunshine of her old age. Although my great grandfather was by this time retired, he used to take him to his old workplace where he and my father's uncle let him watch while they made him wooden toys.'

'So what could possibly go wrong?' inquired Elspeth who remained listening intently.

'By the time my father went to school he had been allowed to get away with developing a bad temper when his will was thwarted. He threw temper tantrums, as little children do, but he was never prevented from throwing and breaking things including his toys. He was laughed at and found amusing when such behaviour should have called for his parent's intervention. His father, of course, was out of the house working when many of these outbursts took place, he was a good and conscientious policeman enforcing the law while his young son was becoming more and

146

more unruly. By the time he was four or five, his older siblings were growing tired of witnessing what he was being allowed to get away with and more was to come. When he began school his mother, still knowing nothing, or failing to believe in any connection with the Mafia in her family, was delighted when my father was placed in the same class as his cousin Marco, who was a month or two older.'

Elspeth thought back on her own childhood and her adoring grandmother, but Gran, as loving as she was, would have corrected bad behaviour and she thought how her brother's innocent behaviour had been harshly treated.

'So what happened when your father began school?'

'Marco had been born around the same time as my father, they had known each other from babyhood and from starting school they spent everyday together. At first things went well, my father was good at Mathematics, it was a natural ability he developed during his life, but he also lacked discipline and his cousin was little better. They began being disruptive and as the years went on they were continuously in trouble both inside and outside of school. When they were ten years old they were found stealing and my grandfather as the local policeman was outraged. My father was not allowed out for some weeks after being incriminated but attempts to control his behaviour were long overdue and efforts to discourage his friendship with Marco failed.

The two boys' years as adolescents were a nightmare for my father's parents, for while the pair avoided committing crimes, they became something of a menace in the town and increasingly earned unsavoury reputations. My father would turn up home drunk in the early hours of the morning and he also had a reputation for hanging around with women of ill repute. My grandfather meanwhile continued to be respected and liked and managed through his friendship with a local bank manager to get my father a job as a bank clerk and for a while it seemed that things had calmed down. My father didn't lack intelligence and as I said he was proficient in mathematics and so he soon earned promotion. The bank manager praised him and indeed liked him, my father never lost his ability to charm and he was very attractive looking.'

Elspeth thought of Maeve Donoghue. 'What happened to change things?' she asked.

'This is the worst part of the story but I want to share it with you Elspeth. My father worked at the bank for five years and his family began to believe that their problems with him were in the past, they thought that he was settling down and they relaxed. Then my grandfather was called into his friend the bank manager's office and was forced to hear about the probability of his son's involvement in a sizeable embezzlement. Worse, he told my grandfather there was a real possibility of Mafia involvement. The rumours surrounding his wife's family had finally surfaced and his son was implicated.

My great grandparents had tried to alert him years before of their suspicions and he had refused to listen saying it was idle gossip and nothing had ever been proved against them. With his parents now dead, he was facing the possibility of investigating his wife's family and his own son. He knew that this would lead to prison sentences if it was found to be true. He discussed it with my grandmother and decided that he would hand the investigation over to a colleague so that he could appear impartial but he confronted my father and made it clear to him that he had no intention of defending him. It may well have been the wisest thing to have made my father pay for his crime but my grandmother pleaded with my grandfather and got him to agree to sending my father out of the country before the investigation got underway.

My father's sister had married a Spanish army officer and was living in Madrid and my grandfather, possibly believing that he had had his own part to play in my father's indulgent upbringing, allowed himself to be persuaded and my father left for Spain. When the investigation was complete my father's cousin, Marco and other members of his family were sent to prison and it was alleged that my father had been drawn into the situation against his will and out of fear.

Everybody was fully aware of the Mafia's tactics and my grandfather's honourable reputation remained intact. Tragically, however, he and my grandmother were to pay a terrible price for their son's criminal involvement. Some months after the trial ended they were taking an afternoon walk along a quiet road close to the coast when a car came apparently out of nowhere and drove straight into them and they were killed instantly. There were, of course, two or three witnesses but this was obviously the work of the Mafia and nobody was prepared to speak out.'

'It's shocking!' Elspeth felt that she had just been listening to the story of a film or TV drama. 'What was your father's reaction to his parent's death?'

'He was devastated. He knew he would have to live for the rest of his life knowing he was indirectly implicated in their deaths. He returned to Sicily for the funeral accompanied by his sister, her husband and their two eldest children. His two brothers refused to speak to him, his eldest brother, Andrea was a doctor and his other brother Luigi, was a lawyer and they had no doubt about my father's criminal activities. They both emigrated to America with their young families soon afterwards.'

'And your father?'

'He returned to Madrid with his sister. She is soft hearted and felt for her brother who was traumatised and seemed to have undergone a sea change. Despite his behaviour he had loved his parents and according to my mother and my aunt always blamed himself for their deaths. He never returned to Sicily and never again contacted his cousin Marco.

It appeared for a long time afterwards that he had finally learnt his lesson and perhaps he would have maintained the change if he had stayed in Spain living close to his sister who always loved him. He took up teaching mathematics to private pupils to begin with then he managed to get a post in a private school and this situation continued for five years which he was to assert were the happiest years of his life. Then fate once again intervened! His uncle Georgio, as I said earlier, owned a restaurant in Rome and his wife had died suddenly. The couple were childless and he had known and loved my father as a child and indeed my father and his brothers and sister had spent holidays with him and his wife as children, now that he was wishing to retire he sent for my father and requested him to join him in Rome and help to take care of the restaurant. And so my father came to live in Rome, but I'm going to break off here, it's growing late and getting chilly. We'll go and get a drink and then I'll see you home and I'll tell you the rest of the sorry tale another day. By the way, don't walk alone in Rome late in the day, Italian men are likely to approach you and it's unpleasant, their reputation, particularly with foreign girls I find distasteful, we're not all the same.'

II

Anton was taken up with his teaching and his choir but they met up whenever he was free and the following weekend Elspeth asked him to continue with his father's story. Why, she asked did things go badly in Rome and how did his father make victims of his mother and himself? Anton looked sad and was silent for a while and she wondered whether she had spoken out of turn or that he had later regretted telling her about his family, but after a while he went on.

'Things should have turned out excellently and again things were good to begin with. My great uncle still looked in at the restaurant from time to time and remained the proprietor but he was by this time old and wanted to fully retire, so he left things more-or-less in my father's hands. My father could have made a wonderful job of managing, he was attractive and charming and more than capable of dealing with the financial aspects of the business, but his character was weak and he should never have been left fully in charge of anything. During the first two years of his being in Rome he met my mother, Rosa, her eldest sister, my aunt Sara, had been best friends with my uncle Giorgio's wife and my mother had visited the restaurant frequently.'

'Is your aunt Sara, Maria Rosa's mother?'

'Yes, she is the eldest of the three sisters, my aunt Beatrix is the youngest'.

'Then I've met her she came to Lourdes one of the years I helped out there, she was with her husband who was in a wheelchair'.

'That was my uncle Pietro, he had cancer and died actually the same year as my parents. My mother was a dressmaker and excelled at a number of skills, embroidery, lace making, she could turn her hands to so many things and she was a wonderful cook! She was five years older than my father and was thirty-five years old at the time of her marriage. She had been engaged to be married in her early twenties but her young fiancé had contracted a serious illness and died. I have no doubt she was charmed by my father and I believe she genuinely loved him and continued to, she would have learnt his story, he would have confided in her and she would recognise his pain and as long as she lived she made excuses for him. They married a year before Uncle Giorgio died and they were left very comfortably. My father's brothers and his sister were well established and my parents were left the restaurant and my Uncle's apartment. It's where I still live – it's large and in a good neighbourhood, I haven't invited you there yet but I do intend to and I'll prepare you a fine meal, I cook well'

'I'm afraid I'm a pretty useless cook'.

'You'll learn to be good if you continue to live in Italy, all Italians love good food, we have some of the best cuisine in the world, along with our ice cream! It's in our genes.'

'I don't think it's in mine,' she replied, but go on, I'm interested to learn the rest of your story'.

'If only it was a story! Almost from the beginning of my parent's marriage things went badly – even before they were married he became controlling and he was drunk the night they married and he was physically abusive.'

'Did she tell her family?'

'Not for years. She had a miscarriage two years after they were married and my mother confided in my Aunt Sara and said that my father's behaviour had led to it, whether that was the case I don't know, of course, but he apparently mocked her and blamed her. My mother was forty years old when I was born and by that time she was more-or-less running the restaurant.'

'You said in Lourdes that your family helped Jewish people and saved their lives, during the war.'

'It's true. My father wasn't altogether bad and he knew what it was like to be a fugitive himself. The restaurant employed a Jewish chef at the time and my mother's family had a Jewish maid and my parents and my mother's family became involved in finding places of refuge for them. My father had attended Fascist meetings during the thirties and openly admired Mussolini, but fortunately he didn't sign up to any stronger allegiance, however, he had several recordings of his speeches, which were still in circulation for some years after the war and when he felt inclined to make my mother or me suffer and feel uncomfortable he would play them in our presence and say things would have been better in Italian society if Mussolini had remained in power. Perhaps he even believed it. I destroyed those recordings after he died. He tormented us because he couldn't come to terms with his misery and guilt and instead of facing up to it he tried to escape by drinking and eventually gambling and drowning his moral conscience. He was totally undisciplined. He was a tragedy really and I felt sorry for him and disgusted with him by turns.'

'Did your mother's family help at all?'

'My mother tried to get me as a child out of the situation and I spent much of the time with my aunts and cousins. Maria Rosa and I became very close, but by the time I was in my early teens I was spending more and more time in the restaurant helping out, waiting on tables and helping in the kitchen washing dishes. My dream was to go to university and it should have been possible but the business was failing and we were having to get rid of staff. It was my mother's family and our Parish Priest who knew that I could sing well and who heard about the American Scholarship and encouraged me to apply, but it was the university education that I wanted more than anything. I find it difficult to forgive my father, he only had one child and it should have been financially possible'.

'Lots of people go to university far fewer are awarded Singing Scholarships! You have the voice of an angel. Did you never dream of becoming a professional singer?' asked Elspeth.

'Thank you for the compliment but I am no Pavarotti or Placido Domingo! I know my capabilities,' Anton laughed.

Do you keep in touch with your aunt in Spain?

'What of your father's brothers, did they welcome you?'

'Yes! I visit most years and am friendly with my cousins. When I won the scholarship to America my Aunt Maria contacted her two brothers and her mother's – my grandmother's family – and I stayed with one of my great aunts.'

'It would have been wrong to blame me for my father's misdeeds but while they were kind they never once inquired after my father. It was as if he was dead and I suppose to them he was, they had simply erased him from their minds. My uncle Luigi said one day that I resembled my grandfather and I thought that's the only way he can accept me and I took it as a compliment. Both my uncles have prospered in the States. Their children, my cousins, are older than me by at least ten years, and they have all received the kind of education that I dreamed of. They were kind, yes, but I had little in common with them and preferred the company of my grandmother's family. I keep in touch with them all at Christmas but I feel as cool towards my uncles as they feel towards me. I don't have many warm emotions for two brothers who could not forgive their youngest brother and through all my young life, despite hearing about me from my aunt, they never attempted to contact me or make any enquiry about me'.

'Have you ever visited Sicily? It's so beautiful. I visited with my parents a few years ago.'

'I found the address of my grandparents' house among my father's things after he died. He kept a photograph of them in his wallet all his life – that made me very sad – and their address was written on the back, so I went to Sicily six months or so after his funeral. I saw the house where my father had been brought up and my grandfather's Police Station. I suppose there were people who knew the family still around but I didn't inquire. I spoke to the Parish Priest and had a Mass said for all the family, but I felt dejected and a part of me wished I hadn't gone. Perhaps one day I will return.'

'So things in your home never improved', stated Elspeth.

'The year you say you met my aunt and uncle in Lourdes my mother fell ill with cancer. By the time she was admitted to hospital it was too late to save her life and when she was discharged her youngest sister said that she must not go home, where my father was incapable of looking after her, but stay with her and that's what happened and my mother could have died peacefully. Unfortunately, my father who completely depended on my mother for everything was furious. He went round to my aunt's home and finding my mother dressed and sitting in a chair he began shouting and saying she was perfectly capable of being at home with him. My aunt's husband told him to leave and threatened to call the police if he refused to control his behaviour which was becoming increasingly threatening. In the end he left but managed to get drunk on the way home. I was in the house by myself while he raged against my mother and her family and at that moment I hated him, I grabbed my jacket and left the house and went to my aunt's house, I was very anxious about my mother, as you may imagine. When I returned home I thought my father had taken himself off to bed and to sleep, and I went to bed myself. The following morning he still wasn't up and he was in the habit of rising early so I looked into his room and he was lying on his bed with his mouth wide open, he had had a massive stroke during the night and I had heard nothing! I feel guilty, I go over and over it in my mind, he was a broken, tragic human being who never grew up or took responsibility for his life. I torture myself sometimes thinking that night when he came home I should have offered him love and understanding and perhaps he would have come to his senses and responded. My mother felt equally guilty saying she should have accompanied him home that night. She died herself two months later. When I looked at my father lying dead my anger and disgust evaporated, I thought he's been like that small indulged child all his life, he never grew up.'

'We both have fathers that need forgiveness.'

Anton looked at her with some surprise. Elspeth began by saying that she was fortunate in that her father seemed to be sorry for his behaviour and was trying to make amends so she was being enabled to forgive him though she still experienced times when she thought back on his behaviour and while she forgave him she could not forget. She told Anton about her father's harsh treatment of her brother which she believed had led to his death. It should not become the way to deal with our own misery by taking it out on the innocent but unfortunately it happens. Then she described how she had been raped and how her father had not asked any questions but had behaved in a way that was unacceptable. I realised eventually that I love him and that I was not doing my brother any good by not forgiving him. I made myself understand what he had suffered because of the war and his brother's cruel death.'

When she had talked of being raped, Anton was very quiet and then very gently he put his arm around her and cradled her head on her shoulder and kissed into her hair. It was a truly tender gesture that spoke so much louder than words could have done and it was a gesture of healing. She thought I've cemented this relationship and yet I'm not sure how I want things to develop. She liked Anton and enjoyed his friendship but did she wish it to go any further? She knew that Anton clearly did. She also remembered Sister Maria Rosa's words, he's 'something of a troubled soul'. But for this afternoon she felt close to him and loved him, but was the love for him more than she would feel for a friend?

Anton spoke up, 'I'll take you to the restaurant for our evening meal! '

'Do you still own it?'

'No. I had to sell it after my parents died to pay off my father's gambling debts. With the money I had left I renovated and redecorated the apartment. The chef, Cosimo, bought the restaurant.

He's a good friend and you'll love him. He has a large family and he has managed with the help of his family to turn the business round and it's doing very well. His food is superb, you'll see. We've been friends for years, he's worked at the restaurant as chef for almost twenty years and stayed put through the difficult times when he could easily have found a better placement. He got on well with my father actually and he adored my mother, so did his wife.'

The restaurant was full when they arrived and Elspeth liked its family atmosphere. It didn't have wooden beams like a similarly aged restaurant in England – she thought it was a round the turn of the century, but possibly older but before she could ask Cosimo had left the kitchen when he heard they had arrived and came towards them beaming and gave Anton a hug. 'Where have you been I was beginning to think you had deserted us I haven't seen you for weeks. And who have we got here! You have been hiding her away – ah! such a beauty!'

'Elspeth is English she's come to Rome to work for a time in Maria Rosa's school,' said Anton introducing her.

'English, a real beautiful English rose, it's my delight to meet you, I'm enchanted. You mustn't keep her secreted away, Anton, you must bring Elspeth to meet the family. Now sit down both of you and you must have the meal on the house, I will make you something special!'

True to his word he did, it would have been impossible not to be charmed by this bear of a man. He was large and exuded happiness and warmth. Elspeth didn't know about his singing voice but his size and natural exuberance reminded her of Pavorotti.

When she and Anton left the restaurant they sauntered happily towards her home. The meeting with Cosimo had mellowed and relaxed them both. At the entrance to her block of apartments

Anton held her and kissed her and she returned his kisses and he murmured, 'I love you'.

'Please don't let's hurry things.'

'I won't, but I will hope you will learn to love me too, I want you to be sure. I'll wait here while you go up and put your light on and I'll know you're safe.'

'It's as safe as houses as we say in England! The apartments all belong to old people, I'm the youngest here! But thank you I've had a wonderful time and thank you for seeing me home'.

When she arrived to her room she put the light on and went to the window and waved down at him and he blew kisses back at her before turning and walking away. She thought that he looked a lonely figure and she wondered about what deeper part his 'troubled soul' played in his life. He had said once that she had a sad expression sometimes, and it was true that she felt a depth of sadness. Was she just oversensitive? She could never abandon herself fully. She must always be serious, it wasn't depression it was sadness. And she asked herself how far she could make someone else happy.

There was always she thought something deep within her that would always be apart, some inner sanctum kept only for herself that she could, not share. Only once had she emptied herself and laid bare her soul. One cold winter's day in a sparsely furnished room to a holy priest. Louise had said to her that she had thought Father Dominic was in love with her. It was not 'in love', it was a knowledge of each other that was there that afternoon and grew over the following months and years, as if their two souls were not only in harmony, but were one. It would never be spoken or expressed because it didn't need to be. She sighed. Her relationship with Anton was not at that depth or of that nature and she feared that it never would be, but did it need to be?

Relationships for me, she thought, are either a communion of souls or a communion of minds, they never seemed to be both. They had both suffered, she did not want to increase his suffering she wanted him to be happy and she wished, not for the first time that she had inherited something of her mother's optimism and light heartedness. But she thought we are what we are and I am not sure that we can change our essential nature and after all, she thought, Anton is falling in love with me not with my mother or with anybody else. I wonder if he has ever been in love before. Today had been special and they had shared something very precious, something timeless, and she realised with instant certainty that she would never walk away from him that he would always be there in her life, and she thought, one day I will be his wife, I know him better than he knows me and she felt it as something inevitable. Then she thought of Jamie, he was still in her life as was Gran, they have simply moved into the place before and out of time, she thought. Her little brother's time within in time had been short and beautiful. She found herself recalling the lines of Ben Johnson's poem:

> "A lily of a day
> Is fairer far in May,
> Although it fall and die that night;
> It was the plant and flower of Light.
> In small proportions we just beauties see;
> And in short measures life may perfect be".

And so she drifted to sleep.

Chapter 10

"The rainbow comes and goes"
(Ode: Intimations of Immortality - Wordsworth)

Soon Christmas was upon them. In the school all the preparations for the feast were being made. There was the tree in the Entrance Hall and Elspeth helped to decorate her room. A Nativity play was rehearsed with one of the nuns narrating the story while the children mimed the parts and parents helped and were invited along with visitors to see the finished play. Anton prepared the music and there was singing and the jingling of bells and the priest said the final blessing. There was a small party arranged by the parents and the exchange of small gifts and then just as quickly it was all over and the school was closed until January. Anton's choir put on a concert and Elspeth sang in the choir and afterwards he travelled with her to Switzerland to spend Christmas with her and her family.

She would remain forever grateful for that Christmas and for the reception that her family gave Anton. It was not just for her sake that they took so kindly to him, that might have been their initial response, but her parents, particularly her father, liked him immediately and the two men became and remained friends. She was amazed and delighted. Anton, she thought, probably regarded her father as a father figure, for despite her having told him about his behaviour to her brother and herself he recognised a disciplined and ordered human being and admired him as he had not been able to admire his own father. However, she was not sure about Nan's feelings. She had inherited, she thought so much of her grandmother's character, the way she knew things and was intuitive in a way other people were not. It had, Elspeth thought, little to do with education, intelligence or even experience, it was just the way some people were, it was an innate giftedness.

But then when she was alone with her grandmother a few days into the visit her grandmother said that she considered Anton a good young man, adding, 'I believe that you will marry him, I said to you last year that life would open up for you as it does when we are young, but take your time and remember there is a difference between being committed and being sure. Of course, few of us can be absolutely sure but we must be able to ask ourselves whether we can rely on the person we marry to see us through difficult times when they occur and they do occur in every marriage, and we must also ask ourselves if we can make the person that we plan to marry happy and fulfilled too. There are some marriages where a couple just fit together like a hand in a glove, it has been like that for your parents and they are the lucky ones. It was not like that for us, your Grandda and I had to grow together over time, but we have weathered the storms and difficult times and our marriage has grown stronger with the years. You are a lot like me Elspeth so remember, that sometimes a sudden flame goes out while embers go on glowing'.

Elspeth knew she herself was intuitive and could perceive how life was likely to turn out for others though rarely for herself. It had nothing to do with fortune telling, it was the reading of character and Louise had sometimes been amazed at how perceptive she was. So she took Nan's words seriously, thinking, 'I can't keep anything from Nan she knows me better than I know myself'.

II

Anton, Elspeth thought, had never looked so happy and confident. He had persuaded her that they should ski while they were in Switzerland and said that it was something he loved. She tried saying she was hopeless but he laughed it off.

'There you go again! You have a brilliant degree from one of the best British Universities and you constantly distrust yourself!'

'Do I?'

'Yes, you do. You have a beautiful singing voice, you describe as 'not brilliant', you joined an Art class and told me you that you have no talent, when I mentioned cooking you make out that you can't cook, though I suspect you've never tried, and now you say that despite having spent winters in Switzerland on ski slopes, you can't ski! I'll make sure you're safe, I promise. I wouldn't make it to the Olympic Games either but it doesn't stop me from enjoying the sport'.

'I'm sure you're right. I began to acknowledge the importance of sports when I was teaching and to see what I'd missed out on because I never liked sports as a child. We'll go skiing and you can judge my competence for yourself but don't say afterwards I didn't warn you!'

She enjoyed the time they spent on the ski slopes more than she could have imagined. She wasn't sure if she was any more competent but she had a wonderful time with Anton and by the time they returned to Italy she knew that she only ever wanted to be with him.

They had travelled by train and on the return journey she was silently gazing out of the window when Anton broke into her thoughts, 'If I had enough pennies for your thoughts, I'd be a millionaire.'

Elspeth laughed and moved her head onto his chest and he put his arm around her and she thought I've never been so happy.

III

The Spring arrived and Anton asked her if she would marry him and she had agreed. She thought this is my fate and I do love him but there are times when I feel irritated and hesitant and question him. She was aware of his insecurity and she knew, of course, from where it had originated, but could she change him? He laughed if men in the street made complimentary comments as they passed her and he said how much they must envy him with such a beautiful girl on his arm, but he visibly stiffened if a young well educated man in the choir or of his acquaintance, showed any obvious interest in her. Jealousy is one thing, she thought, and natural enough, but making a point of saying something disparaging about someone afterwards was thinly veiled envy, which she considered an unpleasant characteristic in anyone. It was an attempt to control her opinion of someone and she resented it.

One young man in the choir, Giovanni, had a fine bass voice and in conversation with him she learnt that he had studied in Harvard; he was polished and she surmised well placed in society and while she was not particularly attracted to him she found him interesting. He had auditioned for the choir in much the same way as she had and for much the same reasons, he enjoyed singing and he sang remarkably well. He was the obvious choice for bass soloist in the coming Oratorio but Anton passed over him and placed a far less accomplished singer in the part. Elspeth asked him when they were left alone why he had made the choice he had and his answer set an alarm bell ringing. He passed her enquiry off, saying Giovanni had too high an opinion of himself, that he was privileged and too many things had come his way too easily.

She knew she could not let this matter fester so she told him how she had been misunderstood herself, she had had an expensive education and all the trappings of wealth and she considered Giovanni by far the best singer for the bass part though she realised that she was not in charge of the choir and perhaps should not comment. He replied sulkily saying that she was right she was not in charge. It was their first disagreement and a day or two later he came back to her saying that perhaps she was right and he would think it over and finally Giovanni was given the part. Afterwards he showered her with so much love and affection and expressed so much pride in her that she put the negative aspects aside and loved him back, and she was reassured, almost. She knew his insecurity.

At Easter they were engaged and Anton told her that she must choose the ring that she liked best and he took her to an expensive looking jewellery shop. She was attracted by a Solitaire diamond that seemed to be reasonably priced, but she thought, 'solitaire, it's too much like me', and she caught Anton looking at a ring with two diamonds entwined and she thought he is recognising the symbolism it is representing and she said, 'That's very pretty, I think I like that best'. She could see how happy he was with her choice and she thought, 'it hasn't just been my choice we've made it together, it's something we both equally like', and she was content. They called in at a nearby church that was old and very beautiful and silent and where one or two people were quietly praying and he placed the ring on her finger and kissed her very tenderly.

The engagement meant their relationship was now publicly stated. Elspeth rang her parents, her grandparents and her friends in England and they said that they had been expecting the announcement and were very happy.

At the school Sister Maria Rosa told the children and their parents who happily received the announcement, and Anton's family began preparations for a special reception for them in the restaurant his parents had once owned, but Elspeth sensed a lack of wholehearted enthusiasm from Maria Rosa and wondered why. A week after their engagement the pair were alone and Maria Rosa spoke up?

'I hope that you will forgive me for appearing to interfere but I wondered if I could speak to you openly about your engagement to my cousin. Anton and I have been close all our lives and I want his happiness above all things yet I think there are matters in his background that you may not be aware of and which I think you should know about'.

'You mean his father's behaviour to Anton and his mother? he has described it to me,' said Elspeth.

'Has he also told you about his father's early life in Sicily?' asked Maria Rosa.

'Yes. He said that he had never discussed it with his mother's family.'

'He hasn't. His mother told my mother and my aunt after his father's death and before she died herself. She wanted to explain his behaviour or try to gain some understanding for him. I have never known how much Anton was told, I thought perhaps she withheld it from him so that it would not allow him to have an even worse opinion of his father than he already held. I understand that his father's sister, Maria, may have enlightened him and, of course he had to learn of his father's early life before going to America and meeting up with his father's family there, but he was already an adult when this happened and more able to cope with what he was told. I don't think he knew as a child.'

'It is hardly an impediment to his marriage,' Elspeth said somewhat in surprise!'

'Of course it's not! But it does have some bearing on his behaviour on occasions. His father was not a youngster when the events in Sicily took place, he was an adult who allowed himself to be persuaded to leave the country and save his own skin while his lifelong friend went to prison for a crime he was equally responsible for. He had to live forever afterwards knowing not only that he was implicated in his parents' deaths but that he had been a coward. His behaviour would have been interpreted as treachery by his cousin, his mother's family, and indeed the Mafia, who have long memories. His apparent admiration for Fascism during the war, I believe, was his way of attempting to appear brave, at least in his own eyes.'

'I don't see what this has to do with Anton,' Elspeth said puzzled.

'All children want to feel proud of their parents. All of us want to think that our fathers will stand up bravely if challenged. Anton's father had to live all his life trying to come to terms with the image he had of himself and he took his shame and frustrations out on his innocent wife and son. So much of the reality of our lives goes on behind our eyes, behind the facade or appearance we present to the world. When Anton went to America, his mother told us that his father wrote to his brothers and asked them to receive him and offer him hospitality and they did but with a poor grace, Anton was made to feel inferior. His uncles never attempted to contact his father, they had changed their name when they arrived in America – perhaps understandably – there is a Mafia network in the States. How influential it is I don't know but I do understand that they wanted to sever themselves completely from its contagion, both for their own sakes and for the sake of their children.'

'I agree but Anton has lived with the knowledge of his father and the misery his father has imposed on him all his life. To make something worthwhile of your life faced with those circumstances is very brave and raises him even further in my estimation. I don't understand your concern. He took up a scholarship in America and succeeded although he would have preferred to study at a university. He has a beautiful singing voice but has humbly said that he is not good enough to be on the world's stage!'

'Or doesn't want to be. Anton knows that if he became famous his family history would be investigated and as I have said, the Mafia have long memories and deep roots. But apart from this,

Anton is a good, caring person but he is no more perfect than the rest of us. He can be bitter, sometimes envious of others that have had an altogether easier passage through life. Children rarely do as their parents say but as their parents do sadly, and this has to be borne in mind. I want my cousin's happiness but his happiness depends on your happiness as equally as your happiness depends on his. Your upbringing has been secure, Elspeth. I'm not, of course, suggesting that you haven't had difficulties, but when our childhoods have been secure and happy we are in a stronger position to deal with the problems that life presents us with. You will always have to be the stronger of the two of you. Perhaps I should not have spoken at all but I sense that my cousin is very deeply in love with you and that you don't feel quite the same. Have I got it completely wrong? You are very lovely, academically clever and I think your background is privileged'.

'I love Anton. When I was at university some of my fellow students believed that I considered myself above them. There were reasons, privileged I might be but I was having to face up to very traumatic events in my life which I have shared with Anton and he has shown me so much kindness and understanding. I am sometimes detached, I sometimes feel an outsider looking in on life, I believe I know Anton better than he knows me and I understand him and shall care for him for the rest of my life. Being 'in love' with someone isn't necessarily the same thing as 'to love' someone, and I believe my love will stand the test of time. If I didn't completely believe that I would not have become engaged. We none of us can say with absolute certainty that we will feel exactly the same always but I shall vow to stay faithful and I fully intend to, I think that is the most any of us can do.'

'That makes me feel much more confident and I hope that you will forgive me if I have offended you for speaking out as I have.'

'Of course I forgive you! You know your cousin and have been close to him all your life and I appreciate your desire for his happiness. I'm glad that he has family who care. I realise that we are from different backgrounds, and countries with different cultures and I am a Catholic convert and to some degree still a novice, all these things may present problems but they are also enriching and positive. My father's parents have settled very well in Switzerland and as a family we are far from being insular. We are planning to settle in England eventually and he, hopefully, can put so many negative things in his life behind him. We can tell any children we hope to have that his parents owned a restaurant in Rome and so leave the past where it belongs.'

IV

Anton's family went ahead and gave them a special reception choosing the restaurant for it and Cosimo's family were all invited. It was a wonderful occasion and the food was splendid. When Elspeth congratulated Cosimo and told him that she was a very poor cook herself and that she was glad that Anton could cook so they wouldn't starve he responded by saying that, of course, she would learn and indeed must and that he himself would take it upon himself to teach her! Preparing good food for one's family, he told her, was an act of love.

'My Clara, my beloved wife is as good a cook as me and she needs to be with seven children, it is a mother's duty to feed her children.' He looked over fondly at his wife, 'she is more beautiful every year. When we married, she had such a tiny, tiny waist but now she is magnificent! You will come to me once a week and I will teach you some Italian dishes'.

Before they left he told Anton what he had 'suggested' or what Elspeth thought, he had commanded, but she was not offended, it was impossible to be offended by him, he was so good natured and kind. I shall be watching my own waistline though, she decided.

The arrangement was made and if it had been made over her head she did not protest. She would attend at the restaurant one afternoon a week to watch and be given simple recipes to prepare.

'It's all very simple, my Maria is only eight years old and she can prepare meals. All you have to do is prepare the ingredients then follow the instructions. Taste the food from time to time to make sure you have added sufficient seasoning – it is not difficult,' Cosimo insisted.

Elspeth had looked with horror at the contraption for making pasta in Anton's apartment and wished she had paid attention to her Gran's efforts to teach her when she was a child. I cannot believe I will ever master cooking, I am just not a very domesticated person, it bores me. But having been offered lessons by a very able masterchef she thought she must, at least, make an effort and she must succeed for Anton's sake. Being made to look stupid did not appeal to her either so she made up her mind to do her best. First ski-img now cooking, her engagement was proving to be a series of passing tests against the grain of her nature. She knew that she was given to being absent minded, she became lost in her own thoughts, it had happened in Gran's kitchen long ago and she feared that this might happen while she was supposed to be attending to preparing food in the restaurant. I have a lot of sympathy with King Alfred and those burnt cakes she thought!

V

The summer progressed and she would look back on it as the happiest time of her life. They visited the coast together and swam together and enjoyed the close physical proximity it gave them. As the summer heat left the sometimes scorching days they would lie together on the emptying beach entwined, silent, sharing each other's breath and experiencing a harmony that bonded

169

them more than words could and a completeness closer and deeper than a physical unity. Surely nothing can threaten this feeling
of wholeness, she thought we are content together.

Chapter 11

....

"What so false as truth is, False to thee?
Where the serpent's tooth is
Shun the tree -

Where the apple reddens
Never pry -
Lest we lose our Edens
Eve and I"
(A Woman's Last Word - Robert Browning)

As the summer progressed so did the love that now bound them deepen and Elspeth began to experience a passion she had never expected to feel. She longed to spend every living moment with Anton and considered every moment away from him as wasted. His physical presence became more and more attractive to her and at last she knew with certainty that she had finally indeed unexpectedly fallen 'in love' and that it was more delightful than she could have imagined. The rape that had so dominated her inner consciousness began to fade though it never disappeared completely. Anton never mentioned it to her and she would be ever grateful to him it enabled her to put it behind her though it was never blotted out.

She had come to believe that her life existed on a mental plane, she had analysed situations and had tended to keep her judgements to herself, now she felt bound to share them, but in doing so she failed to recognise how her approach to life differed markedly to his. In her desire for him she refused to jeopardise her relationship with him by disagreeing on the fundamental beliefs she held. Anton did not discuss or debate things, he made what she inwardly believed were dogmatic statements, particularly about religion, he did not develop his thinking, and expected her to agree with him. In the years ahead she was to think, I should have taken these things up with him and I did not when I could have done and when I should have done. Yet she knew that he loved her totally and if he had offended her in any way he quickly made amends. She knew that he adored her and he was also kind and tender and that long, hot summer before their marriage she had been enthralled and willingly enslaved by the passion she felt for him and she saw how he grew in confidence, she was also fully aware how much he expected her to agree with him.

II

They had chosen the end of August for their wedding day which would take place in England. They planned to honeymoon in Scotland and return to Rome in September when they would both take up their life there again. Anton had agreed to look for a teaching post in England and once he had achieved a suitable situation they would move there but they planned to keep his apartment in Rome which they could use in future years for holidays and visits. Elspeth's parents found themselves more than happy to be involved in the planning of the wedding and her mother. Elspeth knew, would be more than happy to help with choosing her wedding gown when they arrived in England in mid-July. Events began to take over and there seemed so little time for everything. She thought, 'I am sure, why wait, and Anton wants the marriage as soon as possible, and yet at an almost unconscious level I am not altogether sure about the rush? Why do I feel such contradictory feelings, I am not usually indecisive?' She finally put it down to wedding nerves, after all this was the biggest decision she had ever made and she was a long way from home and family and old friends.

Her cookery lessons helped to lessen the tension she felt which surprised her, she had thought they would heighten it. But Cosimo was such an easy going teacher, he laughed aloud at her mistakes and encouraged her successes and they got along at an easy pace, with a relationship that flowered into a happy friendship.

One sultry early evening in late June after a successful cookery session Elspeth wandered contentedly towards home. She felt hot and sticky and decided to drop into a bar close to her flat for a cold drink. She ordered a lemonade with ice and sat down at an empty table in the centre of the bar. When her drink arrived she looked around her and she felt her heart miss a beat. Sitting at a table close to the window was Callum Donoghue holding hands with a simply dressed, pretty young woman about Elspeth's own age. Elspeth drank up her drink quickly thinking I will leave while they are absorbed in each other, they will not notice. But even as she was thinking it the pair stood up and she was relieved believing that they were both leaving together. She was wrong, the girl left and Callum sat down again and ordered another drink and when it arrived he sat with his elbows on the table and his head in his hands. Elspeth thought again, I will leave now and she stood up rather too carefully and doing so managed to brush her glass over on to the table and heard, with horror, it clatter as it fell. She picked it up, but it was too late, she looked over at Callum almost instinctively and met his direct gaze. It was a split second but she knew he recognised her and she was aware of a look of near agony cross his face. She could not just walk past him, she had to speak so she walked up to his table.

'It's Callum isn't it, Callum Donoghue! Your mother introduced us at Louise's wedding? I'm Elspeth Penrose.'

She wondered if she should have addressed him as a priest, but she was not sure that it was appropriate in the circumstances and he was not dressed as a priest. She wondered if there was something Louise had not told her.

'Yes, I remember, perhaps you'd like to sit down. Louise mentioned to me that you were staying in Rome. Can I get you a drink?'

'No, I was about to leave', said Elspeth lamely but taking up his invitation to sit down.

Elspeth felt awkward and embarrassed having obviously witnessed something she very definitely was not meant to have seen but it was too late. It was Callum who spoke first.

'I shouldn't be in a situation where I need to give an explanation to you, but I would like to request you not to mention what you have seen to my sister.'

'You don't have to request it; I have no intention of telling anybody. It really isn't any business of mine'.

'It is. You are a confessing Catholic and I am a celibate priest, you have a right to question what you have seen. It wasn't meant to happen.'

'You were not meant to fall in love with someone is that what you are saying? or you didn't intend to allow a relationship to develop between you?'

'Sofia works on restoration work and we met and began talking, we're both interested in Church Art, it was never meant to go further than that. I wish to God it hadn't! I have never wanted to be anything else but a priest, ever since I was a child. I wasn't pushed into it; it was – it is what I want!'

'And Sofia?'

'Sofia comes from a family very like mine. She's very like my sister, Ann- like my mother too really – deeply confirmed in her own faith but able to reach out to others'.

Elspeth remembered Mrs Donoghue's approach to her and she nodded in agreement.

Callum was speaking again, 'Sofia's family would be as distressed as mine if I were to abandon the priesthood. She doesn't want it to happen either. She says that I would end up hating her, that's impossible, though I certainly might deeply regret it. She has asked me to speak to my superiors and request time away – she thinks I should take a year or so away from Rome – she thinks it would do me good anyway – and make up our minds not to contact each other. If I remain in Rome the possibility of meeting up is more than likely'.

'I went to the Northeast to study, having turned down my place at Oxford because I needed to get as far away from my home as possible at the time.'

'You were running away from a love affair?'

'No. The only desire I had at the time was not wanting to wake up each morning to face another day! I met your sister and through her I learnt of the Catholic Chaplaincy and Father Dominic. He spoke these words to me and I'll repeat them to you if you don't accuse me of being preachy. The English are said to have a streak of Puritanism in them which the Irish I don't believe have but when these words were spoken to me they certainly were not preached and they saved me from myself when I was desolate and close to despair. They are branded into my soul and they are worth repeating: "As you go through life you will find that everybody has a cross to bear, some heavier than others and yours is particularly heavy at the moment, but at the end of the day, it is not the weight of the cross that matters, it is the way we carry it. I have not met anyone worthwhile that has not suffered and neither have I met anyone that is wise that has not learnt to forgive".'

'Father Dominic. He has the reputation of being a saint!'

'He's the finest human being that I have ever known'.

'Have you learnt to forgive and put it behind you, Elspeth?'

'I have learnt that the cross I was handed led me to the One who bore the heaviest Cross of all and I have moved on. Have I forgiven the fundamental wrong that was done to me and to another who was dear to me? – not the wrong perhaps – but I no longer harbour feelings of vengeance, they are long gone!' I hope that you find a resolution to your present situation that you can live with, Callum.'

'Louise has told me that you are soon to be married to someone you have met here in Rome'.

'Yes. Today I have been attending a cookery class. I am hopeless in the kitchen, Louise puts me to shame, and I feel honour bound to make some practical preparations. Anton is a very good cook and I had hoped that might suffice for the pair of us. I've managed to go this far through life without doing much more than boiling an egg!'

'I remember at my sister's wedding thinking you were very superior, in possession of all life's attributes!'

'Thank God, Anton thinks no such thing! I remember thinking that you were very strict and rather smug, I didn't see you smile all that weekend. Love is good for us although it can be bitter-sweet and bring its own agony. I don't have any right to say it but I hope that love will bring you understanding and peace, eventually, whatever decision you arrive at. I really must leave now but I'm very glad we met even if not in the happiest situation.'

Suddenly he smiled and it transformed him, it was a warm, open smile that reminded her of her friend. There was an innocence and goodness in it and it changed completely her first impression of him.

'I'm glad too, Elspeth. I wish you well and I hope we will meet up again sometime in happier circumstances.'

III

The heat was intense and she was glad to arrive home. She showered and as Anton was going to be busy that evening and she was not meeting him, she took a book onto the small balcony and sat down intending to read but the words swam in front of her eyes and she couldn't concentrate. The events of the late afternoon went over and over in her mind. Callum had stated that it was her business, and she thought that she did indeed have a vested interest in the church and she considered seriously the celibate priesthood of the Catholic Church for the first time. She knew that Callum would defend the discipline a hundred percent and he would not be looking for a way out of it while at the same time remaining a priest. She thought of how Anton would regard Callum's situation and she knew that he would state simply as she herself had, 'he's a priest'. Louise's lifelong knowledge had allowed her to say, 'he's also a man', recognising that experiencing love was not the same as expressing that love physically. Louise like her brother, would insist that a boundary existed that should not be crossed. She could almost hear Anton saying, 'You make a vow unto the Lord and you keep it, the same goes for marriage'. But was it the same she asked herself now? The Church would maintain its discipline, believing that the priest would be in a very real sense 'marrying' his flock and the boundary set was a security barrier. Was this the same as with all moral barriers?

She thought back on her conversations with her friends, Helen and Johannes Manasses, and her own experience, and considered how the removing of moral barriers in order to make things easier for people and enlarge their freedom frequently led not to greater freedom but to insecurity. She thought, all freedoms are

limited and they all have inherent boundaries within them whether we want to recognise them or not, and a vow taken is a security that is intended as a safety valve, there to protect as well as
bind. Her thoughts strayed on, individual lives, she considered,
like great Art, are bound by their own parameters, allowing us
to say where greatness is or individual goodness is, even when
we cannot always say where it is not, but I think it is important
to be able to say where it is. Yet also she pondered, the contra-
diction, 'Love transcends a multitude of sins!' And Christ's own
words about the woman who poured expensive ointment onto
his feet, 'For this reason I tell you that her sins, many as they are,
have been forgiven her, because she has shown such great love'.

Elspeth sighed. Christianity is completely based on love and around
love and love has no boundaries, and yet it is so precious that it
requires protection perhaps so that it fulfils and is never used for
selfish or destructive ends. Imogen Beaumont suddenly came
into her mind, the little girl's suffering. It was a long time since
she had thought about her and she hoped that she was happy and
that things had worked out for her. Love is always giving, generous, magnanimous and for the fulfilment of the other, otherwise
it is not love but becomes its opposite. And yet she was glad that
she had been able to maintain that final physical barrier between
herself and Anton, it gave her a sense of freedom that she cherished. She wanted marriage to be its place of fulfilment. I am no
Heloise, she thought, and no child of the Sixties either and then
there was the rape, the rape! that deep down fear of being physically overpowered. She sighed. She wished Callum well and only
hoped that the love that he had found would bring him greater
understanding of others and make him a better priest and suddenly she knew that he would not be leaving the priesthood, there
was no choice for him, he had made it already a long time ago.

IV

Each day of July became more difficult than the day before, the heat in the city was unbearable and at night it became impossible to sleep, Elspeth found herself longing to return to England, not least for its cooler climate. She also wanted to introduce Anton to her friends, and she wanted Anton to know her home and something of her life in England. It was going to be a very busy time, there were lots of final arrangements for the wedding. She would only have one bridesmaid, her cousin Esme. Her mother was surprised but Elspeth said she wanted simplicity above everything and she had so little time she did not want any elaborate plans.

They were both packed and ready and Elspeth found herself assuring Anton, he was nervous and she suddenly realised the enormity of the step he was taking. He had never been in England, even for a visit, and here he was approaching the coming month, in a strange land, and about to change his life forever.

'You weren't unsure of visiting my family in Switzerland at Christmas, my friends will love you, you'll see, and my parents really like you already.'

'I'm not sure they think me good enough!'

'What are you saying!'

'Elspeth, we've never spoken about it but I know your family are wealthy and that you are too. You have had an expensive education and have a brilliant degree. It's all fine between us two, it doesn't make any difference to us, I know, but I also want you to know that I will never allow you to keep me. Any money you have can be for our children – I hope we have a big family – it's what I really want! But I also want to be independent financially from you.'

Elspeth thought back to the conversation that she had had with his cousin, Maria Rosa, and thought this is the first time Anton has shown any kind of insecurity with me and she thought I should take it seriously and reassure him, I must not just dismiss it because it's important for both of us.

'If that's all that's worrying you, you can rest in peace. My darling grandmother, I told you, spent her life helping others. She respected the means she had available to her but she always refused to make them an end in themselves. I feel the same way, I have never been a snob! Gran influenced me more than anybody else while I was growing up and my greatest sadness in returning home and being married, is that she won't be there to greet us and she'll never know you'.

'I love you more than anyone else in the world, Elspeth, you are my life, I just need to know that you are absolutely sure and that your family accept me.'

'You are my life too and you have nothing to worry about'.

Yet even as she spoke she found herself concerned by what he had said. As far as she was concerned he was more than her equal, it had never crossed her mind that he had ever considered her superior in any way. Her family had never attached any particular significance to material possessions, they had taken them largely for granted it was true, but perhaps they were also unusual in that. For the first time she realised that the situation required sensitivity from her. She had only been considering how things were for herself and the relief she had always felt that Anton had never treated her as being in any way too good for him as so many of her peers back home had. She was glad that he had given her this insight into his inner feelings, a vulnerability she had never suspected in him allowed her to feel a greater tenderness towards him and just as he had done when she had told him how she had been raped, she put her arms round him and kissed him and he

tightened his hold on her and reassuring each other of their un-
dying love for each other they prepared to leave Rome behind
and set out for England and the wedding that awaited them.

Chapter 12

....

Arrival in England and their two lives were enmeshed in a maelstrom of activity, weddings Elspeth soon realised, didn't organise themselves. Her parents had sent out invitations and even spoken to the local Catholic Parish Priest she and Anton visited the church and made the final arrangements including booking an organist. Wedding clothes and flowers were chosen and ordered and they found themselves so caught up in all the organisation that the days sped by. Anton was overawed somewhat by her home and said, as Louise had that it was splendid and palatial. She had looked forward to introducing him to Belle and her family and they were delighted, they liked Anton immediately and Anton felt at ease with them. It was as she had expected. Belle's family had a simplicity and did not dwell on complicated intellectual matters and Anton responded – he could be himself and he chatted happily and his 'foreign ness' delighted them. She took him to visit Helen and Johannes Manasses and they formed an immediate friendship. Louise and her family were on holiday in Ireland but would be home for the wedding so an introduction to her friends would have to wait until then. There was so much to do!

Anton loved the room containing the books which they always called the 'Library' and which also contained the fine Piano which belonged to her mother and Elspeth encouraged him to play it. When he was reluctant to do so because he said that her mother's playing put his to shame she reminded him of his insistence that she should ski and take cookery lessons. They practised a duet together and put on a small performance for her parents and her mother praised his ability. He had a better musical ear than she, Elspeth had, and by far a greater competence and when they were alone she told him how proud she was of him and how much her parents accepted him.

II

The day of the wedding there was glorious sunshine. She took a final glance out of her bedroom window as she had on most of the days of her life, the Silver Birch tree was heavy with leaves and the roses were in bloom it was full of life and promise. Esme had already left for the church and Elspeth looked into the long looking glass at herself and was so grateful for her mother's dress sense which had helped her to choose her wedding gown. It was beautiful, a creamy white. It had an affixed long lace like coat that divided at the front with the dress underneath and long sleeves with covered buttons extending from the cuffs. She had always admired the dresses in Medieval pictures of women of the period and she thought her wedding gown resembled their simplicity. She wore the lace veil her mother had worn at her wedding and she had chosen Arun lilies and peach coloured roses. Her father was waiting at the foot of the stairs and he told her that she looked as beautiful as her mother had on their wedding day. She sensed he was close to tears and she pressed his hand. She was surprised how in control she felt. In the car on their way to the church her father told her how lovely he considered her and how proud he and his mother were of her. He expressed his desire for her to be happy and hoped that she would turn to them if she needed help. She thought it was his way of recognising how he had failed her those years before and while neither of them alluded to it she was grateful to him. He also said that he thought she was very like his mother and she agreed and then they were at the church and she placed her arm through his and he held her hand tightly. She had never enjoyed being the centre of attention but today she felt like a queen and Anton turned towards her and smiled. Afterwards she remembered little of the ceremony, it went by quickly and then they were both walking back down the aisle together while the organ thundered a wedding march.

Sister Maria Rosa's mother and two of his cousins along with his aunt Maria and a married cousin and his wife from Spain had flown in for the wedding and Elspeth was pleased that members of Anton's family were there for him. Miss Cresswell had made it too and Elspeth was happy to introduce her friends to each other. She was eager to introduce Anton to Louise and Jerome and to Ann Donoghue and she told Ann that she was sure that she would get on very well with Anton's cousin Sister Maria Rosa and she hoped that she would visit them in Rome.

All the guests were invited back home and given further refreshments after the hotel reception, while Elspeth and Anton got ready to leave for their honeymoon. Elspeth had decided not to throw her bouquet into the crowd that had gathered she had made another plan. On her bed was a second bouquet that she had ordered and when they finally left the house they made a short detour to visit Jamie and her grandparents' graves. She laid her wedding bouquet on her brother's grave and the second bouquet on the grave of her grandparents. The graveyard was silent, serene and calm, still full of the day's sunshine, and she prayed that these her loved ones were resting peacefully and in the knowledge that she remembered them and that they were an integral part of this her wedding day.

III

Would it really have mattered had the weather in Scotland been wet and cold? – as it was it was sunny and warm with the occasional downpour. The Edinburgh Festival was nearing its ending for that year and they intermingled with the crowds feeling at the same time their own blissful isolation from them. They wandered during the days absorbed in each other and grudging any intrusion. Anton adored Scotland saying it was the most beautiful place he had ever known, he said that it had a mystery all its own. They visited the Isle of Skye and thought it wonderfully romantic. And then he was tender and gentle with her and she wanted their short time there never to end and they promised each other that their honeymoon would go on lasting forever and they wanted only to be together in unending harmony. They had known each other only a year they reminded each other, a short year ago they had been strangers, how was it possible! They responded to each other's passion and Elspeth asked herself how she could ever have doubted the totality of this love that she felt, a love that held them both in awe of the other in a mutual joy and fulfilment.

IV

Then before they knew it they were back in her home and making their goodbyes and planning to meet up at Christmas in Switzerland and glad that it was sometime away and that they would not have to share each other for months. Anton's apartment was now their home. It had been left shuttered and it felt cool. She felt delighted with its simple and tasteful furnishings. Anton had told her that she could change whatever she wished but she did not, she said, wish to change a thing. 'It feels like paradise and there is no place on earth I'd rather be', she told him and he laughed and said that he hoped that she would always feel the same.

V

For weeks they jealously guarded their time alone together but as time went on their life of work with its ups and downs once more began to invade and take a prominent part in their lives. Their paradise was not to last, but then did it ever last indefinitely for anyone? Reality eventually intruded and she was to come face to face with it sooner than she had anticipated and with a rude awakening!

Elspeth was to learn that we take our childhood experiences with us, and in one way or another they influence so many of our attitudes to life forever. Anton's childhood had been severely crippled and he was always to feel undervalued. He felt as a music and singing teacher he was unfulfilled. It would always be that lack of a better education, that university background that had been denied him that created his sense of grievance. He complained sometimes bitterly about his colleagues and how well they fared in comparison with himself when he knew he was so much more capable and experienced than they were. He had said little about his work before the marriage and his occasional complaints had not seemed serious. During the early months of married life and when he came home in the evenings moody and angry she had been able to cajole him and he would help her with the evening meal and laughing at her mistakes she thought she was allowing him to recognise her limitations and failures, university educated notwithstanding, but she was also allowing him to put her down. Eventually it all began to wear thin.

One evening a colleague, Carlo, invited them both to an evening meal at his home. Anton said that he had recently been promoted and described him as 'methodical' but with little in the way of initiative. He said that they had two small children and lived in a poky two roomed flat. Elspeth found them charming, the children were impeccably behaved and Carlo's wife, Sara was delightful. The flat was small but carefully decorated and the meal was perfectly cooked and presented. She thought she could easily make a friend of Sara and she praised the couple on the way home. Anton made little by way of reply but invited them to join them for a meal a week or two later. He busied himself preparing a very fine meal and she helped to present it. The couple were impressed and complimented them generously and when they left Elspeth again praised them and said how much she liked them and how she wished them to become friends. But she felt her praise of his colleague was displeasing Anton and that he was annoyed and she wondered why.

One evening a week he arrived home later than she did and she prepared the meal for them without his help and on this particular occasion it happened to be the evening following Carlo and Sara's visit. Anton looked sullen on returning home and sitting down to the meal she had prepared said it was inedible and that she had had more than enough time to improve. Then he stood up angrily and announced that he was going out to a restaurant to eat and taking his jacket he left. It was shocking. The meal was one of her most successful, she had placed the same meal before him a fortnight earlier and she knew that it was far from inedible. The suspicions that she had felt before the marriage and stifled now resurfaced. She thought he builds himself up by putting other people down and she felt wary of him. I cannot compliment a colleague of his or a talented member of the choir. He is clearly insecure but there is no excuse for envy, it's unacceptable and I won't tolerate it but what can I do?

She quickly cleared up the kitchen, her own meal was spoilt. She prepared her things for the next day and picked up a book. When he returned she refused to speak to him, he put on the radio and they sat in silence. It was hateful, she felt a line had been crossed.

The following morning it was if nothing had happened he told her he would drive her to the school and in the evening they would attend choir together. She asked herself if she was taking what had occurred too seriously or was she being too sensitive. She had wanted only to please him and her trust in him was dented. Would he react in the same way again? She knew he undoubtedly would.

After choir practise they went to a small restaurant to eat on their way home and he carried on as if nothing had happened, he did not apologise and she felt disconcerted. She picked at her food and left the main dish half eaten and ordered a coffee. He said nothing. She knew instinctively that she must not mention his colleague and his wife again, they had been summarily dismissed. It is intolerable to me, she thought.

Chapter 13

....

"Elected silence sing to me
And beat upon my whorled ear,
Pipe me to pastures still and be
The music that I care to hear"
(Gerard Manley Hopkins)

With the Christmas term and the Christmas choir concert over Elspeth and Anton left for Switzerland and things went well throughout the holiday. Her family thought them blissfully happy and any misgivings Elspeth held were carefully hidden. On returning to Rome she announced that she was going to have a baby in September and Anton was overjoyed. He treated her like a queen and could not do enough for her. Close to her one evening he told her that he believed that Eastern Christians considered the Holy Spirit a feminine spirit so that parents and their child mirrored the Trinity. 'That's beautiful', Elspeth murmured.

'I'll show you the baby things my mother made for me,' he said and took her to a drawer where he had kept the small knitted garments. They were carefully wrapped in tissue paper and it was clear that he treasured them.

'They are beautiful', Elspeth said handling them carefully. I sew a little, we did have sewing lessons at my school but I can't knit or croquet.'

'You might learn. Maria Rosa and my family would be very willing to teach you.'

'I think not. We'll buy what we need!'

She sensed that he was not happy so she added that her father had had a special cradle made for her as he had no carpeting skills. 'I don't think you have ever learnt to make things in wood either', she said.

'I was never given the opportunity,' he replied, 'I would have liked to have learnt'.

'It won't make you any the less of a good father because you didn't learn to make things in wood, or me for that matter, any less of a good mother because I have never been interested in learning to knit, but I do so admire your mother's handiwork.' She thought I am clearly not his archetypal figure of a mother but this baby means everything to me and I want to be a good mother and a good wife more than anything. But she also thought I have got to begin exerting myself. He had not repeated walking out on her over her cooking but he had stopped helping her to prepare the evening meal and expected her to do it on her own even if she had been away from home as long as he had during the day. There was an uneasy truce between them on the matter. 'A penny for your thoughts' had become of late, 'you really should come down to earth and learn to concentrate'.

She had quickly learnt that he was unwilling to discuss things in any detail. He gave his opinion as if that was all that was required with the expectation that she would meekly submit to what he appeared to think was a superior or obvious point of view. When she asked him to read something that she judged he might be interested in and which she hoped would allow him to consider a differing opinion, he would read a page, or in the case of a book, a chapter or two and then put it down. He was not particularly interested in Literature, he preferred the cinema, the theatre and the opera and he told her once that he would have loved to study Physics. He actually loved anything that was theatrical and she thought not for the first time that he would have been very successful as a professional singer. He never said anything but she sensed his frustration and his impatience with himself, but nothing prepared her for one Sunday in April when her own misgivings came to a head.

The day was warm and sunny and they decided to drive to the coast and attend Mass in a church there. The priest was clearly local and lacking the urbanity of a city priest and he had adopted a liberal approach that he clearly regarded as avant-garde. His vestments appeared to have been put on in a hurry, the music was deplorable and the singing sounded more like a modern pop concert. There was no silence, no sense of the holy, there was little in the way of awe and reverence. The young woman who read the epistle was dressed in clothing more fitted for the beach. Young children were being allowed to run around and make a noise unchecked. Elspeth could sense Anton's growing anger and at the end of the service he told her that he was going to complain to the priest and taking hold of her hand, so she had no way of staying behind, he walked with her towards the Sacristy and entered. There were two young servers and the priest was removing his vestments. He turned and looked at them in some surprise and Anton began a tirade of bitter criticism. The priest adjusted his spectacles and fixed his gaze on them with disbelief. Anton reproached him in near fury. The Mass he said had been celebrated negligently with little or no care given to what should be the highest expression of our Holy Catholic Faith and he accused the priest of a failure to perform the most important of his duties. He added that the young woman, dressed immodestly as she was, should never have been allowed in the Sanctuary of any Catholic Church. The priest spoke quietly but said that he was appalled to be so addressed by a lay person and he asked Anton to leave but Anton refused. By this time he was almost shouting and the situation was turning ugly, Elspeth was squirming with embarrassment but Anton went on. He complained furiously about the music and singing that he said more closely befitted a carnival than a church service and he had every reason as a Catholic to object. This he said was God's House not a concert Hall and he had every right to complain when he witnessed what he could only describe as an offence to God and his people. The priest stared at him and did not reply and at last Anton turning on his heel walked through the door only stopping to allow her to pass.

In her heart Elspeth knew that the Mass had been unacceptably celebrated but she was also horrified at Anton's temper. She wondered not for the first time whether he expressed himself at work in the same way. He had little concern for authority and although she felt that he was justified in speaking to the priest she thought there was a better way of approaching the situation. His temper had frightened her and she felt humiliated and embarrassed. There had been two young children present and she felt that they should not have been subjected to such a display. The priest in the end had remained calm and in control and looked altogether more dignified. The moment one loses one's temper, she thought, one loses control and the argument is lost. The priest might well have responded to a complaint courteously made but he might dismiss being harangued in such a manner.

They entered a restaurant close by but it was obvious that Anton was still trying to gain some control of himself and she felt unable to speak and he took it that she was censoring him and he turned on her.

'Why don't you say something? You were, I take it, as critical as me. You've been saying for as long as I have known you that the Mass must be celebrated with dignity'.

'I believe it should', Elspeth replied.

'Well then how well did this morning's liturgy fare?' He asked in a hostile manner, 'you are hardly being supportive. What we witnessed this morning cannot be tolerated.'

'Perhaps you could have asked to speak to the priest alone afterwards and expressed your dismay,' she said lamely.

'And he would have listened no doubt! Very English. Let's be compliant. Let's tolerate the intolerable, let's live and let live, let's make music while Rome burns. Tolerance carried to an extreme is cowardice and I have been given to understand that 'tolerance' is almost a religion in England'.

This made her cross, 'Tolerant the English may be and we may be many other things besides but no one can accuse us of cowardice.'

'I suppose you think you can leave that to the Italians!' he retorted.

'I didn't say that, Anton and neither do I think it'.

She thought this is dreadful. She thought that he had had some justification in complaining but it had been lost the moment he had become belligerent. She was shaken and she felt sick. She had been sick early in the pregnancy but things had settled. The meal they had ordered arrived on the table and the sight of it and the smells in the restaurant made her suddenly feel nauseous. She stood up, 'I'm sorry, I'm going to be sick', she said as she made for the toilets.

He looked up quickly when she returned but said nothing and finished his meal. She took only a glass of water and sat miserably. She felt weak and close to tears and was relieved when he called for the bill and they could leave.

'We'll go straight back home, you can lie down, you look unwell'.

Nothing else was said and he drove them back in silence. She thought, 'I hate these silences, I can remember Gran and Grandpa disagreeing sometimes but they never lost their tempers with each other or cut each other out. She had hated her father's treatment of her brother but her mother was never made to feel that she had to 'pussyfoot' around her father so as not to anger him. She was isolated, threatened and out of her depth with this situation and she did not know how to react.

When they arrived home he told her to go straight to bed and added, 'you can stay away from the school tomorrow, I'll ring my cousin and tell her that you are unwell.'

'But I'll be fine tomorrow!'

'You don't need to go, you must stay home and rest.' He allowed no response and she felt helpless. She thought he is treating me like a six-year old and I feel trapped.

She lay on the bed and once alone she broke down in tears. England and her own family and friends were so far away and she thought I've never wanted them so much.

She did not hear Anton enter the room and when she became aware of him she buried her head in the pillow, but his voice was gentle and distraught.

'Don't cry, please Elspeth! I'm so so sorry. I didn't mean to up-set you. Please forgive me.'

'You frightened me, I felt threatened'.

'That is unforgivable of me. I know I have a temper and some-times it gets the better of me but I have no right to take it out on you. Please forgive me. I was so distressed by the priest and I thought you were agreeing with me.'

'I did agree with you about the Mass,' she said.

'You think the priest would have listened if I had asked to speak to him by himself'?

'He may have listened but I doubt that he would have changed his mind. His interpretation of the changes that have taken place in the Church are widespread. The only thing one can do is to find a Church that maintains the beauty and dignity in the celebration of the Mass. Both of us prefer the Old Mass but the services here in the local Parish Church do not cause offence, the priest has a sense of the timelessness of the liturgy'.

'There's nothing we can do about the changes. It's hopeless. I was a server myself growing up in the Church. Things were so different'.

She saw the struggle going on in his face, his frustration coupled with the realisation that he had made an undignified exhibition of himself in front of her and in front of two young boys. All the insecurity in him was expressed in that look. She thought I cannot help you. I also felt dismayed, "Suffer the little children to come unto me", never meant that children's misbehaviour should go unchecked. The Sacrifice of the Mass was to glorify Christ and worship Him not a social 'feel good' get together with your friends enjoying a 'singalong'. It saddens me, she thought.

'I'm going to prepare you a light meal, you haven't eaten anything solid all day. I'll bring it to you in bed, you must rest,' he said.

II

The following day being alone Elspeth decided to attend Midday Mass in a nearby Church. It was a very old church and very beautiful. After the service she stayed after most of the congregation had left. There were two or three people besides herself kneeling and praying. She went over in her mind the incident of the day before and she thought back on the conversation she had had with Helen and Johannes Manasses, it seemed so long ago. The age of Liberalism is coming into its own she thought and liberalising the old Truths that are forever new are proving not to be liberalising at all, but confusing. Is it becoming an age of individual opinions vying one with the other for dominance? The ancient walls of the Church were steeped in the Kyrie Eleisons of centuries. Were things always the same? How many thousands of souls had knelt here as she was, seeking answers, perplexed, confused, questioning the problems thrown up by their age and time along with the problems within their individual relationships? She was troubled, she wished she had someone she could talk to and communicate her inner thoughts to. She thought, 'I can't discuss anything at any deeper level with Anton, I love him but we don't establish a dialogue, we don't seem to talk to each other so much as talking at each other'. She closed her eyes and her soul grew into the silence until it totally absorbed her. She prayed softly. She lost track of time and when she finally came to herself she rose and walked to the door and opening it the bright sunlight struck her and she shaded her eyes against it. She felt the new life in her stir and suddenly she was filled with a great sense of happiness and peace. She was aware that she had experienced something profound and that what she had been asking or seeking, and that had barely been articulated, was resolved for the present.

She walked to the shops thinking I will buy some special ingredients and prepare a wonderful evening meal and I will buy some flowers. Once home she went to work and set the table making sure it was carefully presented then she prepared the very best meal she was capable of. Making good food is an act of love she had been told and she was rewarded when Anton arrived home. The look on his face spoke a thousand words. He praised everything and she never forgot his look of gratitude as he told her that she made him feel like a prince! His behaviour of the day before and his treatment of her she was showing him had been confined to history and would never be alluded to by her again. She thought, we are bonded together for better or worse, one in body and spirit if not in mind, in principle I agree with him about most things that are of importance to us but I wish I could share the deeper thoughts I have and explore and develop those thoughts. I cannot just accept things at face value. I want to ask questions of life, I want to have a dialogue, I do not like my contributions to be easily put aside and replaced by convenient formulas put in their place.'

III

Spring advanced and the flowers she and the children at the school had planted flowered and then died only to be replaced by others taking their place in the garden surrounding the school. Elspeth became convinced that these mentally disabled children benefited and developed from their time spent growing things more perhaps than from anything else she did with them. Anton still came once or twice a month to sing with them and make music and she encouraged them to paint and draw and model with clay and plasticine. The children loved the time spent creating things and watching and caring for plants and flowers as they grew and she enjoyed seeing them happy and occupied.

As summer advanced so did her pregnancy and soon she would be leaving the school behind though she promised that she would be calling in from time to time and bringing the baby to see them. The mothers had grown fond of her and told her how successful she had been with their children and as the term grew to a close they brought along small knitted garments they had made for the baby. Elspeth was delighted and handled the little coats and garments lovingly. She and Anton had prepared a nursery and Elspeth decided that she would make her own handmade contribution. She bought and prepared the material for a pram cover and pillow. I am no great needle woman she thought but I am going to make the best effort I can.

The heat began to be unbearable and as soon as the term ended for both of them they left Rome for a village in the mountains. The small house felt like paradise. The garden was filled with flowers and there was a lemon tree. As she grew heavier Anton was all solicitude. He brought her breakfast and prepared her fruit and watched admiringly while she sat and sewed. The villagers soon got to know them and welcomed them when they visited their shops and there was no repeat of careless celebrations of Mass as there was a monastery close by that they could attend. The monastery bell for vespers carried across the valley with its timeless and calming call to evening prayer and they rested entwined together in the garden and recaptured their honeymoon and the early days of their marriage. The insects that had glutted themselves on nectar during the afternoons had left and there was the heavy perfume of flowers that scented the evening air and they breathed each other's breath quiet and at one together and wished it could go on forever. The city with the threats and difficulties it posed was left behind and they were happy alone with only each other and Elspeth was content not wishing to discuss anything other than themselves and their future plans and the baby.

'I want this to go on forever, I want us to return here every year, it's so beautiful, so perfect, I wish we didn't have to leave', Elspeth said as August was finally coming to a close. 'Promise we'll come back next year with the baby.'

'Promise!'

It was the evening before they were to leave and return to Rome for the birth and preparing to return he would not allow her to carry anything and she laughed. 'I'm not a piece of porcelain,' she protested.

'And I'm not taking any risks, you are both too precious to me.'

And she thought my doubts have disappeared, when we are alone he is contented and his insecurities disappear and that makes me contented too.

IV

The first labour pains began one evening almost ten days earlier than expected and while Elspeth thought there was no hurry Anton insisted that they should leave immediately for the hospital.

'It's your first birth and neither of us knows what to expect', he said and she decided that he was probably right and as it turned out he was.

'The hospital was a religious foundation and its atmosphere was peaceful, things seemed quiet and unhurried and Elspeth felt calm. The sister who attended her on hearing that the baby was not expected for ten days told her that it was possibly a false alarm and added that this frequently happened but she asked her to lie down so that she could examine her. Within minutes it seemed to Elspeth, looking back on the situation later, the labour was well and truly underway. She suddenly experienced the worst pain she thought possible and she cried out in agony almost in disbelief. The sister re-entered the room, she asked Anton to wait outside and she made to begin an examination and Elspeth found herself shaking uncontrollably and she thought how can I bear her to touch me.

The next events became a blur in her mind she remembered that she was given some kind of injection and the shaking stopped and she was asked if she had felt a large lump at the top of her stomach. She did not understand what exactly she was being asked and why and she replied that she did not think so. Another sister arrived and she was being told that the baby had turned and they were going to attempt to change its position. When they failed, they informed her that it would be a breach birth and they would be close by throughout the labour and they sent for a doctor.

The hours that followed were difficult to recount afterwards, how long the labour took she did not know. She could not have imagined such pain neither could she remember its intensity afterwards but she remembered how concentrated her whole being was on the child whose birth and life was dependent on her and how nothing else mattered. She would have been unable to recognise the sisters and doctor who attended her or when they came into or left the room. The hours went by in a daze and sometime the following morning her baby was delivered safely and her small son was laid into her arms. What was also unexpected was the overwhelming love that filled her, she would defend this little life to the death if necessary.

When Anton entered the room to greet his tiny son he looked pale and shaken.

'All through the night I didn't know what to expect when they said it was going to be a difficult birth. The doctor told me that you were calm and very brave. I'm so proud of you both.'

He bent down and kissed them and spoke in awed tones as he tenderly gazed at his child's tiny features and remarked on his head of dark hair.

At this point a sister entered the room and told them that the baby had been shocked at birth and she had come to take him to a special ward for twenty-four hours and Elspeth was taken to another ward and fell immediately into a long dreamless sleep. When she woke she went to find her baby, he was being held by one of the sisters and looking at him she thought how wide awake he looked and how sure she was that he recognised her. The sister smiled when she told her and said all new babies knew their mothers.

V

The weeks following their return home were a jumble of new experiences. How was it Elspeth thought that babies are born every day but no one ever tells a new mother what to expect. It had never occurred to her how much her whole life would change having another life completely dependent on her and how effectively her own independence diminished. She had no sooner finished changing him and completing the washing when he required feeding. They arranged for the baby's Baptism and her parents came from England. She and Anton had agreed to call him John – after her father – and Antony. They were still planning to live in England and wanted English sounding names and her parents were looking out for a suitable position for Anton in England, The baby, however, was always to be known as Gian by family and friends.

Once her parents left Elspeth found herself alone and any idea that motherhood was a case of knowing what to do by instinct was quickly put aside. She was particularly afraid of bathing her tiny baby in fear of him slipping from her grasp and was happy to watch Anton taking over when he was home. She was constantly tired and wondered how mothers managed with two or three children. Louise now had a son, Sebastian, born some three months before Gian and she thought about how well she would be managing. She tried hard to make sure that she took the baby for an outing each day and that she had a meal ready for Anton when he arrived home from work but it was all taking its toll. She had managed some weeks after his birth to establish a routine of a sort and after Gian's lunch-time feed she would put him into his pram ready to take him for an outing after the siesta hour. The baby would cry for a while and she would go into him but did not pick him up and he would cry for a further five minutes before going off to sleep. She was quite proud of this routine until one lunch-time Anton arrived home unexpectedly having forgotten something he needed for the afternoon. When he heard the baby crying he went straight to him and picked him up and Elspeth protested.

'I won't have him crying! He's distressed! What do you think you're doing allowing him to cry'?

'He's not distressed, he cries for a short time after he's been fed and before I take him out for some fresh air' Elspeth retorted.

'I won't have him left crying, he's too tiny to understand. How is it you can't cope that you are forever worn out. Perhaps you thought you could sit down every afternoon and read a book! There are plenty of other mothers with a house full of babies and children. You even have someone coming in during the week to help with the housework! It's beyond me that you seem unable to cope'.

He was angry and unjust and his criticism stung.

'Why are you so keen to make me feel inadequate?'

'Well you'd know everything there is to know about making others feel inadequate wouldn't you Elspeth. You with all your superior learning, forever presenting me with books that just might interest me. You're my wife not my teacher. Always questioning, always wanting to know', he all but sneered.

She was shocked, 'It is about trying to understand'.

'Oh really! it's about considering yourself superior! I overheard my pathetic colleague, Carlo, remember him? recounting our visit to his home and his visit with his wife here. Apparently another colleague has a friend with a child at Maria Rosa's school and she told him that they had met your mother when you arrived here. She said you and your mother were from the English upper middle-class, clearly made of money, and I had clearly landed on my feet! Obviously I'm not good enough for you, my dear.'

The baby was howling by this time and he handed him over.

'I have to get back to work. I'll be working late and going on to the choir, I'll get something to eat on the way home so don't put yourself out preparing me any supper!'

He stormed out and she sat down and tried to soothe the baby. When he stopped crying and fell to sleep she placed him in his pram tidied up and got ready to take him out. Anton had lost his temper before but had rarely been so unjust.

She sat down on a park bench, she felt shattered and asked herself if he had been unjust. She wondered how long Anton had harboured these grievances against her. She thought I am innocent of his accusations, I do not think of myself as superior but she knew that it was hardly the first time that she had given that impression and she found it unbearably hurtful to be accused by Anton. What had taken place was not just irritation on his part it was serious and she could not dismiss it. She felt undermined and began to question the sincerity in his feelings for her and then she pulled herself up sharply. His love and tenderness towards her was not feigned, she had known of his insecurity before she married him and he had not hidden the difficulties of his upbringing he had shared the shame he felt about his father. But Maria Rosa had had misgivings. She wished not for the first time that she had someone to talk to. She thought, he never allows me to go near his place of work, I know he hates it, and it dawned on her that the conversation between his colleagues that he had overheard must have taken place soon after Carlo and Sara's visit and had been the cause of the anger he had displayed the night he had walked out of the house saying that the food she had prepared was inedible. The staff of his college must meet together at the end of terms or at Christmas but he had never invited her to join them and he did not attend himself. I will ask him if they are meeting together at Christmas and I shall insist that we take part. If only a suitable position would come up in England, if only I could get us away from here.

She sat for some time watching a group of children playing. Their mothers were sitting talking together and she felt suddenly lonely. She thought I do not know how to deal with the situation between Anton and myself. Yesterday I felt a growing confidence I thought I was dealing so much better and now I just feel tired and depressed. I do not know what I am going home to, I do not know if I can really trust him. His behaviour may be understandable but it is no less acceptable.

The baby was beginning to stir and she bent over and smiled down at him and began the walk home. I will not allow Anton to hurt Gian's life like his father hurt his and how my father hurt Jamie. I will do everything it takes to protect my child!

When Anton arrived home she had finished feeding the baby and was singing a lullaby to him to get him to sleep. Anton crept into the bedroom and bent over her and kissed her, 'I'm sorry, I was out of order this afternoon'. She felt in no mood to forgive him so easily and she did not reply. Once the baby was asleep she laid him down in his cot and went into the living room.

'I had a bad morning.'

'And that's your explanation is it?!' She was angry and felt he should know it. 'You never mention the college or your work without complaining. I can't believe all your colleagues are against you – well with the exception of Luci.'

Luci taught Science and they had met once or twice.

'I was not aware that I made you feel inadequate, perhaps your colleagues are not aware of it either. Perhaps it's in your own head. I certainly don't think of myself as superior, they probably don't either. Why didn't you tell me what Carlo had said?'

'I felt humiliated if you want to know! They spoke as if I had taken advantage of you. They implied you were out of my league. Luci was there and she told me that she had been very annoyed. She said they were jealous and that I should ignore it and she was right of course. Carlo had laughed saying that Sara had said that she considered me good looking and suggested that I was attractive to women. They scoffed and all but insinuated that I had seduced you'.

'That's ridiculous! When two people fall in love they are not taking advantage of each other. You should dismiss it as silly gossip! I'm sure they meet up together at Christmas time. This year you will attend and take me with you. It's time I met these people. In the mean-time don't allow yourself to be bothered about it or to take it out on me. It's of no importance to either of us and certainly not to me'.

'I couldn't bear it if I lost you,' he said weakly.

'I'm not going anywhere. You and our baby are more precious to me than anything else but make sure that the next time you are feeling distressed about your work or your colleagues you talk to me about it and I'll stop handing over books for you to read if you think I'm trying to teach you'.

VI

Anton had not protested when she had said that they would attend a social end of term gathering with his colleagues and while he sounded reluctant when informing her about the Christmas function he did not disagree about attending.

Elspeth prepared for it carefully. They asked Anton's cousin to babysit, the baby knew her and she said she was more than willing, but it was the first time they had left him and they agreed to only stay for the meal so that they would be back home in just over two hours. Elspeth had a dress that her mother had insisted on buying her some Christmases before. It was a rich dark red, simply cut with her mother's impeccable taste stamped on it. Anton had persuaded her to grow her hair long and she decided to wear it loose. Her only jewellery would be her engagement ring and wedding band and a pearl ring Anton had given her on her birthday, worn on a finger of her right hand.

They were ready when Clara arrived and Anton told her that she had never looked more beautiful and she laughed and told him that he looked pretty irresistible himself.

A large room had been booked for the gathering and several round tables were arranged each set for six guests. They were shown to a table in the centre of the room and Anton introduced her to the members of his staff. Belle's sister Chloe had once remarked that when she or her mother entered a room other women immediately felt overdressed. There was a silence in the room when they arrived and Elspeth felt the eyes of the other guests glued on them. She greeted Carlo and Sara and enquired about their children and Sara asked about the baby as they made their way to their places. The seating arrangements had clearly been thought out carefully beforehand and she and Anton were seated with Daniella and Frederico, the two colleagues that had along with Carlo, made the comments about them both that had so distressed Anton the year before. Also sharing the table were the Principal and his wife, Francisco and Irena. Anton had told her that they generally kept a distance from the staff which had earned the couple the title, 'The Ivory Tower Duo'. They both belonged to old Roman families and moved in influential circles. It was rumoured that one of Irena's brothers was a Cardinal. She and her husband greeted them warmly and she was introduced to the other couple sharing their table. Irene, sitting next to Elspeth soon engaged her in conversation and Elspeth felt an immediate liking for the older woman who she took to be in her early forties. She enquired after the baby and Elspeth explained that she was feeling somewhat anxious as this was the first time they had left him with a babysitter.

'The first child is always the most difficult! but don't worry he'll be fine,' Irena assured her. 'We have four children, our youngest is just entering his teens. No one ever tells you that you'll never be free again! One goes on worrying about them at every age they reach. We were fortunate we always had our parents around and grandparents too when our children were very young but your parents are still in England I think, that must be difficult for you. What about Anton's parents?' Irena enquired sympathetically.

'His mother and father are both dead but his aunts and cousins are happy to lend a hand,' Elspeth replied.

'Do you have brothers and sisters?' asked Daniella.

'No. My only brother died when he was fifteen and Anton is also an only child. How about you?'

'Two brothers and a sister.'

'Do they live in Rome,' asked Irena.

'They live in Anzio, thirty miles or so down the coast. It was a beachhead during the war and I'm afraid the people don't like the English very much'.

It was hardly a kind comment and Irena immediately spoke up, 'We certainly don't feel that way in Rome, we think well of the English. The War was a dreadful business my own father was injured quite badly'.

'My father was a bomber pilot in the RAF and his brother, my uncle died in a Japanese concentration camp, but we cannot go on hating for ever.'

'I wholeheartedly agree!' added Irena.

Anton was engaged in conversation with Francisco but at this point Frederico who had been listening spoke up.

'You speak very good Italian, Elspeth, do you and Anton always speak in Italian?'

'No, we always speak in English, Anton's English is much better than my Italian and he also speaks fluent French and Spanish. He has an excellent ear for languages.' She was determined to compliment him in front of his colleagues and Anton overhearing gently squeezed her hand saying, 'She flatters me'.

'I have a niece who went to school in England – an excellent school by all accounts, my niece was very happy there. In the West of England, called Oak something...' began Irena when Elspeth broke in.

'Oaklands! that was my old school!'

'Really, what a coincidence, Liliana must be about your age'

'Liliana Rossi?'

'Yes, you knew her?' asked Irena.

'Yes indeed! We sang in the school choir together. My home is in the same city as the school so I could go home for weekends and Liliana sometimes came to my home so we could practise together. My mother is a musician so she used to help us to rehearse. Liliana is a year younger than me. I understand that she was hoping to become a cellist'.

'That's right. She is in Rome staying with her parents for Christmas, she was engaged during the summer to a musician and she will be coming to me this coming Monday for lunch. Do you think you could join us? I'm sure Liliana would enjoy meeting up with you? Of course you must bring Gian.'

'I'd love to come!'

'That's settled then. You must give me your address and I'll send our driver to collect you. 'Our driver' sounds rather grand actually I had some ill health last year and I along with a group of friends engage a driver between us. Can you be ready by 12.30?'

'I'm sure I can and thank you, I'll really look forward to it,' and Elspeth quickly rummaged in her handbag for notepaper and a pen and wrote down her address.

'We'll look forward to it too'.

Soon after the meal was over Anton explained that they needed to be home for the baby and saying their goodbyes they prepared to leave.

'Well goodbye my dear 'til Monday,' said Irena kindly.

Once they were outside Anton asked her what it was all about as he hadn't heard the exchange between them. When she explained he was amazed, 'they never mix with anybody on the staff, she's from a noble Italian family. If Daniella heard your conversation it will be around the college before I turn up tomorrow, she's a Socialist and adamant feminist. You really are a star, Elspeth, I'm so proud of you. I think everybody in that room will be envying me tonight!'

He overwhelmed her with his praise and said that the evening had been a great success but always there was that hesitation in him and the belief that she would be moving into circles he felt himself barred from. His father was always there at his back watching over his shoulder but Elspeth, if she sensed it, chose to ignore it.

She renewed her friendship with Liliana and Irena was set to become a lifelong friend, a relationship that outlived her and Anton's decision to move to England the following year.

Irena was closely involved with the church as her family had been for centuries and learning that Elspeth was a convert she introduced her to some of her friends. Several of them were young mothers like herself and she was able to take Gian with her when they met together. Irena told her that as a teenager she had believed that she had a vocation to be a nun and had joined a Carmelite closed order but it had not worked out for her and soon after she left she had married Francisco. They had known each other most of their lives as their families were close and she said theirs had not been a grand passion but an ever deepening friendship. They were she said soul mates and frequently knew what the other was thinking and they had never had to explain themselves to each other. She said that it was a commonly held belief that marriage frequently thrived on disagreements but that her marriage was not included in that.

It was also a commonly held opinion Elspeth knew, and certainly among the staff at the college, that Irena considered herself above them all. Elspeth could sympathise with her new friend because she had experienced the same misunderstanding herself. Irena was elegant and regal looking owing to generations of fine breeding but she was as Elspeth learned also humble and much loved, her eyes were brown and velvety with an expression that was both caring and wise and Elspeth learnt a lot from her. She also met Francisco but he remained a distant figure to her and while Anton remained a member of his staff the couple never invited him to their home. As Principal he had the reputation for being fair and impartial and was generally respected rather than liked, but once Anton had gained a position in England Irena arranged a farewell dinner party to which they were both invited and Elspeth was happy for her husband to meet 'The Ivory Tower Duo' in their own home and he received a warm reception.

Chapter 14

. . . .

*"Yahweh, my heart is not haughty, I do not set my sights too high. I
have taken no part in great affairs, In wonders beyond my scope.
No, I hold myself in quiet and silence, like a little child in its moth-
er's arms. like a little child so I keep myself - Let Israel hope in
Yahweh Henceforth and forever."*
(Psalm 131 The New Jerusalem Bible)

Early in the Spring following the Christmas Staff gathering, information of a position in England came from an unexpected
quarter. Johannes Manasses wrote and told them that a teaching post was to be advertised around Easter time, in the college
where he worked, for an applicant who could teach music and
who would also be able to offer a further subject adding that an
applicant who could offer a foreign language would be looked
upon favourably. He told them that his colleague was retiring
at the end of the summer term and if Anton was interested he
would tell him the moment the post was advertised. To Elspeth
and Anton, it seemed too good to be true and Elspeth allowed
herself to dream about a successful outcome. She also attempted to keep her hopes to herself thinking if he fails he is going to
feel very vulnerable. By this time she was wary, she frequently
considered that he had a chip on his shoulder and he could be
moody and short-tempered. It was the baby that usually raised
his spirits, the little one would glow with pleasure when his father arrived home in the evenings, he would be picked up and
smothered in kisses and told how wonderful and unique he was.

In mid-February they travelled to Switzerland for a long weekend and they joined her parents who were spending an extended holiday there. Elspeth was eager for her grandparents to meet

their third great grandchild her two eldest cousins each having a child by this time, but Esme, her favourite cousin, was showing no interest in marriage. She was working as a doctor in an Indian Mission hospital and she was dedicated to the work and to the poor. It was destined to be her life's vocation and she only rarely returned to Europe.

Her grandparents were now in their early eighties and Elspeth felt they had aged since they had last seen them though they seemed lively enough and they said that but for a few aches and pains, which were to be expected at their age, they were fine. They were thrilled with the baby.

'He's a Penrose that's for sure. He could be one of yours and mine, Nan! exclaimed Grandda, 'what do you think Nan?'

'I think he's like himself', Nan replied. As always she was aware of the other's feelings and she didn't want to offend Anton.

Anton wasn't in the least offended. Elspeth remembered them taking Gian to meet Cosimo and his family and the lovable chef had said innocently that the baby was a beauty and resembled his old boss and friend, Anton's father. Elspeth had felt Anton stiffen and as they walked home he said the baby might resemble his father in looks but that was where the likeness ended, now he added that he saw something of his mother in his baby's eyes and that he wished his mother could have known him.

Elspeth could never tell what her aunt Elspeth thought of Anton. She was, as Nan had described her, 'a good soul' and she had married her uncle Walter, a man as dependable and hardworking as herself. Her aunt was down-to-earth, practical and capable and Elspeth thought she and her aunt had in common was their name. She felt her aunt considered her to be living in some fanciful world of her own and that Anton was far too Latin for her tastes and she was shy in his presence which somewhat amazed her niece. Her aunt cared for her mother devotedly but had much more in common with her father and she secretly thought that her clever niece along with her mother were much alike impractical and in need of managing. She expressed something of surprise at her niece's handling of her baby son, however, and was generous in her praise. Elspeth thought that she would be excellent to have around in an emergency and felt more comfortable with her than she had in the past though her aunt had always been kind and what had appeared to Elspeth as silent criticism had actually only been a lack of understanding as they were so different in temperament.

Soon after arriving home they received the news they had been waiting for. Johannes was as good as his word and they received the advertisement about the college post in good time and sent for the Application forms. Elspeth helped Anton to complete them and write an accompanying letter of Application then all they could do was to sit back and hope for news of an interview. It took time in coming and Elspeth did not want to admit how much she wanted a positive outcome. She loved Rome, she loved Italy but she wanted, more than she was prepared to say, to return home to all that was familiar to her. When Anton was at home she would busy herself with odd jobs knowing that the post had arrived but reluctant to appear too eager. Just when she thought the application had been unsuccessful and she was beginning to give up hope and Anton was telling her that they were much more likely to choose a British candidate, the longed for letter arrived and an interview was offered. It was to take place at the beginning of April giving a successful applicant the time to resign from his or her post and leave sufficient time for a replacement.

Anton travelled alone to England and stayed with her parents while she stayed at home waiting anxiously. The baby took her mind off things during the day and during their outings she took to paying a visit to the church offering up prayers of petition and lighting candles! The day of the interview came and the evening and she had to make herself concentrate on feeding the baby and getting him to bed and yet the awaited telephone call did not come. She estimated that it was seven thirty in England and at last the longed for ringing sound! He had been successful! The job was his! He apologised for not having rang earlier but he had met up with Johannes and had only just arrived at her home. She wished he was there so that she could throw herself into his arms. He told her that he was to spend the following day at the college so that he could acquaint himself with the curriculum and he expressed his relief and delight in the college and the hospitality he had received but adding that he could hardly wait to be back with her and felt lost without her and the baby.

He arrived home with gifts for herself and Gian and talked long into the night. Johannes had shown him wonderful friendship and Elspeth was always to wonder during the coming years if it was indeed a Mediterranean understanding that they had in common as their friendship remained close. She was to experience a different side to Anton who listened to this new found friend and was happy to allow his opinions to take president over his own. They never argued, Anton seemed always to agree with, what he told Elspeth, was his friend's learned point of view. He rarely mentioned his lack of a university education again, it was not a case of 'happy ever after' but England was to give him a confidence in himself that Rome had failed to give him and along with it an opportunity to reinvent himself.

II

They began immediately preparing for the move. Elspeth's parents wanted them to take over the 'big house' which her father had stated would eventually come down to her. They asked if she would be willing for them to take over part of Gran's house which was at present let out as separate flats. It had, of course, been where her mother had been brought up and her parents pointed out that they required something smaller.

'You will be the fourth generation to live in the big house and I would be reluctant to sell it', her father reasoned.

Elspeth thought how blessed she was, she loved the house while recognising how very fortunate she was and she and Anton spent no time in agreeing to the proposal. The short term lease on the lower ground floor and ground floor of Gran's house – which of course was in her name – was due to end within months and Elspeth gained the impression that her mother was delighted. She wanted something smaller and she began to take the necessary steps to redesign and draw up plans for the redecoration of the house where she had been brought up. They would be close by and her father was enthusiastic about being close to his grandson.

As the summer vacation grew close Elspeth asked if they could take a holiday in the mountain village where they had spent such a magical time the year before.

'You promised', she said.

'Yes, why not. We can stay for a fortnight or so,' replied Anton.

This year, however, their 'Lemon Garden' cottage had been rented out for the summer to an elderly couple and the only house available for them to rent was small and rather dark. Elspeth knew before they were due to leave Rome that she was again pregnant and when they arrived she was already in the throes of morning sickness. But they were both delighted with the knowledge of another baby and a sibling for Gian. The villagers were happy to see them and made a fuss of their little boy but the fine memories they had from the year before did not live up their expectations this year.

They were soon to begin a new life and a new life was beginning inside her and then they received news of an old life ended. At the end of their first week in the mountain village her father contacted them to tell them that his father had suffered a massive coronary and had not survived and they quickly gathered their things together and journeyed to Switzerland to attend the funeral.

'I'm so glad we visited my grandparents and that Grandda met Gian,' stated Elspeth sadly. She had not been as close to her grandfather as she was to her grandmother but he had always been kind and she wondered how her grandmother would fare without him.

The funeral service took place in the Protestant church Elspeth remembered being taken to as a child by Nan. Her Aunt Elspeth had managed the arrangements and to her niece's surprise her aunt broke down during the service and cried pitifully. Nan stood calm and dignified and refused the offer of her father's arm both on entering and leaving the church saying quietly that she could manage. Her uncle Walter supported his wife along with her older cousins. Esme was unable to attend and had sent a special message which was read out during the Service. Elspeth felt it was a forlorn little gathering but was happy that her grandfather had chosen burial and not cremation. After the ceremony and the committal, they returned to her aunt's house and Elspeth was glad to find herself next to Nan's sister May, and was happy to engage her in conversation. She had always liked her and knew Great Aunt May like herself had been a teacher. She was two and a half years younger than Nan and the two had remained very close. Their father had also been a teacher and had died when the two children were very young and they had had a very close relationship with their mother who Nan had described as a wonderful manager. It had been a contented little household Nan had told her and we very soon learnt how 'to make do and mend'.

'Were you very poor?' Elspeth remembered asking as a young child and Nan had said that there had been a shortage of things but she could not remember being very poor and she had never minded what restrictions their financial state had imposed on them. Their mother had grown vegetables and the garden had also had some beautiful flowers she remembered and fortunately they had their own house so they were very much better off than so many other families left without a breadwinner. For that they were very grateful because it had been a time of poverty and there had been families that had ended up in the Workhouse which people dreaded almost as much as death and disease.

Elspeth turned to her great aunt now asking her how she was and the old lady told her that she was intending to stay with her sister for a month or two and hoped that Nancy would join her in England for Christmas.

'I'm pleased and I hope that you will both come to us for over the Christmas period. We would love to have you both'.

'Well If I can persuade your Nan to come to me I hope that you will bring your nice husband and the little one to visit me! I was so pleased to learn that you were returning to England and that Anton has got himself a lectureship'.

Elspeth's great aunt was shorter than her sister and her great niece observed her while they talked. She was carefully and 'properly' dressed Elspeth thought to herself and the adjective 'properly' seemed most appropriate, Aunt May was very much of her class. She was wearing a navy blue skirt and jacket that she would refer to as her 'costume', altogether less masculine sounding than 'suit'. On her head was a straw hat of the same shade as her jacket and a Victorian cameo brooch that had once belonged to her mother was pinned at the neck of her blouse. Elspeth was glad to see that none of the family and friends attending the funeral were wearing black the occasion was altogether sombre enough without being bleak. Looking around the thought came to her that her grandparents and great aunt belonged to a generation that by and large took the hand that life had played them and got on with it, and she looked fondly at her great aunt. Perhaps today her generation would consider that she was stereotyping an older generation but looking at her Aunt May she could not help thinking that she could so easily have stepped out of the pages of 'Cranford', an unmistakable member of that gentile Middle Class that was fast disappearing. And then her aunt surprised her as she began talking about the subject that interested both of them: education and teaching.

'I'm so glad that I retired when I did,' her aunt was saying.

She had, of course, retired all of two decades ago.

'I really don't like these new Comprehensive schools, so big and noisy, I don't know how the teachers survive more than a term in them. I taught primary school children, of course, and I like to think I was firm though I was never a disciplinarian. My school catered for poor children and many of the little mites were indeed poor. Disadvantaged is how educationalists might describe them now but we didn't think of them in quite those terms then and we always insisted on courtesy and good manners and almost all teachers could enter large classes and be met with respect. I like to think that we respected the children in turn and believed that courtesy and quietness in our classrooms were good in the long run for children'.

I remember the thirties and the fifties and know that there are those who consider the fifties as being boring, but I remember that decade and the thirties as altogether gentler times – unless you were living in the fast lane and most of us weren't. The population was also chastened in the years following the war and while the class system still persists there was a movement that allowed for greater advantages to be given to everybody and of course I agree wholeheartedly with that but we had the opportunity, in the late fifties and early sixties, it seems to me, to have allowed young people the possibility of upward mobility and well, I ask myself has that really occurred. In these big schools they seem to have focused almost entirely on 'equality' and as a consequence they put all the youngsters together and don't pay sufficient attention to differences – children have different abilities, needs and attributes and one size does not fit all – or so it seems to me, and I don't think it works, I think it is more likely to fail children.

'Some children should be stretched academically and others need special teaching at a slower pace. We have politicians who are theorists and the majority have never been in a classroom since they left school and too many of them went to Public schools and know little or nothing about the vast number of youngsters and the backgrounds they come from. I'm not thinking of you, my dear, I'm not particularly against private schooling as it happens but I do wish that politicians could learn something from the experience of the past instead of thinking it was all bad. The moment these 'educators' come up with a new educational theory they always manage to bring forward adults that were at school decades ago to inform the public how they suffered from ignorant teachers who thrashed them into subservience and failed them. There were bad schools and poor teachers then – I expect there still are now – but I remember a different situation and children who succeeded against the odds of their upbringings and who became fine citizens and parents in their turn and it distresses me profoundly when I hear some of the rubbish that is sometimes presented to us as if we had never had it so good and as if material goods are all we need to be happy. I don't think people are happier'.

Oh! I've no doubt my generation got a lot of things wrong, don't misunderstand me Elspeth, but we also got many things right and some of those things will stand the test of time.'

It was a strange conversation following a funeral Elspeth thought and her Aunt May's thinking on 'equality' reminded her of Johannes' words and his use of the terminology 'mythical common denominator', and she thought that the experience that the two shared had led them to the same conclusion and her admiration for her aunt grew. She was experienced and she thought and questioned and was outside her time, above it in a sense, and certainly she had never been a prisoner of it and her great niece was impressed.

Her aunt had not quite finished her argument, however, and she went on to surprise her great niece further.

'Pursuing equality as it is pursued today never seems to me very Christian. There's the Parable of the Talents, of course, but what I have always found comforting is the outcome Jesus states at the end of the Parable of the Sower when He says: "And some seeds fell into rich soil, grew tall and strong, and produced a good crop; the yield was thirty, sixty, even a hundredfold." There's the recognition there or so it seems to me that we are all different and yet if we try our best to be good Christian people we will be acceptable to God even if our "yield' falls well short of "a hundredfold"'.

Elspeth looking at her aunt was reminded of her friend Belle and she thought that what Great Aunt May had expressed and knowing how she had lived her life, and how doubtlessly she saw herself as a hopefully "thirty-fold crop", was surely yielding "a hundredfold". There was such humility and acceptance in the old lady's life.

'I think you are right Aunt May. I had never recognised what you have pointed out in the Parable. It's all about God's love for us really and His acceptance of our littleness'.

Two days following the funeral Nan joined her for a walk. Gian had fallen asleep as she pushed his pram and when they reached a suitable spot they sat down on a bench. It was a warm sunny day and the shade was provided by a large tree. They faced a mountain range and Nan was the first to speak.

'Mountains on a day like today look almost benign and it's as I like to see them. On stormy overcast days they look forbidding and even threatening'.

Great mountain ranges are majestic like mighty oceans but if I could choose my favourite environment to live in I think I would choose a woodland with a quiet stream and hills rather than mountains,' replied Elspeth.

'I can remember the day we took you to the seaside for the first time, you must have been about two years old and you exclaimed, 'it's a big bath!' said Nan laughing.

Elspeth smiled, 'Really!' then she became serious, 'Aunt Elspeth seems very distressed'.

'Yes, she was always a favourite with her father, they had so many things in common, being so very alike'.

'And you Nan, how are you?' Her grandmother, she thought looked pale but calm.

'It still doesn't seem real. When you have been married for close on sixty years, I keep on expecting Grandda to be there, to come into the room or be sitting in his chair, we had become part and parcel of each other – perhaps taking each other for granted, but at the same time each other's refuge. A good marriage and family can be like that, sharing the children in a way that it is impossible with anybody else, for example sharing the joy in their successes and covering their failures too. During the War we shared, of course, in our friends' anxieties and it brought them very close to us and then there was James' death and that brought your grandfather and myself very close.'

Elspeth looked down at her little boy sleeping peacefully and remembered Nan saying that mothers saw their children in a way that others did not and she thought it's true I would stand by Gian whatever happened. I love him.

'I had a chat to Aunt May after the funeral. Did she never think of marrying?' asked Elspeth.

'She used to walk out – that's how we termed it then – with a farmer's son from our village, she was only sixteen at the time and Chas was eighteen. He was killed on the Somme. Mother and I thought and hoped she would meet somebody else but she never did. She was always the most soft hearted of the two of us and the children she taught became her life. We both had managed to get a scholarship, which was quite something in those days and when she left school she went to help in the village school. She finally managed to get a grant – quite a few years later – and she got a place at a Teacher Training College. When the Second World War began and so many male teachers were called up, May got a Headship in the next town and she remained at the school until she retired. I like to think that she has had a fulfilled life, we've always been very close and now I think that we'll be spending much more time together.'

'So you never thought to teach yourself Nan?'

'No, it wasn't what I wanted.'

'How did you meet Grandda?'

'I worked as a waitress in the Tea Rooms in the next town and one afternoon your Grandda came in with a young lady. I thought she was his wife but he called me over and made a point of saying that he and his sister would like another pot of tea! Two days later he came back again and asked me out. I was very surprised, and very shy, it was clear to me that he belonged to a very different world from me. Your Great Grandmother came from a family of landed gentry and she didn't approve of your Grandda's choice of wife. She was very proud. Your Great Grandfather was a gentle soul and he made me feel welcome but it took a tragedy in their own lives that finally broke down the barrier between your great grandmother and me.'

'What happened?' All Elspeth knew of her great grandparents was their photograph hanging in the hallway of her home.

Your great grandparents had two daughters, Ursula the eldest – the young lady who was accompanying your Grandda to afternoon tea the day I've just mentioned – '

'Wait a moment isn't she the one still living in Australia?'

'Yes, indeed! She married a fine and very likeable young man, Wilfred, and after her parents died they moved with their young family to Sydney. Wilf's been dead some years now and Ursula is living in a Nursing Home. Two of their sons have visited us in the past and the family have all sent telegrams this last week. Your Aunt Elspeth keeps in touch with them all'.

'So what tragedy occurred to change things with my Great Grandmother?

'Their youngest daughter, Elspeth, died. She didn't become ill with influenza during the 1918/19 epidemic but she caught influenza in 1922. It was a serious attack and she was dead within days. She was their youngest child and believe me she was beautiful and adorable. People frequently say of a loved one that everybody loves them in the case of young Elspeth it was true. Your Great Grandparents never fully recovered from her loss'.

'Did you live with them after you and Grandda married?'

'Certainly not at first. They owned so much property – you know the saying: Speculate to Accumulate, they applied it! It was your Great Grandmother's money and her mind and energy that mainly drove the business. She saw the opportunities around at the time and they bought up houses and properties and renovated them and offered them for rent. They were good, and fair Landlords it must be said and, of course, your mother's family were in the same line of business which is how your father eventually met your mother. Grandda and I lived at the beginning of our married life in one of his parent's houses, it was there that your father and Uncle James were born and I loved that house. It was a solid Victorian Villa and I was sorry to leave it, but after Elspeth died your Great Grandmother begged us to move in with them. Ursula was married by that time and living in London and the big house seemed empty and so we went to live with them. Elspeth's death changed her mother particularly and she was glad to have our young family around her and although I can't say we ever became close exactly I served a need and she was grateful.'

'What about your mother, Nan'.

'Oh she played a loving part in our children's lives. Aunt May stayed at home and she and Mother shared the little cottage where we had been brought up until Mother died and your great aunt moved into a house in the town where she taught'.

'And Elspeth became a family name! There's so many of us it can become confusing!'

'I understand that Elspeth is the Scottish form of the name, Elizabeth and that is my middle name, the family can't get rid of us', laughed Nan.

'Nancy is not the name you were Christened is it?' asked Elspeth.

'No, my name is actually Anne Elizabeth but when my sister May was just beginning to speak a friend of my parents used to

225

visit with their little girl called Nancy and May hearing the name must have thought it applied to being a girl! We'll never know but May insisted on calling me Nancy and it stuck! And now the youngest Elspeth and family is about to move into the big house so I understand. How do you feel about it?'

'It's always been my home and daddy has always intimated that he wanted it eventually to become mine, he would be very reluctant to sell it and I love the house so it was an easy decision which we readily agreed to.'

'It half surprised me because I know you also knew difficult times there – Jamie and the terrible trauma you experienced. You were raped inside your own home I understand.'

'You were told about that!' Elspeth said shocked.

'Perhaps I should not have referred to it, my dear. Your mother told me. She was horrified and distraught both for you and your father. She said your father broke down completely and that she had never seen him so devastated, she said that he hardly spoke for weeks and said that he been a total failure as a father. He went to see the young man that had violated you –.'

'What!' Elspeth gasped.

'You didn't know but according to what your mother told me you had stated in a letter that you wanted him cautioned and believed he would benefit from psychological counselling and your father paid for it, however, he warned the young man that if he ever dared approach you again he would not hesitate to have him charged. I'm sorry Elspeth I've distressed you.'

Elspeth had paled, 'I thought it was in the past but it never goes away. I have drawn a line about that dreadful summer and think, 'before' and 'after''.

'You have told Anton?'

'Yes, of course and he has always been very gentle with me. His tenderness when I told him has played a large part in helping me to accept what happened and in coming to terms with it. It never goes away completely and I doubt it ever will. For a long time it felt as if I had survived my own murder and that I would never trust anyone again. But it has also helped me to support Anton. His father was physically abusive to both his mother and himself – his father had his own demons to contend with – and it has left him needing assurance so we help each other. I will never go so far as to subscribe to there being 'some good in all things evil', when it comes to rape however'.

'Anton's a good man and it's very obvious how deeply he loves you. Try not to get too distressed when you don't agree about things I think he's altogether a simpler person than you and he sees things in black and white where you'll be forever asking questions. But you are strong, stronger than you know and you would never have chosen an easy way, you didn't even as a child. It doesn't make for a painless existence but it can prove to be a better part.'

'Does anybody ever manage to hide anything from you Nan,' Elspeth said somewhat in amazement.

'Oh, your Grandda and I had our disagreements believe me and you are so much like me – more so than any of my children and other grandchildren, you are the child of my soul, a strange way of putting it but I think you understand.'

'Yes I do. I don't have to explain things to you. Daddy said to me on the way to my wedding that I was like you and I thought it was very insightful at the time. What particularly did you and Grandda disagree about?'

'Quite a few things, we were brought up very differently and I objected very strongly to sending the children away to school. Your grandfather had attended a public school and he was determined that his children would too. He said that his school had been the making of him. I don't think it was a bad thing for our children in the long run but I'm still not in favour of sending children away. He didn't understand the value of money either in the way I believed I did. I had to learn its value very early on in my life and then there was the question of class. My father had been a school teacher in a poor boys' school and when he died Mother had to make the pennies go a long way. She brought us up gentile middle class and the wealthy family circumstances I married into were a revelation to me. I sometimes had difficulties adapting and sometimes we argued. I always loved and admired your Gran, she taught me a great deal. Wealthy she may well have been but I never knew of anybody more dedicated to the needs of the poor. She was kindness and generosity itself.'

'She was. I think of her every day. I've been very fortunate in my grandmothers! I'm eternally grateful.'

'It's time we got along home, your aunt will be preparing the evening meal and she won't want us to be late'.

As if on cue, Gian stirred and woke up and Elspeth helped him to sit up.

'Gian is not going to be an only child for much longer, Nan, we have our second baby due in the Spring, there's going to be new beginnings for all of us in the old house!'

'I'm delighted for you and the big house needs children'.

When they arrived home they found Anton in the kitchen with Aunt Elspeth happily producing Italian food magic and the younger

Elspeth was surprised and pleased to see her aunt finally at ease with her husband.

Later when they were alone Anton expressed his liking and admiration for her family and his pleasure that they liked and accepted him.

'I feel so relaxed with them. I've developed a sense of paranoia almost in recent years which I don't remember having when I was young. I've grown to distrust people. I think that it developed in America when my father's family didn't think me good enough and looked down on me. I think I've been trying to prove myself ever since. Y'know during the funeral service I found myself thinking of my father. I remembered once when I was about twelve years old being bullied on the way home from school. A group of lads, a couple of years older than me and from the same school set on me and really beat me up. When I arrived home bruised and crying and with a torn shirt my father who was alone in the house was so kind. He washed the blood away and cleaned me up and the following day he met me from school and he asked me to point out the lads who had bullied me and he went to them and told them that if they ever dared to approach me again or hurt any other child they would have him to deal with. He didn't report them he just calmly and quietly stood his ground with them. He must have loved me in his own way'.

'Perhaps he just didn't love himself very much,' Elspeth said.

'I can't get out of my mind seeing him that morning lying dead. If only I had not reproached him and been so unforgiving. It makes me reproach myself.'

She didn't attempt to commiserate or say his reaction was understandable but she went to him and told him how much she loved him. He gathered her to himself then and said that she was the best thing that had ever happened to him.

'And now we have a new life on the way and new beginnings ahead of us!'

'Yes! New beginnings! he replied.

Chapter 15

....

*"How much I must criticise you, my church and
yet how much I love you!*

*I should like to see you destroyed and yet I need your presence.
You have given me so much scandal and yet you alone have
made me understand holiness.
Never in this world have I seen anything more compromised,
more false, and yet I have never touched anything purer,
more generous or more beautiful.
Countless times I have felt like slamming the door
of my soul in your face - and yet, every night,
I have prayed that I might die in your sure arms!
No, I cannot be free of you -"*
(Taken from the ode written by the renowned spiritual writer
Carlo Caretto in his old age)

They approached the old house as the late August sunlight shone on its solid grey stone, softening its outline. So it had stood for over a century welcoming members of the Penrose family and the earlier families that had lived and loved and died there. So many lives, so many secrets and now it had been prepared for this new chapter.

Elspeth's parents had wasted no time in making sure everything was ready for them. Elsie's friend's daughter had been employed in getting the place to rights and had agreed to take over from Elsie who was now needed by her parents who had already moved out. The furnishings of the house, always elegant were showing the signs of age but while they gave the appearance of being lived in their familiarity was loved and added to Elspeth's peaceful sense of homecoming.

After an evening meal together her parents left assuring them that they would be more than happy to be called on if they were needed but recognising that the young couple now needed to rest and to settle into their new situation. Her father had brought her and Jamie's old cot down from the attic and it had been carefully cleaned and a new mattress, sheets and covers had been added and very soon Gian was carefully laid down to sleep. The moment he was silent Elspeth took Anton's hand and together they went from room to room while she re familiarised herself with her old home and pointed out the things she loved.

'We are so fortunate, so privileged, the house is so big!' Anton was saying, 'we will need to have lots of children!'

'And hopefully we will, but just one at a time, if you don't mind', and Elspeth laughed, and then grew serious, 'The first thing I want to do is ask the priest to come and bless the house. It's old and seen the births and deaths of so many family members'.

She didn't mention the violation she had suffered and she had never told Anton just where it had taken place but Nan's mention of it had brought it forcefully once again into her mind and she wanted it exorcised from the house. She wanted a blessing too for the peaceful spirits of her loved ones that pervaded this place that was now her new family's home.

And so the following weeks went by in a hive of activity, there was so much to do and things that had to be bought before Anton's term began. Her mother had taken the grand piano with them and Anton needed one for his work and Elspeth reasoned that they both required new cars and she noticed that Anton looked disturbed and finally he questioned the spending of so much money.

'Do we really need the best of everything? Shouldn't we be able to manage on so much less?'

'I didn't spend anything from the capital of the investments Gran left me while I lived in Rome, I only spent the rent from the flats and the interest has grown so we can manage very well.'

'I suppose I feel guilty; we have so much.'

'We need to be wise but the money is there and there are things we need. Believe me I understand your misgivings. I have gone over in my mind so many times: what IF my brother had not died that summer and the frightful event that followed had not taken place, I tell myself that I would in all likelihood have taken up the place in Oxford and mingled with other privileged students and I may well have remained ignorant and aloof about, 'how the other half live', as my friend Louise put it. And IF Gran had not left me her estate I would probably have stayed teaching in England and we would never have met. 'IF' is a very small word adding just one small letter to 'I' and both these words encompass so much of our lives. So IF I use the means at my disposal I tell myself, for good purposes, perhaps I should not have to feel guilty. What do you think? You mustn't think I have never considered these things or that I lack a conscience'.

'It's true and it makes one think about the means by which we arrive at particular places in our lives. IF my father had not committed the crime he did I would probably be living in Sicily if I had been born at all. I suppose we just have to try to do the best – morally speaking – in the situation that we are born into or find ourselves in'.

'I suppose that we always have to ask these questions to prevent ourselves from becoming complacent or indifferent to the needs of others.' And so they reasoned.

II

When time allowed during the September weeks Elspeth took Gian into the garden and began planting bulbs for the Spring. Her little boy looked on and handed the bulbs to her until he grew bored and began pulling up the plants near him and then she stopped and played ball with him and when Anton was around he joined in. She left him with his father while she planted a herb garden which the garden lacked and sometimes when the child was asleep and she was alone she sat under the Silver Birch tree as she had as a child and as she had sat beneath the Oak tree at school and dreamed dreams about the future.

Then unexpectedly she felt unwell and found herself threatened with a miscarriage. Gian's birth had been difficult but the pregnancy had been easy and straightforward now she found her legs visibly trembling as they had during her last labour and she felt unaccountably weak and exhausted. Anton told her she was doing too much and insisted that she rest and her mother came of an afternoon and looked after Gian though usually he slept too. When the hospital sent for Anton and took blood tests and told him that he was passing antibodies into her blood she felt her worst fears were being realised although the hospital did not seem to be unduly alarmed. She confided in Belle who told her not to worry and said Alistair knew something about the transmission of blood and it probably just meant that her blood was negative or something and that the doctors could deal with it, but it was inevitable that she thought about Jamie and she asked her mother about her pregnancy and labour with her brother. Her mother said everything had been perfectly normal and they had not realised there was anything wrong at the time but on looking back Jamie had had some difficulties from the very beginning.

She still had two months of her pregnancy to go and she tried to keep her anxiety to herself. Anton was working hard and remained enthusiastic about the college and much to his surprise he was becoming very popular with the students. 'The female students are falling for your Latin looks', Elspeth joked and she was happy for him as she noticed the harassed expression that had become habitual with him, while he taught in Rome, beginning to disappear.

The labour despite her anxiety was finally over and had been reasonably easy, she had been more concerned about the baby than she had been for herself. As she looked down at the tiny child lying in a cot at her side she was filled with wonder and was to say afterwards that he had looked up at her with an expression that seemed to say that he already knew the world he had entered and was content. He was to wear a look of calm serenity all his life, the future might well produce difficulties for him and sadness but it did not alter the look of calm and his appearance of serenity deepened with the years. He would always remain the child she felt closest to and he brought a sense of tranquillity with him into the home. He was self-contained and the most original of her children and she considered him a blessing as she thought back on her anxieties for him prior to his birth. They named him Joseph and he soon became 'Joey' to family and friends but to Elspeth he was always Joseph, she felt the name was perfect for him and she would not shorten it.

III

Elspeth's life slowly settled into its old furrows and her old friendships were soon resurrected. Belle was by this time the proud mother of a second son, David and a baby girl, Susan, and the two friends and their children were often together. Meg's two daughters frequently joined them so the children had plenty of readymade playmates. Chloe, the youngest Honeyman daughter, had surprised the family by recently marrying a titled young man, Christopher, heir to an Estate in the Scottish Borders. His main interest lay in breeding race horses which particularly appealed to Belle and Alistair but the title clearly perplexed Mr Honeyman when he spoke to Elspeth about his youngest daughter's new husband.

'I'm a simple grocer by trade Elspeth, it's really all I've ever been. I'm not in his family's league. If it had been you it would have been understandable given your background. Still he's a nice enough young man, and he clearly loves Chloe and I suppose he meets up with folks from all walks of life in horse racing events', this last comment was stated by way of an explanation.

When Elspeth and Anton met up with Christopher a few weeks later they liked him immediately, he was open and pleasant and fun loving and his eyes followed his young wife round the room. Chloe still had the same dreamy expression, her light fair hair was still long and she wore loose dresses that she had designed herself. She seemed to glide rather than walk and Elspeth thought she would grace the dinner tables of the rich and famous with ease. Neither she nor her husband were intellectual their conversation on subjects other than horses, avoided any topic that might prove confrontational or which might offend but Elspeth would have been reluctant to describe them as lightweight though she was aware that others might. She considered them incapable of being deliberately unkind, it was a characteristic that typified the Honeyman family as a whole and it was no small virtue in her view.

It was Louise and Jerome that Elspeth hoped Anton would forge a close friendship with and here she was disappointed. Anton liked Louise but remained critical of Jerome from the beginning. Elspeth initially thought it was Jerome's Cambridge Double First but realised she was being unjust. Jerome appeared to totally embrace the changes that had taken place in the Church without questioning. He came from an old English recusant Catholic family a branch of which had escaped to the continent during the long years of persecution and had returned after the French Revolution when the family had again faced danger.

When Elspeth and Anton told Louise and Jerome that they were attending the Latin Mass and that Anton was now singing Gregorian Chant in the choir that Elspeth had been a member of before going to Italy, Jerome had been somewhat disparaging. He seemed to accept Elspeth's adherence to the old Mass since she was a convert and she found herself feeling indignant by what he apparently considered his superior judgement. The Church he stated – quite dogmatically, she thought – had introduced changes for the benefit of all and the new Mass being in the vernacular could be understood by all. He added that they were sending their children to what they considered an excellent Catholic school in the Parish they attended. Elspeth could not be sure what Louise made of all this, it had not been the way she had thought when they were students together but she was not, apparently, prepared to offer a point of view that differed from that of her husband and while Elspeth would always remain firm friends with Louise they rarely and for long into the future discussed church matters.

While this exchange was taking place she observed Jerome. She had never considered him arrogant or paternalistic but Elspeth recognised a slightly bemused expression that would seem to refute any possibility that his reasoning could be questioned, it was an unspoken assumption but nevertheless clear and she sensed Anton's anger and she squeezed his hand in an effort to show solidarity with him. When he responded he was calm but he spoke coldly saying that, despite the upheavals in Italy throughout the centuries, his family had remained faithful Catholics from time immemorial and that he considered many of the changes in the modern church to be indeed 'modernist' and the new Mass to be unacceptable. He added that the Second Vatican Council documents had not rejected Latin or Gregorian Chant, indeed all the opposite, and the changes in the Church were heading for division in its unity. He added that as for sending his children to a modern English Catholic school or allowing them to attend the Modern Mass, he would not allow it adding that his wife was a born teacher and an excellent Catholic and they would be educating their children at home during their early years.

So it was at around this time that Elspeth began to consider for herself the very real dangers inherent in Liberalism and indeed in Democracy with its proneness to elitism and individualism and the assumption of liberal democrats that they were obviously and almost unquestionably 'right'. There was she thought 'Authoritarianism' but also 'Inverted Authoritarianism' and the latter, she began to consider, was as dominant, overpowering and unpleasant as inverted snobbery. Anton might fit into the former category while Jerome into the latter. Where she stood in all this she was not altogether sure, somewhere in the middle she surmised. She would have liked to discuss the whole matter with Father Dominic as she still corresponded with him and she had long sensed he was unhappy about the changes taking place for although he had never spoken directly about them he had entered a monastery of a contemplative order in France, explaining only that this had long been a desire of his and as his mother had been French and as he loved France this seemed the obvious place for him to be. At Christmas during their stay in Rome she discussed the situation with Irena and was happy to find that her older friend also had misgivings about the modern church. Elspeth learned that the 'family Cardinal' was not Irena's brother but a cousin of her mother's aunt who had died of old age soon after the end of the Council and who had expressed his grave doubts about many aspects of it. Irena said that she had several friends who attended the old Mass which she herself considered beautiful and timeless.

'The Church is not a Democracy – that's the problem for Western political thinkers – the Church is based on the absolute authority of Christ and sadly there is an attempt in the Western church to politicise religion to the detriment of its spiritual mission but where there are people there will always be contradictions,' Irena said and Elspeth felt reassured.

IV

Elspeth had remained a close friend of Louise's sister Ann who had visited them while they lived in Rome. She had become a friend of Maria Rosa and she had joined the yearly pilgrimage to Lourdes. Elspeth also sent Christmas and greeting cards each year to Louise's parents so that the following summer, Louise invited them to join a family celebration. Her parents had recently celebrated a special wedding anniversary and following a party at home in the Northeast they had been invited to continue their celebration at an event put on by Louise. Ann was joining her parents and Louise informed Elspeth that Callum was also going to be present as he was home for three months.

'We haven't seen him for years, he's working as a priest in Brazil now and this celebration I'm planning will serve a dual purpose. You must come and with the children, of course, my mother always talks well of you and she will love meeting Anton. We always look forward to your visits and Gian and Seb being the same age will hopefully become good friends.'

So on a glorious summer's day in late June, Elspeth and Anton with the two children, joined the family gathering in the Cotswolds. There were tables set out in the garden and while the three eldest children played – Joseph was, by this time, some sixteen months old and too young to join in the games of the older children – the adults found themselves drawn into small groups of their own. Anton was soon engaged in an animated conversation with Mr Donoghue and appeared at ease. Perhaps the two felt themselves 'outsiders' in this very English middle class setting. Elspeth sensed that Louise's father was not altogether at ease with his son-in-law who was himself at this moment engaged in conversation with Callum. She, herself, had joined Jerome's parents and unmarried sister, Angela, and Mrs Donoghue and Ann had drifted into the small group too. Louise was in and out of the kitchen. It was a peaceful scene, but after a while Joseph began feeling restless and Elspeth taking his little hand began a short walk around the garden with him. She was pointing out the 'pretty' flowers to him when Callum joined them.

'It's good to see you Elspeth, I wanted to snatch a moment or two with you, I just wanted to say, 'thank you'.

'Thank you for what?'

'For keeping my confidence. For not betraying even with a look the last short sad encounter. This is the 'happier situation', I hoped for. You helped me make up my mind and I have found a fulfilling position in Brazil. It's very hard work and the scale of poverty is huge but I feel I can dedicate myself to my priesthood more completely than I did with all my academic learning'.

'I'm glad – and Sophia – what has happened to her, have you heard?'

'She married eighteen months ago, an architect, a fellow she has known since she was very young. When I heard I felt a pang of pain I admit, it was almost instinctive and impossible to dismiss, but it passed more quickly than I stubbornly wished to own and I'm very happy for her. She deserves to be happy and that would have been impossible with me. And this little fellow is Joseph? Son number two.'

She had shared a short and deep confidence with him that none of his family shared, so it is, she thought, that hearts and souls are bound across continents.

Suddenly there was loud crying and Anton dashed up. 'Gian has fallen and hurt himself and he wants you', he said and took charge of Joseph while Elspeth rushed off to deal with her eldest child's mishap.

Louise was already in the kitchen with the three children and reaching up to the cupboard for the 'The First Aid Box' and seven-year old Ellie had taken charge.

'Mummy keeps the First Aid Box in the cupboard, you'll need some antiseptic on your cut'

Louise handed Elspeth some cotton wool and a bottle of antiseptic- Gian's little lip was trembling but he had stopped crying when his mother arrived and kissed him.

'It will probably sting so you'll have to be brave,' said Ellie giving a running commentary, 'it won't need stitches it's just a bad graze but I expect you can have a plaster on your knee', this was spoken with a sense of awe as if he was receiving a badge of honour, 'I expect mummy has some sweeties for us'. Louise gave Elspeth a grin and went to look for some sweets. All the time Seb looked on silently. He was a dark haired child with large eyes which held a soulful expression. He rarely smiled and Elspeth thought there was something tragic about the little boy and she longed to pick him up and give him a hug.

'I want to show Papi my knee and plaster,' said Gian and off he went looking like a little wounded soldier with Ellie and Seb trailing across the grass behind him.

Elspeth was not particularly demonstrative but Anton showered his children with caresses. He would lift them onto his shoulders then lift them high above his head, he would get down on the floor with them and let them climb on his back. They had recently bought the children some percussion instruments and even little Joseph sat shaking a tambourine with a face wreathed in laughter. Anton had a natural rapport with children and while he could be stern about poor behaviour he was gentle and the children adored him. At this moment he was picking Gian up and hugging him. He was still quick tempered and he passed over her questions without giving them due thought, he was not intellectual in the way she was, but she recognised that their home with their children was happy and there was plenty of laughter.

She turned to Louise, 'your parents look well and very happy, has your father retired?'

'Not for another four years. They have a right to be happy, they've done well, all their children are more or less independent now. Catherine will be married in the Spring, she's a lecturer and the two youngest boys have finished university and medical school, one is a lawyer and the other is a doctor and thankfully Maeve has finally settled down. She'll always be Maeve, of course, but now with a second baby daughter and happily married she is a good mother. She and her husband's sister have opened a hairdressing and beauty parlour together. She completed a hairdressing course while she was pregnant and she also helps out at an Irish dancing class where Marieanne, her eldest, is learning to dance. So yes, I think my parents have a right to feel proud and it's good to see them having some time to themselves.'

Maeve had married a teacher, Seamus, from the school in Dublin where Louise's brother-in-law Tom taught.

The afternoon slowly wore on, the children began to tire and after everyone had thanked their hosts and commented about their good fortune in having such lovely weather and such a beautiful garden to enjoy the day in, it was time to return home.

'If you find yourselves in the Northeast you must visit, you will always be welcome', Mrs Donoghue assured Elspeth and Mr Donoghue readily agreed.

242

'We would be more than happy for you to visit us too,' replied Elspeth, 'Ann has promised us a visit during the autumn half-term'.

V

The two children were soon fast asleep as they made their journey home Elspeth asked Anton how he had enjoyed the day.

'You seemed to get on very well with Louise's father.'

'He's a good man, a man after my own heart, I like Callum too, I think he's a fine and very dedicated priest, I admire him. Pity about the son-in-law!'

'You still don't like him but I think it is a pity you didn't meet him in Lourdes, he was very kind to the sick and they loved him'.

'English Public Schoolboy, Oxbridge scholar living in his own little private paradise!'

'That's a bit harsh!' Elspeth retorted, though it had been said without either bitterness or envy.

'Perhaps'.

'My father went to an English Public School'.

'Your father's a man not an overgrown schoolboy'.

'I went to a Girls' Public School and I dare say folks would consider that I am living in a sheltered little paradise'.

'Not if they were to get to know you. You're not insulated from the world, you go out – I don't know – mentally I suppose. You seek to understand people and consider where they came from and why they end up the way they do. You could have married anyone and you married me.'

I didn't want to marry 'anyone', I married you because I love you.'

'And I know I'm the luckiest man on earth and how far I am from deserving you!'

His compliment made up for his sudden outbursts of temper and occasional bad moods. She never doubted that he loved her. 'I happen to think that I am very fortunate to have met and married you and that the children are very, very fortunate to have the father they have'.

Chapter 16

....

"When I consider everything that grows
Holds in perfection just a little moment."
(Sonnet XV Shakespeare)

Gian was five years old and Joseph three when Michael was born. The birth had been straightforward but the baby had to be in an incubator for almost a fortnight to clear the antibodies passed into his blood. Nobody in the hospital explained the cause, and all Elspeth was told was that any further baby would require a complete blood change at birth. She thought that perhaps less than a hundred years ago her baby would have died or been severely handicapped and she thanked God for the medical advances that had allowed for her healthy baby because by the time she left the hospital with him he was the picture of health. He was a sturdy, beautiful, handsome looking child with an abundance of dark curls and it was inevitable for Anton to compare him with what he knew about his father. Michael from the beginning was a sunny natured child and although he attracted attention he remained unspoiled and happy. He was the most uncomplicated of the children, generous and loving and Elspeth thought it was his father that he most resembled not his grandfather. The child adored Anton from the beginning and his father doted on him and as Michael grew he adored his brothers in equal measure and it was impossible not to respond to his all-embracing affection, he was soon the centre of the home.

Michael was born five months after Nan's death and Elspeth while she was sad did not mourn, her grandmother was very old and Great Aunt May had died twelve months before her sister and Nan had never really recovered from her death. It was the slow passing of a generation Elspeth thought and when people lived to be very old the personal memories of lives shared ceased to have the same significance for others and more often than not remained unspoken while the young were intent on building up their own store of memories. On the day of her funeral the mountains were covered in snow, the sky was a cloudless blue and the sun glistened on the mountains like thousands of diamonds glorious and serene. Nan had told Elspeth that she was 'her soul's child' and Elspeth felt that Nan was an inner part of her being, a gentle, peaceful presence that would always remain with her and which death was incapable of erasing.

II

With three young children, Elspeth's life was full and busy. She set up a room with small tables and set about teaching her children herself. Her parents were proving to be much better at being grandparents than they had ever been as parents and while her mother introduced them to piano lessons her father was more than happy to take the children for walks in the nearby park.

The years sped past and two years after Michael's birth a longed-for daughter was born. It was an anxious time facing the feared blood change but it proved to be a straightforward procedure and Anton was overjoyed.

'She's like a little flower,' he said awed as he bent over the cot.

They had considered calling her Emma Rose after her two grandmothers but Anton said that she was unique and he would prefer her to have her own name and they decided on Marie Fleur and so Fleur she became.

These were memory making times and Elspeth wished that some of the memories could be held in the present moment forever. She recaptured with affection Gian reaching up trying to take hold of cherry blossom in the Spring, Joseph shaking his tambourine, Michael's plump little legs running ahead of her with the sun catching his curls and Fleur reaching up to take Anton's shock of hair, that fell across his brow, into her tiny hands. I will keep these images of the children in my mind forever, she thought.

Having no siblings she found that she had plenty of offers of help. Ann Donoghue, Louise and Jerome were godparents to Joseph, which helped to keep their friendship intact, Johannes and Helen were godparents to Michael and Belle and Alistair were delighted to be asked to be godparents to Fleur. Johannes and Helen played a very full part in all their children's lives, being denied children of their own, and were more than happy to make themselves available. Johannes had recently published a book and Anton had obtained it the moment it was off the press and studied it avidly. Johannes was the only person he debated or shared ideas with.

'The English are reluctant to talk about religion and politics, they regard the two subjects as private and personal and to be avoided in polite society! They are, of course, the most interesting of subjects and infinitely more enlightening than the weather!' Johannes said.

Neither of them attempted to convert the other, however, and since each respected the other's allegiance to their respective Churches the friendship flourished.

'I'm Catholic born and bred,' Anton told Elspeth, 'but the Orthodox Liturgy is very beautiful and most Orthodox beliefs are my own anyway.'

Elspeth was relieved that the move to England had been such a resounding success knowing that this was in no small way due to Anton's friendship with Johannes. He was happy teaching at the college and worked hard. He built up a choir of students and each year collaborated with the English and Drama Departments in putting on a Musical. These were so successful that they were advertised in the Local Press and proved to be very popular. When Elspeth could engage her parents in looking after the children of an evening she helped in the final rehearsals and grew to know his colleagues; she was determined that a similar situation that had occurred in Rome was not repeated here in England.

Anton she recognised, was above anything else, a family man. His home, his wife and his children took priority over everything except his religion and she knew that he needed her and as the years passed she recognised how dependent she in turn was on him. She still raised objections to his easy dismissal of people he did not like, he was critical of Jerome particularly which annoyed her. After one visit to her friends he was irritated by Jerome's treatment of his young son, Seb, and on reaching home and when the children were out of earshot he expressed his annoyance.

'He has no idea how to treat his son, there he is giving lengthy explanations when a simple directive is all that is required!'

'He's trying to make him understand, I can't see what's wrong with that,' she retorted angrily.

'He confuses the child! The boy's intelligent and reasonable and will work out things for himself left alone. You tell your children to keep away from a fire and you expect them to obey, there's no requirement for a narrative, they will gather why by themselves and as adults we should make sure that the fire is out of reach anyway. It's the same with a good many things, you don't tell very young children that by practising scales on the piano they may one day be able to play piano concertos or by learning their times tables they may one day become Mathematicians. Most young children practise these things happily enough because they wish to please their teachers or parents. I didn't understand most of the Catechism when we had to learn it off by heart as young-sters, but it makes sense now', he was irritated and expected her to agree but she refused.

'There are some things you have to explain to children. You are far too hard on Jerome, he's a caring and loving father, you just don't like him'.

I don't actually dislike him I just don't think he knows how to treat his son, Ellie and Siobhan (Siobhan, Louise and Jerome's youngest child had been born when Ellie was ten years old), don't present a problem, Louise manages them and Ellie seems to manage them all, her mother included, but Seb is a sad little boy, I don't see how you don't see it,' Anton said.

Elspeth sighed, she did see it, she had a sadness within herself, the uninvited guest at the table of her soul, she silently thought, and it was this very sadness within her that wanted to reach out to Louise's young son. He was a quiet child who seemed to be-come animated when he was with her sons and her family. He was a particular friend of Gian's and eventually of Joseph's and she made a point of inviting him over for weekends.

Her own father, who had never been very keen on football was passionate about cricket and had played in a team when he was in the RAF, he had a season's ticket at Lords and he had put a bat in his grandsons' hands as soon as they were able to hold one. One weekend when Seb was staying with them he was encour-aged to play along with them and her father was full of praise for their young friend's ability.

'With practise young Seb will end up playing for his County!'

Elspeth stood by delighted to see the boy's face light up.

'Has your father been coaching you?' her father asked.

'My father doesn't like sport', replied Seb.

'Well you get him interested young man. Make him proud.'

III

When Gian reached eleven years they found him a place in a lo-cal Independent School. Anton remained adamant that the chil-dren would receive their religious teaching at home and at the Traditional Church they attended. Gian and Joseph were already altar boys and served the Mass most Sunday mornings and Holy Days. Each evening at home they said the Rosary together as a family. When a disagreement had taken place between Anton and Elspeth and they remained quiet with each other in the chil-dren's presence Gian would call attention to it.

'We squabble and have fights and we are expected to make up and get over it why don't grown-ups do the same? Why are you two not speaking to each other? it's a bad example!'

Invariably they were forced to laugh at each other and by the time of the evening Rosary they could all put the difficulties of the day where they belonged, behind them. Anton criticised the Modern Church for laying the Traditional Sacramentals along with Religious Processions aside saying that the 'modernists' no longer paid atten-tion to them and at a cost, 'they think such traditions are for peas-ants and illiterates – they believe they are intellectually superior but throughout the history of the church it has been the unsophisticat-ed pilgrims who have remained faithful and carried the Faith on'.

Elspeth, for her part, was only too glad that she had never al-lowed any feelings of resentment to linger and fester and when they were alone after a serious disagreement, Anton was usual-ly quick to gather her to himself and kiss into her hair and they would whisper their own secret language of love to each other and she thought that despite her private misgivings at the beginning of their marriage it had proved a success. Father Dominic had said that forgiveness gave greater blessings to the one forgiving than the one needing forgiveness and she had learnt too that she was frequently at fault herself and if she was slow to acknowledge the fact the children as they grew older were more than happy to enlighten her. Nan too had been right and had undoubtedly faced up to very similar situations in her marriage that could so easily have failed because she had told Elspeth that she and Grandda had come from very different walks of life. If there is love and good intentions between a couple, she had said, then difficulties can be sorted out. And Elspeth found herself feeling a deep sympathy for couples where one or the other presented problems that were impossible to accept and continue living with. She and Anton she thought were among the fortunate ones, she had parents and grandparents that had enjoyed good marriages and the strength it had given her had allowed her to reach out to Anton so that his own unhappy childhood did not cause him to destroy his children's lives, all the opposite, his children's happiness was his chief concern and he could not do enough for them. Over and over again over the years he told her how fortunate he had been that she had married him jokingly adding now and again, 'you got a decent bargain in return mind you'.

IV

Gian was enjoying school and Joseph was about to join him in the Autumn term and Elspeth told Anton that she would like Fleur to go to Oaklands school once Michael was ready to join his brothers, 'I shouldn't want her to be alone at home, she's a sociable little girl and I think she would love Oaklands as I did', and Anton who was never prepared to deny his only daughter anything readily agreed.

Fleur was Anton's greatest delight, the little girl was the only one of their children who had inherited Elspeth's mother's musical ability. Unlike herself growing up, Fleur was happy to spend time in the kitchen especially if she could help her father prepare a meal. Helen Manasses, Elspeth learnt to her surprise, could sew and knit and was more than eager to pass on her skills to Fleur and Anton was overjoyed, 'She's just like my mother! She could turn her hand to anything! You'll see, mind my words, she'll make us proud.'

The children were growing up fast and making suggestions already about what they wished to be when they left school. Elspeth heart dropped one day when Gian arrived home after being with her father, saying, 'I know what I've decided to be when I grow up', and knowing how much her son admired his Grandfather she thought he's been talking about the RAF but she could not have been more mistaken. 'I'm going to be a doctor. Grandpa's brother James was a doctor and Grandpa says he was the best person in the world and the person he admired most, so I've decided that's what I will be, a doctor'.

It was her father who made a telling comment about Joseph too. One weekend he took the boys to visit an Aerodrome and he told them that Joseph was very much more interested in the design and mechanics of the aircraft than he appeared to be about flying an aeroplane. 'I think the boy will make a designer or engineer,' he said.

V

Elspeth was to look back on the years of her children's childhoods and their shared family life and wonder if she was telescoping her memories and viewing them through rose coloured spectacles, things were surely more problematic at times than she remembered or was prepared to admit and she thought often of that last glorious summer, the summer of Gian's fourteenth year.

Louise asked Anton and Elspeth if they would like to join them in a holiday on the coast in Wales and Elspeth agreed immediately without thinking it through sufficiently, the children were clearly in agreement and she gave her consent without taking Anton's feelings into account.

When they arrived home Anton was furious, 'A week! a weekend once in a while or an afternoon now and again, but a week! Jerome and myself have very little in common and a week will seem like eternity and under the same roof!'

'It's a very short time and the children are enthusiastic', she replied, feeling for the first time doubtful.

'Well I'm not and neither am I happy that you make arrangements over my head. I'd be much happier going on holiday with Belle and her family, their children and ours get on very well'.

'Belle and family are going to her sister Chloe's for a month. They and their kids are all mad on horses and will no doubt be spending their days riding and mucking out the stables. You would really enjoy that!'

As things turned out Anton was given a good reason for not joining them, the wife of one of his cousins in Spain was terminally ill and died a few days before they were due to leave for Wales and he set off for the funeral. Elspeth felt a sense of silent relief, it would give her time to be alone with her old friend and she liked Jerome sufficiently well to spend a week's holiday under the same roof that being the arrangement. They had rented a huge holiday villa with enough space to accommodate them all in comfort and she was looking forward to it.

One afternoon, a day or two into the holiday, Elspeth and Louise climbed an embankment overlooking the beach. Jerome was contentedly building sand castles with the two little girls on the beach below and the four boys were nearer the water's edge, where the sand's surface was firmer, playing cricket with yellow plastic bats and stumps. Ellie now sixteen was sitting by herself reading. The year before she had been happy enough to join in the boy's games, but she was now feeling herself grown up and was looking with painful disdain at their boyish immaturity. Elspeth sensed that Ellie wasn't particularly pleased either with a holiday planned above her head, she was an adolescent and wanted friends of her own age.

Once they were seated Louise, as of old, opened the conversation, 'Did you ever imagine how our lives would turn out? Here we are approaching middle age, you with your boys and daughter and me with my three. I always thought I would have lots of children like my parents but it hasn't turned out that way'.

'I don't remember thinking of children of my own at all, there was a time when I thought I might end up an old school marm', Elspeth replied.

'That was never going to be the case! I remember saying to you before you went off to Italy that you would meet the love of your life and you did. The grand passion, Elspeth, you were born for it'.

'Elspeth laughed, 'The grand passion, one in body and spirit if not always in mind, even our disagreements tend to be passionate!'

'But you're both very obviously happy!'

'We are, I can truly say I am married to the love of my life, and you too, I believe'.

'We are content certainly', her friend replied, rather too hastily.

Elspeth sensed a certain lacklustre in her friend's response and looked quickly at her and then quickly away.

'We worry about Seb', Louise confided, 'he's a loner, he looks more animated these last two days than we've seen him for weeks. It's the main reason I wanted this holiday, he always comes home happy after staying with your boys. Perhaps if he had had a brother, things may have been different. Jerome got him to join a cricket club for youngsters y'know, after your father praised him, but it didn't last.'

'Doesn't he get on well with Ellie?' Elspeth asked.

'They've never been close. Ellie loves to organise him – to organise everybody really – and he resents it, he shows a lot of affection for Siobhan and is happy to play with her.'

'What does his school say? He's bright I think'.

'He's very bright and academically capable but he's very quiet at school and he doesn't make much effort. He's talented at Art his teacher says and that would seem to be why he appears to get on with Joseph. I just wish he was more open with his father and myself.'

'Youngsters change as you know better than most. Let him get through adolescence. Changing the subject, what is Ellie planning to do after school?'

'She should make it to Oxbridge, her teachers are very confident. She's keen to study modern history but it's her management and organisation skills that are her chief forte. She's marvellous in the house and she was great when Siobhan was born, she changed her and helped with feeding her as a baby, Siobhan must have wondered which one of us was her mother. I can imagine her joining an international Charity like Cafod.'

'She sounds like my Aunt Elspeth,' Elspeth said.

'Your aunt in Switzerland?'

'Yes, my father's sister. She manages and organises the whole family and works hard in her local church too on committees and things. We get on very well in nowadays but like young Seb I resented her when I was growing up, she considered me an impractical dreamer. The relationship between Ellie and Seb will no doubt resolve itself in a similar way.'

'I hope you are right! What happened to your cousin by the way, the one who wanted to become a journalist, did she?'

'Jackie? Well there's a turn up for the books if ever there was one! Perhaps what she absorbed from her Salvation Army upbringing proved stronger than a tabloid salacious scandal. The year after she graduated she met and fell in love with a young man entering Holy Orders they married and have five children. He graduated from Oxford and is rapidly scaling the Ecclesiastical ladder, there may well be a Bishopric on the horizon. The only writing Jackie involves herself with nowadays is Church and Diocesan news. I often ask myself what Gran would have made of it all! Folks always have a habit of surprising us. What about Maeve and her five children, does she and her sister-in-law still have the hairdressing salon?

'Yes, she has endless energy. They now have three assistants, all with young children and they all work on a part-time basis. Maeve, I may say, keeps her own children on a tight rein! We'll be off to Dublin in a week or two, my parents are already there. Ellie is joining Ann on her annual pilgrimage to Lourdes'.

'I remember Ellie went last year – she impressed Maria Rosa. We're joining my parents in Switzerland, Anton is going straight there from Madrid. If the weather is favourable we'll be spending most of the time outdoors with mountain walks a plenty.'

The afternoon conversation left Elspeth feeling inwardly dejected, for although her friend chatted openly she sensed a listlessness that was new to her character. She was as always neat but her hair was already greying and she wore it in a tight bun that did nothing to enhance her looks. The lively, intelligent expression which had been her most attractive feature was gone, her skirt and blouse were drab. She and Belle, Elspeth thought, were the same age as Louise and they both still felt young! We are only thirty-eight for goodness sake, we're not middle-aged yet! I still love beautiful clothes and Anton encourages me to buy them and he notices them and compliments me on at least a weekly basis.

Before calling everybody together to return home, Louise asked Elspeth if she had heard from Father Dominic recently.

'I heard last at Easter, he sounded very tranquil and generally at peace with himself. Why do you ask?'

'Just out of interest, I suppose. Things have changed and not entirely for the better I think. Callum has returned to Rome, I told you he has been unwell. Total exhaustion I believe. He's teaching and back as an academic and is happier with the world of books. What has happened to the world we knew, Elspeth?' Louise sighed and Elspeth left the question unanswered, she was not sure how to respond, it was obvious that her friend was not as content as she made out. Perhaps it was just her anxiety about Sebastian and if that was the case she hoped it might resolve itself in time and she would make sure that the young boy was invited home more frequently.

Chapter 17

....

"Lead kindly light amid the encircling gloom
Lead thou me on."
(Cardinal John Henry Newman)

When the two friends met up during the autumn following the holiday in Wales Elspeth was pleased and relieved to see that Louise looked altogether happier. Her hair had been cut and she looked younger.

'I do like your haircut, it suits you!' said Elspeth.

'My sister Maeve's doing. She insisted on taking me along to her salon telling me that I was looking old before my time. She chopped the bun off and got rid of the grey.'

'Good for Maeve.'

'When we returned home Ellie received her GCSE results and gained the highest grades in her school so there was a general rejoicing, she works hard and deserved to do well.

But Elspeth had her own concerns. Superficially things were much the same as always but as the autumn slowly merged into winter she felt burdened by a sense of foreboding that she could not dispel. She felt glad that they were remaining in England for Christmas she wanted her family safely around her. The week after Christmas they invited Louise's family for lunch and she felt reassured by their presence. Louise had kept up her sister Maeve's good work and looked younger and happier, even Seb looked content and Anton and Jerome chatted amiably. Anton loved these occasions, he made himself responsible for producing the meal and refused Elspeth's offers of help telling her that she had the time off.

'I have been helping Fleur to cook the meal', he said smiling.

'I have been helping you Papi', the little girl looked up at her father laughing and with an expression of perfect trust, her thick, dark curls framing her pretty face. Elspeth caught the image and stored it in her memory of unforgettable memories just as Joseph remarked, 'Michael has been setting the table again, you'll all need to change your knives and forks round he doesn't know his right hand from his left'.

It was true, he was told every week but the fault persisted. It was surprising, Michael was the cleverest of the children and usually practical. He wasn't a dreamer as Joseph tended to be.

Once the meal was over Anton told the four boys to clear the table and they groaned, 'What about the girls, girls like that kind of thing?'

'And which girls are you referring to may I ask?' said Elspeth.

'Fleur for a start and Ellie,' replied Gian.

'That's because they are by nature more responsible,' put in Anton, 'and today they are having the afternoon off. As quickly as you finish the four of you can go and play with the new football game, but make sure you leave the kitchen clean and tidy'.

The boys moved off reluctantly but did not protest any further. Fleur and Siobhan went off happily to play with Fleur's collection of dolls. They were a source of amusement for Elspeth and Anton who had listened in on Fleur's conversation pieces with her dolls since she had been very small; she acted the part of their teacher, – Anton said that he didn't need to go to the classroom Elspeth had set up Fleur copied her mother perfectly – she became the dolls' hospital nurse, their dentist and she took them on shopping excursions.

Ellie got up quietly and went to the kitchen without being asked and just as quietly established some order there before asking if she could go to the 'library' to read.

II

They celebrated New Year with her parents but Elspeth's sense of foreboding persisted. She did not speak of it but as January got underway it got worse, she could not throw it off so that Anton noticed it and he put her mood down to the time of year. 'You usually feel depressed during January darling, it's the weather at this time of year and it's the anniversary of your Gran's funeral'.

'You're probably right'.

'West Side Story' had been chosen for the Musical production and the performance was scheduled for the end of January, 'It will cheer you up, it promises to be a really excellent performance this year,' Anton said and he brought home recordings of the lyrics and they sang them together. It had long been Elspeth's favourite Musical and she looked back with fondness on the occasion at Oaklands when she had taken two young firebrands to see the film.

'I'm going into college this Saturday for rehearsals,' Anton announced the second week into January, 'you've got Belle and the children coming round, they should cheer you up'.

Yes, Dave and Susy are coming with their mother, Jonathan is staying at home helping his father.' Jonathan was now eighteen and on a gap year, he had a place at university lined up, he was planning to be a vet like his father.

The morning of the Saturday arrived and she and Anton serenaded each other with the musical's lyrics during the morning. After a light lunch Anton left for the college saying, 'I shall be dropping into town for some things I need but I hope I'll be home before Belle leaves'. He liked Belle and her family. He blew her a kiss as he went out of the door whistling, 'Make of Our Lives One Life', and she set about getting the tea things ready for her friend's visit.

It had been dark all day. A mist had lifted leaving the atmosphere damp and dismal while the clouds hung grey and heavy. The weather never failed in affecting her mood and she was glad when Belle and her children arrived.

The children made short work of the sandwiches and cakes and once things were cleared away Susan took charge of Fleur. She was much older than the little girl but she was kind and planning to work with young children. The four boys were keen to watch a film on video and Elspeth watched Gian make off with a box of chocolate biscuits under his arm, 'In a few years' time it will be cans of beer and potato crisps!' she said laughing.

Her children and Belle's youngest two had been friends all their lives. It was a carefree, easy-going friendship with none of the tension that existed in their friendship with Sebastian and Elspeth felt herself relax. She prepared a fresh pot of tea for Belle and herself, put the light on in the sitting room and drew the curtains to hide the darkness and was about to sit down when the doorbell rang.

'I wonder who that can be, I wasn't expecting anybody,' said Elspeth moving quickly to answer it and knowing instinctively that something was very wrong. She opened the door and let the night in.

Standing on the doorstep was a young policewoman and a policeman.

'Mrs Spadaro?'.

'Yes. What is it?'.

'May we come in and have a word?'.

Elspeth moved aside to admit them and led them into the sitting room. Belle stood up as they entered and Elspeth motioned for them all to sit down before sitting down herself.

'I'm afraid we have some bad news, Mrs Spadaro,' and Elspeth felt her blood run cold.

'There's been a serious accident and your husband has been very badly injured. A heavy truck swerved and skidded across a road in town. A small girl was in its direct path and would certainly have been killed had not your husband pushed her out of the way. It happened in a split second and unfortunately your husband received the full impact. We are so sorry.'

'Where is he? I must go to him at once.'

'Of course, we are here to take you, he is in the hospital, close to the town.'

Elspeth could hear the children happily laughing as she spoke to Belle, she was surprised at how calm her voice sounded, 'can you ring my parents? – the children!'

'Of course. I'll stay here with the children. I'll take care of everything here.'

Elspeth automatically dragged on a jacket and put on a pair of outside shoes while slipping her house keys from the hall table into her pocket. She could not remember getting into the police car only the journey as the car raced in the gathering darkness across the town. Her mind was reeling, the policewoman had said Anton was badly injured, she had not said that – she refused to acknowledge the worst possibility and she felt reassured as the brilliantly lit hospital came into sight. It stood out she thought, solid and comforting as a lighthouse must appear across dark and dangerous seas guiding seamen into a safe harbour. The police made brief enquiries and she followed them still without speaking as they led her to a corridor and left her with a doctor.

'Do sit down, it's Elspeth I believe', she thought he looked very young but he spoke gently and carefully, 'I'm afraid that you must prepare yourself for very bad news, Anton has been very badly injured, I'm afraid. We have done everything we can but he has sustained serious internal injuries and he is haemorrhaging internally.'

His voice seemed to be coming to her like a foreign language from a great distance. 'Surely you can stop the bleeding, you must be able to do something, you can't let him die'.

'Sadly there's nothing further we can do. We have made him comfortable, he's not in any great pain. He asked for a Catholic priest and the Catholic Chaplain is with him at this moment. He is still conscious and we told him that you had been sent for and he is expecting you.'

The doctor got up and led her to a small side room. The Chaplain spoke to her softly, 'Anton has received the Sacrament of the Church and is very peaceful, should you need me I can be contacted very easily'.

Elspeth approached the bed and sat down and Anton smiled weakly. His face was white and drained of blood and his eyes stood out like dark pools, the unruly shock of hair was falling as always across one side of his forehead.

'I knew you would come, darling. I wanted to explain, the child, a little girl, I had to push her out of the way, she would have been killed. It could have been one of ours and we would have wanted someone to help. It was an instinctive reaction. You understand?'

'Yes! You don't need to explain, my love.' She sounded more certain than she felt.

'I want you to tell the children how much I love them, that my last thoughts were for them.'

Elspeth stifled a sob, she would not cry.

'I am leaving them in the best hands, you are strong, Elspeth. I have loved you more every day, I loved you from the moment I first saw you. When I came across you sitting on the embankment in Lourdes I had not come across you by accident, I never told you, I followed you. I know it was not love at first sight for you darling, I never thought I could ever be good enough for you, and then you loved me back – '

'And we've never wanted to be out of each other's sight for long, ever since', she said, the sadness seeping into her voice.

'It was like a strong current between us. Other people dream and long for such a love that we have shared. I haven't always been as understanding as I should, I'm sorry, mentally I'm a clumsy fellow. I'll love you forever, death won't end my love for you.'

'You have never failed me and there is nothing for you to be sorry for we're passionate people we feel passionately about things and you have made me happier than I ever imagined possible'.

His voice was growing weaker, he seemed to have said what he had wanted to express, he closed his eyes. and she heard him half murmur in Italian, 'Into your hands Lord I commend – the final words were mouthed and his lips moved for the last time. He fell silent and was still.

She thought I should pray but no prayer came instead the words from the Musical went over and over and over again in her head, "There's a place for us, somewhere a place for us – hold my hand and we're almost there, hold my hand and I'll take you there, somehow, someday, somewhere." Was it only this morning that he had sung it to her, this morning now a lifetime away, his lifetime away. She looked at the monitor, he was still alive but had fallen into unconsciousness and she cradled his head in her arms and the lyric just went on over and over again in her head. He had kept himself alive so that he could speak to her for one last time and it had taken an enormous effort. He gasped suddenly and a harsh sound came from his throat and he fell back on the pillow and she saw that the monitor had flat-lined and she sobbed.

A nurse came by and turned off the monitor and established his time of death and went quietly out and left them. She looked at him and saw that his face was peaceful, the stress lines had smoothed, he looked as if he was merely sleeping as Gran had done the morning she had died. She held his hand in hers. Where was he? Somewhere, where? He was next to her and gone from her, she would never hear him speak again. It was impossible she could not believe it.

How long she sat on the side of the bed with him she did not know and could not say afterwards, time had stopped, had ceased to exist. Finally a nurse looked in and said that her parents had arrived. She learnt later that they had not been at home when Belle had first rang them and they had come as soon as they had heard.

'Elspeth!' Her father raised her from the side of the bed and held her, 'oh! we are so, so sorry".

What was there to say? She caught sight of her mother's horrified expression and her father must have indicated to her that she should draw up the sheet and cover Anton's face. When Elspeth drew away from her father she moved to turn the sheet down again and realised the futility of the movement and at the same the finality of Anton's death.

'Your mother will take you home now'.

'I can't just go home. There are things I will need to do here – I can't leave Anton alone'.

'He won't be left alone. I'll take care of everything here. You and your mother will take a taxi and I'll follow later and call in at home and collect things, we'll stay over, you and the children must not be left alone.'

It sounded so prosaic to her, every day and practical and she was reluctant to leave. It was unreal, unbearable, impossible to believe.

'The children will need you at home now Elspeth'.

The children! How was she going to explain to them what had happened! She nodded and without looking back she followed her mother out of the room. The lights had been dimmed for the night, the whole hospital seemed cloaked in a grave silence. The lights of the hospital earlier had been a welcoming relief to her, now she wanted the darkness to cover her pain. What time is it she wondered? It had been late afternoon when she arrived at the hospital, now it appeared to be very late. All the life of the city and the enclosed life of the hospital had gone on as always, in a different time zone unaware and outside of the momentous event that had changed her life forever.

She remembered that her keys were in the pocket of her jacket and she opened the door for them and Belle stood up and moved towards them as they entered the living room, a questioning look on her face that immediately changed as she caught sight of Elspeth's expression.

'No!'

'There was nothing they could do'.

'You look very pale, you'll need something hot to drink, I'll prepare something.'

'Where are the children?' Elspeth asked, her voice a monotone.

'Alistair came by earlier and took ours home. I went up ten minutes or so ago, Fleur is fast asleep but the boys were still awake'.

But the boys had heard their Grandmother and herself arrive and were on their way down the stairs. Elspeth took control of herself in an instant, she had to be calm and she had to be strong for them. When the three children entered the room she asked them to sit down and sitting down herself with them as quietly as she could she explained what had happened placing emphasis on their father's bravery in saving the life of a small child. She told them that their father's last thoughts had been for them and she told them that he was now peaceful and with God. She held them as they sobbed and they wept together. It was her mother that finally made a decision, she said that despite it being late she was ringing the doctor. They were very shocked and the doctor could give them something that would help them sleep, because sleep they must, she refused to listen to Elspeth's protests and Belle told her that she agreed.

So it is, Elspeth was to think later, that life changing events take place against a backdrop of the ordinary and mundane: whatever happens we still eat and drink and sleep. The mechanics of living.

'Belle you must get home,' Elspeth's mother said.

'I'll come back tomorrow morning early and take the children back with me. There will be things to do and it will be best for them to be with their friends', replied Belle and Elspeth wondered what she would do without her.

When the doctor arrived he gave them mild sedatives and told them that they needed to sleep and Elspeth feeling very weary as if she had grown suddenly very old in the space of a few hours followed the children up the stairs to bed.

She fell almost immediately into a troubled disturbed dream. She was in a large building and was searching for something she had lost. The maze of rooms went on and on and at last she came to a police station that closely resembled the photograph Anton had taken of his grandfather's police station in Sicily when he had visited there after his father's death. Standing outside were the policeman and woman who had come that afternoon to take her to the hospital. When she finally awoke it was morning and she turned instinctively and the full realisation of the day before struck her and she recoiled in horror. She realised a moment later that it was Sunday morning and they would normally be rousing the children for church and Anton would be going in to wake Fleur and she would have been hearing him as always saying, 'time to wake up my little rosebud'. The boys never objected to their father's spoiling of their little sister, they also adored her and were careful for her. Elspeth got out of bed quickly saying to herself, I must go to her she doesn't know what has happened.

Fleur stirred as Elspeth sat herself down on the edge of her bed and waited for her to wake up. When she did she had that tousled, sleepy expression of a child just awakened from a dream and she looked at her mother in some surprise recognising something was unusual.

'Where's Papi, is he better, is he coming home today?'

Elspeth helped her out of bed and when she was sitting next to her she put her arms round her small daughter and as gently as possible she explained what had occurred. 'Papi has gone to be with Jesus'. It sounded trite and unconvincing.

'Why does Jesus want him in heaven when we need him here, I want him here'.

Years later when Elspeth spoke to the children about their father's difficult childhood and the part their grandfather had played in his parent's deaths, Joseph asked if their father had forgiven his father and Elspeth had replied in the affirmative saying that it had been very hard but she believed he had and that his father's death had troubled him greatly. If we do not forgive, she added, we allow the past to poison the present and the future. Joseph had replied that perhaps their father's saving a child's life in some way redeemed his father. What, Elspeth thought would the world make of such unworldly reasoning? yet it comforted her. Logic and the world's reasoning counted for nothing when confronted with death and sorrow and the big questions of life. But that Sunday morning as she held her daughter's little body shaking with sobs, she could find no answer to give her.

Belle came as she had promised and took the boys and Elspeth's mother took charge of Fleur and Elspeth began ringing family and friends. It gave her something to do and she listened to their exclamations of shock but she did not cry, it was if the well of tears within her had dried up as they had once before after Jamie's death. Johannes and Helen had heard of their friend's death from the local news and came straight round offering their help and support.

By Monday morning Anton's death had reached the National news and Elspeth caught sight of a Headline stating: "Hero Dies

After Saving Life of Child." There was a photo of Anton that her father had supplied the press with and in the Local Press there was a photograph of herself and Anton with the children that had been taken at Christmas. Elspeth read the account and thought the event it described sounded like something that had happened to someone else.

Belle's two youngest children were back at school and her children were back home and Elspeth allowed her mother and her helper and cleaner to see to them. She was not sure how they occupied themselves during that long painful week but the house was strangely silent and they seemed to be whispering among themselves, afraid of grief and unable to escape it. Her father took all the arrangements in hand, Anton was to be laid in the same grave as Jamie and Elspeth was glad. She contacted the church they attended and arranged for the Traditional Requiem Mass and for refreshments afterwards in a nearby hall. Her father managed to arrange for the funeral to take place on the Friday morning following Anton's death and those of his family who could make the journey began arriving. Aunt Elspeth and Uncle Walter came almost immediately and Elspeth was relieved. Her aunt was, as Nan had said, good in an emergency and, of course, her niece's house was where she had grown up and she helped to take everything in hand. She handled things quietly and without any unnecessary fuss and Elspeth was grateful and her appreciation of her aunt grew.

III

If anybody had asked Elspeth about the funeral afterwards she would have been able to say very little. She remembered that the day was dry and cold with no sun but on this occasion it had fitted her mood. Yet she drew comfort from the ageless words of the Antiphon for the Burial with their grace and dignity: "May

the Angels lead thee into paradise – May the choir of Angels receive thee, and mayst thou have eternal rest with Lazarus, who
once was poor".

She only half heard the short speeches made in the hall set aside
for refreshments. She did, however, listen to the Principal of the
college who spoke of Anton as 'one of our most popular teachers' and one of Anton's students spoke about Anton expressing
his love and admiration for his beautiful wife and children. She
thought back on his experience of his college in Rome and was
thankful that his years in England had been successful and more
than anything else, happy, and in this knowledge, at least, she
could find comfort.

IV

She mentioned to her aunt her plan for visiting Rome after Easter
with the children and her aunt made to question the wisdom of it
but drew back from making any criticism saying only that there
would always be a place for them at her home if and when she
wished to visit. And so immediately after Easter she and the children set off for Rome and their second home there.

Elspeth realised immediately on entering the apartment that it
was a mistake. Anton had been brought up there and his spirit
seemed to pervade every room. He was there in everything and
his absence seemed more intense. It had been here that they had
spent those earliest years of their marriage and she loved the place
and remembered how she had declared it 'perfect' and how she
had not wanted to change a thing and it had, in fact, changed
very little. She was aware that the children felt it intensely as if
their father was at one and the same time present and absent and
their grief overwhelmed them. When Elspeth went to bed that
night she sobbed herself to sleep.

On the second day they visited the restaurant and Cosimo now largely acting as proprietor while his eldest son managed most of the work, greeted them with tears in his eyes. 'I remember him as a youngster', he said, 'he was like my son.' He sat them all down and he himself prepared them a meal. They visited Anton's cousins and most importantly, Maria Rosa who spoke to Elspeth out of earshot of the children.

'I expressed my reservations to you before your marriage, Elspeth, but I was proved very wrong. You made my cousin very happy. He loved you and the children and together you made a wonderful family and that will never be lost. I have such lovely memories of your two years working here at the school, and of Anton coming to make music with the children, he was like my brother.'

They were invited during their stay to Irena's home and after lunch they walked to a park close by and the two friends talked while the children occupied themselves in a somewhat desultory fashion close by.

'It was a mistake our coming, the children are distraught, they don't complain but I feel it. At home in England there are my parents and friends around. I'm thinking to take return tickets,' said Elspeth.

'It was too soon for you to come. It will take time,' Irena replied. 'You have said that you have arranged for Michael and Fleur to begin school when you get back and Gian and Joseph are already at school. I think it is wise. They need to be out of the house and to make friends and you too, dear, need to take up the reins of life again for the sake of the children to begin with and then for your own sake. You have always told me about your love of teaching, perhaps you should consider returning to Oakland School where you were so happy.'

'No, I don't want to go back there, it would be like living in the past. Miss Cresswell, the Headteacher, has retired. My friend Helen who I've spoken to you about is still teaching there and as I have arranged for Fleur to begin school there in three weeks' time Helen will keep a lookout for her but I want Fleur to begin to stand on her own feet and to be completely free. I think my being in the background might prove an obstacle to that'.

V

Returning to the apartment Elspeth told the children that she thought it might be better to return home earlier than they had planned and she sensed a general sense of relief. They helped her to cover the furniture again with sheets but before they left she went quietly to the drawer that held the small baby garments that Anton's mother had made and which he was always so proud of. They were lying there carefully wrapped in tissue paper and she gathered them up thinking 'I'll have them vacuum packed when I get home'. Sentimentality or just a refusal to let go? She didn't care. Anton had looked after them for years and she was determined to do the same now.

Chapter 18

....

"Out of the depths have I cried Unto thee O Lord.
Lord hear my voice: let thine ears be attentive
to the voice of my supplication."
(Psalm 130 The King James Bible)

Michael had begun school with his brothers at the beginning of the summer term and Elspeth felt a pang of regret as she handed him over to his form teacher. There was, she thought, always something stoical about her youngest son he never complained, he took things in his stride and soldiered on. Fleur's term was not due to begin for another week and Elspeth was glad to have her mother usually on hand giving music lessons and trying to make things as normal as possible.

One morning towards the end of the week she was alone in the house Fleur having taken herself into the garden with the doll she had been given at Christmas and which she refused to be parted from. Elspeth found herself in front of the family photograph of her Great Grandparents in the hall studying it carefully. It had hung there all her life and she considered that she knew it intimately and all the people in it, now she looked at it as if for the first time. The photograph had obviously been taken sometime after the death of her Great Grandparents' youngest daughter, Elspeth, her namesake, because there was only her Great Aunt Ursula with her husband Wilfred and their young children in the photograph along with her Grandfather and Nan and their children when they were very young. Elspeth found herself staring intently at her Great Grandmother's face and her proud, detached expression. Had the old lady always worn that distant sad look and was that the likeness with herself that Louise had recognised all those years before?

Had she always looked so detached or had the look become habitual after her daughter's death? Was she always so distant or had it become her means of protection, a mask to hide her feelings behind? She would never know but she felt she could identify and empathise with the woman in the photograph whose blood flowed in her own veins. Elspeth sighed and moved into the kitchen to prepare lunch for herself and her daughter.

She stopped again suddenly in her tracks as she caught sight of Fleur sitting under the Silver Birch tree much as she had done so herself as a child but she had usually had a book in her hands and had felt happy as far as she could remember. Fleur was sitting silently holding her doll and staring into space, she looked a small, lonely, vulnerable little figure and Elspeth felt a stab of pain. Anton had been the most important person in her little girl's life and she had been the apple of her father's eye. Her trust had been sorely dented and Elspeth wondered if she would ever again regain that look of unparalleled happiness she had witnessed all of her youngest child's life, was it really gone forever? She thought, 'I can't let her be so alone, I can't bear it,' and she hurried out into the garden.

'Would you and dolly like some refreshments before lunch?' she asked.

'It's not just dolly, she has a name, she's Victoria!' Fleur replied affronted.

'Well perhaps you and Victoria might like to come indoors for a fruit drink and a biscuit'.

Fleur stood up and accompanied her mother indoors and the pair of them sat down together at the kitchen table.

'How about the three of us taking an outing and getting lunch somewhere in town?'

The little girl's face brightened.

'Perhaps when we've eaten we can go and look for a dress for you to wear at
Siobhan's birthday party. It will be her birthday in a fortnight.'

She watched Fleur's expression cloud over. 'I don't think Siobhan wants to be my best friend anymore.'

'Why not? You never said.'

'Siobhan doesn't like dolls, she says they are childish and we are too big to be playing with them'.

'Did she indeed! Well I don't agree and neither does Susy, she enjoys playing with you and with dolls and she's much older than Siobhan.'

'Susy makes up plays and she's good with different voices,' and Fleur laughed.

'What does Siobhan like playing with?' asked Elspeth.

'She quite likes animals, she is going to get a puppy for her birthday'.

'Would you like a puppy do you think?'

At the moment Elspeth thought that she would be happy to give her little girl the moon if she requested it or if it made her happy. She watched Fleur consider the possibility.

'No, I don't think so. I couldn't take a puppy to school. The dolls won't mind being left at home while I'm away from them but a puppy might. I suppose we could have a hamster or a rabbit, for all of us, I mean. Susy has a hamster and rabbits.'

Elspeth thought back on Susy's mother Belle and her small menagerie of animals and smiled. We'll talk to your brothers about it.

II

The days following Fleur's first months at school were long and wretchedly unhappy and Elspeth thought about the summer holidays ahead and how they would spend them. She did not want them to go to Switzerland there were too many memories from the year before and she was not ready for them. At the beginning of May her mother told her that her cousins, Freda and Frank, Jackie's parents, had been in touch suggesting that they might like to join them and Jackie's family on holiday on the south coast where they spent their summer holidays every year. Jackie and her husband Adam had three daughters and two sons roughly the same age as her own and if Elspeth thought it sounded like setting up a Sunday School holiday camp she considered that it might offer a solution for them all. She was grateful that her cousins had thought of her and after considering the possibilities it offered she accepted.

Jackie and Adam and their children stayed for three or four weeks each year in a large Boarding House, Freda and Frank usually stayed for a couple of weeks in a small family hotel close by and finding that there were places there for her parents and for herself and the children, they booked rooms for four weeks.

Elspeth was thankful that Adam and Jackie were open and approached the situation with understanding. They made it clear that none of them must allow themselves to feel that they were getting under each other's feet. Adam had experience of church relationships and pointed out that it was a holiday and each family group was free to make their own day-to-day arrangements but that they were to be there for each other. He was a thoughtful and serious man and Elspeth was also appreciative that he was prepared to speak openly and did not, on any occasion, shy away from speaking on topics that others of her acquaintance felt embarrassed of approaching in case they distressed her.

One afternoon during the second week of the holiday her parents along with her mother's cousin Freda had taken themselves off on an outing into the nearby town leaving Adam, Jackie and Frank to set up a beach game of rounders with the older children. Fleur had made friends with the youngest of her cousin's children, Isabelle, and they were happily playing together. Elspeth had excused herself and strayed away from them alone, taking a book with her further up the beach. She liked her cousin's children, the two eldest girls, Miriam and Catherine, wore their hair in loose plaits and reminded Elspeth of the characters she had encountered in the Girls' Boarding School stories she had read avidly as a ten and eleven year old. They had mainly been set she believed in the 1930s and there was she felt something old worldly in her cousin's daughters. They were a close knit family and Elspeth liked the way the eldest two girls watched over their youngest brothers, William and Frank, each named after their Grandfathers. Sitting now with the book in her lap unread, Elspeth's attention was focused on the beach in front of her where the children were enjoying their game and her eyes filled with tears. She watched her sons' concentration and responses to her adult cousins who were supervising them and an overwhelming sadness filled her. Anton's children, he should be here with them, he should be here with us, she bent her head and covered her eyes with her hand. She was in an alien land forced to listen to a language she did not understand. Her body ached with longing and her heart and spirit yearned. Sometimes she had found herself in a room by herself and been surprised by someone entering or thought she had heard a familiar step on the stairs and for a split second her heart had responded and then her whole being had been crushed in the cold reality of his absence. The daily anguish consumed her.

'I'm taking a break while they eat their ice creams. Adam had quietly seated himself beside her and she rapidly replaced her sunglasses so he would not see her grief. She resented his intrusion but if he sensed it he did not move away.

'I enjoy sitting watching the sea and considering the ships as they leave from the nearby city port.'

For the first time Elspeth became aware of a ship approaching the horizon far out at sea.

'I like to imagine the travellers setting off on long sea journeys. Have some of them set off from loved ones sadly waving their goodbyes? Then I wonder about where they are journeying to and if they will be welcomed on a distant shore with joy. Somebody, I'm unsure who, has said that ships leaving one place and arriving on a distant shore is a metaphor for death.'

Elspeth was silent and he continued, 'My mother died very suddenly of a brain embolism when I was seven years old. She saw my two brothers and myself off to school saying as she always did, 'take care the three of you', and that was the last time we saw her. I thought you were very wise to take your children to Anton's funeral and to the burial.'

'Didn't you attend your mother's funeral?'

'No, we were sent to school as if it was any ordinary day. My father is a kind, somewhat distant figure. He was a GP and had worked in a hospital for returning gravely injured service men during the war and had witnessed death and pain many times, but he could never express his own suffering and doubtless thought he was protecting my brothers and myself.'

Elspeth thought it was treating death as a somewhat shameful happening as if it was a failure of some kind but she did not comment.

'I shared a bedroom with my youngest brother, Toby, at the time and I would hear him sobbing himself to sleep and I would cry too. Toby was only just five years old. Matt my eldest brother was nine years old and had a room of his own and doubtlessly he also sobbed himself to sleep alone.'

'Are you and your brothers close?' Elspeth enquired.

'Yes. We were always there for each other and we still are. My mother's death bound us together. For the first month or so my father employed a housekeeper and the household functioned but without warmth and then my father's unmarried sister, Auntie Peggy, came to live with us. She had spent years looking after her parents until they died and she gave up what may have been a longed for freedom to come and take care of us. She was crotchety and fussy but essentially kind and selfless. Toby was the first to accept her, just five he perhaps needed a surrogate mother the most but eventually we all settled down into the new regime and grew to love my aunt. My two brothers and their wives each have two children and there are our five youngsters and they all look at my aunt as their grandmother, a position which she has a very fair claim to.'

'And you became a priest. Are your brothers also believing Christians?' Elspeth asked caught up in the story and forgetting her own distress for the moment.

'Matt, my eldest brother, is also a doctor and like my father is not hostile to religion but he doesn't practise any faith. Toby's wife, Grace, belongs to the Evangelical wing of the Church of England and they and their children attend church and come to our church when they visit us.'

'Did you attend church yourself when you were young?' Elspeth asked.

'No. My aunt attended church but I can't remember any of us ever being expected to go along with her. I and my brothers at eleven years old began our secondary education at a local Independent School. It was a late nineteenth century foundation and provided education for the sons of lower middle class professional parents. The school housed a Chapel where school assemblies took place and we were told that it was open for personal visits if we wished to make use of it during our free time. I was around fourteen years old when I decided I would make a visit. I had had a dose of flu' and my father had insisted that I was not sufficiently well to attend games so as I was passing near the chapel I decided to drop in. I can remember quite clearly everything about that afternoon. It was a bright sunny day and inside the chapel the trees outside the window sent dappled shadows across its walls. The chapel was empty but for one student kneeling near the front and I sat down near the back. I knew the outlay of the chapel, of course, but my attention that afternoon became focused on a cross on a wall near me. It was a crucifix! There was the figure of Christ on it and this is unusual in a Protestant Church, such crucifixes are considered Papist as I expect you know. This crucifix had been bequeathed to the school by the parents of a past student who had been killed in the Great War and who had perhaps been a Catholic. I stared transfixed at the crucifix and I found myself believing in the image I was contemplating. It was overpowering, a sudden overwhelming recognition of a truth realised in an instant. I knelt down and I can only quite simply say that I gave myself over to God that afternoon in that school chapel I had entered on a whim. But Elspeth I have been talking so much about myself! You are a convert to Catholicism. How did that come about?'

'Perhaps for me it was the image of the Blessed Virgin and Child in a Catholic Chapel and the understanding given me by a Holy Priest when I began at university shortly after the death of my brother, Jamie'.

'I remember Jackie telling me about the loss of your brother. So death is not a stranger for you Elspeth.'

'No. I think we're being required to deal with the children! But thank you for talking to me. This afternoon I feared I was about to fall off the edge of a cliff.'

The holiday had been a success. Perhaps, Elspeth considered, it might not be so successful if repeated but that year it served a huge need and she felt she had made a lifelong friend in Adam and the children, being taken as they had been from an unbearable situation at home, had made new friends too. She had been very wrong about Adam, if others appointed him to a Bishopric in future years it was because he was worthy of such a position she had not observed any ecclesiastical ambition on his part.

III

Once the children returned to school that September Elspeth left them in the care of her parents and took a flight to Rome. She had decided that she would let the apartment on a short term lease and she set about having it redecorated. Maria Rosa knew of two students that were looking for accommodation while they studied in Rome and Elspeth let the apartment to them. She removed any personal objects and made replacements and she thought I'm becoming a woman of property. She had taken over her investments at home investing in city properties as her father had advised. She now had the children to consider and like her family before her she would make sure they were well provided for. 'I'm more like my Great Grandmother than I believed', she thought.

She felt she was going through that sad year largely on autopilot and when she returned from Rome she applied for a teaching post on the far side of the city. Looking down the lists of adverts giving the details of available teaching posts she saw that an English teacher was needed at 'The Beeches' Comprehensive School and the name stirred a memory; it was the school's netball team that had drawn in a netball match with the netball team at Oaklands all those years ago and she applied and was successful in securing the job. Her feelings were divided, she was unsure about the appointment she felt unsure about almost everything but her friends were encouraging and she almost reluctantly took their advice knowing that they wanted her re-adapt her life.

Her funny, gentle, sensitive cousin Esme was spending three months away from India and Elspeth along with the children and her parents journeyed to Switzerland for Christmas. Esme was Elspeth's favourite cousin and she and the rest of the family had grown used to and entertained by Esme's enthusiasms over the years. This year perhaps she sought to act as an antidote to Elspeth's grief and also knowing how her cousin was always keen to ask questions she explained to Elspeth her new found interest in Physics.

'Y'know how I almost decided on studying Physics at university, Elspeth?'

'Yes, I seem to remember and then you changed your mind at the last minute'.

'Well now I'm really into Parallel Universes'.

'Parallel Universes?' replied Elspeth, 'who has put that theory forward? and how has it been received by Physicists?'

'Well many of them consider it crazy but some are coming round to it and more will', Esme continued seeing her cousin showing some interest.

'But it can never be proved'.

'That's been stated about many mysteries of the Universe. Have you never considered what occurred before the Big Bang? That always seems to me the most intriguing question. There is a new theory being put forward that this universe came into being on the embers of a previous one and that there is no beginning or end just a continuum. I think it's fascinating. I've been reading up a lot, I'll be happy to let you have some of my books that explain these theories, you'll enjoy them. After all we are all familiar with parallel lives, perhaps the mysteries of the Cosmos mirror what we already know about existence here on earth.'

'It sounds plausible,' said Elspeth amused despite herself.

Esme did not say, it will take your mind off things, but she wanted her cousin to begin to take an interest in life again and she continued to enlighten her about mysteries of the universe and Elspeth knowing her cousin's kindness realised that she was deliberately attempting to by-pass her grief by engaging her as she so often had in the past in one of her enthusiasms and she was grateful.

There was one final postscript to her tragic year. Elspeth had written to Father Dominic after Anton's death and she had received a beautiful letter from him which she would always treasure. 'God loves those He chastises', he had written but what he had failed to tell her was that he was himself ill with a heart problem. When she had failed to receive his greetings at Christmas she contacted his monastery to be informed that he had died suddenly in September and she felt doubly bereft. Father Dominic had played a vital role in her life, he had given her the spiritual guidance that had directed her life and she mourned him.

Chapter 19

....

"I sometimes hold it half a sin
To put in words the grief I feel; For words, like nature,
half reveal And half conceal the soul within.

In words, like weeds, I'll wrap me o'er,
Like coarsest clothes against the cold;
But that large grief which these enfold
Is given in outline and no more."
(In Memoriam A L Tennyson)

On a January morning Elspeth drove herself to 'The Beeches', to begin her first day of teaching in the large Comprehensive School some miles from home. The day had a cold, crisp edge to it but she was relieved that the sun was shining. She had arrived early and she sat outside and attempted to come to terms with her own feelings. What exactly was she doing here? she had no deep sense of commitment. She felt marooned in some lonely, forsaken place, becalmed in the doldrums of her own being. She had dressed carefully by habit. Her clothing was a form of protection. If members of the school staff knew of her recent history she wanted no pity. She slowly took in the scene before her. The school had been built during the 'Sixties. It was a low, pale brick building composed of shapeless blocks interspersed with windows but an effort had been made to plant trees and shrubs. Some of the trees were much older than the building itself and lent some gravitas to the purpose of the place. The architecture was uninspired and uninspiring. She sighed and as pupils and staff members were beginning to arrive she made her way into the school.

The atmosphere inside the building was warm and welcoming with teachers greeting each other and sharing their Christmas experiences and groaning at the thought of a holiday past and a new term of work. The teaching staff she was to learn were friendly and she soon found that they were quick to offer help and advice, but teachers, of course, are essentially on their own facing up to classes of varied intake. Her past teaching experience had not prepared her for problems of discipline. She had never lost control of a group because she had never been placed in a position where she had had to be responsible for acceptable behaviour. She had considered the difference between the terms 'schooling' and 'education' and for the first time she recognised that they were not synonymous: the term 'schooling' incorporated the understanding that becoming educated required self-control. It was in those first few weeks at 'The Beeches' that Elspeth realised a few things about herself that she had been previously unaware of. She could stand up to poor behaviour without being intimidated and she could be as uncompromising as steel when the situation demanded it.

The first few days she was not particularly tested, her pupils were reasonably well behaved but on the Friday morning she was taking a class of fourteen/fifteen year olds in the lesson before lunch when three boys took it upon themselves to be disruptive and rude. She sensed that most of the class was resentful of their continuous interruptions and after giving a second warning she told the three trouble makers that she wanted them to stay behind at the end of the lesson. The class filed out and the three boys stood in front of her desk.

She spoke calmly, 'The three of you stand up straight! Now what are your names?' she asked addressing the first of the three.

'Jack Horner', he replied impudently and his two friends sniggered.

'I'll ask you again, what is your name?'

'Jack Watson'.

As each of them gave their name she looked them up on the register in front of her. She made sure that she took her time and she began to sense their impatience.

'How long are you going to keep us Miss? We're going to lose our places in the dinner queue'.

'And whose fault is that? I am waiting for an apology'.

'Sorry Miss'.

'I have a name'.

'Sorry Mrs Spadaro'.

She refused to hurry. 'If you three choose to disrupt any further lessons of mine you will not only lose your place in the dinner queue.' She gestured for them to leave and not risking to be delayed any further they took to their heels. They were adolescents, the same age as her own sons, they weren't bad; they were simply childish and she shrugged her shoulders, gathered together her belongings and thought the first week is almost over and I've survived.

II

The catchment area for the school was large and took in pupils from middle class homes along with children from a sprawling council house estate and the fifth year tutor group that Elspeth took over from her predecessor comprised youngsters from differing backgrounds and a with a wide range of abilities.

At the beginning of her second week at the school two members of her tutor group, Tracey and Simone, approached her and said that they had been speaking to their parents about her over the weekend and Tracey's mother had told them that the surname Spadaro was the name of the man who had saved the life of Jenny Anderson who had been a neighbour of theirs. Elspeth was shaken. She vaguely remembered the child's name but she had no idea that she had lived in the neighbourhood of the school.

'Your husband was a real hero we reckon', said one of the girls, 'and we are going to do our best for you', she added.

'Jenny's sister died of meningitis and if her parents had lost Jenny as well it would have been terrible. Last summer they moved back to Scotland to be close to their family', said Tracey.

Jenny Anderson had been one of theirs and it was a strange logic that motivated the girls to extend their consideration to her. She returned home that evening in a turmoil. The little girl that Anton had saved could still have been in the neighbourhood where she taught. She was not sure what she would have felt about it. Would Jenny's parents have tried to see her? She was relieved they had left. But whether it was the knowledge about Anton's heroic death she was never sure but she sensed that the story got around and perhaps was one of the reasons that she had an easier time with potentially difficult classes than she might have done that first year.

She found that she learnt a great deal about herself as well as her pupils. She had experienced traumatic events in her life it was true and yet she had also been cocooned against some of the hazards of life that some of her pupils faced. While almost all her pupils came from caring home backgrounds she became slowly aware of the dysfunctional backgrounds of others. Young truants that had little in the way of parental supervision. Parents who almost savagely protected their children against school and any kind of discipline it attempted to impose. One mother had six children by five different men and her children shared a house where men came and left as suddenly as they had arrived. One or two pupils became pregnant and it was the opinion of several members of staff that 'the poor girl' just wanted something of her own to love. Sexual morality was not the school's business though lessons in Social Care were given regularly.

Elspeth was beginning to become involved in the life of the school but she remained as unconvinced about the Comprehensive system as her Great Aunt May had been. She was not at all sure about very large schools where children could so easily become lost in the system as they moved around from one end of the large building to the other, or it seemed to her that they did. With such a large intake any one teacher might only teach one third of the pupils, during their time in the school, and the rest remained strangers. Also they were largely neighbourhood schools which was fine if the school was in a pleasant leafy suburb but many were situated in very poor deprived city areas and despite being 'comprehensive' many of the youngsters could remain all their secondary school life within one impoverished environment. She felt strongly that some of the children required a greater sense of security. Worst of all the school practiced 'mixed ability' teaching which meant that very bright children shared the same classes with groups of children who required a different educational approach and these children became disruptive, as well they might, when they were left behind and subsequently failed.

There must be a kinder and more effective way of teaching children she thought. If the general intention was equality and integration, it fell far short of realisation. If 'equality' was based on 'fairness' most people Elspeth mused, would agree to it but the definition of 'equality' could be just as readily placed on 'sameness' as in 'two and two equals four' and children being different, different approaches were required if education was to deliver on 'fairness'. In small classes, such as those in a public school it might be possible to teach children in one undifferentiated group but in classes of over thirty, children she felt, were being frequently failed. Educational theories were one thing reality was another. Perhaps when dealing with school children three plus one equals four or one plus three equals four might prove more appropriate, Elspeth thought.

The children at The Beeches formed groups generally with children of similar ability and although she never encountered any serious prejudice within classes – children accepted each other and their different abilities well – they did not mix outside of lessons. She thought about her cousin Esme's parallel universes and parallel lives and she thought once again that there was a difference between 'human rights' and 'equal rights'. She remembered her aunt saying that new educational theories were frequently advocated by people who had never been in a State School in their lives and she thought I may very well have looked favourably on some of these theories myself once upon a time.

Yet teaching had always come to her aid. It was a job she loved and she slowly became involved in the ups and downs of the school and by becoming closely involved in teaching and in the development of her pupils her own problems and sadness could at least be shelved in the hours she was away from home.

What never ceased to amaze her was the openness of her pupils in regard to herself: 'You talk posh Miss', and the sixth formers would freely comment on her clothes and hair. But there was no malice in these personal comments and most of them were meant as compliments.

By the time the summer term was coming to a close she felt she had become part of the school's environment and was accepted and on the last day of term her fifth year tutor group, most of whom were leaving school, presented her with a bouquet of flowers. She believed Tracey and Simone were behind the gesture and they presented the gift. She found herself moved almost to tears as she thanked them and she told those leaving that she hoped they would drop by in the future and how happy she would be to see them.

Elspeth did not go straight home, she made a detour to Anton and Jamie's grave and carefully placed the flowers into the vase there. She stood quietly and thoughtfully for a time contemplating the changes in her life and the children's lives which were never far from her thoughts. Her parents had organised a holiday for them all in the States and the children were very excited and she found that she too was looking forward to the holiday and the experience of America.

Chapter 20

....

*"Sweet love of youth, forgive if I forget thee While
the World's tide is bearing me along:
Sterner desires and darker hopes beset me,
Hopes which obscure but cannot do thee wrong.*

*But when the days of golden dreams had perished
And even Despair was powerless to destroy,
Then did I learn how existence could be cherished,
Strengthened and fed without the aid of joy."*
(Remembrance - Emily Brontë)

The years following her return to teaching were so full that occasionally Elspeth lost track of time. There was her work at the school that took up much of her life and most essential of all there were her own children that were growing up fast and whose futures were a major concern.

She became at one and the same time amused and saddened when it was hinted to her that she was still young and attractive and could perhaps consider marrying again. A second marriage was the very last thing she wanted and she rejected the idea without a second thought; it was impossible for her. Anton had been the love of her life and she did not require or desire a replacement. She was also asked if his death had affected her faith at all and after a passage of a year or two she could say with certainty that if anything it had deepened it. When Christ had cried out in anguish during His crucifixion, "My God, My God why hast Thou forsaken me", there was embodied within His cry an acknowledgement of His Father, not a denial. 'It is not the weight of the Cross that matters but the way we carry it', had been the

292

foundation of her faith from the beginning of her conversion and she found deep within herself a certainty that she was not alone, that she was accompanied. Eighteen months after Anton's death she joined the choir in the Church she and the children continued to attend and found an inner peace and grace in the quietude of Gregorian Chant and the beauty of the Tridentine Mass.

In time she was offered the possibility of promotion as a Head of Year or Head of Faculty but she was not interested. She was needed at home and in addition she had never wished for anything other than to be an effective classroom teacher. She had become convinced that literacy was the most important factor in becoming educated and she placed the greatest emphasis on it. She encouraged first year children that she taught to bring a library book along after lunch to her classroom and while she marked work she allowed them to sit and read. On the whole it was girls that turned up and she felt that as the year progressed their reading ability improved and she watched them as they grew in confidence and self-esteem.

Her mother asked if she was perhaps working too hard: 'You are very thin, Elspeth, are you perhaps doing too much?' And she had laughed it off and said that she was fine and wished to be busy.

The children fortunately were strongly involved in their own pursuits of one kind another. Gian never deviated from his decision to study medicine and worked hard at school to achieve the results he needed to become a doctor. He had grown tall and as his teenage years progressed he matured into a thoughtful, caring young man. He was also handsome as Elspeth noted proudly though it was the quieter Joseph who attracted a following of young girls! For her second son it was not so much that he chose a profession so much as the profession chose him. Her father had been correct, Joseph's gift lay in design and with very little in the way of outside encouragement he was set to study engineering. But it was Michael who surprised her the most. She had recognised from the days of home teaching that Michael was academically brilliant, he also had an aptitude for sports and was a much required figure in his school sports teams. One day when he was still in the early years of adolescence Elspeth asked him what he intended to study for in the future. She had some idea that he might say that he was dreaming of becoming a Cricketer in the National team but to her amazement he answered with a surprising degree of certainty that he was planning to become a priest.

'You sound very sure', Elspeth said.

'I have never wanted to be anything else,' he replied.

Elspeth considered her third son. He had an open personality and she thought he had little of the adolescent angst that beset his older brothers. He had a freedom of mind and outlook that might well enable him to reach out to others and he had suffered his father's death and was sensitive to grief and unhappiness. The days of placing the cutlery the wrong way round were long past. Joseph might know the design and inner workings of objects but Michael gave them a practical application. He had learnt somewhere how to mend a fuse and had put up shelves to accommodate books in his room, frequently when he saw her arrive home tired he would tell her she looked jaded and made her sit down while he prepared her tea. From his early childhood he had established peace between his older brothers when they had squabbled and had been generally loved. He had, Elspeth conceded to herself, the attributes of a priest and not for the first time she thought about Gran and how she may have disapproved though she thought that she may have been won over; these after all were her granddaughter's children and Gran had always delighted in everything she had done.

Then there was Fleur to think about. Her young daughter was a prodigy according to her grandmother and was already far ahead of where she had been as a pianist at the same age. Elspeth recognised her child's gifts and would listen to her. The depths and fullness of Fleur's soul was in her playing and sometimes Elspeth would hear the plaintive strains and sometimes the pathos within the music and would be filled with sadness. Her daughter might well become a renowned concert pianist and yet Elspeth thought such a position might well be lonely and while she recognised Fleur's undoubted talent the image of her little girl sitting under the Silver Birch tree holding her doll, lonely and vulnerable, still resonated with her. Her daughter was surrounded by love it was true but she did not want her to be lonely and her mother's heart went out to her. When do one's children become fully fledged adults? At which point does a mother cease to see the child in her grown-up offspring, Elspeth mused? She wanted them to be independent and to have fulfilled lives and she would never hold them back but they would nevertheless always be the children she and Anton had nurtured and she would always treasure those memories of their early childhood when they were for a short time entirely and only theirs.

II

Gian decided that he would go to Medical School during the autumn that he finished school and without taking a 'gap year'. Medicine is a long course, he reasoned, and he had visited and stayed in several foreign countries. He went up to London at the same time as Seb who had gained a place in Art School. Louise was pleased that the two would be studying close to each other and Elspeth caught a hint of relief in her old friend's comments. Louise never fully confided her anxieties about her only son but Elspeth sensed that Seb was emotionally, at least, estranged from his parents. He had given up on religion during his teens Gian had told her and his father had taken the view that he should approach the situation with understanding and he made no demands of any kind on him.

'Seb has no respect for his father he openly ridicules him' Gian had said and Elspeth felt sorry for Jerome, 'his father has never stood up to Seb he lets him get away with anything', and Elspeth thought back on Anton's criticism but she made no comment.

Towards late autumn of the following year Gian unexpectedly turned up one Friday evening at home looking serious and Elspeth thought somewhat disturbed. She waited for his brothers to disappear to Joseph's room to play video games before asking him if something was wrong.

'Is your friend Jill OK?' she inquired. She had been introduced to Jill on a recent visit.

'Jill? she's fine I think. I don't see a lot of her. No, it's Seb I'm very worried about,' he replied somewhat uncomfortably.

'What's wrong with him? Louise and Jerome paid him a visit recently and Louise didn't mention anything being amiss'.

'They didn't see him at all during the long summer vacation because he went to Europe on an Art study course.'

'I remember his mother saying,' said Elspeth, 'what's happened is he ill?'

'Soon after beginning his course he took up with a student, Lexie. He fell head over heels in love with her. Seb introduced me to her and I thought trouble! She's the daughter of an oil tycoon of a father. She spent her early years in the Middle East, from what I could make out, and was sent over here when she began school. She was apparently expelled from one place. She has little in the way of talent, she's spoilt silly, glamorous in a brassy sort of way and she was simply playing around with Seb, she's completely out of his league. She introduced him to drugs, probably just pot to begin with. When they were in Europe this summer she dropped

Seb or expected him to stand by while she began an affair with a foreign chap. It was then or just before they left England that they began taking cocaine, whether she had been experimenting with heavier drugs earlier I don't know. When I met up with Seb one weekend in October he was high on something and he reacted aggressively and told me that if I told his parents it would be the end of our friendship. Then last weekend I rang him and went round and he looked really frightful and I said I was going to tell you to inform his parents and he just shrugged. He needs help, I'm afraid he may overdose. Can I ask you to tell Louise?'

'They need to be told. I won't find it easy but I can't take the risk of not informing them now I know,' said Elspeth, 'this will be terrible for them!'

'So I can leave it with you?'

'I'll ring Louise this evening and arrange to see her this weekend. Seb! I'm afraid he's presented his parents with problems most of his life, things, I suspect, have never been straightforward. Will you be staying for the weekend'?

'I'll drop round and see the grandparents tomorrow morning and tomorrow afternoon I'll go to the football match with Joe and Mike, and Dave will be joining us. Good to know Dave never changes! His business studies are going according to plan and he says when he's made his millions in Retail he'll buy up a football club! Susy's been accepted for a nursing course in a top London Hospital, Auntie Belle's over the moon.'

'Yes, I know, so is her father.' The children still called Belle and Alistair Aunt and Uncle and she remained Auntie Elspeth to Belle's children. After all Elspeth thought Belle's more a sister than a friend.

'They received the best of childhoods and like us they have always been fully accepted for themselves, the way they are,' Gian went on. 'I felt angry about Pa for a long time because we all needed him and I wish every day that he was still here for us but then I grew to realise that the way of his death was characteristic of him. He would see someone in need and he wouldn't hesitate he'd just respond without a second thought for himself.'

Gian spoke seriously, he'd said very little over the years about his father's death but Elspeth was aware of how deeply all her children had grieved and she was moved and comforted by her eldest son's words of appreciation about his and his siblings' upbringing.

At this point of the conversation Fleur entered the room, 'and how is my beautiful little sister?' Gian asked.

'Not so little,' she replied giving him a hug. 'I've brought the video of the film down. Mama and I usually watch a film together on a Friday night.'

'Yes, I'm looking forward to it,' her mother replied, 'I just have a phone call to make, I'll be with you in five minutes.'

'And I'll go and join my brother's, they have a new video game,' Gian said as he ambled off.

III

The following morning Elspeth drove to the coffee and tea rooms where they usually met to see Louise. She felt miserable at the prospect of telling her friend about Sebastian, she thought I've known him all his life and I've always nursed the feeling that there was something tragic about him.

Louise was already sitting waiting when Elspeth arrived, she looked anxious and as if she had not slept and Elspeth thought she's aware of something being very wrong and she knows it has something to do with Seb. She spoke immediately as Elspeth sat down, 'It's Seb isn't it?'

'Gian came home this weekend he's very concerned'.

'It's that girl isn't it? He introduced us at Easter. She's no good Elspeth!'

As calmly as she could Elspeth explained the situation to her friend. 'I wish I didn't have to give you such information but I couldn't withhold it.'

'Of course you couldn't and I'm glad it's come from you, you're my oldest and best friend,' replied Louise.

'What will you do?'

'We'll go immediately! I hope – Oh Elspeth!'

'It won't be too late and if taking drugs has been a recent thing he may not be completely addicted. I don't know a great deal about these things but we can hope that things are not as bad as we imagine'.

Elspeth observed her old friend, she looked pale and dejected but when she watched her walk away she recognised the old resolute spirit reassert itself. It was as if Louise had made up her mind, her son's problems were now fully out there in the open and Louise had never been one to run away from things. Her son was urgently in need of help and she and his father would be there for him.

IV

In the months following Elspeth heard from her friend from time to time and Louise conveyed her gratitude. The situation had been serious but not, as Elspeth had hoped, impossible or beyond repair. She and Jerome had journeyed to London immediately to bring their son home and they had met with no resistance from him. Jerome found a place for him in a rehabilitation unit close to where they lived and he gave his son all the time, love and care he required. He never censored him or attempted to change his son's attitudes to life he was simply there for him and eventually, if at first reluctantly and silently, Seb acknowledged his father's goodness of heart. Perhaps, Elspeth thought, it was the moment when Jerome finally grew up and was no longer the overgrown public school boy that Anton had criticised. But the friendship with Gian and her boys was never renewed and the four of them went their separate ways.

V

Seb was eventually offered a place in an Art School nearer to his home and after completing the course he set up in a partnership with a college friend and supplied well designed home products. The business was successful and in his mid-twenties he married his sister Siobhan's friend and they had a beautiful daughter, Alicia, who became destined to be the centre of his parent's lives but this was well into the future.

Chapter 21

....

"The old order changeth, yielding place to new"
(The Passing of Arthur - Alfred Lord Tennyson)

The second Millennium was greeted with celebrations in Elspeth's household. It was impossible not to feel the growing excitement as fireworks exploded in a myriad of colours and lights and patterns around the globe. Elspeth was gladdened by her parent's presence, they were, of course older now but showed little sign of slowing down. All the children were with them and Gian had invited his girlfriend, Diana, to join them in a special Millennium dinner. It was a joyous occasion, old doubts and fears were laid aside with the old century as they found themselves caught up in the mood that prevailed all around them.

'And Times They Are a'Changing', announced Gian, 'we watched as the Berlin Wall came down and there was general rejoicing and now we have a new Millennium. We should drink a toast to the new century and an end to World Wars and wars of all kinds'.

'I'll say Amen to that,' said his grandfather.

They finally broke up their celebrations and went to their beds in the early hours and once there Elspeth lay awake for a long time. There was the hope of new beginnings but equally and as inevitably, she thought, the century passing had a strong hold on her; there was sadness as much as joy. The twentieth century had seen more deaths in its wars and conflicts than had the previous Millennium in all of its thousand years and it had given to her and taken away from her too, the irreplaceable lives of those she had so deeply loved. The twentieth century formed me, she reflected. During the meal she had glanced from time to time at her father and had noticed the deepening lines of sadness etched into his face.

I stated all those years ago that I would never forgive him and was told that 'never' is a long time. She thought of Jamie and an image of his innocent, trusting face came into her mind and she thought too of the harsh treatment he had received. And yet she had forgiven, her father had made amends a thousand times over and she wondered how she would have managed without the strong and calm support her parents had given her and the children since Anton's death. Her last and deepest memories that early morning of the new century were for her dead husband and the life they had shared. She felt he would be proud of his sons and daughter. Gian was completing his medical studies, Joseph's degree in Engineering was excellent, Michael was reading Greats in Cambridge and was still determined to enter a Seminary after university and Fleur was following her dream of a musical career. This coming decade will see all our children fully grown adults she thought and probably I shall become a grandmother, and finally she thought of Gran and Nan and the part they had played in her life, before falling to sleep telling herself that New Years, new centuries and new Millennium were as much about looking back as looking forward.

II

The new term began much like any other and Elspeth wondered if it was only in her imagination that she sensed an undercurrent of excitement, after all it was not merely a new decade beginning but a new century and a new Millennium. It was understandable to speculate about changes and hopefully changes for the better. Two World Wars and other conflicts had torn the twentieth century apart, was it too much to hope that people had learned from the carnage? Or are most of the memories in the minds of the old and do the young start all over again making many of the same mistakes? The thought distressed her. Her own life had been lived around family, friends, her church and teaching and she had taken little part in the wider life of the world and the questions it posed. She supposed it was the same for most people, parents sought security and peace with the strong desire to give their children stability. She lingered over her thoughts while nursing the knowledge that the seeds of the twentieth century had largely been sown in the century that had preceded it and that life was a continuum. Elspeth had never forgotten the conversations she had shared with Johannes Manasses all those years before and she considered them now, in many ways they formed the basis of her thinking. He had said that Liberalism would become the dominant ideology of the Twenty First Century and it was impossible not to be aware of its effects; the climate of everyday life was liberal and while it produced a positive acceptance and care for others it also gave rise to a negative tolerance of things that should not perhaps be tolerated. She believed that up until a short time ago, even during her own childhood, there had been a consensus of what constituted right and wrong in morality generally and life seemed simpler. If that was true it was no longer the case. These were the thoughts that occupied her mind as she embarked on the new term and met its demands. Soon she was caught up in the presentation of lessons and the challenges of the external examinations ahead for her pupils and these of necessity took president.

III

When she looked back on that first year of the Millennium, Elspeth's day to day life remained much the same as it had in earlier years until the end of the year when Gian and Diana announced their engagement and the family met up once again in celebration.

Elspeth was glad that she thought well of Diana though she was not sure she had a great deal in common with her. She was also studying medicine and the pair were planning to marry the following year once they graduated. Diana was bright and optimistic and was committed to the profession she had chosen, she genuinely wanted to serve the sick particularly Elspeth learnt if they were poor and destitute. Diana was not religious and had been brought up without any recourse to religious belief but recognising the part the Catholic Church played in Gian's life and in the life of his family and loving Gian as she did she had agreed to have a Catholic wedding and to allow him to bring up their children in his faith. Her own family's raison d'etre was politics. Her father was a lawyer who had once stood in a local By-Election as a Labour candidate in a strongly held Conservative Seat and had been unsuccessful but it had not deadened his ardour and his daughter shared it while her mother remained, perhaps wisely, silent on the subject. It was a similar situation to that of Gran and Grandpa Elspeth thought. She had never, of course, known Gran when she was young but she recalled her Grandmother's Suffragette credentials and her belief in the Labour Party and her dedication to the poor and she had to admit that Gian's choice of a wife would have pleased her Grandmother immensely. Elspeth had never been a very practical person and she was conscious of others regarding her as something of a detached dreamer and sometimes she wondered how much of her life she had spent sleepwalking through it. Diana certainly made her feel something of the kind and she remembered Nan saying how her daughter Elspeth had made her feel as incompetent as a young child.

But it was the September of the following year that Elspeth considered the rightful year of the new Millennium. The conflicts in the world had continued largely unabated but it was that September when they came closer to home. She had stared fixedly at the television screen, scarcely believing as planes full of people had slammed into the Twin Towers. They looked like a sequence of still photographs in a catastrophe film destroying the protective sheltering of minds, crashing into ordinary lives. Perhaps the announcement of the Second World War at eleven o'clock that fateful September morning some sixty years before had had a similar effect breaking through and into the everyday lives of those gathered round their wireless sets listening in silent dread. Elspeth taught Muslim children and considered them some of her best and pleasantest pupils. She was aware of colour and usually of race but she saw individual people not creeds and she hoped there would not be a backlash against the innocent. She wondered like thousands of others whether this was an isolated incident or the beginning of a fresh terror. Gian and Diana's wedding was planned for the middle of October and the young couple were starting out on their lives together and she was saddened that it was to coincide with such a tragic world event.

She discussed it with her father and he was of the mind that any military incursion into Afghanistan, where the cause of the attack on the Twin Towers originated, and a battle with the perpetrators was a mistake. 'The geography of Afghanistan is very difficult,' he said, 'and the battles fought there during the nineteenth century ended in defeat. Wars don't solve problems they just present the world with fresh ones,' and he had sighed deeply.

Yet life goes on as Elspeth had learned after Anton's death and the family wedding planned for October went ahead. Gian and Diana chose Italy for their honeymoon. They had decided to make the apartment in Rome a base and planned to travel around the country from there and Elspeth felt a special feeling of contentment as if life had gone round full circle; the Rome apartment having been her eldest son's first home.

IV

The main events of those early years of the new century stood out clearly in Elspeth's mind and she made her own important personal decision the following year, she decided to take early retirement from teaching. She still enjoyed her work and she was not ill but she felt inwardly disturbed by several occurrences taking place in the world around her and she felt restless. Her children were forging ahead with their own lives and she felt a growing desire to return to her books and to ask questions and look for answers about the changing world around her. She wanted to study and read more about religion and politics and then events from her past that she believed she had largely come to terms with began to surface once again in the light of disturbing news stories that were beginning to abound.

Elspeth's Catholic faith remained of prime importance to her and was not shaken as she was drawn into a discussion with Louise and her sister Ann. The question of the sexual abuse of children by Catholic priests was impossible to ignore for any Catholic learning of them for the first time and during a visit from her friends Ann described the distress her mother had expressed on hearing of the cases of abuse coming out of America and the accusations that were beginning to surface in Ireland.

'I have never seen my mother so distressed. She spent a very happy childhood in Ireland and thinks there couldn't have been thousands of cases or she would have known something of them'.

Elspeth found herself empathising with Mrs Donoghue's feelings of anguish not because she thought the abuse was exaggerated but because she believed the sexual abuse of children was beyond wickedness. For the first time in years she confronted her own rape. She had been rendered helpless in her late teens but in the case of children it was almost doubly dreadful. She had been given to believe that sexual abuse largely took place in families but from priests it was impossible to countenance. They were acts of total hypocrisy and deception by men she firmly believed handled the very Body and Blood of Christ. It goes to the very heart of my Christian Faith, Elspeth thought, and she felt it as a physical pain

'Catholics are leaving the Church because of what they are hearing', said Louise.

'It's not a time for leaving the Church and abandoning Christ to suffer alone, Elspeth replied. 'I don't know a great deal about the modern Church because we have always attended the traditional Mass but I remember that you once said that liberalising the church doesn't necessarily lead to a greater freedom. Sexual abuse has perhaps always occurred, it's difficult to know, and one person can do a great deal of harm but one cannot tar every priest with the same brush. I have known some very holy priests.'

'So have we! At the end of the day we shouldn't be too judgemental perhaps about a minority of individuals, we cannot forgive the sin but we have been called on to forgive the sinner,' concluded Ann.

The Church is also a family, Elspeth thought and each time she read or heard of a further case of the sexual abuse of children by a priest she felt her family, the Church she loved, had been in a very real way physically bruised and fractured.

Three days before the school broke up for the Easter holiday she faced a further sense of miserable confusion. The mother of one of her Year ten pupils rang her and asked if she could drop by and speak to her. She was the mother of Gareth Lewis a clever and sensitive boy that Elspeth had believed was destined for a top university but something recently, she suspected, had gone sadly wrong. For the past term he had been regularly truanting and his work had become careless and slipshod. As his tutor she had written on his term report that his results were disappointing and he had not attended school for over a week when his mother spoke to her and requested an appointment to see her. Elspeth arranged for the meeting to take place in her tutor room after school. When Mrs Lewis arrived she was clearly distressed and she sat with a handkerchief in her hands which she screwed up nervously. Elspeth engaged her in small talk for a minute or two and waited for her to speak. When she did she spoke with a soft Welsh accent.

'I am very worried about Gareth', she began, 'things have become very difficult at home. My husband, Gareth's father has left us, he's gone to live with someone else – a man! Gareth always had a close relationship with his father and the week after he left Gareth met up with him and his father insisted on introducing him to his new partner. Gareth came home and went straight up to his room and refused to come down all evening. We've brought our children up to respect others and I don't know how to deal with this situation, he refuses to see his father and he's become quiet and withdrawn and so unlike himself. A fortnight ago I discovered he was self-harming and I made arrangements for him to go to my parents in Wales.'

'Gareth's sister, Laura is at university in Cardiff isn't she?, how is she reacting to the situation?' asked Elspeth.

'She's nineteen and has her own life marked out. She hasn't spoken about it much and I'm not sure what she thinks. There's the belief abroad that homosexual people have been victims unable to express themselves as they should be able to and that they have suffered abuse and bullying at school.'

'Did you suspect your husband was homosexual?' Elspeth asked.

'No! not at all. We met at school in Wales, he was a keen Rugby player and was popular. Our parents know each other, old mining families, humble, chapel people. When Aled got a place at Cardiff Dental School his family were so proud, the whole village was happy for them, it's a close community. All I've told my parents is that Aled has left us and I haven't told them anything else, they wouldn't understand and it would be round the village in no time and I don't want that particularly not for Gareth and not for Aled's parents either. I have felt so utterly confused and unhappy myself, I thought we had a good marriage. I feel betrayed. Last week I spoke to Aled and told him that Gareth refused to see him and that I was anxious about him and had sent him to my parents. He said I should get myself into the twenty-first century and he accused me of influencing Gareth against him, he also said that we should arrange for Gareth to see a therapist who could help him to understand and come to terms with the situation.' 'How did you reply to that?' asked Elspeth.

'I refused. Gareth, in my view, and I may be criticised for it, would be asked to live with embarrassment among his friends and made to defend his father out of enforced loyalty. It's a parent's place to defend their young children not children their parents. My son's education is suffering. I told Aled that I considered his behaviour to be adultery and he just scoffed and said that it was a naive point of view and that he had simply been born in the wrong body and it was impossible to commit adultery with someone of the same sex.'

'You don't have to agree,' Elspeth replied and then stopped herself from saying anything further.' I refuse to take sides, she thought, Mrs Lewis has got to deal with the situation, I really do not wish to be drawn into this. 'Have you discussed the situation with a friend or with anyone else?'

'No, I haven't spoken to anybody. I haven't felt able to. I have been unable to sleep, I just lie awake troubled not knowing what to do for the best and I told Aled last weekend that I am considering returning to Wales. I have been working part-time as a nurse and my sister is also a nurse. She lives with her husband and children in Pembrokeshire, I would have no difficulty finding a nursing job there or nearby. I can't leave Gareth with my parents and in the same village as Aled's parents, it would end up being worse than it is here. I have been thinking of putting the house on the market and I could always rent some place in Wales until things are sorted out and Gareth gets on well with his cousins and could perhaps attend the same school. It could work out. I don't hate his father and I don't want Gareth to hate him either, I just want him to have time to get back on track with his own life.'

'His father will always be his father there's no way anyone can change that and no way anyone should try to. I'm not against removing oneself from a very difficult situation and environment if one is in a position to do so. Your husband has made his choice so he surely will recognise your right to do the same,' said Elspeth.

'I think just talking about it has helped me towards a decision, one that was in the process of being made before I came to see you. I do apologise for taking up your time with my problems Mrs Spadaro. Perhaps I ought not to mention it but I know as all the parents do that you were faced with a terribly sad situation and left with four young children.' Mrs Lewis spoke kindly and with sympathy.

'I had lots of support from my parents and family and friends, one takes one day at a time and one morning one wakes up and finds the clouds have cleared, the sun is shining and the children are laughing again. But it takes time,' said Elspeth.

'Your children can regard their father as a hero', said Mrs Lewis sighing.

'My husband was simply the father that they loved and lost,' replied Elspeth sadly.

'I understand. Thank you. You have been more helpful than you know and I am very grateful. I still love Aled, I've loved him since my school days and it's one of the reasons I don't wish to encourage others to pass judgement on him. I feel protective of him too. I have felt quite desperate but I haven't criticised him to the children. As you have said it is their father and they will come to terms with things in time but I won't have them forced. I have a feeling that Laura may well end up criticising me for not accepting her father for what he is, but I know Gareth was relieved when I sent him off to his grandparents last week. He loves them and is also very close to Aled's parents. And now, Mrs Spadaro I've taken up enough of your time but I also wanted you to know what had happened, you have always been Gareth's favourite teacher. I'll leave you to get along home.'

They left the school building together and Elspeth wished her well and hoped things would go well for Gareth. She had liked the young boy and she liked his mother too. She herself had never confronted homosexuality she was glad only that it had been decriminalised but breaking up a family as Aled Lewis had done was surely adultery and she felt very sorry for his wife and children, particularly Gareth. She had not been called on to judge nevertheless she considered his behaviour wrong and his justification of his actions misguided. Almost inevitably she thought back to her time teaching at Oaklands and little Imogen Beaumont once again, came into her mind. She wondered how life had turned out for her and hoped that she was happy and fulfilled somewhere. Overlooking the needs and rights of children was anathema for her.

She had been invited to visit Helen and Johannes Manasses that evening. They were now both retired and although they had planned to live in Greece after their retirement they had not been able to break away completely and were still spending several months a year in Britain. She thought that what she needed was a discussion with her friends and to give some airing of her own feelings of growing restlessness and she couldn't think of better people to talk to.

Elspeth had worked out for herself over the years the distinction between ideologies and religion: ideologies were built around ideas and were, as such, constructs of the human mind, the Christian religion, she firmly believed, was revealed Truth and was based on the belief that God was the author of life. Ideologies came and went and a consideration of Communism, Fascism and Liberalism suggested that they all ended up in the same place: in silencing an opposition. Liberalism she thought was destined to end up the same when the Liberal Elite's beliefs and practices were opposed and Liberalism might ultimately become undemocratic. Christianity on the other hand had never claimed to be democratic being based on the absolute authority of Christ and it seemed ever more clear to Elspeth that faith in God was diminishing on an almost yearly basis and the State was replacing the Church's influence and passing ever more laws. She thought to put this to Johannes that evening and was interested as always in his response.

'The Church is the arbiter of moral transgressions and we as members of the Christian Church accept Her teaching on sin,' Johannes said. 'The State's Justice System is the arbiter of crimes and confusion frequently arises between the two since sins are not necessarily crimes. Moral transgressions against the Commandments or sins, are primarily about personal, inward struggles with conscience and it seems to me that as religion loses its influence the State becomes more and more the arbiter of sexual morals and the proprietor of souls. I think the Church must stay firm on its teaching. Handing sexual morality over to the State not only creates confusion in the hearts and minds of the Faithful but the Faithful become not more liberated but more enslaved and confused. People can leave the Church – they are free to do so – and to go their own ways but pressure placed on the Church and other religions by the State should be resisted in my view. The Church has been entrusted with the mission of saving souls and it is a sacred mission. Christian Truth doesn't have to be false because an ever larger number of people reject it and in any case attempting to uphold its Truth has always been unpopular. Christ wasn't universally popular in His lifetime and at present the Church is facing a martyrdom. Holding fast to its teaching will, I believe, eventually strengthen it. Doesn't the Catholic Church have a saying, "the blood of martyrs is the seed of Christians"? It's worth bearing in mind because things are going to get much worse.'

Elspeth considered what was being said and while Johannes spoke her decision grew.

'These questions about morality and the Church are becoming increasingly important to me and I am thinking seriously about taking early retirement from full time teaching and concentrating on study. I would like to explore these questions and to study the Scriptures and Church Teaching further. Teaching allows me no time for these things'.

And just as Mrs Lewis earlier that day had said that putting her partially made decision into words had helped her to make up her mind, Elspeth returned home with her mind made up. She slept well on her decision and the following day she offered her resignation to the Headteacher. He was surprised and questioned her and she said simply that her parents were now growing old and she wished to be there for them which was more than partially the truth and she began the Easter vacation with a sense of renewal.

Chapter 23

....

*"Freedom is the freedom to say that two and two make four.
If that is granted, all else follows".*
(Nineteen Eighty Four, George Orwell)

*"If the world hates you, you must realise that it
hated me before it hated you.
If you belonged to the world,
the world would love you as its own –"*
(John Ch 15 vs 18-19)

In the weeks following the Easter vacation, Elspeth discussed her decision with her parents and children. She explained her reasons for leaving teaching and told them what she was planning to do with the house. 'It's very large but it is our home,' she said, 'and I am hoping that one day in the future one of you with your family will come to live here but in the meantime I am planning to make a large flat in the lower ground floor and to let it on short term leases and I'm going to get builders in and have the work done during my last term of teaching.'

Her father was particularly pleased, 'I want the house to stay in the future generations of the Penrose family – I like the thought that there will be a continuation of our family here even if names change.'

So by the time the summer term came to a close Elspeth's new way of life was established and during August she met up with Maria Rosa in Lourdes and Fleur joined them. When the others left Elspeth stayed on for a further two weeks and one afternoon she retraced her steps to the embankment above the Grotto where she had first talked with Anton. Little has changed here, she thought, but for me everything has changed and she wondered if Anton would approve her latest decision and believed he would. I want to ask questions finally, questions that have lain largely dormant for years and to look for answers, she thought and perhaps I shall write about my life, my thoughts and reflections and leave them for the children. She stared ahead of her but her thoughts were elsewhere she was reliving that first encounter and seeing in her mind's eye Anton's boyish good looks and she thought how it seemed such a short time ago and she did not feel like a separate person; he was still with me. He had told her that death would not sever his love for her and she felt the closeness of that love. There was no way to reverse death but that first unbearable agony had given way to a calm sadness of loss and that afternoon she remembered other losses too. She thought back to the Catholic Chaplaincy and the image of the Blessed Virgin holding out the Christ Child and her first encounter with Father Dominic. The statue would still be there holding out the Child for others, always, unchanging, eternally loving and she contemplated the mystery of it in her heart.

II

It was strange waking up at the beginning of September knowing a new term would be beginning without her but she had no regrets; on the contrary she felt a sense of freedom. She joined a Biblical study class at the nearby university and she signed up for a series of lectures on political and philosophical ideas and she bought books and studied them. She felt a sense of luxury having so much time to herself and also time for her friends. But that autumn there was also growing talk and news about Iraq and that country's supposed arsenal of weapons of mass destruction and there loomed the possibility of an invasion. Elspeth placed it at the back of her mind believing there was little risk to western

315

nations and was genuinely shocked as she learnt that an invasion was being seriously considered. As in the case with Afghanistan she discussed it with her father and registered his concern as he said that a military invasion would destabilise the whole of the Middle East. By February it had become less of a probability and more of a grave reality.

Elspeth had never joined a public protest before and had never imagined that she ever would. Michael had already entered a Seminary on the Continent and would not be in England for the planned London Anti War March but Gian and Diana and Joseph along with Fleur had informed her that they intended to join the protest and she agreed to be there too.

It was a cold February day as she drove to London and arrived at her children's meeting place. Gian and Diana and Fleur were already there and within minutes Joseph arrived with his girlfriend Madeleine. It was the first time that Elspeth had met her and she liked her immediately. Madeleine had studied Art History and was now teaching in a London university. Her father was English and she had a French mother. She was pretty and had lively grey-green eyes, a gentle expression and a sensitive mouth. Joseph had talked eagerly about her and described her so enthusiastically that Elspeth felt that she knew her and she met the young woman's open smile sure that this would be her new future daughter-in-law.

The Anti War March comprised hundreds of thousands of people of all ages and from all walks of life and Elspeth was impressed at the friendliness and good nature of the crowd. She thought politicians cannot ignore this obvious will of the people but they did and a month later she watched aghast as bombs rained down on Baghdad lighting up its night sky, destroying the city's infrastructure and setting into effect a chain reaction that spread slowly and surely across the entire region.

When Elspeth met Belle one afternoon in town they chatted over coffee about the new phase in both their lives. Belle was now a proud grandmother and she talked enthusiastically about Jonathan's two girls and Susan's baby son. David had also recently been married and so hopefully there would be further children soon.

'How are you enjoying being free to study again, Elspeth, I always believed you would have become a Lecturer and become absorbed in research?' Belle said.

'I never wanted to lecture but yes, I do want to spend my time asking questions and in researching. The children, of course, are grown up but they still turn up home on a regular basis and Fleur being still a student comes home each month if she can make it,' replied Elspeth.

'I am still helping Alistair in the surgery one or two days a week and I think I mentioned to you that I had taken up some voluntary work attached to the church,' Belle said.

'Caring and attempting to get help for single mothers who have decided to keep their babies. How is it going? It sounds so much more philanthropic than my studying'.

'Elspeth you've spent years teaching and you've had a much rougher time than me. You deserve some time to yourself to do, well stuff I would be incapable of. I just want to provide practical help to these vulnerable young women because I'm against abortion. I can understand in the case of rape and incest, of course I can, but I just find it difficult to justify in most cases.'

'In the case of rape, is it justified to destroy the one completely innocent life, there's the sticking point?' said Elspeth.

'I also find that there is so much misinformation surrounding the subject. It never seems to be corrected when so many young people are left with the notion that what they are aborting is a number of cells looking something like frogs' spawn, at least one young girl I spoke to believed that until she was given a scan. Since most abortions don't take place until the twelfth week of pregnancy by that time the baby is fully formed'.

'I suppose you are also faced with criticism from Women's Rights groups saying that these young single women might very well face financial hardship and other difficulties and folks in positions like ours have no idea and should stay well away'.

'Yes, we certainly have to contend with that, but we also meet with women who have gone through with an abortion and they cannot come to terms with what they have done and they require help and healing. What I find most objectionable though is women from protest groups saying that a woman has the right to do as she wishes with her own body. Well strictly speaking it is not just the pregnant woman's own body to do as she likes with it's a body that belongs to another person with a potentially independent life that is being nurtured by the woman for some nine months. It seems to me that the unborn baby is being looked upon as a parasite. I find that really difficult to accept. Do you remember the two of us finding those butterfly eggs under the cabbage leaf and you finding a book describing the life cycle of a butterfly and the pictures of the emerging butterflies from their chrysalises? They were so beautiful! I find the thought of killing anything impossible'.

'Yes, of course I remember and all your pets!' said Elspeth smiling, 'if you need some help, funding or whatever you only have to ask.'

'Thank you, I just might do that,' replied her friend.

It is said that by the age of fifty, people have earned their faces and Elspeth watching Belle's face while they were speaking noted the calm peacefulness in her friend's expression. Her hair was cut short now and the blonde of her earlier years was now a light shade of brown and her hazel eyes looked thoughtful as she spoke. She remembered that Belle's father had commented about his daughter and Alistair before their wedding saying that there was not an unkind bone in either of their bodies and Elspeth knew that it was true but she also knew that her friend had an inner strength and could stand up to be counted when popular opinion was against her. We have been best friends and companions since childhood, we have literally gone through life together, she thought, and I hope we will eventually face old age together too.

IV

Elspeth frequently wished she had kept up with a diary, she had began to do so on occasions in the past, usually around a New Year, it was one of those resolutions that was usually dropped by the end of January. But when she looked back on this phase of her life she wished she could remember at what point she had come to realise that there was a new spirit abroad in society. When had she become fully conscious of Political Correctness she asked herself? She had been given to believe that Free Speech should be taken for granted and opposing views respected, now it was becoming clear to her that opinions voiced that were disliked by a growing liberal elite were being, not just opposed, but effectively silenced. A nurse offering to say a prayer for one of her patients was reported, another worker was reprimanded and almost lost her job for wearing a cross and chain. Religion, particularly Christianity, was under attack from an increasingly secular society determined to prove a case against a Church it claimed promoted indoctrination and oppression. If I am asked for my point of view, Elspeth thought defiantly, I will give it, I will not be silenced! How could anyone be offended when told that a care worker would say a prayer for her or by a colleague wearing a cross and chain! It is beyond pettiness! She looked askance on two young homosexual men caught leaving court after taking a middle-aged Christian couple to court because their guesthouse refused them a room together as they considered it against their Christian beliefs. They had not been judgemental and they had not expressed any personal hostility and when Elspeth saw the two young men on television leaving court looking for all the world as if they had scored a victory she thought it a very hollow victory; destroying the livelihood of a decent couple who had never committed a crime in their lives and yet being made to appear as criminals. It was a case of getting one's own back, but where was the spirit of magnanimity in all of it? Are the souls of mankind diminishing in the clamour of modern life? Is society descending into ever greater mediocrity?

She took to reading personal accounts recently published by women and others who had been exiled in Communist Russia on trumped up trivial charges that were far from being crimes, the real criminals being Stalin and those in power. She read about purges and torture and thought we are far from such atrocities here but people are being silenced and there is a growing indifference to morality. Then she wondered if things had always been the same. When had the vast number of people who made up the population really been given a voice on the world stage? For all my education I am a simpleton she thought, what do I really know about anything? Anton had once in a rare moment of insight said that she was so simple she was a positive complication. She smiled to herself at the memory, perhaps he had known her better than she had frequently given him credit for. Yet she continued to question the present society. Conscience clauses had been dispensed with, reason frequently distorted and what were once considered Christian virtues were being looked upon as crimes.

Then as this particular year advanced all her attention was once again and of necessity, focused on her family.

At the beginning of autumn she became aware of her father's cough which seemed to worsen within a very short time. One weekend when Gian and Diana were visiting and following a bad bout of coughing, Gian voiced his concern, 'You really must see a doctor Grandpa, that's a very nasty cough.'

'I have told him but he just says it's a cold', said Elspeth's mother, looking anxious. 'That's not a cold,' said Gian, 'you must make an appointment with your doctor straight away.'

Elspeth had never known her father to be ill, her parents were now in their early eighties and owned to having a few aches and pains that were due to age and to be expected, but on the whole they seemed remarkably healthy. She studied her parents closely that afternoon. Her father remained an upright, handsome figure, his steel grey hair was still thick and the expression in his eyes had softened. Her mother still insisted on having highlights in her hair, her beautiful hands were carefully manicured and she still wore expensive, elegant clothes. Together they still made an impression on entering a room and they still had an active social life. For the first time I am seeing them as old people, she thought, and recognising mortality in relation to them and I cannot imagine life without them both. Growing up I was always closer to my two grandmothers than to my mother but over the years both my parents have become an irreplaceable part of my life and I cannot bear to think of them gone.

A chest X-Ray three days later confirmed the family's fears, her father had lung cancer and the prognosis was poor, he was terminally ill. Elspeth expected the illness to take its course over several months but she was mistaken, it all happened quickly. Her father within weeks was so weak that he was unable to walk or dress himself and was admitted to hospital. Elspeth sat next to his bed some days before his death when he looked sadly at her and spoke quietly, 'Elspeth, I'm so sorry, Jamie and…'

'Jamie is at peace Daddy and everything was forgiven long ago. Don't be sad or regretful on my account.'

Shortly afterwards he spoke again, 'Can you ask Adam to come and see me? I know he is very busy but I would like to speak to him.'

'Of course, I'm sure he will be glad to come'.

Adam had not become a Bishop but he had been made a Rural Dean and his services were much in demand but when Elspeth rang him he did not hesitate and so her father, she believed, made his peace with God and she was silently thankful.

V

It was the change in her mother that grieved Elspeth most after her father's death and when her mother had agreed to move in with her. Her mother became listless and on sorting out her clothes and possessions before the move she put most of her finery aside saying, 'I no longer require so many things, I won't be wearing many of these things again', and she donated what she now deemed unnecessary to charity shops. The following spring she brightened up and pottered around the garden helping and Elspeth hoped that she might regain her old spirit of optimism but it was not to be, her mother soon complained of being too tired and she seemed to age almost overnight. She visibly lost weight and Elspeth tried to coax her into eating but after a mouthful or two she would say that she had no appetite. Occasionally she played her beloved piano and would break off in the middle of a piece and Elspeth would find her quietly weeping and putting her arms around her thin shoulders she would say that there was a television programme on that she was sure they would both enjoy and her mother would follow her like an obedient little child. 'It's breaking my heart, she's dying before my eyes and

I can do nothing yet I'm sure she's not physically ill', Elspeth thought, 'my father was her life and she doesn't want to go on living without him.'

One Autumn evening, two years after her father's death the two of them were sitting quietly together, Elspeth was reading and her mother appeared to be looking through a magazine. When Elspeth looked up she saw that her mother seemed to be staring into space and then she suddenly crumpled forward and Elspeth rose and went to her. Her mother had died soundlessly. She had lived only long enough to see her first great grandchild, James, Gian and Diana's son, but her memory had become weak and she called him Jamie and Jamie he became as Diana said she preferred Jamie to having his name shortened to Jim. Two months before her death she had dressed up elegantly to attend Joseph and Madeleine's wedding and she had leant on Fleur, her favourite grandchild's arm. It was the last family occasion for her when they were all present and Michael now ordained a priest had married the couple.

Her mother's death saddened Elspeth more than she could say, her mother was her last physical link with Gran.

Chapter 24

....

"In the end the Party would announce that two and two, made five and you would have to believe it. It was inevitable that they should make that claim sooner or later: the logic of their position demanded it. Not only the validity of experience, but the very existence of external reality, was tacitly denied by their philosophy".
(Nineteen Eighty-Four – George Orwell)

Johannes Manasses was destined to play one further significant role in Elspeth's family life. Johannes had made friends with a Russian student during his time at university and they had remained close. Vladimir, the friend in question, attended the Russian Orthodox Church and following his marriage with his Polish wife, Nadia, had several children who were now adults. The youngest of these was Alexei, born when the couple were in their late thirties, and this young man had recently completed a PhD in Theology and been selected for a lectureship in the Faculty of Theology in the city's university. His parents had journeyed from the South coast where they lived and were staying with Johannes and Helen who were planning a celebration for them. Fleur happened to be playing the piano for a Festival Concert in the nearby city and Helen suggested that they should attend and she invited Elspeth to join them. At the end of the concert they all made their way to a restaurant for a meal together.

Fleur at this time travelled the country giving piano recitals and was making a name for herself but she had confided in her mother soon after graduating telling her that she had no ambition to become an international concert pianist, and that celebrity status was not what she sought.

'It can be lonely and I'm not sure I'm any more suited to such a life than Grandma was, in fact she once told me that she was indecisive about opting for a musical career at the time she met Grandpa and she made up her mind very quickly: she chose to marry Grandpa and she said she never regretted her choice.'

'I'm certain she didn't', responded Elspeth.

'I want a family like the one I've been brought up in. I love home life, I'm not very career orientated I suppose I'm not really very outgoing.'

So it came as no great surprise to Elspeth when Alexei, soon after taking up his lectureship, contacted her daughter and they were soon meeting up regularly and within six months they were engaged to be married.

'We are planning to be married in the Russian Orthodox Church, I'm not sure how you feel about it. We could have a second ceremony in our Church,' Fleur confided, I don't want to offend anybody, I'm not sure what Michael will say.'

'I doubt he'll object, why would he? I certainly shan't whatever you decide. While he was at university he spent a lot of time in Greece and attended Greek Orthodox Liturgies and he said how beautiful they were. Johannes Manasses was your father's best friend and indeed Michael's Godparent. I believe the two churches regard each other as schismatic but not heretical.'

In the end they decided to marry in the Orthodox Church as Fleur decided that she wished to become Orthodox, saying the Russian Orthodox Liturgy was out of this world, and Elspeth did not disagree.

'You held a very special place in your father's heart', she told her daughter, 'I'm sure he's been watching over you'.

And so the young couple after the wedding moved into the family home which had long been Elspeth's dream. She continued to live in the lower ground floor flat which she had come to love. The flat opened onto her beloved garden and she thought, I'll never have to leave my home and my father would have been so happy that his descendants would be living in the house that had been his family's home for several generations.

II

So many hopes for the new century, Elspeth thought, and they seem to be in the process of unraveling. When the Madrid bombings occurred she rang Anton's cousins who she remained in contact with and when the tube bombings happened in London, Gian helped some of the injured that were sent to his hospital. There was twenty-four-hour news coverage for a time then people who were not personally affected put it behind them and got on with their lives. There was little else they could do.

But Elspeth was after all a committed Catholic and there was subtle but very real evidence that the old suspicions against Catholicism remained and came to the fore once again in the early years of the new century. She was shocked when Catholic adoption agencies were targeted and instructed that it was unlawful for them to refuse same sex couples from applying to them as prospective parents. Once again it was Louise and her sister Ann who brought the matter up.

'How many same sex couples do you imagine will apply to a Catholic adoption
agency!'

'Couples that have an axe to grind and want to bring the Church into disrepute. The sexual abuse cases have caused huge harm.

'But how likely is it that people working in these agencies can be penalised? They can hardly be sent to prison all of them it would be ludicrous! Sent to prison for providing for vulnerable children?! this was from Ann. 'It's a law that cannot be enforced surely and Catholics should quietly resist it. These agencies place the most vulnerable children into stable homes. It is also the case that a Catholic parent seeking to have a child adopted will wish to have their child placed with Catholic parents. This 'right' of theirs is being totally ignored'.

'Young children like the unborn have no vote and apparently no rights either in a society that prides itself on its record of human rights. Human Rights being one thing, Equal Rights being another and eventually our society needs to have an open debate on Equal Rights and the implications inherent in Equality. One person's rights are not necessarily another person's rights, in fact all the opposite in many cases. What saddens me in the case of the adoption agencies is the silence on the part of same sex couples. One might hope that if they genuinely have vulnerable children at heart they would say disregard us and deal with the children', said Elspeth.

'That might require the wisdom of Solomon and wisdom in our present society is in short supply,' said Louise. 'We have to recognise that we are a minority and not a particularly popular one and the gay lobby is becoming very strong and has the backing of the media and Parliament and together they can successfully manipulate public opinion. There's little we can do about it'.

'So we sit back and do nothing while the needs of vulnerable children are ignored?' asked Elspeth scandalised in spite of herself.

'We can do what Catholics have been doing for centuries in this country; lie low and live our faith without allowing others to think we are attempting to impose our beliefs on them. I would like to believe Catholic Adoption Agencies will still operate quietly they have the needs of children on their side and I still believe that if a particular Agency is reported it might hopefully backfire on whoever reported it'.

'We are also citizens in a Democracy and it seems like a case of injustice to me,' said Elspeth, 'and people who oppose what they recognise as an injustice should not be silenced'.

It was also around the same time as this that Pope Benedict announced the validity of the Old Mass explaining that it had never been abrogated and Jerome asked Elspeth if she felt vindicated.

'Vindication on my part doesn't come into it. What has been perpetrated is deliberate misinformation by certain high ranking members of the hierarchy foisting their ideas and their own brand of banality on many churches in their efforts to embrace the modern culture. I ask myself why Catholics have gone along with it all, was it misplaced obedience?'

Elspeth liked the shy, scholarly Pope and considered him wise, she thought he was being martyred by the media, blamed for sexual abuse cases as if he were the author of them. But what still concerned her most at this period of her life was the way in which falsehoods of one kind and another were brought about in society and then accepted for being the truth. It became impossible to be unaware. Plausible reasoning and arguments were being used to manipulate emotions and it seemed to Elspeth that deception was widespread and increasing. It rankled with her.

III

Yet the first two decades of the century brought Elspeth personal blessings. She had longed to have grandchildren and soon she had several and she aspired to be good grandmother and to spend as much time as possible with them. Gian and Diana had a son and two daughters, Joseph and Madeleine had three sons, and Fleur and Alexei two daughters and were hoping for further children. Her grandmothers had been a great influence in her own life, they had been generous with their time and loving.

Elspeth looking back on her time spent with her own children had been so busy that she had lacked the time to observe them closely now she found that with more time on her hands she was learning new things about very young children. Staying over at Joseph's house and being asked to babysit for their eldest son, Luke, when he was some ten months old and reluctant to be put down to sleep she thought that she should provide him with some activities to tire him out but he was not interested. She thought he must be bored then realised that far from it he was perfectly content. He has no concept of time, Elspeth thought, he is living in the moment and as long as I am here sitting close to him he is happy. We as adults are conditioned by time but time is different in different situations. There is something particularly satisfying about living in the present.

Elspeth also had time for travel and as her cousin Esme had finally retired they took holidays in far away places together and so she found plenty of things to do and she felt she had found a new contentment.

IV

Elspeth was careful not to criticise her daughter and son-in law and she refused to take sides or offer an opinion unless she was directly asked for one. She remembered her own misgivings before and at the beginning of her own marriage and believed that her children should make their own decisions so she was caught somewhat unaware on one occasion when visiting Gian and

Diana. Elspeth admired Gian's wife but had always been somewhat wary of her. Diana was confident and efficient and so she was surprised when she suddenly spoke up as if she was requesting an opinion. They were alone one afternoon, Gian was still working in a hospital and at work, and Diana had taken up part-time work as a GP in a Health Centre and was at home that afternoon. She came out with what she clearly considered a tricky situation she was finding herself in.

'One of my male colleagues has invited Gian and I to his wedding. He is marrying his long term partner Mark and while I feel happy to attend Gian is not. He maintains that there is no such thing as same sex marriage, he says there are same sex unions but that marriage is a union between a man and a woman and that as far as he is concerned it's a definitive definition'.

'And I take it that you don't agree with that', said Elspeth.

'My colleague is a lovely man and a fine dedicated doctor and he loves his partner. I think he has the right to be happy, but I know same sex marriage is against the teaching of the Catholic Church and it's not going to change any time soon.'

'I hope that it will never be accepted, it is not possible to change a fact of reality,' said Elspeth.

'But it's indoctrination to try to impose this teaching on others.'

'Who is imposing it? There's been an Act of Parliament making Same Sex Marriage legal but I don't remember it being in any Manifesto, it is simply being foisted on the electorate and we are being expected to accept it whether we agree with it or not and many of us don't agree with it, and not only Catholics. If any enforcement has taken place here it hasn't been by the Church.'

The following morning when they were again alone Diana said that she had decided to decline the invitation.

'I don't need to give a reason but I don't wish to distress and embarrass Gian. He never tries to impose his beliefs on me and it's not worth arguing and making an issue of it when I don't feel strongly about it either way.'

Elspeth did not respond and the matter was left as it was.

Elspeth had a very different relationship with Joseph's wife, Madeleine. The two talked easily together and had soon established a rapport. She was a Catholic which helped so she never felt she was speaking out of turn and together, and sometimes when Joseph was present, they discussed topics that were of interest to them all.

Some six months after Elspeth's conversation with Diana when Joseph and Madeleine and their three children were staying with her and Fleur's family and the children were all in bed, Madeleine expressed her concern about a measure that had been taken at the university where she taught.

'I find it difficult to believe that a debate, that had been planned about abortion – and after pro-life speakers had already been invited – was suddenly cancelled. The powers that be at the university decided that the debate was too sensitive and would cause offence to some students and that it had been generally agreed that abortion was not a suitable subject to debate at a university.'

'That's scarcely credible!' said Alexei, 'I would have thought that a university was precisely the place for discussing all subjects of public interest whether they offend one group of people or not.'

'We think things are bad here but my cousin who read Philosophy at university has spent this last year doing research towards her

PhD in the States', said Madeleine. 'She learned of cases where people lose their employment if they speak up against abortion and same sex marriage. Gender Ideology is growing in popularity – did you know that Facebook have sixty definitions for gender – and people can choose their own gender depending on the way they perceive themselves? Some students in some philosophy departments are arguing that there is no such thing as 'Truth' and each person can define reality for his or herself. Young people they maintain are redefining everything.'

'The young cannot redefine reality! Or facts. It's absurd! Some of the cases I've read about lately, coming out of America and spreading here border on pathological delusion,' said Joseph, 'and people are expected to be respectful in the face of them'.

'Certainly at the university where I teach one has to be cautious about expressing an opposing point of view from the one popularly held,' said Madeleine. 'Free speech can very easily be interpreted as hate speech depending where one offers a point of view'.

'I want to believe that 'Truth' finally triumphs', added Alexei, 'after all my great grandparents fled Russia at the time of the Revolution and the terror that took place there, particularly during the Stalin era, defies belief. People were betrayed and sent into exile and to Gulags on trumped up charges sometimes for decades and most of them didn't survive. The lies, pretence and corruption were widespread, people became afraid of their neighbours denouncing them. But I've visited Russia in recent years and people walk freely again and there is a resurgence of religious faith and the Orthodox Church is strong'.

'However, the situation here will I fear be different,' said Elspeth. She had remained quiet but now she spoke up and slowly expressed her thoughts. She had long studied Political Ideologies and she now felt that she was qualified to speak as Johannes Manasses had been all those years before.

'It is interesting to realise,' Elspeth began, 'that in Antiquity the Jewish people never considered the sophisticated philosophies of the Greeks or the illustrious history and faith of the Egyptians to be greater than their own teaching and understanding of the world. They recognised themselves as God's Chosen People – a people that God had made a Covenant with – and the Torah as the eternal wisdom of God implanted for all time in their race. Judaism is Theocentric. The Decalogue given by God to Moses was and is central to their faith as it is to Christians throughout the world today. The Decalogue is centred around obedience and Worship of God as opposed to idolatry indeed it serves as a safeguard against idolatry, and every time the Jewish people departed from the worship of God they faced exile and death and were continually being recalled by the prophets back to the Truth that resides in God alone. The second Commandment is intriguing and frequently passed over with the forbidding of 'graven images' but it's not just graven images in wood and stone that are forbidden but any 'likenesses' – 'make not unto yourself any graven image or likeness – do not bow down to them and serve them' – is what is stated here'.

'Likenesses do not have to be 'images' they can be ideas, ideals or ideologies, the acceptance of which can appear to be in the best interests of people such as those that have plagued the twentieth century, Communism, National Socialism and now most popular of all of them today, Democracy. Each of these ideologies, at least in their conception, are based in and around 'Liberalism'. They were originally intended to be in the best interests of people, to serve the people, by recognising their 'human rights' but they have ended up with people serving them. Ideologies are secular and potentially atheistic. They give rise to idolatry. In opposition to the worship of God ideologies are the worship of ideas and also readily become the worship of material things in their numerous forms, in other words idols. They replace God and humankind created in God's image and likeness and return to the pagan gods made as they were in the image and likenesses of human beings! We no longer have black and white but 'Fifty Shades of Grey' – and during the twentieth century, attempts to build societies around ideologies has left human life on a collision course with destruction.'

'We live in a representative democracy which is based on Liberalism and we rarely question its ethos. An increasing problem posed by Liberalism is in its inherent belief that each individual's belief system is equal to anyone else's and living as we do in a democracy we are conditioned to respect the beliefs and opinions of each other and so Liberalism gives rise to any number of conflicting and opposing beliefs and opinions and so we have in its wake the cult of Individualism. Liberalism offering a right and freedom to choose has given rise to abortion, euthanasia, a culture of death and destruction. This is what is happening now. Liberalism incorporates 'Liberty' but as the present century progresses Liberalism is in the process of destroying the very freedom its followers unquestioning and ostensibly profess to'.

'There is no longer 'Truth' but any number of 'truths', with new ones being continuously generated and fostered. Of late we have Gender Ideology which we are expected to not only respect but to accept. An increasingly illiberal elite expects us to do so and this elite now forms a powerful place in our representative democracy. Liberalism has finally become inverted authoritarianism effectively silencing opposition. There's a growing tendency that a vote democratically arrived at is spurned by the Liberal elite and when the same elite resorts to violence then it heads irrevocably towards dictatorship and totalitarianism. People are unwittingly finding themselves trapped and mentally and spiritually enslaved. There is a lessening in the freedom of speech or conscience and I fear that things are set to implode. There seems set to be a general uprising against governing liberal elites and there is no unity in what might follow. There is no Orthodox Church waiting in the wings, the Churches in our Western democracies are divided the modern Catholic Church, once a bastion of

Orthodoxy, has allied itself with modern society and there is no clear vision about how to replace what we have. The many factions in our societies are disunited, clamouring to be heard and at loggerheads with each other. There could be impending chaos.'

'Armageddon', said Fleur softly.

'It's a sobering possibility,' said Elspeth, 'we have to hope and pray that Alexei is right and that God and Truth will again be acknowledged, but in the meantime we should make ourselves fully aware of the dangers a world faces that disconnects itself from the Truth of Reality and which embraces idols. Ideology and idolatry are closely linked. We really cannot sit back and be complacent.'

V

Elspeth had taken to driving herself to Tintern Abbey when she wished to think things through and three days after the discussion with her family and when Joseph and Madeleine had returned home, she made her short journey to her favourite spot. She felt disturbed by what she had learned and usually the abbey and its surroundings calmed her. But on this occasion she was too disconcerted for contemplation and the abbey ruins added to her feelings of gloom. It was an autumn day and overcast with heavy grey clouds. The abbey stood with the skeletal beauty of an oak tree in winter and witnessing to the condemnable destruction that had been inflicted on it and the centuries of lies and falsehoods that had been woven around its violation. Those who would have defended the sanctity of the life it had stood for had been silenced, terrorised and threatened and so a myth had been devised and through the centuries that had followed there had grown up tales of the immoral lives of monks and their addiction to wealth and easy living. In recent years, historical truths were finally coming to light: a profligate monarch had found a source of riches and historians were at last saying that the Dissolution of the Monasteries was the greatest act of vandalism in English History and that the monasteries had provided employment and help for the poor, indeed they had been a form of Medieval Welfare State that had taken some four hundred years to replace. "Bare ruined choirs where once the sweet birds sang", had Shakespeare visited such places, Elspeth wondered, surely he had or seen them there in the landscape, and was the line he penned his reaction to the monstrous destruction?

There was rain in the air and her sense of sadness deepened. She left the abbey ruins troubled and made for home. She went upstairs to read a bedtime story to her two small granddaughters in an attempt to lighten her mood and afterwards took herself early to bed.

But her mind was overcharged and she was unable to sleep, she tossed from one side to the other and when sleep finally came in the early hours she fell into a deeply troubled dream. She found herself following the White Rabbit and she saw him stop and consult his watch and say he was late and as he disappeared into the rabbit hole she found herself falling in after him but instead of finding herself at the fantastical tea party in 'Alice in Wonderland', she found herself in a warren of passages. Each passage was filled with different groups of people and her feelings of horror grew. The first group of men and women she encountered were all dressed the same and were genderless, they looked at her with undisguised contempt chanting 'WE ARE THE ENLIGHTENED ONES. WE HAVE ACHIEVED EQUALITY' At the second passage were same sex married couples who looked with loathing at her and spat at her as she tried to pass them. Finally, she came to a central place where a large fire was burning and men and women dressed in black were throwing babies into the fire and a group of old people with dementia were queueing up awaiting their turn to be cast into the flames. As she watched mesmerised she saw the White Rabbit standing in the middle of the fire, but now he was no longer white but slowly turning to gold and as he appeared to melt in the heat he metamorphosed into a golden calf. The shouting of the men and women around the fire grew louder as they chanted, 'GOD IS DEAD. TRUTH IS DEAD. WE ARE NO LONGER OPPRESSED AND TWO AND TWO MAKE FIVE!' It was a holocaust. There was a loud cacophony of babbling conflicting voices.

Elspeth woke, the wind was blowing the curtains and they were billowing into the room and rain was lashing loudly against the windows. She got up quickly and opened the curtains and closed the windows. She reached for her dressing gown and put it on and drew it round her and sat on the edge of the bed shaking. She looked round the room and was relieved to see that everything was as it had been the night before, nothing was changed. Eventually she took herself to the kitchen and made herself a hot drink. It had been a bad dream but the images were vivid and graphic and lingered in her mind all day as the images of a bad dream do and for some days afterwards she felt discomforted.

Epilogue

....

We are such stuff
As dreams are made on;
and our little life Is rounded with a sleep.
The Tempest Act 4, scene 1 (Shakespeare)

It was one of those perfect mornings in early spring full of sunshine and light and Elspeth had asked Fleur and Alexei and Gian and Diana and Joseph and Madeleine who were visiting with their families to accompany her to Tintern Abbey. She had not visited since that depressing autumn day and she was anxious to see it once more and on arriving she asked them to leave her for a while alone. She was dying having been diagnosed with inoperable bone cancer a month before. Michael had come home as soon as he had the news and on leaving her the week before told her that he would return immediately when she needed him. She was not afraid of death, after Anton's death she had longed for oblivion and had clung onto life for the children. Now she was saddened at leaving them. She had written for them her memories and reflections many of these would be familiar to her children but would be new to her grandchildren and she had to be content with this.

Elspeth looked towards the Abbey, its ravished beauty stood against a cloudless blue sky and this morning she thought it once more bore testimony to the peace of holiness that time had been unable to destroy. It was silent and tranquil its quietude subduing the senses and dispelling any lingering distress she felt. She turned and walked towards the Wye. Her pain killing relief medication was effective but she limped as she walked. The river had flowed, she thought forever, long before the Abbey had been built and it would go on flowing. The sun touched the undulating water and ignited sparks of light, the riverbanks were a newly minted green and a bird flew across the sky and back to its nest carrying food for its young. It was the yearly renewal, it was the renewed promise of life, it was resurrection.

She retraced her steps back to the Abbey and heard her family returning and little Eve, Fleur's three-year old daughter, was beside her playfully taking her hand and laughing, her thick dark curls framing her pretty face, 'Come along Gran, come with us'. Elspeth laughed and allowed herself to be lead. As she joined them the look of concern in her family's faces cleared seeing that she had not suffered in their absence only to be replaced by sadness knowing that she was going from them.

....

"My beloved spake, and said unto me. Rise up, my love, my fair one, and come away. For, lo, the winter is past, the rain is over and gone;
The flowers appear on the earth; the time of the singing of the birds is come, and the sound of the turtle dove is heard in our land."
(The Song of Songs ch2 vs 10-12)

The author

Author Carole Leret was born in Middleborough,
Northeast England in the middle of WWII in 1941.
Her first memory is of her home being bombed
when she was 18 months old. Sadly her father died
a year later and her widowed mother brought up
Carole and her two sisters. She went to school in
Middlesbrough and to Teacher Training College in
Kingston upon Hull. It was during this time that
she received into the Roman Catholic Church. She
married her Spanish husband in 1967 and moved
to Bristol. She completed her degree in education
in 1979 and in 1983 was awarded a Master's in
Education from Bristol University.

Now a retired teacher, Carole is married with three
grown up sons and seven grandchildren. Carole
enjoys reading, current affairs and is a member of
the Woodland Trust. Before some ill health over
recent years, she was an avid walker. During her
teaching career, Carole taught children of all ages
from primary to sixth form.